UNHOLY FOOLS

Also by PENELOPE GILLIATT

NOVELS

One by One

A State of Change

SHORT STORIES

Come Back If It Doesn't Get Better

Nobody's Business

SCREENPLAY

Sunday Bloody Sunday

UNHOLY FOOLS

Wits, Comics, Disturbers of the Peace: Film & Theater

PENELOPE GILLIATT

THE VIKING PRESS NEW YORK

First published in 1973 by The Viking Press, Inc.
625 Madison Avenue, New York, N.Y. 10022
SBN 670-74073-x
Library of Congress catalog card number: 72-79000
Printed in U.S.A. by Vail-Ballou Press, Inc.
All of these articles originally appeared, in somewhat different form, in the following:
The Guardian, *Harpers/Queen*, *The New Yorker*, *The Observer*, *Spectator*, and *Vogue*.

for EDMUND WILSON

Contents

LAST-DITCH WITS

PHYSICISTS

FARCE-MAKERS

SCAMPS

THE DANDIES, THE BUNGLERS OF CASTE

DISRUPTERS

UNHOLY FOOLS

MAROONED

Tati

There is a particular mutinous mumble in the ordinary course of events which can suddenly sound like W. C. Fields; there are debonair acts of stoicism which evoke Keaton; and there is an overweening electronic buzz which reminds you of the films of Jacques Tati as strongly as a particular kind of starched lope summons up Tati himself. When M. Hulot's author balances a sound track, the human voice plays a small and outclassed part in the din of the inanimate. A while ago, at some stiff dinner party on the beach in California, where the outdoor Ping-Pong table was made of marble ("Because marble doesn't warp in the sea air," said the owner gravely), I remember a nearly unnegotiable ten minutes when the roar of twenty-four people's chicken bones being ground up by the garbage disposal in the grandly enlightened open-plan living room was entirely victorious over the twenty-four brave souls who went on pretending to be able to hear each other. The sound track was Tati's, by any right, and so was the politely programed lunacy of the people ignoring the racket. No other director has ever pitted the still, small voice of human contact so delicately against the nerveless dominion of modern conveniences. Some noisy hot-water pipes become a major character in *Jour de Fête*. In *Mon Oncle* the buzzings and hissings and gulpings of peremptory gadgets are prodigious.

Tati's father originally wanted him to be a picture-framer, in the family tradition. He riposted with Rugby football. Between games, he filled in with what were, by all accounts, some marvelous mimes of athleticism. It would have been fine to see him on the field: six foot four of him, apparently always with a way of being able to lean alertly in any direction, as though he were balanced against a gale. The tilt is generally forward, exposing an eager five or six inches of striped sock, but it has been known to go just as far to the side. There is a sweet minute in *Mon Oncle* when, without interrupting the talk he is having with someone ahead of him, he keels neatly to the side to hear his four-foot nephew mutter something into his ear, and then quickly straightens up again to get some money out of his pocket so that the boy can buy a supply of crullers. The famous figure with the umbrella makes the stances of other and more ordinary people—and indeed, of other and more ordinary umbrellas—look rather peculiar after a time. The umbrella, which he sometimes holds like a low-slung rifle, can also suggest the taut string of an invisible helium balloon or the company of a thin aunt sprinting ahead. Now and again, he will hold it by the ferrule and seem to have to tug against it, as if it were a leash with a hidden dog straining on the end. For himself, he seems to have learned nothing from the gait and posture of others. He is not one of the upright bipeds, because he slants; he doesn't so much walk as get ready to dive. And he hardly ever seems to sit. There is too much leg around, perhaps. Or maybe his hip joints have never taken to the suggestion of the right angle. Sometimes—very occasionally—he will lie down, and the effect is spectacular. He tends to do it wearing his hat, with the jutting pipe remaining in the mouth. To my recollection, none of his films show him lying on anything so commonplace as a bed, although he has been seen supine on a road in *Les Vacances de M. Hulot* and curved amazingly along the serpentine front of a tormenting modern sofa tipped over onto its back in *Mon Oncle*. This is no ordinary man. He can make asphalt look quite like an air mattress; he can also make it clear that a modern piece of furniture feels uncommonly like asphalt.

Mon Oncle is an attack of blistering docility on the generally unadmitted discomfort dealt out by house pride, contemporary design, and high standards of dusting. Hulot's sister, called Mme. Arpel, who is seldom seen without a duster, lives in a balefully mechanized and hygienic house, where a speck of dirt would be like an oath in the Vatican. Her husband, who is in plastics, is a quail-shaped man who wears thick clothes however bright the sun. They live a life of unvarying merriment and pep. The front gates open by remote-control buzzer, and at the same time, if the company merits it, a sculptured fish in the middle of the unnatural little garden starts spouting water. For trade deliveries, and for her brother, the fountain subsides. The Arpels live in a world of ceremony but no actual fun, of regal fuss with two convoluted chairs that are placed in throne positions for the Arpels to watch mere television, of flavorless steaks cooked in two seconds by infrared rays, of high heels clicking on polished floors. Clothes are like the poor in the New Testament—always with them, and quite a trial. A severe-looking guest whom Mme. Arpel casts as a splendid possible future wife for Hulot, and as a certain admirer of the house, is dressed in a sort of horse rug or table runner. A dog leash then gets impossibly tangled in one of her long earrings. The women in the Arpels' world are perpetually harassed by their bags and stoles and hobble skirts, and M. Arpel throws his wife into a panic by nearly forgetting his gloves when he drives to work.

Hulot, on the other hand, is curiously absented from his clothes, which regularly include the familiar short raincoat and ancient hat whatever the weather. He also seems agreeably unemployable. His natural allies are mongrel dogs and dirty children, who follow him in drives. His nephew, Gérard, adores him. Gérard's chirpy mother tends to sterilize the boy out of existence; Hulot is a comrade, being muddle's natural kin. The uncle lives on the top floor of a charming, ramshackle house in an old part of Paris, with windows that he arranges carefully before leaving every day so that his caged canary will get the sun's reflection. Until the last shot of the film, one never sees the inside of this house. All one catches are glimpses through half-open stairways and hall windows of people's heads and feet, or a segment of a girl lodger in a bath towel waiting to scuttle across a corridor when Hulot's legs have disappeared downstairs. Tati is visually very interested in bits of people. If he were playing the game of pinning the tail on the donkey, I think he would tend to find the dissociated tail too engrossing to go any further.

Maybe all funniness has a tendency to throw settled things into doubt. Where most people will automatically complete an action, a great comedian will stop in the middle to have a think about the point of it, and the point will often vanish before our eyes. In *Mon Oncle*, Hulot has this effect very strongly about the importance of holding down a job. His sister, who is bothered by his life as if it were a piece of grit in her eye, has put him to work in her husband's plastics factory. The place produces miles of red plastic piping, for some reason or other. Various machines pump out rivers of it. Hulot is mildly interested. "Keep an eye on number five," says a workmate mystifyingly, wrapped up in a piece of cellophane like a sandwich in an automat, and taking no notice of the fact that Hulot is slumped over a table and half moribund because of a gas leak. Number five, a rebel machine, starts to produce piping with occasional strange swellings in it, like a furlong of boa constrictor that has slowly eaten its way through a flock of sheep. The thing then takes it into its head to start tying off the piping every few inches, as if it were a sausage machine. Hulot goes on manfully keeping an eye on it, which is all he has been told to do, and quite right. Care for plastic can go too far.

His sister is a living witness to that. For her wedding anniversary, she has given her husband an automatic and doubtless plastic garage door that opens when his car goes past an electric eye. M. Arpel is overjoyed, in his plastic way. "No more keys. Happy?" his wife chirrups. Their dachshund then sniffs the electric eye and shuts them in the garage, yapping amiably while they try to persuade him to sniff again. The new door, like the bedroom floor of the house, has two round windows near the top; the Arpels' disembodied faces appear, yelling inaudibly for help, and bobbing about behind the windows like air bubbles in a bricklayer's level.

Husband and wife are content, mostly. They represent a new order of happiness. Hulot represents the old disorder. The Arpels, who rather grow on you, are funny partly because they treat themselves as if they were machines and partly because they have lost the defining human sense of relative importances. Trotting around with their gadgets and their dusters and planning tea parties, they have no grasp of their scale in the universe; they are a counterpart of the sort of endearing Great Danes who will try to fit all four legs onto a lap in the delusion that they are the size of Pekes. These proud owners of this awful model house, tripping around on an artistic but farcically unwalkable pattern of paving stones and being careful not to put a toe to the grass, conduct themselves with a sober sense of import and duty. When they entertain, they might be the President of the Republic and his wife welcoming the signators of a peace treaty. The difference that they are only having some neighbors to a paralyzingly difficult tea party at which everyone is spattered by a minor debacle with the spouting fish destroys no one's aplomb and no one's sense of occasion. It is part of Tati's humor that the Arpels' perception of things is fastidiously concentrated and only a trifle off the point. Who is to say, in fact, that their absorption is not the norm, even if it does screen out what seems more fascinating to the casual observer? They are in the same comic position as the plumbers in one of Robert Dhéry's films, who stalk backstage through hordes of stark-naked showgirls without paying them the slightest heed while talking about nuts and bolts. In *Jour de Fête*, the postman played by Jacques Tati is entranced by the idea of Americanization of the mails through speedier transport. Speedier transport means, to him, bicycling instead of walking. The bicycle suits Tati. He uses one in *Mon Oncle*—a rather dashing one, with a puttering little motor. The shape of the thing fits his legs, which are long enough to turn the bike at will into a quadruped. Bicycles also meet a certain stateliness in his style and a certain disinclination for any vehicle that outsizes the human frame. You feel that he much detests the shiny cars in *Mon Oncle*. He prefers doughnut carts and horse-drawn wagons. The failed plastic piping is hurriedly taken away in a cart drawn by a strong-minded gray horse that exerts a will of its own about going to the right when the driver wants the left; its mood is not so unlike the recalcitrance of the obstreperous plastics machine, after all. Hulot has his own rules about mess. When he trips his way through the rubble of his part of Paris into the antiseptic modern quarter, he is careful to replace exactly a dislodged piece of wreckage as he goes.

Tati's droll, elegant films (there are two more to come here—*Playtime*, long since seen in Paris, Rome, and London, and held up in the United States only because of wrangles about the cost of importing an ambitious picture made in seventy millimeter; and *Traffic*, brand-new) establish that one doesn't have to be a comic to do a gag. There are plenty of professionally uproarious people who come on signaling that they are funny men, that they are the life of the party. Tati seems to believe that it is in the nature of all mankind to be funny. High dignitaries have committed some of life's greatest physical gags. Hulot himself—like Keaton's heroes but unlike Chaplin's—is the least patently comic character in his author's scheme. In fact, he is extremely serious. His style is the inversion of the circus tradition, and of that silent-film tradition in which a normal world is ravaged by a comic personality; in Tati's case, the world is made comic by the sobriety of Hulot.

The films express the subtlest sympathy for other people's moods. In the company of the decorous, Hulot is as correct as a furled umbrella. With someone scared—like the maid in *Mon Oncle*, who is petrified by the electric eyes in the place and backs away from them as if they were basilisks—you can see him slowly submerging in fellow cowardice. With dogs, small shopkeepers, and kids, he starts to borrow jauntiness. Everything in the films is meticulous and spare; nothing is pushed, and there are no set pieces. Some of the prettiest moments in Tati's work vanish as fast as a scent, recollected but not recoverable. In *Mon Oncle* there is a promising beginning to a comic sequence when a long shiny car is trying to back into a space between a ramshackle lorry and a vegetable cart. An old, old man carrying a bag with a French loaf sticking out of the end of it shuffles backward and forward with the car two or three times to signal the driver in, courteously shifting the bag from the left hand to the right as he changes direction. And then he simply gives up, and shrugs a mild "The hell with it," and leaves the sequence gently in the air.

AUGUST 28, 1971

Extinguished Salon

Luis Buñuel's *The Exterminating Angel*, from a story by him and Luis Alcoriza, is clumsily acted—his films often are, partly because this master has habitually had to work in a hurry with tenth-string casts—but it is hallucinatorily funny and very much his own. A dinner party for twenty is about to begin. In the kitchen, servants putting glasses on trays and shoveling caviar onto a swan of solid ice start to sniff trouble, and quit the place with the instinct of rats on a ship about to draw away from the quay. The party nevertheless proceeds on its mummified way, with little clicks of cutlery and meaningless pleasantries that sometimes warm up into exhilarated savagery. Something is happening that hasn't anything to do with the strapless satin dresses and the party faces, which look like the heads of suckling pigs glazed in aspic. Men talk secretly about an overdressed woman who has cancer, and say that it won't be long before she's completely bald. There is a concert—"I beg of you, something from Scarlatti"—and then people speak of getting their coats, but no one actually manages to leave. In the end, they bed down for the night. They are inexplicably trapped in the room as if it were surrounded by fire. "This is the hour of maximum depression," says someone at dawn; the lamps are still on, and the milkman doesn't call. The hostess, managing on her last cylinder of a butler, gathers together a semblance of coping and calls for cold cuts. Soon the guests are hacking at a water pipe with an ax, to find something to drink; more satin, bare feet, a woman with hair clips stuck into the top of her strapless dress; and the butler eating a plate of paper frills to fill his stomach—a trick that the undoubtedly metaphor-minded Buñuel makes him describe as having been learned from the Jesuits at school. A hypochondriacal woman flights off into a fantasy of going to Lourdes; a man complains sharply to a lady that she smells like a hyena; and the civilized start looking like bundles of laundry on the floor. "Hell is other people." Well, yes; hell is a *lot* of other people—people who won't go. These people start to repeat some of the things that they said when the party was still apparently normal, desperately attempting to get back to the point where they went wrong. "I beg of you, something from Scarlatti," the same woman says again, sounding quite wild. A man has been quietly shaving his legs with an electric razor; an occult woman plays games with chicken claws that she keeps in her evening bag; beyond the gates, a priest with a nose for the newsy carts along a tour of children to see the hermetic house. Sealed off by what? Superstition? Conventionality? The habits of pretense with which the human personality can wall itself up and finally suffocate? Buñuel's prefatory note in the film declines in advance to spell anything out. Back at the purgatorial party, the guests are now walking round and round in their mysterious confinement like attempted suicides being forced to move in order to keep alive. Next door, a brown bear skids up a column. A small flock of sheep skelter up the handsome staircase. The occult woman has been doing battle with a disembodied hand, trying to stub it out as if it were a wasp. One of Buñuel's oddly shoddy props, it looks like something off a cheap-jack window dummy.

The Exterminating Angel hasn't the weight or the care of *Viridiana*, mostly because of the acting; if ever a film needed filling with a thousand ferociously accurate details of manners collapsing under stress, this one does. The framework seems made to contain more observations of ludicrous hauteur than it actually produces. The rather wooden actors, to whom the exiled Buñuel is often fated, visibly bring no sophistication of their own to his screenplay. It is because of this, I think, that the surreal references sometimes look more autonomous than the film-maker perhaps intended—as if the baaing sheep had drifted in from elsewhere, and the lopped hand had come to grip the throat of the film from some other movie.

AUGUST 26, 1967

Tony Hancock

Like all great comedians, Tony Hancock has the bearing of a solitary. He is a marooned man to whom the rest of the world looks impossibly remote. His distinction is that this does not worry him in the least because, as he yells at the end of *The Rebel*, he regards the world as raving mad. An American in the same position tends to react nervily, remaining apprehensively watchful, like Keaton; a Frenchman will create an introverted dream-life instead, like Tati; but Hancock stares balefully at the distant majority and maintains an unbudging antagonism.

Contrary to the legends about English restraint, of course, a strain of guileful rudeness is a feature of the nation's character, in fiction and in life. The painter whom Hancock creates in *The Rebel* is a brother-in-arms to Joyce Cary's Gulley Jimson. He also has a strange glint of Augustus John.

Without Hancock's presence, the story of *The Rebel* sounds misleadingly mawkish and worked out: a bowler-hatted clerk who is a secret artist suddenly throws away his ledgers and takes off for Paris, leading him into baffling comedy situations about Existentialism, action painting, tycoon art collectors and chi-chi art pundits. If Tony Hancock were a comedian of the little-man sort, sentimentality could hardly be avoided because one would feel that a shy genius was being trodden under. But his script-writers—Alan Simpson and Ray Galton, as on TV—know him inside out, and their judgment is perfectly right; one is in no doubt that he is an appalling painter, and applied to art his lugubrious terseness is marvelously funny.

"Your color's in the wrong shape," he says flatly to a fellow painter in Paris. After a brief glare at the canvas, a nude, he strides up to it and unsettles the artist by saying that he likes the sense of humor in the foot. Then suddenly, with curt authority, pointing to a shadow behind the left heel: "*There's* your picture."

His attitude to his own work is also gustily insulting. Hacking away in his London digs at "Aphrodite at the Water Hole," a concrete nude wickedly suggestive of an Epstein, he shouts excitedly, "A little bit more off the old choppers, I fancy," and knocks a haggish incisor down the throat.

When his landlady (Irene Handl) objects to his representing ducks as beetroot-colored, he points out severely that she obviously can't ever have tried painting birds getting out of the water. "They're off in a flash. You just have to thwack on whatever you have on your brush at the time." This house decorator's view of art, which leads him to look at his canvases as beadily as he once regarded a bubble under the wallpaper during a paper-hanging session on TV, goes down with great *éclat* in Paris, in this film, where his way of talking about his work as "filling in a quick twelve-by-eight" is also much admired.

The Rebel depends perilously on Tony Hancock's personality; the surrounding parts are stiffly written, and played in a chaos of conventions. After the first hour the brilliance begins to sag, partly because Robert Day lacks any sure directing style and partly because the farcical yacht-society dénouement, with a millionaire's wife making a dive for the hero, is an alien situation better suited to Groucho Marx. But it is churlish to pick holes in a film that is the most robust move in British comedy for years. If we had any comedy directors who were up to working with Hancock, there would be no holding him.

MARCH 5, 1961

Renoir's Flophouse

There exists a rare old Russian screen record of Gorki's *The Lower Depths* as it was played long ago by the Moscow Art Theatre, with the great Kachalov, now dead, as the Baron. Renoir's marvelous *Les Bas Fonds* of 1936 compares interestingly. The Moscow Art Theatre picture is entirely Russian in the wit, the buffoonery, the richness of idiosyncrasy, the profusion of swollen, hallucinated faces, dreaming and condemned. Renoir's version has Louis Jouvet in the Kachalov part and remains entirely French, where any other director would have tried to confect Russianness. "Bresson has said that originality is when you try to do the same as everybody else but don't quite make it," Renoir once remarked to me, apropos something different. The old flophouse in his *Les Bas Fonds*—built around one of the courtyards he loves—is unconsciously just as much Renoir's original issue as Gorki's. Renoir's character is all there in the film: in the response to a story about a dandy who has been stripped by the bailiffs and fallen among guttersnipes who recognize and fear his class; in the minute social details; in the bitter tenderness; and in the breadth of temperament and curiosity that fills the frames of any Renoir film with unmistakable flickering life. He begins with a long shot on Jouvet, the debonair Baron in military uniform, hearing out a voice-over lecture from a superior officer about debts. The shot is held daringly, as Godard often holds one now. In the Baron's palatial home, run by a sadly grateful, class-conscious servant who is never going to get his back wages, a burglar played by Jean Gabin comes in to pinch the valuables and sits down with the Baron to a comradely glass of champagne on tick. The Baron knows what is going to happen to his life, like everyone else in his circle. He has squandered a fortune. In the gambling rooms, his unamiable friends can always tell when he has lost: he walks out calmly enough with a cigarette, but it is unlit, whereas he unconsciously lights it if he has won. The slope now leads only downwards, and he already knows himself to be in Gabin's shoes.

When he gets to the flophouse, after leaving his empty mansion and his unpaid servant with an air, he finds himself at an irreparable distance from everyone else there. Gabin leans on an elbow in a field and talks to him about being fed up. "The mattresses . . . saucepans . . . every word that is spoken is rotten to the core," Gabin says, talking beside a river with a grass-blade in his mouth, in one of the interludes that Renoir directs as no one else can. The Baron and the burglar have escaped for the moment from the flophouse—from the girls desperate to get married as a way out, from the jammy-mouthed government inspector promising to make a princess of one of the down-and-outs if she will have dinner with him, from the crazed alcoholic actor who sees visions of a cure. The Baron has disabused the drunk of those visions, and the drunk has hit back: "You're a real baron. Even with holes in your shoes, you're destructive." Lying with Gabin on the bank, the Baron says that everything in his life has seemed like a dream, consisting mostly of changing clothes—beginning with being a schoolboy, then being married, then a government official—and he looks down at his tramp's coat, the sleeves ending four inches above his wrists.

Les Bas Fonds is unmistakably Renoir's. He shot in deep focus long before Orson Welles and Gregg Toland, because he wants to see everything in motion at the same time and because he prefers not to commandeer your eye. He always likes to see what is going on in the next room, through half-open doors or across a courtyard, so his compositions often have the tunneling perspectives of the great Flemish interior paintings. The scenario of the film was presented to him by Jacques Companeez and Eugène Zamiatine, and he responded to it at once. The adaptation and the dialogue are by Renoir himself, with Charles Spaak, who later collaborated with him on *La Grande Illusion*. He seems always to have been interested by the idea of a beggars' kingdom, like Gay, Brecht, and Weill before him. More than this, his version of the Gorki play becomes, through his temperament and intellect, a heart-rending poem about the loss of caste. The delicate comprehension it proffers to the resolves and wounds of class that are often made light of now by progressive film directors puts it thematically with *La Règle du Jeu* and *La Grande Illusion*, his two masterpieces. (And, indeed, with practically every other film he has ever made. He said to me recently, about another director, "Probably everyone makes only one film in his life, and then smashes it into pieces and makes it again.") Renoir's feeling in *Les Bas Fonds* for the fop deposed, for the grandee who has lost his birthright in high style and will always be mistrusted by his new familiars for that very stylishness, expresses the ideas and the love that led him to his greatest works.

SEPTEMBER 6, 1969

Fellini Himself

"Signor Fellini," says an interviewer in the middle of Fellini's *The Clowns*, "what message are you trying to give us here?" A bucket instantly falls over Fellini's head, and then another over the interviewer's. Splat, wham. Trip over a basin of paste, explode another clown's explodable trousers, turn the fire hose on the elephant. We are in the circus world that Fellini has often taken to be the world itself all the time, as in Gelsomina's march behind the musicians in *La Strada*, and the gay, idiotic strolls along the beach in *I Vitelloni*, and the moonstruck mask of Giulietta Masina exchanging stares with us in *Cabiria*, as if she were a clown who had clambered into the audience. It is the buffoon's world, the arena of mock gladiators, where combat is mortal one minute and gone the next, the Inquisition that doesn't count, because the fatal questions proceed like a schoolboy riddle in some dream of rudeness from long ago. "What message are you trying to give us here?" says the film. A bucket over the intellect, please. "How do you lose ten pounds of fat?" goes the schoolboy catch. "Cut off your head."

The film starts with the sight of a small child in a nightgown—obviously the small Fellini—leaning out of a window in the dark. There is a joyful vamp-till-ready by Nino Rota. Ropes screech. The circus big top is going up. Prisoners listen from the local jail. The circus draws children and convicts because it sabotages authority. The ringmaster is a figure of pomp without power. The white clowns—the symbolic grownups in the scheme of clowning, with blanched indoor faces and black lips and majestic sneers—are overdressed, overprivileged, and no match for the clowns called the *augusti*, their impossible charges, who wear the same dirty costumes the whole time and refuse to recite a nice poem when the vicar comes to tea. Of all the water sloshed around in circuses, the augusts slosh the most. They are the kindergarten criminals, and crime pays in gallons. Their energy includes an empty, splendid braggadocio that Fellini must always have doted on and found touching. It is there in the swagger of his wife, Masina. *The Clowns*—commissioned by Italian television—is slightly a documentary-within-the-entertainment, with Fellini himself appearing as the head of a camera unit recording retired clowns, but mostly a spectacle, with young Italian clowns playing the tricks and wearing the make-up of famous forebears. The spectacle is full of showing-off undaunted by fatuity. Jungle men come on and ripple their muscles before doing no harm whatever. The ringmaster keeps helpfully interjecting things like "Anyone with a weak heart had better leave." The strong man challenges a large opponent called Miss Mathilde, who looks much like Brünnhilde, though with tights slightly baggy above her sandals, and breastplates like two pressure-cooker lids. "And now," announces the ringmaster, "in a *terrible experiment*, the fakir will be buried in the glass coffin." It all seems very Italian. I once saw a magnificently costumed policeman in Florence directing traffic as if he were Napoleon, although the traffic was already successfully following identical commands of tame mechanical traffic lights. He was a figure of military brilliance, with a massive chest, though not much leg.

Fellini is not saying that the circus represents anything else, not indulging the sawdust-among-the-sequins heartache, not making any point except that he adores clowns. The subject is extravagant; the match of style to subject is exact and tonic. We are pitched into the entertainment like tumblers. There are clowns all over the place. This is Fellini pure. In the ring or out of it, say his films, nothing is absolute. He believes profoundly in the redeemable, and clowning is the system where there is always another chance and where damage never matures. It is his native land, and we are in it. Clowns with tear ducts like water pistols, clowns with exploding cars, clowns with hammers, clown dramas with single lines of dialogue like "The cow's loose!" to introduce some ideal muddle, clowns promising to make the smelliest cake that ever was, clowns pumping themselves up in red-and-yellow-striped sweaters, clowns who cry softly to themselves and bay in the ring like dogs at the moon.

After a while, that turn is over. A Fellini bent on homage and learning goes with a camera unit to talk to great clowns in old-age homes. They remember little. They seem more absorbed by their canaries. He looks at a film of one of the historic performances, but it breaks and burns in the projector. Another rare fragment of the film is run for him by a tidy-minded woman archivist who winds up the insufficient record of a career as if it were a remnant of ribbon in a draper's shop at closing time. We are told that the best clowns are Spaniards and Italians, and then there is a somber cut to a young tiger being trained. With the switch from the real life of recollections to the real life of a circus in rehearsal, the ancient ritual of entertainment has a moment of seeming satanic. Fellini's color photography—by di Palma—sometimes has the same effect. Now and then, the sumptuous tone is disquieting. "The clowns didn't make me laugh. They frightened me," says a child in the film, speaking for Fellini. The picture will suddenly darken for a moment, as if a bird's wing had covered the sun.

Fellini makes connections between clowns and village dunces which look as if they were first made when he was small. There is an image of a fool tramp being threatened by a countrywoman with a scythe. Another of a midget nun, always in a hurry on some task, who says that the saints don't trust anyone else. Another of a drunk's wife: "You should drop dead, and I for marrying you." The dirty threats of clowns, their dedicated scuttling on peculiar errands, their savagery about midgets, and the eternal abuse by the elegant white clown of the unemployable bungler he is coupled with sometimes remind Fellini all too much of things outside the circus. Clowns express a peasant dislike of those who don't work, and a peasant cruelty to the abnormal. There is a wonderful shot of a villager creeping along a wall and being jeered at by the local kids. He can be panicked into behaving like this only by seeing war films; then he goes slightly mad, and puts on a soldier's uniform and acts as if he were in occupied territory. In fact, of course, when the clown characters in any of Fellini's other films chance to look around them they always find themselves in the most heavily occupied territory imaginable. But the moments swiftly pass, and they are back in their own beguiled systems. Like much else that is lyric in Fellini, *The Clowns* celebrates quick recovery in its characters, and the film itself has that gift. The mood spins upward fast. Antonioni cherishes the enervating and hangs on to it with the grip of some high-strung insomniac insisting on eight hours' restlessness in bed every night; Fellini shakes off melancholy in a second and behaves as if he wanted the day never to end.

Like Claudia Cardinale in *8½*, Fellini's clowns express the idea of something unspoilable. Nothing alters in their world. Nothing hurts. Mistakes are blissful. A clown bashes another one with a hammer. "You missed!" cries the hammered one in triumph, but holding up a finger with a swelling as big as a grapefruit, and then, after a second hit has wrecked a second finger, he yells, still more victoriously, "You missed again!" But these immune people we are watching, who seem to have no age—we also hear about terrible accidents to them, and some of them are very very old. Fellini gives his film double vision. For half an hour at a time he makes clowns seem the theater's version of dunces and lunatics, but when we suddenly see real dunces and real lunatics they are not like the clowns at all. There is a scene in an asylum. Up above, clowns fly on high wires, anxious to divert, playing Lear's Fool; below sit real fools with catatonia, closed in on themselves, clenched like sea anemones. The sequence has a piercing gentleness and no grotesquerie. There is a wonderful observation of nerve being mustered in a vacuum when a woman patient draws the edges of her coat together and raises her chin. Fellini once meant to make a film about a *vitellone* young doctor working in an asylum, to be called *The Free Women of Magliano*. He wrote an account of it in *Cahiers du Cinéma* in 1957. If he had made it, I daresay he might then have glamorized madness, and he could have been accused of joining the giddy current quest for enlightenment in the psychotic and the stoned, which is a direct parallel to the taste of the Romantics nearly two hundred years ago; all the same, the essay suggests a thicker sense of character than that, like a novelist's.

Fellini's clowns are discards of modernity. So are all the characters he has cared for most in his films, sometimes risking banality. The richness and speed of his gift rescue *The Clowns* and make it a glory. Clowns are his pagan seers, like the character played by Richard Basehart in *La Strada:* divining anarchists, convivial, without guilt. Fellini is the most pre-Freudian of directors. If his characters are unhappy, any cure has nothing to do with "adjusting." The augusts in their run-down clothes are cheeky losers without complexes, and they are also not political in the slightest. They embody revolt, not revolution. The white clowns, sumptuously dressed and stern, like popes, are the authoritarians who are their other half. The complicity of opposites is a cause of endless trouble, but so is marriage, so is family. The augusts suffer squalls of weeping. Their eyelids are sometimes as red as their noses. Nobody pays any heed. One of them cries into a bucket; another says cheerfully, paddling, "Oh, good, your sorrow will refresh my feet." Fellini's film is full of blithe cross-purposes and bathos. The script girl in the film-within-the-film is a rotten typist who tears a sheet of script as she pulls it out of the typewriter; a projectionist can't work a projector. Nobody minds. *The Clowns* happens in a world of not-minding. The aptitude for fun is virgin and carnival, as it was for a moment in the hand-linking scene near the end of *8½*. There is a chaotic circus funeral for one of the clowns: a loafer severely eulogized as having been unfaithful to his friends, and a torment to the gas-and-electricity company. The funeral march mysteriously turns into a triumph. Everything is correctable. Colored paper shoots down from the roof—for once, enough paper streamers. The sound track rustles as the procession pushes through the ribbons. At his best, Fellini catches the look of loss on a million faces, and, beyond that, a kind of felicity.

Now I put a bucket over my head.

JUNE 12, 1971

Beckett

Beckett's *Waiting for Godot*, revived in a production as fine and keen as its own prose, arrived in London ten years ago like a sword burying itself in an overupholstered sofa. The serious theater in London then was a theater of posturing and flab; the English Stage Company didn't even yet exist, and the sheer frugality of Beckett's play seemed an affront. He had done far too much on far too little. It was hard then for people to sit comfortably in such an ascetic presence, watching a drama that had no plot, no climax, no star parts, no rousing rhetoric, not even a dilemma apart from the dilemma of how to live, which had long since dropped out of the repertory of questions that could properly be asked in a modern play in England.

Now there seems to be nothing formidable about the play technically at all. The people who called it obscure or pretentious must have been finding labels for their own disquiet, for the method of the play is as clear and clean as a plucked bone, and if it were pretentious the situation of the two tramps waiting on the road for a key to their lives could never have become the powerful myth that it has. The only puzzling thing about *Godot* now is not the play, but the way we take it: why on earth has it ever accumulated such a reputation for determinism?

Part of the trouble is perhaps the way Beckett has been bracketed with Ionesco. Ionesco's characters often do talk like ticker tapes, and they are indeed pushed around helplessly by the circumstances of the world, by goods and chattels and uninspected banalities; but Beckett's characters are freely eloquent, with a speech that flies up out of the mundane and tugs in the air like a kite, and they live in a void which they alone have any power over or any obligation to change.

Whereas Ionesco's plays are crammed with disagreeably dynamic objects, cupboards that assume the initiative and chairs as fertile as rabbits, Beckett's plays habitually happen in an unfurnished void where the only significant object is the human figure, more or less ugly or infirm but all the same often wonderfully oblivious to it. Beckett's characters are anything but pure-dyed pessimists: like most people in real life, they are capable of feeling at one and the same time that existence is both insupportable and indispensable, and that they are both dying and also amazingly well.

"How like a man, to blame on his boots the faults of his feet." Beckett keeps insisting that the tramps' predicaments come out of the dialectic of their own characters. The tramp called Vladimir —marvelously played by Nicol Williamson, with whirling arms and the vast skimming lope of a town-born tramp moving over pavements as though they were heather—is prohibited from laughing, but it is a right he has waived, not one that has been removed. The urns and mounds that encumber the people in the later plays are not imposed; they are annexes of the characters' temperaments, traps created by their own past. Their physical equipment may be grotesquely inadequate for their tasks, but it is all they have, and they are constantly and comically pulling themselves together to mount another feeble attack on the objective, which is "to represent worthily for once the foul brood to which a cruel fate confined us." Beckett's characters are perpetually trying to carve out of the boundless gray flux a piece of time that will have some form and gaiety. They are devoted, in fact, to trying to make art out of the unpromising material of life, and to bringing off at least one achieved stylistic feat as a way of beating the dark. This isn't determinism.

In *Godot* the two tramps behave as though they had a sacred obligation to turn the day into a piece of music hall. It is impossible for them to sustain the effort for long, but they keep nerving themselves to have another go, standing back after a burst of backchat to have a look at the result as though they had to be their own audience in the void. "That wasn't a bad little canter," says Estragon encouragingly to them both after one spurt. *Godot* is a very affectionate play.

Vladimir and Estragon are locked together in a relationship that is a haunting celibate replica of a marriage. They are pitiless in waking each other up for company because they are lonely, for instance, thereby restoring one another to the horror of their situation. Part of the great power of the second act is that by then each has discovered that the other is better and happier without the other, and is trying not to admit that the same might be true of himself, for fear that this might force solitude finally upon him.

Anthony Page's production—much less broad than Peter Hall's English original of ten years ago—is characteristically self-effacing, with a marvelous ear for the rhythms of the text. Pozzo is played by Paul Curran in clothes like a Jorrocks groom, with a boss's accent that crumbles quickly into brotherhood with the tramps: this Godot-substitute of theirs is in fact as beleaguered by panic as they are, and linked inseparably to an idiot who was once his good angel and is now tormenting him to death. In the first act the idiot—Jack MacGowran—has a twitching tirade that employs a breakdown of language with more grief and horror than any other speech I can think of in our half century of experiments with incoherence. Placed where it is, it might well have subdued the whole of the rest of the play if it weren't for Pozzo's great outburst in the second act. The tramps ask Pozzo when his idiot went dumb:

> When! When! One day, is that not enough for you, one day like any day, one day he went dumb, one day I went blind, one day we'll go deaf, one day we were born, one day we'll die, the same day, the same second, is that not enough for you? They give birth astride a grave, the light gleams an instant, then it's night once more.

When a man writes with this noble comic stoicism he can break any rules he likes.

JANUARY 3, 1965
LONDON

Ionesco and Feydeau

Ionesco's *Le Piéton de l'Air* begins rockily but ends as magnificently as *Exit the King*. Like the earlier play, it is about a man called Bérenger who is suddenly aware that he is going to die. Along with the rest of us, he has managed for most of his life to obscure from himself the prospect of extinction, and when he arrives in England with his wife and daughter at the beginning of the play he is absorbed by naïvely seen appearances. The landscape he drops into looks like a primitive, with glowing toy-farm trees and a grape-juice sky like the one in Chagall's "Poet Reclining"; and the grazing is occupied by a set of characters who are deliberately simplified English archetypes.

For the first part of the play—which Jean-Louis Barrault in celery-green plays in a dehumanized mood—the hero behaves very like Ionesco himself in a puckish mood. He gives morosely funny interviews about being tired of actors and of playwrights fighting yesterday's injustices, and there are moments when the play scatters apart like shrapnel and turns into an author's apologia. But when it does start to group itself—when Bérenger speaks of "the years going by like a lot of sacks we send back empty," and a middle-aged lady suddenly voices the universal thought that it is only other people who ever make us know that we are older—the comedy grows as powerfully as *Les Chaises*. It moves from the waking to the sleeping world: back to the skills we have in dreams, which make Bérenger joyfully able to fly, and to childhood nightmares of lost parents.

At his best, which he is in this play, Ionesco is a transcriber of dreams, a witness to fears that we spend a third of our lives inexorably remembering and can forget only in the daytime. In a scene that could be dangerously like J. M. Barrie but works in fact with a child's sense of play, Bérenger levitates and cycles off into the cosmos to explore the afterlife: his report of heaven, which no one believes, is of a monster's world full of columns of guillotined men, men with the heads of geese licking monkeys' behinds, a Paradise where the blessed are burned alive, and beyond that nothing but abysmal space. *Le Piéton de l'Air* follows a difficult split scheme—seized in the second part by vertigo and anguish.

With the Ionesco there is a ravishingly funny thirty-five minute farce by Feydeau called *Ne te promène donc pas toute nue*. The sense of people sealed into the past is as crucial to it as it is to P. G. Wodehouse. Like most good farce—even a farce as apparently antitraditional as Henry Livings' *Eh?*—the play is about a set of people who are impeccably servile to custom and who are called upon suddenly to face a single unmissable gaffe which they can deal with only by behaving as though it isn't there. The gaffe in *Eh?* is the central character: the gaffe in *Toute nue* is a nightdress, which is worn with Sunday hat and button boots by an otherwise devotedly conventional woman, and which every man in the play does indeed consumingly regard as though it weren't there: Madeleine Renaud is naked to every imagination on the stage while the dialogue trots desperately around the point, chatting about civic affairs and the weather.

The appalled fusspot husband, a Deputy with ambitions of becoming a Minister, talks to his election rival with a ghastly lack of conviction about dressing lightly for such a clammy day, while his wife uses the skirt of the nightdress to whisk a wasp out of the marmalade. Madeleine Renaud plays the character with the crushing energy of a woman spring-cleaning, using a bossy trudge that is very funny when it is conducted in lingerie and putting down male dreams as though she were swatting them. The Deputy is played by Jean Desailly, who so perfectly incarnates the bourgeois Frenchman's spirit that even the shape of his tiny mustache begins to look like an irritable shrug of the shoulders in the *mairie*. Like the rest of the company, he understands the crossness that is the cardinal mood of farce: not neurotic, merely ratty.

MARCH 28, 1965
PARIS

Prince Hal's Boon Friend

The Royal Shakespeare Company, which is on its uppers for want of the price of a small tour by the Royals, opens the season at Stratford with magnificent economy by reviving the two parts of *Henry IV* from the 1954 history cycle. Anyone bored by the saving must be badly bored with Shakespeare.

Detail by detail the production isn't perfect; Norman Rodway's Hotspur is strained and square, for one thing. But over-all it is meticulously intelligent, a true expression of the double play that is one of the great marvels of the canon. No other work of Shakespeare's has the same extraordinary twin mesh of historical and personal ethics. The sense of a kingdom on the edge of change is engulfing. Politically the play is even more complex than *Coriolanus*, more expansive, less jaded; and the course of the friendship between Prince Hal and Falstaff is recorded with feelings far beyond the grief in *Romeo and Juliet*. In the capacity that *Henry IV* expresses for simultaneous pain and magnanimity, one sometimes seems to be in the presence not of one man's creative process but of the imagination of humanity itself.

Ian Holm's brilliant Prince Hal, a cool, trim watcher, makes the betrayal of his past with Falstaff seem a deeply rooted act of temperamental necessity instead of an expedient piece of ditching by a new monarch. Quite early in the play, Hal has begun to inspect himself and to cast off his old judgments. He is no longer altogether rapt by Falstaff. The roisterers in Eastcheap are sometimes a whole world for him and sometimes nothing but a tiny faction of subjects. The scene when he refuses to recognize Falstaff is stunningly prepared for in the deathbed scene with his father, which Hal plays drunk. It is a piece of production insight that makes instant sense of Hal's mistake in thinking his father already dead. The vulgarity makes him sober for the rest of his life.

Henry IV is about many things: power, friendship, the withering of fun, the smothering of conscience; but most of all it is about occasion and timing. The old King—a fine performance by Tony Church, red-eyed and querulous—has come to power by fostering a moment of public opinion. His enemies in Northumberland, Scotland and Wales are motivated not only by envy but also by a suspicion that he has dangerously misread the clock of the State. It is because Falstaff behaves as if he were immortal that he becomes a sacrifice; the people who survive are the ones who sense the machinery of time moving on.

Hal grows into a good king when he knows that something is over, and Hotspur has to be killed because he is a "Mars in swaddling clothes," arrested at a stage of infant aggression and thinking that the engine of England can be driven by brute strength.

The losers in the play believe that power is something static, like the throne itself; the victor knows that it is a process.

Paul Rogers' Falstaff is elegiac from the beginning. He is funny not because he is simple but because he is hideously shrewd, screwing up his eyes when he is in a fix because he has a horribly intelligent double vision about himself. He pretends to be irritable when he is abused or caught out in a lie, but he is really rather gratified by insults; they are a sort of compliment to his baby's ego, which is ravenous to be noted and intrigued by any mirror that is held up to it. Hal's insults are a game to him. Jokes about his size give him no pain since they are never aimed at the cause of it; other people take it that he is fat because he is greedy, but he himself feels swollen by a heroic attempt to banish melancholy ("grief blows you up like a bladder"). He boozes to warm his blood, so he tells himself, and to sharpen his wits for Hal's sake; and in the prince's presence in the first play he seems indestructible, alive with the young man's affection and almost floating with fatness.

But in the second half of the play his mass acquires leaden weight, and in the scenes without the prince the joker begins to lose his way. His sensuality becomes wan, his body aches, and his gout draws on. A hole is cut in his boot for the swelling, and his movements hurt him. With Doll Tearsheet on his lap he revives for a moment with thoughts of bed, but in the next half line he is gripped by self-disgust and fear of death. Apparently safely wrapped in an eternal present, he feels in fact the chill of mortality more keenly even than the king. He is like a toddler gifted with some appalling edge of adult apprehension.

"I shall be sent for soon," he says furiously after banishment, telling himself that the king's betrayal was only a passing mood; "at night." Their ancient night, "a lion," is what he yearns for all existence to be like, out of time, drowned in sack, a limbo of private life and immortal license; but for Hal it becomes a dream to be shaken off, a deceiving infancy that he leaves behind to see his avid boon companion as a profane and surfeited old man.

Like all Shakespeare's greatest plays, *Henry IV* is immensely complex and also very simple. To a child seeing it, the production by John Barton, Trevor Nunn, and Clifford Williams might shake down into a series of pictures: a crowned father in a narrow black bed envying a political enemy for his son, a red-headed family with split Northumbrian vowels plotting rebellion in the North, a prince mimicking his father's disappointment while he is sitting in a fat man's chair in a tavern, grown men pretending to be children around a tarred gibbet in a screaming wind, and an archbishop playing deadly politics in a wood with rooks cawing over his head. The sight of Ian Holm on the field at Shrewsbury after killing Hotspur, sobbing with hysteria and exhaustion after a fight with buffoonishly heavy broadswords, is one of the best things in the production. It is meant to earn laughs, and the fact that it made some schoolgirls giggle on the first night shouldn't put the producers off. John Bury's sets are superb.

STRATFORD-ON-AVON
APRIL 10, 1966

Of all the probably apocryphal stories about royalty, the one about Shakespeare having written *The Merry Wives of Windsor* to the instructions of Queen Elizabeth seems among the likeliest.

Shakespeare would have known better than anyone that for Falstaff to fall in love would be ruinous. In *Henry IV*, where the character stands pure, the knight's egotism is dedicated and inviolable; this is one of the things that set him outside the time scale of ambition in which the historical characters are trapped. For a queen to cause him to be dragged out of comic eternity and attached to the apron strings of a Windsor housewife must be one of the most philistine acts in the history of feminism. It is as though Queen Victoria were to have insisted that Conan Doyle make Sherlock Homes fall for Irene and botch up a case.

And so emerged the only bourgeois-spirited play that Shakespeare wrote—and in fourteen days, if the legend is right, though if *Hay Fever* took Noël Coward only three days I don't know that *The Merry Wives* can have cost Shakespeare more than a morning. From a tradition of writing in verse about kings for a popular audience, he abruptly set himself to producing a prose spectacle about the middle classes to titillate the Queen's Court.

As many people have said ever since it was first produced, *The Merry Wives* is not a good play. Much of it is perfunctory, and the travesty of the knight is painful; he should have stayed in the smoking room, for the whole secret at the heart of the Falstaff scenes in *Henry IV* is their easy and exclusive maleness. In the "Henrys," it is when Doll Tearsheet and Dame Quickly have left that the men are free to be themselves; on their own they can abandon wit, which is an exhibition, and take up humor, which is self-addressed.

In John Blatchley's beguiling new production of *The Merry Wives* he has excised a lot of prancing and subplotting and summoned up instead a lot of Lewis Carroll and Widow Twankey. It is an evening full of magic and horselaughs, with fable pipings by Malcolm Williamson scored for flutes and trumpet and glockenspiel, and tender comic designs by André François. The black-and-white sets are like school children's drawings, unapologetic and unexplained, including a gauze dropped into the tavern scene that seems to represent a disembodied trudging foot and that reminded me of the lone gum boot that used to stand in the window of an old leather-shop in Piccadilly Circus with a label saying that it had been in water without leaking since the Battle of Waterloo.

The characters are dressed in the colors of crayons: lilac and chalky pink and sulphur-yellow, with baggy tights and lamb-cutlet ruffs and cheerful antiwalking shoes that have heels like clowns' noses. The men's codpieces, usually the most knowing bit of costume ever devised, in this case look more like lumps of Plasticine plonked onto dolls by a playing child.

All the way through, it is the trace of pantomime in the play that John Blatchley has enlarged on: in the fight scene, for instance, the foppish French doctor gets his sword joyously stuck in the mud. The laugh at Falstaff's inept declaration to Mistress Page—Brenda Bruce, looking beautifully put out in a Tenniel court-card dress and a minute ostrich feather—is the laugh of kids at adults putting their feet in it. The characters lug the scenery around themselves, fall up nonexistent stairs, and crash onto their bums because the walls give as easily as the one at the beginning of the Marx Brothers' *A Night in Casablanca*. Brenda Bruce struggles downstage for ages with the basket, and then says brightly, "Look, there's a basket."

In this atmosphere of lucid innocence there is a pathetic seriousness about Falstaff that restores some of his lost dignity. Though Clive Swift is underfueled in the part, he makes you hear that the scene after the ducking is marvelously written; the feeling of physical self-loathing in it is almost as anguished as it is in the Sonnets. In this production, the scene begins with Falstaff lying on his side in the tavern like a whale and swimming sadly in his sleep, breasting his way up to the daylight through the suffocating barriers of flesh, and landing gasping on the beach. "I have a kind of alacrity in sinking. . . . Thrown into the Thames and cooled like a horseshoe, hissing hot. . . . Water swells a man. . . ." The melancholy encumbered vision of himself is very clear. It is the characteristic vicious insight of the fat, like the self-portrait of herself as an aged load spilled onto the garden path that plagues the heroine of Angus Wilson's *Late Call* when she has fallen on her way to a party.

DECEMBER 20, 1964
LONDON

The Golden Girl

In *Let's Make Love*, sitting at rehearsal in sweater and tights with a textbook on her lap, Marilyn Monroe explained that she was studying geography so that she would know what a person was referring to. Arthur Miller's *The Misfits*, directed by John Huston, is pervaded by the same defiant comic idiom; Marilyn's waifish intensity is somehow transferred to the other characters, especially to the cowboy played by Clark Gable, and the bronco-rider of Montgomery Clift. Their despairing directness with each other becomes a metaphor for immaturity that is often poetically touching.

From the text of the screenplay, one expected less. The dialogue can seem disconcertingly awkward on the page, and Arthur Miller's view of his characters sometimes so sentimental as to be unintelligent; but the film is made under such a spell that even Eli Wallach's impossible line as a guilt-stricken ex-pilot—"I can't make a landing and I can't get up to God"—becomes speakable. Some of the spell, of course, must be put down to Marilyn Monroe's physique, which the cameraman dotes upon as openly as everyone else in the picture, particularly upon her backview in jeans on a horse and her technique while hitting a ball attached to a piece of elastic. But the mood of the film is chiefly cast by her curious, childish urgency, which holds her three squires in thrall. "You're really hooked in. Whatever happens to anybody, it happens to you," the pilot remarks, considering her. "People say I'm just nervous," she says anxiously; to which he replies, "If it weren't for the nervous people in the world, we'd still be eating each other."

As Lionel Trilling once pointed out in writing about *Lolita*, the concept of romantic love in fiction depends on unattainability, and in the twentieth century this is a difficult point to make credible. To turn the beloved into a twelve-year-old girl is one way of doing it; another is to make her physically available but emotionally out of reach, like the heroine of *The Misfits*, which is a deeply romantic film. Marilyn Monroe plays a lost, questing woman waiting in Reno for her divorce, and her final conciliation is not only glib but also runs right against the form of the piece, for her character lies in being wayward and alienated: doing a melancholy drunken dance alone in a dark garden, twisting her head away during the furious sequences in which the three men catch wild horses to be sold as dogmeat, and finally yelling hysterically at them in a remote long-shot, irate in a hostile desert.

It is perfectly obvious that, in writing with this desperate perception about an impossible golden girl, Arthur Miller was writing about his wife. But art is often semi-autobiographical, especially about love, and the fact that the associations here are gossip-reporters' property is no reason to belittle the film. With reservations about some ineptly overcharged lines, *The Misfits* is a sad, beguiling allegory made with unmistakable truth of feeling; if it weren't, the caustic comedy of Thelma Ritter's performance and the hard violence of the mustang sequences could scarcely be accommodated so smoothly.

JUNE 4, 1961

After she had been working with her on *The Prince and the Showgirl*, Sybil Thorndike said about Marilyn Monroe:

> On the set, I thought, surely she won't come over, she's so small-scale, but when I saw her on the screen, my goodness, how it came over. She was a revelation. We theater people tend to be so outgoing. She was the reverse. The perfect film actress, I thought. . . .

O wise and piercing sibyl. The long to-and-fro about whether or not Marilyn Monroe is an actress is really a question of semantics. If acting means the ability to project the idea of a big role through a proscenium arch, the answer is obviously no: on a stage, I doubt whether she would have a fraction of the extraordinary sweet power that she has on the screen. But then nor would Garbo, with whom she has, in fact, a good deal else in common: the same curious phosphorescence on film, the same hint of sympathy for the men who fall in love with her, and the same mixture of omniscience and immaturity, though where Garbo is half ice-goddess and half a surprisingly athletic boy, Marilyn is a tragicomic blend of a sumptuous courtesan and a stammering small girl. In a way, her sheer gift of poignant physical presence is an essence of film-acting, for the weight that cinema gives to sensuous detail is one of its great potencies, distinguishing it sharply from the theater. When this characteristic fuses with an actor who has as much physical magnetism as James Dean, or Marlon Brando, or Marilyn Monroe, the effect is transfixing. It is also much more than simply sexual. Apart from the "flesh-impact" (Billy Wilder) and the "tortile, wambling walk" (*Time*), Marilyn Monroe's abundant physique has the most subtle and perfected comic implications.

One comes, with a pair of tongs, to Maurice Zolotow's noxious book. Apart from the style, a peep-bo prose that uses "the bovine" for "cow" and constantly scampers off to hide its face in French (the *mystère*, the *jeunes gens*, a magnificent *derrière*), the material of the book is an unseemly pile of private anecdotes, leering asides, and cheap psychological speculations, bolstered by a personality that seems, on the evidence here, to be pretty self-important even in the context of the ironclad trade to which the author belongs. The phenomenon of the show-business gossip-writer who sees himself as the star's dear personal friend is becoming a familiar one, but Mr. Zolotow is the first reporter I have read who actually casts himself as his subject's lover.

> I found the room—or rather myself—growing unbearably hot. The jersey blouse was cut loosely, or perhaps it was my mind that was cut loosely that day. . . . A combination of literary curiosity and lust sorely tempted me to fling myself on the bed and make love to her. What would have been her reaction? And how inspired was she as an *amoriste?* . . . The world will never know.

MARCH 24, 1961

Marilyn Monroe had, to say the least, a moving personality, but *Marilyn* leaves you tearless. The film clips that Twentieth Century-Fox have gummed together aren't a memorial to an actress; they're a memorial to a contract, a sort of votive offering by Fox to the star system and the big-studio machine. Thank god for the success of *The Longest Day*, you seem to hear the board of directors muttering, and please don't let Elizabeth Taylor be ill again while we're shooting.

The commentary between the clips is spoken—"personally narrated"—by Rock Hudson. At the beginning of the film the cameras happen, by great luck, to catch him on one of Fox's sound stages, wandering about with a raincoat over his arm as though the weather had been bad in his dressing room and crumbling the artificial snow with a sad look in his eye. As you would expect, he is made to go in for lots of rhetorical questioning about "the magic quality that makes a star." When he has settled into a private viewing room and given the OK to the projectionists, he struggles to define what it was that made Marilyn famous. In the end the script hits on it and calls her, in a triumphant ungrammaticism, "more unique," which somehow deftly suggests the uniqueness of all the other Fox stars too.

There are fifteen clips, starting with Marilyn in the chorus line in *Ticket to Tomahawk*. Nothing from *The Misfits*, or *Some Like It Hot*. They weren't Fox pictures. At the end, to make everyone happy again after some meaningless and painful clips from her unfinished last picture, the film shows her singing "Diamonds Are a Girl's Best Friend," a piece of whipped-up Hollywood exuberance that she actually does rather woodenly. But as the Personal Narrator says, with a final spurt of sincere-type acting, it's the way he likes to remember her.

The only nice thing one can say about this horrible picture is that it does a certain amount of credit to the skill and sympathy of the best Hollywood script-writers. This is one of the good aspects of the system: the dialogue that Marilyn was given, even very early in her career, really did seem to come out of her own humor and character. In *All About Eve* and *How to Marry a Millionaire* and *The Seven Year Itch*, you feel the lines might have been breathed by her own goldfish mouth. Marilyn's style always had a comic moral charge: a remark from her about keeping undies in the icebox, or about not saying "hey, butler" to a passing butler in case it happens to be a person's name, can seem a principle of living.

JULY 28, 1963

Woody Allen

Take the Money and Run, written by Woody Allen and Mickey Rose and directed by Allen, also stars our Woody as a lad named Virgil who has insane hopes of being a great criminal. He bungles it from the start. As the commentary of the film proudly trumpets, not listening to a word it is saying, "Virgil is an immediate failure at crime." The commentary sounds like one of those Log-Cabin-to-White-House specials on television. It is intentionally quite deaf to the central fact that its hero is awful at everything. His cello teacher, interviewed for reminiscences, as people on this sort of earnest biographical program are, admits that even Virgil's cello-playing was terrible. "He would just saw it back and forth," says the teacher, in a grieved Viennese accent. "He had no concept of the instrument. He was blowing into it." When Virgil falls in love, it is with an unendowed girl who has, he says nicely, a sort of genius about T shirts; he never *saw* anyone who knew so much about T shirts. His mother and father, wearing false noses, have a row on camera about their famous son, whose complete unfitness for fame hits them in the eye even in public. "If he weren't rotten, why would we be wearing these false disguises?" they say, ignoring the camera and fighting like hell. Virgil's father sticks up for himself in the end and says, "I *tried* to beat God into him." At this, Virgil's mother only sobs. "You're a very dominating person," she says. My favorite part of this sweetly dopey picture is a holdup sequence in which Virgil, after standing nicely in queue, presents a polite note to a bank teller, apparently saying, "I have a gub. Abt natural." The problem is one of handwriting. The snooty teller, sniffing an illiterate, say disbelievingly that he wants to see this gub. "That's a plain 'n'!" Virgil yells to the bank manager, who also reads "gub." It is like being back at exams, when the stupid professors can't even decipher the junk you're churning out for them. Later, on the run to Mexico, he grandly reassures his new wife that she's not to worry, because he knows how to use a gub. The "b" has now got into his speech. "Did I say 'gub' again?" he says, frowning at himself behind the misleadingly brainy-looking spectacles. When he fails to make the Ten Most Wanted list, despair sets in. He starts saying he is a gynecologist. It's true that the picture goes by fits and starts, and that some of the plot is parochially limited to sending up idiot remarks of the kind made by people on idiot television programs, but the film has a lot of wild charm.

AUGUST 30, 1969

There is a new Woody Allen film called *Bananas*. He wrote it (with Mickey Rose), directed it and stars in it, and goes on somehow endearingly to imply that he has thus dropped three bricks in a row, though concealing from us any mood of apology and devoutly hoping that his lost nerve will be found beneath a cinema seat and returned under the impression that it is nothing more signal than a dropped pair of spectacles. He plays an overparented, politically flustered character called Fielding Mellish. Below the surface he seems to be coping with a secret feeling that the whole project of the film is loopy and he is damned if he is going to let us in on that ignominy. The Woody Allen style characteristically lies in keeping his end up in circumstances obviously doomed, and obvious to him most of all. His spry and eager efforts to have a stab hide the most unsullied absence of worldly optimism. Left to himself, you feel, the Woody Allen comic character would have no ambition, drive, or social hopes whatever. He would lie on his back and play with a yo-yo, which is a very difficult thing to master, or look at a nude magazine in a spirit of besotted awe about the professionalism of the beloved, like a dumb sweetheart mooning over a book of her fiancé's calculus.

Fielding Mellish is a poor but patriotic specimen, dressed in a shirt shyly striped in quite thin bars of red, white, and blue. In the presence of a girl, he finds that the other sex these days is likely to be attracted by the mere guise of intellect and won't notice for a second if a man's conversation goes off the rails. "I have dabbled in Kierkegaard," he says airily to a sumptuous girl activist while swinging a couple of mugs from his fingers and leaning against a kitchen doorjamb, as I remember. "Well, of course, he's Danish," says the girl with agreeable fatuity. Thrilled at the way things are going, gnawing at this crumb dropped from the rich girl's table, Mellish says with largesse, "Well, he'd be the first to admit that." No flies on Woody, and not many on Kierkegaard either, and if a pretty girl wants to chat about *Kierkegaard*, then OK, she's welcome to be an ass. The funniest things in Woody Allen often seem to depend on his sweet brotherhood with people who are being nits, his sense that this is life when talk runs amok, his effort to fit in with rules that are visibly daft but enforced nonetheless by the everyone-else whom he dearly wishes to please. This is no comic loner; this is a trudger in the wake, stumbling after the rest, accommodating like anything, and picking up any scraps of alliance going. The film exudes the greatest sympathy over the terror on a television newsman's face when his colleague Howard—"Come in, Howard"—takes an immortal four seconds to come in. This thin-skin, ill fitted to be on camera, is a true brother to Woody Allen; in the same situation, Woody Allen would be wearing the same look on his face.

Like the modern possibilities of screen fame, the open feast of bookshop filth now spread before us strikes into Woody's soul respect and panic. Near the beginning of the film, we see Mellish in a bookshop, dotingly fingering a pornographic magazine and then buying *Newsweek*, *Time*, *Commentary*, the *Saturday Review*, and "Oh yes, the one underneath." The cashier, a bolder man, yells to the back of the shop, "How much a copy of *Or-*

gasm?" You can see that Mellish, while stricken, is entranced by the courage of the chap. It is confessed later that in his youth Mellish bought pornography in Braille and used to rub the dirty parts with his fingers. He admits this on an analyst's couch. The analyst is a puff-faced woman who seems to be taking dictation rather than doing any doctoring, with her mind elsewhere on something in the range of a small mistake in her account at the butcher's.

Like a lot of comics now, Woody Allen is deeply fascinated and affronted by the reign of jargon. Sociologists who write about the death of the word in America must have poor ears; American wits at the moment have the antennae for details of cliché that the English have for details of vernacular. In *Bananas*, which is slightly about revolution in a banana republic, the plot is ropy and can seem flailingly right wing when it probably thinks and means something reforming; the one-liners therefore run out of steam halfway through the picture, and too many scenes tend to come out on a bit of *esprit de l'escalier* when they would work better if the person on the staircase would shut up, but the film really *is* funny about automated language. A broken-accented interpreter, translating into American as he stands at the bottom of plane steps between two dignitaries speaking perfect American, painstakingly repeats, "I am looking forward with great anticipation." Mellish is keen on Eastern philosophies for the earnest reason that "they're metaphysical and redundant." The television news reporter in the film has a passion for dead adjectives and a sort of fatal creative urge to describe what one can already see perfectly well on the screen. He covers the assassination of the President of San Marcos with exquisite ham-fistedness. "A word with the next dictator of San Marcos," he says bravely, using his mike in a mob as if it were an ice-cream cornet, "if I could get through this noisy and demonstrative crowd." He is showing us, as he says in a voice uniquely dead even in the cemetery of television news reporting, "a land of colorful riots."

Mellish/Allen is absorbed by people's quick infectability with language. "Pity," his girl compliments him; "Full of pith," he agrees; "Lithen," she says, not even tailing off. Mellish's own character is also absolutely trapped in habit. As he sets out to dine with the dictator of San Marcos, memories of politesse stir in the back of his mind and he brings a cake. He then argues matter-of-factly about the bill for dinner, which the butler has brought to him with due courtesy in the dictator's own palace. In a bewitchingly unexplained sequence about Mellish as the Messiah, undergoing his own peculiar Calvary and being carried through traffic by cop-scared monks, he takes it for granted that metropolitan life means that there will already be another Jesus lying there, nailed to another cross, to argue with him about a parking space. But still, for all the odd glories of the film, it has to be said that the Castro jokes are often miles out of control, that the blackout lines get lame, and perhaps that the use of a comic personality dependent on being humbly distraught may be holding back this wit from the soaring and fearless lunacy that he can sometimes flight to.

MAY 15, 1971

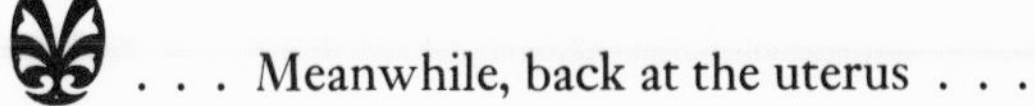

. . . Meanwhile, back at the uterus . . .

The above unforgettable line is taken from Doctor David Reuben's book *Everything You Always Wanted to Know about Sex but Were Afraid to Ask*, a waggish tome now turned into a cockeyed and sometimes insanely funny film of the same name, written and directed by Woody Allen. There are moments when you think he must also have written the original book, as a send-up of all the chatty medical textbooks that manage to make something quite simple loom with complications by dragging in homely metaphors, in the manner of those treatises on economics that muddle you by representing the national income as a pie. The best sketch in the movie—the last—exactly catches the surreal jauntiness of the book. It is called "What Happens During Ejaculation?"—a question dreamed up by Dr. Reuben that you never thought of asking. In it, Woody Allen fastens on the doctor's fondness for technological jargon derived from Cape Kennedy. The answers in the book are full of words and phrases like

"Central Control," "blowing a fuse," "fail-safe design," "cylinder," "crankshaft," "another reproductive rocket ready for launching." The temptation to Mr. Allen was obviously irresistible. In this closing sketch, his cheerfully diseased mind shows us a brain designed like the war room in Kubrick's *Dr. Strangelove.* We are in a quite unerotic world in which mechanisms that seem to us to operate in a perfectly gentle way are shown and described as if in a live TV program about a moon shot, copying the style of Dr. Reuben's best-seller, which includes the magical sentence "When the ratio of FSH to LH reaches the critical point, a rapid countdown begins, and the ovum is hurled into the abdominal cavity." Everything in this book is always being hurled. Dr. Reuben has written the first work truly combining sex and violence. Maybe that's why it has become a best-seller.

Allen's closing sketch seizes with beady-eyed lucidity on the good doctor's mechanistic view of sex and makes it as lunatically anti-sensual as it is in the book. ("Copulation is not fly-casting or kicking a football," writes Dr. Reuben sternly somewhere, changing the impressions he has been busy giving us.) In the splendiferously solemn sketch Allen bases on this question of ejaculation, the war-room brain is a madhouse of computer data and interdepartmental grumbling. Everyone is answerable to Central Control; different departments responsible for eyes and ears and innards are perpetually blaming things on one another. Events proceed on an immensely magnified and hefty scale. Stomach Control reports that his staff "did very well with the fettuccine" (which we see being heaved around the floor of some melancholy lower quarters in shovelfuls by groaning workmen), but that two men were injured by the veal scaloppine. The effort being serviced is the seduction of a girl in a car. The endeavor is Herculean. A tongue is rolled out: it looks like a hundred yards of deep-pile carpet. Atrocious interdepartmental mistakes arise. Subject should have been blowing into the girl's *ear*, comes the message from ratty Central Control, not into her *nose*. Far below, men in hardhats with their shirts off sweat to get the crucial organs going. They make it clear that theirs is the donkeywork, shoving heavy winches around and bawling rather despondent sea ditties. "Heave-ho!" is not the most lyric accompaniment to the tentative efforts in the car. You feel that the hardhats are about to put in a wage claim, and that the physical process of sex must be contributing to the economic spiral as well as to the psychological problems of millions of sperm. The sperm in this sketch are hard-working but nervous parachutists dressed in what look like rabbity versions of wartime siren suits, as if they were a lot of skinny Winston Churchills visiting the site of a blitz. They have helmets to keep their ears warm, and tadpole tails that the parachutists at the back keep treading on. Woody Allen plays a sperm who seems to be having a crackup about the idea of lunging into space.

The film opens with "Let's Misbehave" on the sound track and a sort of soft background counterpane of pink-nosed white rabbits behind the credits. The first sketch is called, in Dr. Reuben's sober style, "Do Aphrodisiacs Work?" Anthony Quayle plays a testy Tudor king who keeps his wife in a softly contoured iron chastity belt. Lynn Redgrave, looking beautiful in it as his padlocked queen, talks very rapid Elizabethan gobbledygook to the court. Woody Allen, wearing a jester's velvet suit that seems too big for him, plays a woebegone Fool silently despairing about his own wisecracks and carrying a desolate-looking puppet in matching velvet. The king is an athletic despot who charges irritably around the royal corridors and is said to be the only man in the palace who swims the moat lengthwise. His suspicions about the queen's ardor are perfectly just. Aphrodisiacs do indeed work. She nearly swoons when she is given some orange juice that the Fool has laced with an erotic ingredient handed out in the dungeon kitchen by a knowing sorcerer. "It goes down bubbliest," the queen chatters gaily, quaffing the fizzing goblet. (The sketch has some fine parodies of the style of Shakespearean prose as spoken by elocutionary actors trying to make unspeakable words sound vernacular.) Running at the chastity belt with a candlestick and calling for a halberd—he has to do *something* fast, because the Renaissance will be here before he knows it, and they'll all be painting—Woody Allen mostly makes the old gag work because of his doggedness of purpose. There are moments when his frozen face looks like a Jewish Buster Keaton's, though less august and more hounded.

"What Is Sodomy?" is a love story of delicate charm about a Jackson Heights doctor (Gene Wilder) and a sheep belonging to an Armenian shepherd patient. I have always thought that Gene Wilder was a wonderful actor; the shy dawn of love in his face as he looks at the sheep (called Daisy, which must be a rare name among Armenian flocks) should be recorded for improvisation classes all over the world. The hell with the Actors Studio. Imagining you're a lamppost or a mailbox is as easy as falling off a log; try convincing an audience you're smitten by a rather large-headed and brainy-looking sheep. Daisy has a happy resemblance to Voltaire. "Let's be gentle with each other," says the doctor after taking a hotel room for Daisy and himself at a politely unsurprised equivalent of the St. Regis that blandly accepts an order for chilled white burgundy, caviar, and green grass. Felled by love, the doctor throws to the winds his earlier quavered remonstrance to the shepherd in his office that it's not normal to experience mature love with anything that has four legs. Woody Allen's cavils are so temperate.

Some of the sketches run out of steam, but they all have fine moments. There is one very classy-looking episode, spoken in Italian with English subtitles, on the knotty subject of women's frigidity. Woody Allen plays a peanut-shaped husband airily attempting caddishness, wearing dark glasses and with a jacket slung around his shoulders. The immovable wife, who suddenly reveals herself to be immensely turned on by lovemaking in public places, has her hair done like Delphine Seyrig's in *Marienbad*. Woody Allen takes swift-spoken advice from other husbands across smart white rooms; he talks at a great distance without looking at the person he's speaking to, like a character in an Antonioni film. The longest sketch—which gets strained at the end, and devolves into a sci-fi parody about a forty-foot-high marauding breast run amok in the countryside—begins beautifully with a sequence about a mad sexologist, played by John Carradine. He lives in a Gothic mansion among his experiments, attended by a Frankenstein monster of a butler who has been deformed by one of the doctor's more lunatic tests in the pleasure principle. The butler has been left limping at an angle of forty-five degrees and looking as if he lived in the belfry of Notre Dame. "Posture! Posture!" whispers Woody Allen encouragingly as he passes. Allen plays a visiting prospective assistant. The doctor's house looks as if it were about to sprout a lot of carved-oak theater organs played by spooks. "Is your decorator still living?" says our Woody, softly to the point.

His unmatched style is extremely modern and extremely American. It is partly a humor of bashfulness—a kind of bashfulness that resides only in the very clever. It seems to relate to the whole immensely solemn body of American literature about male impotence and dither, which in turn has given rise to hundreds of Broadway and Hollywood comedies and to dozens of truly funny fictional best-sellers (by, for instance, Neil Simon and Philip Roth). *Everything You Always Wanted to Know about Sex* goes by fits and starts, but at its best it is recklessly absurd in a way that no one can rival. Woody Allen himself sometimes has dreams as wild as the imaginings of the fanatic doctor played by Carradine, whose experiments-in-progress include the transplantation of the brain of a lesbian into the living head of a man from the telephone company. (Allen's imagined illicit activities for the Cosa Nostra in "A Look at Organized Crime"—an essay that appeared in *The New Yorker*—cover gambling, narcotics, and the transportation of a large whitefish across a state line for immoral purposes.) His funniness is a marvelous blend of muttered good sense and extreme battiness, best when it keeps deludingly within the bounds of the ordinary. Nothing that a supermarket couldn't cope with. A supermarket manager could certainly come up with a corkscrew suitable for attacking a chastity belt, would look askance at some of Dr. Reuben's sillier questions ("Why do women have only two breasts?"), and would be inclined to reply shortly that he was fresh out of grass for sheep. The hangdog face of Woody Allen gazes stoutly at us from the screen. It is the face of an energetic shopper in mourning over inferior brands of daftness like Dr. Reuben's, abashed by girls less spry about love than he, alarmed by women who just lie there like a smoked salmon, perturbed by much of life, but infinitely resourceful.

AUGUST 19, 1972

COGITATORS

Buster Keaton

"When you take a fall," the ailing Buster Keaton explains to me from the top of a bookcase as he is nearing seventy, proceeding then to zoom towards the window, "you use your head as the joystick." The poetic human airship grounds delicately, and coughs.

He often seems to see himself rather distantly and as if he were some mechanical object. I suppose this is partly because of the physicality of a stage career that began in vaudeville as a manhandled toddler called "The Human Mop," and partly because he has an exceptionally modest notion of himself, including his suffering. Hollywood after the talkies treated the decorous genius like a goat.

"You don't go out of your way *not* to talk in a silent film," he says, "but you only talk if it's necessary." Two-minute pause. He is sitting in his rather poor ranch house in the San Fernando Valley, quite a drive from the stars' hangout in Beverly Hills. He always talks about work done long ago in the present tense. You wouldn't use any other.

He has been less canny than Chaplin or Harold Lloyd about retaining possession of his pictures and preserving himself from the new producers, and after the halcyon time his working conditions were ruthlessly taken from him, followed by the sack from Louis B. Mayer and the boot from a chilling wife, who changed their son's surname when the gloss went off it. But with his back to the wall and drinking enough to kill himself he still seems to have been practical and even rather dashing, with much the same spirit as his fighting Irish father, who once dealt with an impresario's humiliating order to cut eight minutes out of the family vaudeville act by setting an alarm clock to go off on stage in the middle of the routine. It seems entirely characteristic of Buster that he should once have escaped from a straitjacket during the anguish of DTs by a music-hall trick learned from Houdini. As an infant he was plucked out of the window of his parents' digs by the eye of a cyclone, and deposited intact a street away. Maybe it was this incident that planted in his father's head the theatrical possibilities of throwing the baby around. Joe Keaton started by hurling him through the scenery and dropping him onto the bass drum. When the child bounced, he began wiping the floor with him. One of his costumes had a suitcase handle on the back of the jacket so that he could be swung into the wings. Joe Keaton's wife, Myra, a lady saxophonist who seems always to have been at the end of her tether, used to refer thinly to the human-mop rehearsals as "Buster's story hour."

Buster is now sitting down, his back away from the back of the chair. The pause goes on. He is trying to explain, on the basis of what he started learning this way in vaudeville when he was rising three, the machinery of silent jokes. The beautiful head looks out of the back window, on to the plot of land where he has built his hens a henhouse that has the space of an aviary and the architecture of a New England schoolhouse. The great master of comedy, who is one of the true masters of cinema, suddenly gets up again and climbs onto a dresser and does a very neat fall, turning over onto his hands and pretending that he has a sore right thumb. He keeps it raised, and then stands stock-still and looks at it, acting. "Suppose I'm a carpenter's apprentice," he says after a while. Chest out, manly look, like a Victorian boy with his hands in his pockets having his photograph taken. "Suppose the carpenter hits my thumb with his hammer. Suppose I think, God damn, and leap out the window. Well, I'm not going to *say* my thumb hurts, am I? That's the trouble with the talkies."

He sits down in his chair again and thinks. He is wearing a jersey with piratical insignia on the front, and the sort of jaunty trousers that people sported on smart yachts in the 1930s. "The thing is not to be ridiculous. The one mistake the Marx Brothers ever make is that they're sometimes ridiculous. Sometimes *we're* in the middle of building a gag that turns out to be ridiculous. So, well, we have to think of something else. Sit it out. The cameras are our own, aren't they? We never hire our cameras. And we've got a start, and we've got a finish, because we don't begin on a film if we haven't, so all we've got to get now is the middle."

He lays out a game of solitaire. The room has a pool table in it, and a lot of old photographs. On the table between us there is a card that a studio magnate left stuck in his dressing-table mirror one day soon after the talkies had come in, giving him the sack in three lines. "In the Thirties, if there's a silence," says Buster, "they say there's a dead spot." Stills from his films come to mind: images of that noble gaze, austere and distinctive even when the head is up to the ears in water after a shipwreck, or when Buster is in mid-flight of some sort. Partly because of his vaudeville experience and partly because of his temperament, he obviously reserves great respect for those who retain a stoic attitude toward calamity and imminent death in the middle of being flung from one side of life to the other. He admires the character of a performing animal—a chimpanzee, as I remember, called Peter the Great—who expressed a Senecan-sounding serenity as he was being thrown around the stage of Buster's childhood.

Keaton's first film entrance was in *The Butcher Boy*. His character is clear at once. We are in a world of slapstick chaos, but he emits a sense of wary order. The scene is a village store. Everyone else moves around a lot, to put it mildly. When Keaton enters, the unmistakable calm asserts itself. He is wearing shabby overalls, and big shoes with a hole in one sole (which later turns out to be usefully open to some spilled molasses), and already the famous flat hat. He then goes quietly through a scene of almost aeronautic catastrophe and subsidence, the whole parabola photographed in one take. Only a child brought up in music-hall riot from toddling age could have done it. The shop—hung with posters promising "Fresh Sausages Made Every Month," run by a Roscoe Arbuckle who puts on a fur coat to go into the freezer locker (Keaton never calls him Fatty; it is always Roscoe), and inhabited by a club of aloof cardplayers with Abe Lincoln faces clustered around a stove—turns into a whirlwind. Molasses sticks, and bodies fly, and flour powders the air. We are in a world of agile apprentices and flung custard pies and badly made brooms that Buster scathingly plucks by the individual bristle as if they were suspect poultry. And through it all there is the Keaton presence: the beautiful eyes, the nose running straight down from the forehead, the raised, speculative eyebrows, the profile that seems simplified into a line as classical as the line of a Picasso figure drawing. After a bit, Roscoe Arbuckle throws a sack of flour at him. Throughout his life, to many people, Buster has repeated his admiration of the force and address of that throw.

In spite of the peculiarly heroic austerity of his comic temperament, Keaton maintains firmly that he is a low comedian. This is a simple piece of old vaudeville nomenclature. "The moment you get into character clothes, you're a low comedian," he says. There are also, among others, tramp comedians and black-face comedians—a category that was stylized for purely technical reasons but that drew some of Keaton's shorts into looking Uncle Tom-ish. "What you have to do is create a character. Then the character just does his best, and there's your comedy. No begging." This is the difference between him and Chaplin, though he doesn't invite comparisons and talks a lot more eagerly about technical things. The system of vaudeville comedy that he works by is methodical, physically taxing, and professionally interpreted. "Once you've got your realistic character, you've classed yourself. Any time you put a man into a woman's outfit, you're out of the realism class and you're in *Charley's Aunt*." There are one or two films of Keaton's, early in his career, in which someone wears drag; leaving aside modern unease about transvestism, the device goes against what Keaton can do.

Keaton's logical and vitally realist nature gradually got rid of the farfetched, or what he amiably calls just "the ridiculous." His whole comic character is too sobering for that, though infinitely and consolingly funny. Nothing much changes, it says. Things don't get easier. He will be courting a girl, for instance, and have to make way for a puppy, which the etiquette of the girl's demonstrativeness demands that she hug; the proposal that he meant to make to her goes dry in his mouth. He leaves with an air. Seasons pass, the puppy grows to frightful size, and he is still outwitted by her intervening love of pets. Finally, against every sort of odds, and only by great deftness, he manages to marry her, but the chance of kissing her is still obligatorily yielded to others—to the minister, to the in-laws, to the rival suitor, and to the now monstrous slobberer, who ends the picture by sitting between the wedding couple on a garden seat and licking the bride's face. All the same, whatever the mortification, Keaton is never a pathetic figure. His heroes stare out any plight. Perhaps because he has an instinctive dislike of crawling to an audience by exploiting any affliction in a character, including any capacity for being victimized, his figures never seem beaten men, and after a few experiments in his early work he never plays a simpleton. He has perfected, uniquely, a sort of comedy that is about heroes of native highbrow intelligence, just as he is almost the only man who has ever managed to establish qualities of delicate dignity in characters with money. Comedians don't generally play the highborn. The fortunate, debonair, tongue-tied central character of *The Navigator* is one of the rarer creations of comedy: rich, decorous, possessed of a chauffeur and a fine car that makes a U turn across the street to his fiancée's house, infinitely capable of dealing with the exchange and mart of high-flown social marriage, jerking no heartstrings. Keaton's world is a world of swells and toffs as well as butcher boys, and mixed up in it are memories of his hardy past in vaudeville that give some of his films a mood of the surreal. In *The Playhouse*, which he made after breaking his ankle on another picture, he plays not only nine musicians and seven orchestra members but also a music-hall aquatic star, an entire minstrel show, a dowager and her bedeviled husband, a pair of soft-shoe dancers, a stagehand, an Irish char, and her awful child, among others. We see the Keaton brat dropping a lollipop onto the Keaton *grande dame* in the box below; the dowager then abstractedly uses the lollipop as a lorgnette. He also plays a monkey who shins up the proscenium arch—something that must have been rough on the broken ankle. The film has a peculiar aura, not quite like anything else he made. It is dreamlike and touching, with roots in a singular infancy that he takes for granted. Vaudeville is what he comes from, as powerfully as Shakespeare's Hal comes from boon nights spent with Falstaff. In *Go West*, there is a music-hall set piece about a slightly ramshackle top hat that is kept brilliantly in the air by repeated gun shots. "It has to be an old hat," says Buster. "You couldn't use a new hat. Otherwise, you don't get your laugh. Audiences don't like to see things getting spoiled."

Keaton has a passion for props. Especially for stylish things like top hats, for sailing-boats and paddle steamers, and for all brainy machinery. He finds ships irresistible. A short called *The Boat* forecasts *The Navigator;* there is also *Steamboat Bill, Jr.* Facing many calamities, Buster as a sailor works with a sad, composed gaze and a resourcefulness that never wilts. In *Steamboat Bill, Jr.*, he leans on a life preserver that first jars his elbow by falling off the boat and then immediately sinks; Keaton's alert face, looking at it, is beautiful and without reproach. In *The Boat*, where he is shipbuilding, though deflected a good many times by one or another of a set of unsmiling small sons, his wife dents the stern of his creation with an unbreakable bottle of Coke while she is launching it; Keaton helps by leaning over the side to smash the thing with a hammer, and then stands erect while the boat sinks quickly up to his neck, leaving us to watch the august head turning round in contained and unresentful bafflement. In *Steamboat Bill, Jr.*, his last independently produced film, he turns up, looking chipper, to join a long-lost father who runs a steamboat. The son will be recognized by a white carnation, Buster has bravely said in a telegram delivered four days late. He keeps authoritatively turning the carnation in his lapel toward people as if it were a police badge. No one is interested. His father eventually proves to be a big, benign bruiser, and not the man his son would have expected; nor is Buster the sort of man his father instantly warms to. He is much put off by the beautiful uniform of an admiral that Buster wears to help on the steamboat. It is not, maybe, fit for running a paddle steamer, but it is profoundly hopeful. It represents an apparently mistaken dapperness and an admission of instinctive class that turn out to be as correct in the end as the same out-of-place aristocratism is in *The Navigator*, that poetic masterpiece of world cinema.

There is nothing anywhere quite to equal the comic, desperate beauty of the long shots in *The Navigator* when Buster, the rich sap, is looking for his girl on the otherwise deserted liner that has gone adrift. The rows of cabin doors swing open and closed in turn, port and starboard in rhythm, on deck after deck; the noble, tiny figure with the strict face and the passionate character runs round and round to find his dizzy girl, who is looking for him in her own quite sweet but less heartfelt way. The flower-faced fiancée played by Kathryn McGuire is a typical Keaton heroine. She is rather nice to him when he has got into his diving suit to free the rudder and has forgotten, with the helmet closed, that there is a lighted cigarette in his mouth. (This is a mistake that apparently happened while Keaton was shooting. "They've closed the suit on me," he says, coughing, the memory bringing on his present bronchitis, "and everyone just thinks I'm working up a gag.")

Keaton's characters are outsiders in the sense of spectators, not of nihilists or anarchists. He isn't at his best when he hates people (unlike W. C. Fields, for instance—whom he talks about with regard, doing a brotherly imitation of the voice of men who are martyrs to drinkers' catarrh). A short called *My Wife's Relations* has some of the Fields ingredients, but Keaton muffs the loathing. The picture has its moments, though. The wife is a virago with Irish relations who are devout but greedy; the only way to get a steak, Buster discovers, is to turn the calendar to a Friday. The blows that he manages to give her in bed when she thinks he is only thrashing in his sleep are pretty funny. So are the hordes of rapacious brides in *Seven Chances*, rushing after him on roller skates and wearing improvised bridal veils to make a grab for him because he will inherit a mint if he marries by seven o'clock.

But Keaton is really at his best when he is being rather courtly. He has great charm in a feature called *The Three Ages*—about love in the Stone Age, the Roman Age, and the Modern Age—when he stands around among primordial rocks in a fur singlet and huge fur bedroom slippers chivalrously helping enormous girls up boulders. In that Age, prospective in-laws assess the suitors by strenuous blows with clubs, and people ride around on mastodons that are clearly elephants decked out with rococo tusks by Keaton's happy prop men. In the Roman Age episodes, Wallace Beery as the Adventurer has a fine chariot, and Keaton has a sort of orange crate drawn by a hopeless collection of four indescribable animals. The Romans throw him into a lion's den, but he thinks of only the pleasantest things to remember about lions, which is that they behave well if you do something or other nice to their paws. He takes a paw, washes it, manicures it, and dries it. The interested beast responds affably. We switch back to the Stone Age. Keaton, looking more than usually small in the surroundings, is dealing courageously with the colossal opposite sex while hoping privately for more lyric times. He gets them for a moment in the Roman sequences; there is a wonderful shot of a girl's worshipful face as she thinks of Buster when she is in the middle of being pulled by the hair in some impossible Roman torment. But nothing vile in antiquity, Keaton implies by the sudden, pinching end of this revue-film, can equal the meager-spiritedness of Los Angeles; the Stone Age and the Roman Age episodes both finish with shots of Buster and his bride surrounded by hordes of kids in baby fur tunics and baby togas, but the Modern Age episode finishes with the happy couple walking out of a Beverly Hills house followed by a very small, spoiled dog. Such minutes of tart melancholy are often there in Keaton. They go by fleetingly and without bitterness, like the sad flash in *The Scarecrow* when a girl takes it that his kneeling to do up a shoelace means that he is proposing. His beloveds sometimes have overwhelming mothers; one battle-ax, in *The Three Ages*, causes a pang when she makes him produce his bank balance, which is in a passbook labeled "Last National Bank" and obviously not up to scratch. One thinks, inevitably, of the hard time that Keaton was to have with his ambitious actress wife, Natalie Talmadge, which left him flat broke when the talkies came in. The Keaton hero, with the scale he is built on, and with his fastidious sense of humor, is obviously the born physical enemy of all awesome women. The girls he loves are shy and funny, with faces that they raise to him like wineglasses. But his idyllic scenes are very unsentimental. There is a nice moment when his loved one in *The Navigator* says to him, in reply to a proposal of marriage, "Certainly not!" Chaplin was once said to have given comedy its soul; if so, it was Keaton who gave it its spine and spirit.

"They have too many people working on pictures now, you know," says the aging, unsoured man whom the talkies threw on the dustheap although he could probably have gone on making great films in any new circumstance, and on a minute budget, and editing in a cupboard. "We had a head electrician, a head carpenter, and a head blacksmith." The blacksmith seems to have been crucial. There was a lot of welding to do. Keaton himself did his stunt work, magically and beautifully. Who else? He could loop through the air like a lasso. When he is playing the cox in *College* and the tiller falls off the boat, it is entirely in character that he should dip himself into the water and use his own body as the tiller. The end of *Seven Chances* is an amazing piece of stunt invention, inspired by cascades of falling boulders, that would have killed Keaton if he hadn't been an acrobat. Most of his stunt stuff isn't the sort of thing that can be retaken, and Keaton doesn't care much for inserts. "I like long takes, in long shot," he says. "Close-ups hurt comedy. I like to work full figure. All comedians want their feet in."

He has just been asked to the première of *It's a Mad, Mad, Mad, Mad World*, which he has a part in after spending decades doing nothing much but commercials. *Mad World* is in the mode of wide screens with a vengeance. Buster has seen the picture. It can't be much to his taste, but he doesn't say so. He likes working; even making commercials doesn't strike him as such a cruel outcome to a life. He wants to go to the première. He looks vigilant and spry.

The wife of his last years thinks he shouldn't go to the première, because he might get a coughing fit and have to leave.

"We have aisle seats," he says.

"You're not well," she says.

"I can take my cough mixture," he says. "I can take a small container. I can get ready to move in a hurry."

MAY 24, 1964
JUNE 18, 1967
SEPTEMBER 26, 1970
SAN FERNANDO, CALIFORNIA

A Good Night

A long view of a youngish man in a dark coat. Black-and-white photography; silence, as after a fall of snow. The first noise is the bang of his car door. Then Jean-Louis Trintignant, the wittily blah-faced engineer who is the hero of Eric Rohmer's marvelous *Ma Nuit Chez Maud*, goes to Mass in Clermont-Ferrand. A glance passes in church, twice, between him and a fair-haired girl. There is a shot of him at home, reading a book of calculations, drinking coffee. Morning alarm clock. Arm out to turn on radio music. Bookshop. Attraction to a title: *Calcul des Probabilitiés*. He runs into an old friend (Antoine Vitez), a Marxist professor, who tots up the chances against their having met after all this time. They sit and talk. The friend holds you. A thin, comic man, very bright, amused by his sex muddles. He has a pleasant, speculative voice and a nose like a pen nib. His name is Vidal. The Trintignant character is called Jean-Louis. It is plain that they have known each other for ages. Rohmer has made a rare sort of film: his intimates really seem intimates. They speak their own thoughts instead of reciting lines, they react to the moment before last, they chat by laminating two monologues, they hang fire wondering about the next thing to say. The intelligence his characters are allowed to have is gentle and true. So is their attention to each other. The two men talk about choice and chance, Marxism, Jansenism. Jean-Louis is a Catholic who has placed his bet. Now he is waiting with his own kind of quizzicality for the outcome of the game. He has no girl, for instance. He wants the blonde from church. Vidal has gambled on "Hypothesis B, the ten-per-cent possibility that history has a meaning," because if he gambled on the ninety-per-cent chance of Hypothesis A—that history has no meaning—his life would be lost. "Someone—Lenin, Gorki, or Mayakovski—said that after the Russian Revolution they were forced to take one chance in a thousand, and that it was worth it," he says, actually speaking touchingly about himself, while he and Jean-Louis are apparently discussing Pascal abstractions. Clermont-Ferrand was Pascal's birthplace. Like Maud, whom the two friends go to see that evening, Vidal and Jean-Louis are steeped in the ideas of the thinker who proposed the famous Wager about believing in God: the notion that if you win you win everything, and that if you lose you lose nothing; the argument that since you are obliged to play the game anyway, you renounce reason if you hoard your life for the sake of a calculable, finite stake rather than risk it for an incalculable, infinite gain.

Maud (Françoise Fabian), a great beauty, meeting Jean-Louis for the first time, watches and cooks and smokes. His determinism is not for her, or his rigor, but she likes him. She tells him that her ex-husband had a mistress—a blonde with a character "rather like yours." She herself had a lover, killed in a car crash. Her nature makes her hate Pascal's lottery, but she listens carefully—to the cheerful professor, who is having an affair with her, and to this interesting friend, with his cordial intractability and his poor assessment of himself, who speaks rather solemnly about his mediocrity, about his incomprehension of unfaithfulness, and about his longing for the right girl. "The classified ads?" suggests Maud softly to this last problem. " 'Seeks blonde practicing Catholic. . . .' " It is said with droll affection by this brown-haired, non-Catholic dish, whose habit of sleeping naked under a white fur rug in her living room ("I hate bedrooms") scares Jean-Louis nearly to flight once Vidal has left them together to go home because of the weather. Lust's hour is about to strike, you can see him thinking nervously. He looks at the unforeseeable freethinker wriggling about under her fur rug. "You both reek of holy water," she was saying to the men earlier. He wraps himself safely in another rug. She goes on smoking and talking to him. It occurs to you, as they go chastely to sleep, that this night with Maud confronts Jean-Louis with a problem vexingly Pascalian as well as voluptuous beyond his wits, since the oppressive possibility of making love to her represents a bet in which there is nothing to be lost and maybe a kingdom to be won.

Next day, intact, he finds the girl he saw in church. "I know I should think of something clever to say," he says urgently, "but how can I get to know you?" The courtship proceeds, clubfooted. Caught in the snow with her that night, he makes tea for her in her place. He does it with exquisite pedantry. Apart from some of the actors in the great Russian companies, Trintignant in this film is better than anyone else I have seen at playing a man amused at himself for being humorless. "No good being more Papist than the Pope," he mutters to himself at some point.

The script is Rohmer's own, one of his six *Moral Tales*. Two were made for French television. Another, a feature film, is called *La Collectionneuse*. Two to go. Sometimes this screenplay is in a literary class near Renoir's for *La Règle du Jeu*. And oh the pleasure of a film that looks at people for long takes instead of going chop-chop-chop, like television; that so often finds a listener's face more interesting than a speaker's; that lets people *talk*, instead of yielding to the cant that talk isn't "visual." A lot of the producers and directors who intone this particular slogan now aren't very talented. Would-be-classy cinema has acquired in them a new sort of middle-brow. They are people so fogged by tenthhand regard for the *caméra-stylo* theory, and yet so far from kin to the *writers* who historically directed *caméra-stylo* films that they misunderstand the theory to mean throwing words out in favor of shock-cuts and zooms. Why is the sight of someone speaking necessarily less "visual" than the sight of someone walking? The word is one of the more inanely used elements in the cinema. You imagine that one day, off camera, your truly filmic hero is going to have to leap out of his chair and say to his girl friend, "Let's go out and do something visual." Like careering around Paris with a bevy of balloons, or eating frankfurters extremely fast on speeded-up film. Well, not many people could have done what Rohmer has. It is a very delicate triumph for the talkies, and the ending of his picture hangs there like the close of a great short story.

APRIL 4, 1970

Eroica

Thinking only of Chopin, we like to regard the Poles as high romantics, which is probably why Andrzej Wajda is their best-known film director here. At home they have another Andrzej, called Munk, steeped black in the sardonicism that is the other half of the Polish character, and it is time we discovered him. *Eroica*, which was made in 1957, is a marvelous film. I suspect it of being the most recklessly ironic satire on modern war that exists in the archives of Eastern Europe.

The theme is the heroic mood of the 1944 Warsaw Rising, which is about as dangerous a subject for ridicule as you can get in Poland: we misread the situation, or perhaps merely read Cold War pop leader articles, if we think that it is more dangerous to ridicule Khrushchev.

In the first half of the film, marked "Scherzo alla Polacca," a flourishing spiv has joined the Resistance, but his surge of *gloire* soon ebbs and he leaves for the country. His wife is entertaining a Hungarian lieutenant, who sends him back to Warsaw with a message that the Hungarians are ready to quit the Axis in exchange for Russian recognition. Behaving often with unwilling intrepidity and for some time totally sloshed, seeing a battle through a pastoral haze of stolen Tokay, the legate eventually finds the Hungarian offer refused; and to avoid being alone with his wife now that the cuckolding lieutenant has fled, again heroically joins the Resistance.

The "Scherzo" is full of glancing blows, but the central character is a bad soldier, so military self-regard could still survive. The second part, marked "Ostinato Lugubre" and set in a Polish Officers' POW camp, is about the copper-bottomed hero-class. After the Rising, a fresh batch of natural leaders is sent to the camp, joining the relics of the 1939 campaign and quickly adopting their intricate fiction of not letting oneself go. The myth that keeps their backs stiffest is the myth of the brave Zawistowski, said to have escaped, but in fact ill in a loft above the washhouse. Only three officers know he is alive: the secret is kept out of shame rather than security, and when he commits suicide the Nazis, in much the same spirit, provide an old boiler to smuggle out his body. Their hunt for him has been too public; their own military dignity is at stake. The legend survives. *Eroica* is comic and searing, full of ungrateful wit and acted with tight, wry style, but what is most striking is the intellectual order beneath it. Munk is a genuine satirist, rash-spirited and level-minded.

JULY 16, 1961

Shaw

Shaw's *Mrs. Warren's Profession* is seventy-one years old, but let no one tell you that it works in spite of the passionate topicality it had in 1894; it works because of it. The play is still flintily apt in what it has to say about our capacity for humbug, our double view of ambition as admirable in men and disagreeable in women, our high regard for greed when it is called the profit motive, and our special conviction that immorality always means sexual immorality. The wit in this play is like a white ray.

Mrs. Warren's profession—bordello madam—was her one social blunder. Her energy and thrift, the ingenuity that rescued her from life in a fried-fish shop in the East End, were virtues that Victorian England deeply admired. If she had no training to live by, no one in 1894 regarded that as a crime, nor indeed does anyone now. The most respectable people still believe that a woman's best bank balance is her body: finishing schools and the laws of alimony are instances of perfectly legal ways of trading in sexuality. Mrs. Warren's mistake was that, instead of marrying for money or milking a living out of a divorce, she agreed to run a classy chain of European brothels to fill the pockets of a nice-looking squire called Sir George Crofts, who tells her blandly not to mention his hotels because the word makes people think you keep a pub.

Every man in the play finds her indispensable, including a portly vicar to whom she has borne a wastrel son; but her job gives everyone the right to patronize her, including the clever daughter whom she has trustingly educated. The last-act combat between the two women is agonizing, and full of charity that isn't often recognized in Shaw. The play is a superb theatrical organism, able to call on the old energies of Victorian melodrama, but gifted with the most even and fine-drawn sense of particular temperaments in conflict. What a play Shaw might have written after the Profumo–Christine Keeler–Stephen Ward case: except that he would be accused now of "mere" sociology, of "attacking well-worn targets" with "Mr. Shaw's wearily familiar wit." The tide has swung away again very fast from social concerns in plays. Shaw would have hated the alternative that seems to be replacing it, a fad for the sort of writer whom he once caustically defined as a hopelessly Private Person.

MAY 2, 1965
LONDON

In the middle of Shaw's *Fanny's First Play* there is a playlet said to have been written by a character called Fanny. Round this is wrapped a discussion between four footling drama critics, who swear between footles that the piece is a characteristically pigheaded and derivative work by Shaw. The whole unmistakable parcel was presented in 1911 as being by Xxxxxxx Xxxx, fooling no one, and giving the author huge pleasure as a device combining modesty, trumpet-blowing, and critic-proofness in one fell swoop.

When the Mermaid Theatre has been under such a spell of bad productions it is pleasant to have to say that Don Taylor's is very good indeed, quick-witted and slyly funny. He finds an exquisite moment of buried bathos in the way a nice bourgeoise chucks over the lesson dealt out of Saint Peter when a high-flown friend has been elaborating on the theme that people who depend on religious dogma are liable to be shocked when they can't walk on the water. Adrian Vaux's set, a black triptych with a proscenium arch crawling with cherubs in the middle and a Turnerish sunset on each side, works equally well for the inner play and the notices.

There is a particularly good performance by Robert Gillespie as an owlish butler called Juggins, who is (as Shaw says, eagerly getting it in first) shamelessly derivative from Barrie's Crichton. The critics are very funny indeed, especially the one called Mr. Gunn, who is a representative of the school that "goes for the newest things and swears they're old-fashioned"; he is played by a long, long man called Douglas Milvain, who twists his knees with the excitement of his fatigue at meeting "more secondhand Schopenhauer."

OCTOBER 3, 1965
LONDON

Shaw, defending himself in advance about his wickedly intelligent *Man and Superman*, said in his dedicatory preface to the critic A. B. Walkley that "your favourite jibe at me is that what I call drama is nothing but explanation." It is true that Shaw is always hugely exegetical. His characters never do anything that another character does not forecast, commentate upon, and then tell us to see as totally characteristic of that sex, that class, that upbringing, that period; but when they do it with Shaw's shrewdness they can be explanatory until the cows come home.

The England here is the one that Shaw most detested, a "moral gymnasium" where we would rather flex our own principles than attend to other people's necessities. His symbol of the New Man, the chauffeur 'Enry, who seems to drop his aitches to oblige a caste system that likes things cut and dried, is played with taciturn aplomb by Clive Swift. Alan Badel as John Tanner sees and solves beautifully the problem of playing a dashing prig (touching about Shaw that his Don Juan character should be a man petrified by women, and one who doesn't do a single piece of adventuring on stage).

Sian Phillips plays Ann Whitefield much too soothingly, but Marie Lohr does the silly mother dead right, giving her expressions of confused quick-wittedness that afford her facial muscles at least the impression of being on the ball. The only commonplace thing in the evening—wittily directed by Philip Wiseman—is Shaw's acceptance of the old saw about women winding men round their little fingers: it would have been more like him if he had stood that truism on its head.

JANUARY 9, 1966
LONDON

Pirandello

The sight of actors at a rehearsal when they are not acting happens to be one of life's natural theatrical draws. Next to men making tea around a hole in the middle of Piccadilly, the prospect that opens Pirandello's *Six Characters in Search of an Author* must be one of the most crowd-gathering spectacles of nonwork that there is.

In the Compagnia dei Giovanni's production the stage is bare. The scenery has all been struck. The cream brick walls of the Aldwych stage, towering and dirty, dwarf the human figure like the perspectives of one of those eighteenth-century Romantic engravings of asylums. The company of actors hectically doing nothing includes an aging leading man, an ancient trouper who says that the lines are the thing, an ingénue in a purple sweater that upsets a superstitious actress, and an old-guard leading lady dressed in a lumpy beaver coat with an artificial flower pinned on the shoulder. On stage are an upright piano, two full-length mirrors, and the characteristic Italian prompt-box downstage, rising out of the floor like a conning tower.

With a typical lick of rancorous humor, Pirandello makes the play that they begin to creak through his own *Rules of the Game*. And Giorgio de Lullo, the producer, has added a conceit of his own: before the actors loaf on to start *Rules of the Game*, he shows them loafing off to make their entrances in *Six Characters in Search of an Author*. The play within the play is within another play.

The atmosphere of the company is obviously tenth-rate, but all the same ebulliently confident. It is a bit like the playing of a Sicilian brass band. Into this amiable chaos of exhibitionism, where an ambitious prompter fails to contain himself during the leading man's best pause, wander six creatures from another system. There is a gray-lipped widow clutching two children, an elder son, a remorseful father played by Romolo Valli with a mustache like mule-panniers and a vengeful red-headed stepdaughter played by Rossella Falk. They are lost souls from an abandoned play, and for Pirandello the salient difference between them and the other characters is that their identities are fixed because they are fictional, whereas the "real" people are suggestible existentialists for whom everything is in flux.

The "real" people feel themselves to exist only through other people's apprehension of them. The characters looking for an author, on the other hand, are in a determinist trap where they feel dependent upon someone else to write the very narrative of their lives. The fierce figments who have wandered onto the stage are apparently consigned to an existence of doodling, re-enacting their characteristics over and over again, and finally watching the purple abandoned draft of their lives being performed by members of the hick company.

The father, a harrowing middle-aged lecher in a gray mac who walks with a flat-footed lope and looks like a rapist on the last tube train, sees himself embodied by a dandy elocutionist and finds that the act of representation has changed everything for him. His own past no longer seems to belong to him. Lines to his stepdaughter that have become unbearably painful keep striking the producer as merely marvelously theatrical.

Pirandello's form is partly a stand against the dead conventions of a theater that subordinated people to plot and pumped out three acts of motives like motor fuel. But it is a lot more than that. It often seems to be suggesting that there are a great many people in the world apart from the six characters whose lives are spent waiting for parts to be written for them. Pirandello's famous braininess and twentieth-century desolation go with a fondness of feeling that is less obvious. Giorgio de Lullo's warm production has some overelaborate comic effects, and the melodramatics of the six characters' life stories sometimes seep into their performances, but there are enormously touching flashes of contact between this group of people who feel themselves to be irredeemably someone else's raw material and the ones whose occupation as role-players has robbed them of the sense that anything is fixed.

The last part of the play always seems rather flogged out and wooden, but some of the rest is extraordinary. Why Pirandello is ever likened to Shaw, apart from chronology, I can't imagine; Shaw asks "What?" and "Why?" and "How?" but Pirandello asks only "Who?", absorbed in fatalist questions about the self that lie in the mainstream of Christian thought and often seem close to T. S. Eliot's.

Earlier in the week this resourceful and bouncing company blandly gave *The Rules of the Game*, the earlier play that the author shows being wrecked by the hams in *Six Characters*. De Lullo's company performs it with lucid aplomb. The plot is a love triangle in which every conventional characteristic is reversed. The lover—Carlo Guiffre—is cautious and punctilious. The husband—Romolo Valli, plump and acquiescent in a city suit—happily gives his wife a freedom that infuriates her. The wife, a slinky post-Cubist beauty played by Rossella Falk with hand movements off an Egyptian jug, finds her lover too subjective and womanishly incapable of impersonal thinking.

Pier Luigi Pizzi's domestic interiors make a stylish setting for the production, hardened into a pastiche of 1918 smartness that is just this side of comedy and drawn with the bright perspectives of a de Chirico painting. Valli's performance, eyes sharp as needles but vacant at the same time, is a very funny study of an Olympian sort of obsequiousness. He cooks augustly in his library and mouths the responses of both sides in turn when he is involved in a fight with the other two people in the triangle. Most of the time he prefers to engage himself in an effort to exist as little as possible, successfully smothering the others with the weight of his self-effacement. It is a very suave play.

APRIL 3, 1966
LONDON

Congreve

Congreve's comedies aren't about people who see sex as a pleasure; they are really about sex used as a form of currency to purchase something else. In the theater of sophisticated periods this often seems to happen. In a lot of modern American plays, for instance, the hero uses sex to buy proof that he isn't a social deviationist. In Noël Coward, sex sometimes seems to be a coin to pay for the company of a wit at breakfast. In Congreve's *Love for Love* it is used to buy money, with every courtship in the plot wooing an estate; love for loot.

Congreve wasn't really a Restoration playwright. His period of work was William and Mary's, when people had stopped celebrating the end of Cromwell's austerity and started to be enthralled by trade. It was the time of the rise of the merchant class, of coffee houses "full of Smoak and Strategems," of emptying churches and growing piety about shopkeeping. *Love for Love* is filled with images of money. Conscience is "a domestic Thief," a poet "sells Praise for Praise," the woman who gives most pleasure is the tart who can be bought. A key passage has a horrible image of sexual vigor as an old man's bank balance, with Sir Sampson Legend pawing a desirable heiress to give her "a Rent Roll of his Possessions."

Peter Wood's production goes at all this oddly tamely. Lila de Nobili's sets, drenched in yellowy Sov-color lighting, look more like an estate agent's dream of the past than Congreve's reeking new world. The clothes seem dry-cleaned, and you could eat off the whoring Mrs. Frail.

Some details seem as right as William Gaskill's work on *The*

Recruiting Officer two years ago: the background of ragged business figures, for instance, the tousled brown wig that makes Geraldine McEwan look like a beautiful miniature, and Colin Blakely as the hero's booby brother, a stinking tar barrel whose dreadful jokes make the wits in the play recoil as sharply as his breath does. The weakness of the evening is that it goes only halfway and is liable at any point to collapse back into the conventional Restoration twitter. A lot of the acting hasn't a fraction of the attack in the text. Anthony Nicholls's lame performance of the monstrous Sir Sampson undermines scene after scene. Much the most pungent character is Olivier's Tattle, a marvelously funny study in the frantic alertness of the really stupid.

OCTOBER 24, 1965
LONDON

Brecht and Company

Although Brecht is dead, his Berliner Ensemble epitomizes the way he wanted the theater to be: skimming, speculative, beautiful, fun, even if received ideas about him teach the opposite (his plays are expected to be heavy because he was German, shut-minded because he was a Marxist, visually like wartime utility china because of his emphasis on use in design, and no fun at all). But the work of this stunning company has an energy and sense of play that hardly anyone but Joan Littlewood working in other countries' theaters now seems to dream of.

To see Brecht's *Arturo Ui* is an experience like watching a bunch of tumblers or men on a trampoline. Physically the actors are phenomenal. Even their moments of relaxation have a fierce life. The substance of the play is an acrobatic feat in itself: it is a farce about the rise of Nazism, mockingly mirrored in the career of an unimpressive American gangster who blackmails a mayor called Dogsborough (Hindenburg) into allowing him to organize a protection racket and move in on a town that symbolizes Austria.

The scenes are played and set inside a circus big-top, and the ringleaders are presented by a huckster. Göring is a cleft-chinned jokester in a white suit who collects the hats of his victims; after a murder he is inclined to open his jaw on a mirthless, cavernous howl. Like all the cast, he is brilliantly made up, with a cheese-green skin that makes his mouth look shrimp-pink. The betrayed Roehm, assassinated in a St. Valentine's Day massacre with car headlamps glaring straight at the audience, wears plus-fours, black lipstick and a magenta scar. Goebbels (Hilmar Thate) looks like an Oriental monkey, with damson-stained lips and an Adam's apple that lurches at religious music. In his performance the big physical images are distinct and unforgettable. In one scene, plotting with Hitler-Ui in a hotel room mined with treacheries, he sits on a very low stool at a very high table, drumming excitedly at a blotter under his chin, and then races Göring for Hitler's handshake, bouncing along on his stool like a satanic toddler. In another he sings a song astride the barrier of the dress-circle, leaning perilously over the stalls with one leg jabbed into the gilt balustrade as if he were using a grappling hook.

Ekkehard Schall's performance as Ui starts from a paradox that is pure Brecht. To define a man incapable of shame, it first records that he is bashful. Ui clearly longs to be an actor, but he is locked in a rictus of stage fright. Whenever he is near a window he goes to it instinctively, like a girl model to a mirror, and prepares to harangue the street; but his gestures fall foul of one another, the left arm ambushes the right, and his feet hang down from his abject macintosh like the feet of a dummy in a shooting gallery. When he is yelling he will suddenly gag, or change dynamic level uncontrollably, as he does in a deafening diatribe where the recurring word "faith" is each time spoken in a soft indrawn gulp. His neck is scored with two black lines of make-up, the tendons of tantrum, like a frantic pullet's, and after a stint with an actor hired to teach him Shakespearean delivery he aquires a Hitlerian clasp of the hands that one suddenly sees to be the primordial gesture of male modesty used by the naked Popeye.

Herr Schall plays Coriolanus just as anti-heroically. Usually the violence of the character has a moral inflection: this Coriolanus employs force as though he feels that any argument but a physical one is a hypocrisy, admiring the persuasion of a blade in a man's guts much as others respect candor. But in Brecht's version the violence has no moral content because it is the expression of a pre-moral and barbarous infant. The victor of Corioli is a plump narcissist who smiles as he kills and has a frightening capacity to cut out when people are urgently communicating with him. When Menenius pleads or Aufidius curses, he looks away and goes deaf. There is a hint of erotic excitement in his feeling for Aufidius, but this passes, like his feeling for his mother. At the beginning he watches her, embracing his wife with his wrists turned fastidiously back because Volumnia is looking, but by the end "he no more remembers his mother than an eight-year-old horse."

In Brecht's version, Coriolanus changes his mind about marching on his native Rome not because of maternal pleas, but because she tells him there is a sizable plebeian uprising to be surmounted, which is rather disingenuously supposed by Brecht to be enough to instill in him the realization that heroic leaders are dispensable. I suppose, though, that Brecht's reason is no more insufficient than Shakespeare's. If either had to be accepted as the single motive for Coriolanus's switch of heart, without the density of other purposes collected behind it, there wouldn't be much to choose for hollowness between them.

When Shakespeare has been translated and his tongue has been cut out, the chief thing left to be defended is his complexity. Without German I can't be sure, but the dramatist in Brecht doesn't seem to have been guilty of giving in to the aphorist in his *Coriolanus*. It seems clear from the delicate expansion of business in Brecht's version that it was Shakespeare's characteristically complex series of mirrors—everyone seen through everyone else's eyes—that he most admired. One of the tensions in

Brecht is the fact that, though he had the polemicist's instinct to pose simplifications, he also had the playwright's instinct to prove them infinitely disputable. It was like the tug between his cool theories and his violent feelings, and between his plain man's sympathies and his very august wit.

The production by Manfred Wekwerth and Joachim Tenschert is the best *Coriolanus* we are ever likely to see. Karl von Appen's designs are incomparably beautiful: all pale chalky grays and the browns of hide and wood, scorchingly lit, with one stupendous red cloak which is dropped and left when Coriolanus is banished. The ironwork is exquisite—slender, stately chairs, for instance, and an avenue of poles that two men decorate with the helmets of the vanquished, reaching up with staves like Victorian lamplighters. The Ensemble must have its own smithy. And each Shakespearean costume looks as though it has belonged to that particular character for a long time. All but one: it was a very Brechtian trick to make Coriolanus play his discomfited electioneering scene in a toga a foot too long for him. The revolve shifts from one camera-angle to another for the vote-catching scene in a way that is almost an image of Shakespeare's way of writing verse; and in the battle it does the same, swiveled round from a side that shows a chalky Roman arch to a side that is a log stockade like the one in Kurosawa's film of *Macbeth*. The battle scenes are spectacular. Leathery soldiers fight with the ritualism of the Kabuki, using a choric bark coming over the speakers, in which the human voice is massed and notated almost as Schönberg did in *Moses and Aaron*. The movements are very stylized, curiously both ferocious and dispassionate: one of the generals suddenly leaps onto the crooked arm of the other and hangs there, like a basket. And what an ending for Coriolanus. His death is inglorious: he is hacked down in mid-chuckle by a ring of soldiers with their arms round each other like a rugger scrum.

The appeal of *Coriolanus* to Brecht must have been enormous. Shakespeare understood in it as much about the power vacuum as any dramatist after Marx, and he was characteristically absorbed by Brecht's same lifelong fascination with historical impulses that mistake the tide. It is part of the structure of *Coriolanus* that each of the forces in it acts without being aware that it is also being acted upon, and this must have spoken to Brecht very powerfully. It is also the narrative point of the Ensemble's production of his *Days of the Commune*, a warm chronicle of a group of Parisians in the winter of 1871, when the workers rose against Thiers and his ally Bismarck, hung out briefly in the cold, nourished only by their historic excitement, and collapsed largely because they still insensibly obeyed the laws of the society they opposed.

"We have resolved in future to fear / Bad life more than death": the revolutionery song, set by Hans Eisler, has Brecht's blackest voice. Unlike most of us, he had the courage to find nothing better than anything. The acting is the best Stanislavskian acting west of the Moscow Arts: so much for the crass myth that the Berliner Ensemble has a rigid style.

AUGUST 15, 1965
BERLIN AND LONDON

Etiquette for Cataclysms

Ivy Compton-Burnett's wit seems made for the theater. *A Heritage and Its History*, adapted by Julian Mitchell with the grace of a fencer, is the first of her novels to be staged and it animates murderously well.

I suppose the reason why good novels are usually such bad dramatic material is that the central character is so often the author's voice. Lose the tangent of Forster's presence from a Forster novel and one has *Hamlet* without the Prince. But Miss Compton-Burnett operates without comment. All she does is stare at people, and in the Gorgon glare of her prose certain crucial interchanges and demands are petrified. The characters' grimaces are all their own, and they react wholly to one another: the author seems terrifyingly absent.

A Heritage is really about what is expected of us, by ourselves, by others and by the process of life, an inexorably opposed triangle in which all the positions are precisely visible to everyone concerned but an infinite number of possibly fatal choices may be made about stating them. This is etiquette on a monolithic scale, the manners necessary at Mycenae. To apply a version of modern upper-class politeness to a plot involving classical incest is a very personal feat. Miss Compton-Burnett has matchless command of the appalling skill of the high-bred Englishman in courteously destroying outsiders, and she has a rather Greek feeling about heirs and births; where a child is born, there is the spearhead of the house, and to her the word "house" is a concept like the House of Atreus.

Frank Hauser has arrived at a fine style for the play, stately and cataclysmic. Miss Compton-Burnett never writes "can't" or "isn't," and the actors deliver the lines so that an apostrophe would be like a stumble in a pavane. They are placed deliberately flatly, drinking clear soup in serried order behind a long table downstage, for instance, and the depth of the stage is used for ruthless interjections, so that a comment can be lobbed suddenly from the back of a drawing room like a hand grenade. The cast is locked into the style as in a rictus. It includes Dorothy Reynolds, smiling like a considerate skull, Pamela Lane as a novice in the family who begets her husband's child, perhaps through nerves, and Jonathan Cecil as an acerbic pipsqueak descendant who looks like a drawing by Beerbohm.

MAY 23, 1965
OXFORD AND LONDON

A Last Drop of the Hard Stuff

George Cukor's film of Philip Barry's *The Philadelphia Story* was made in 1940, with Katharine Hepburn, Cary Grant, and James Stewart. All three give performances of such calm comic judgment that one wonders whether Cukor's legendary reputation as an actress's director does him honor enough. It is true that Katharine Hepburn, cast as a rich girl who thrives on fights and who seems to be marrying her deadneck second husband as some sort of penance for flamboyance, has never seemed more invincible; her faultless technical sense makes one feel that she could play a scene with a speak-your-weight machine and still turn it into an encounter charged with irony and challenge.

But Cary Grant, as her first husband, flourishes under Cukor's direction almost as much. For once his style of unwounding mockery seems to come out of the character; and though it is partly due to the editing that his glances at his recalcitrant ex-wife are as shrewdly fond as they are, they would never have been thrown at all if it had not been for the atmosphere of trust and intimacy that Cukor palpably creates for his cast. One could not imagine them in a Billy Wilder picture.

James Stewart, playing a dryly self-loathing gossip-journalist, head perpetually inclined as though he were going through a doorway in some quixotic Tudor cottage, seems to have bloomed in the same way. For some reason, mutters on the screen are always comic and beguiling: Stewart here is an incorrigible mutterer, tending to wander off into corners by himself and throw low insults like grapeshot at the palatial Philadelphia homestead he has invaded. In the circumstances his abrupt declaration of love for Katharine Hepburn in a public library, spoken away from camera in an undertone that infects her own bronze caw, demonstrates the most precise control of mood. Beneath the stinging repartee he implies a romanticism that makes it perfectly believable that he should work for an equivalent of *Confidential*, and at the same time gently detest himself for it. "We'd love to see those pictures one day," says the engaged couple, having been compromisingly photographed by journalists whom they take to be guests. "You will," says the photographer grimly.

A good deal of the credit for *The Philadelphia Story* must be laid squarely at the feet of the writer. In most sophisticated comedies about sex among the rich the question of money is ignored, as though the author did not really like to remark on how well-heeled his characters are, and the sexual situations are acted out as though they were a mime by uncomprehending children. Neither of these generalities is true of Donald Ogden Stewart's owlishly witty screen version of the Philip Barry stage play, which embodies a view of life as critical and formed as one would expect of any serious dramatic writer. I am not sure why, in a century widely versed in Marx and Freud, we should somehow have agreed to accept snobbery about money and infantilism about sex with little resistance as long as they occur in a comedy; for one reason and another, *The Philadelphia Story* is to be saluted as a rare film as well as a good one.

AUGUST 13, 1961

Summer Judy Holliday

"What's new in the city?" they said.

"The sprinklers are on in the playgrounds," I said. Memory of the famous scene in *The Seven Year Itch* when Marilyn Monroe stands over the draft from the subway—skirt blowing (summer sight), like the skirt of the bicycling girl in Truffaut's *Les Mistons*.

"No," they said. "A film."

"*The Passion of Anna*, then," I said. "The new Bergman."

"Yes," they said. "But we've seen that. What else? Isn't there anything funny?"

"Judy Holliday," I said.

"Oh, good," they said. "Is she on again?"

The new releases of the week are nothing; but the late, great Judy Holliday is alive just now at the New Yorker movie theater in *Born Yesterday*. Like most of the funniest performers in the world, she has an attitude in her films of alert skepticism. There is something fishy about this planet, she implies. She is ready to be grateful for its small mercies and she is infinitely educable to our ways, but we may all, she hints, be nuts. She makes her entrance in *Born Yesterday* with a corsage hanging behind her right ear like a displaced bunch of grapes. Apart from Beatrice Lillie, no one can ever have expressed a more ungodly disbelief in fashion. Judy Holliday is perfectly polite to her clothes, but they seem visited on her, like mannered guests whom she can't wait to be rid of, although native absorption keeps her interested in their arcane reasons for being around. She is not one of us. She behaves toward the corsage, though courteously, as if she were an uncomfortably intelligent horse decked out with bells and flowers for some festival held by another species.

Miss Holliday was one of the most touching American comic actresses. To any luck dealt out to her in the parts she played—diamonds, nice men, high living—she extends a powerful disbelief. Orchids and sequins obviously arouse in her a very strong suspicion that the orchidless and sequinless times must be just around the corner. Her assumption that her grand clothes are a disguise to fool no one and that she is obviously a down-and-out to anyone with eyesight is specifically her country's, and wonderfully funny. She shared it with Marilyn Monroe. Both of them were breakable-looking waifs struggling to stay hidden inside their confidently rubbery bodies. They plainly felt themselves to be pretenders, and they had a very American inkling that they weren't going to get away with it for long. It made them beautiful clowns.

In the *Born Yesterday* story, from Garson Kanin's famous Broadway comedy, Judy Holliday plays the girl of a big-shot junk dealer and swindler called Harry Brock, whose hotel booking in Washington is for a whole wing. Broderick Crawford plays the swindler. Miss Holliday's character is called Billie Dawn. Her given name was Emma; she could never face the test of living up to that one, though. Her man behaves to her like a pig, but she gets through things by pretending not to notice, just as she uses her shortsightedness as a glamour puss's excuse not to have read anything. When Harry is being most boorish to her, she bawls cheerfully to him from a window of their posh hotel wing, opting for comradeliness in this millionaire's hangout that they are trying to browbeat into a slum. The hotel manager, clinging to fake politesse in the chaos like a drowning man clutching at a stone, refers to her cattily as Mrs. Brock. Harry stops that. "Not Mrs. Brock," he says. "There's only one Mrs. Brock, and she's my *mother*, and she's *dead*." He nods toward Billie and briefly classifies her. "She's a *fiancée*." There are Mrs. Brocks and there are fiancées, and fiancées are trash. But this trash is blessed with good lungs and a roaring spirit. She was once in the chorus. And not just the chorus, she protests later, in that ripe, high, expostulatory voice; she spoke lines, actually. Five, she says. Ask anybody. But Harry didn't want to share her with the general public.

Billie Dawn is a fine character for Judy Holliday. It is the character of the girl who carefully copies what the dolts do but who obviously knows more than any of them. When William Holden starts feeding books into her and persuades her to wear spectacles so that she can read, it is clear that her brain is better than anyone else's in the picture, including that of Mr. Holden in the part of this more upright than engaging pedagogue, who has been hired to teach her about Paine and Jefferson and the opus number of Beethoven's Second Symphony. Miss Holliday, you feel, could have *been* Paine, and nothing on earth would incline her to think her life well spent if she put it to numbering symphonies. Her whole comic character is a natural forerunner of Women's Lib, in a way, but managed without weight. When she caricatures the dopey, pampered woman her men think they want, she is throwing a bone to admen's creatures, and she does it partly because she finds the disguise a useful decoy that gives her space to think. Wherever there's a row in her films, the blade of her mind whips out. Harry Brock, the capitalist who supposes he has bought Billie wholesale, finds that her loyalty to him is not such a plangent harpstring to play on as he thought. When she questions a reekingly dishonest contract that he wants her to sign, and he accuses her of double-crossing him, she says back, "If there's a fire and I call the engine, so whom am I double-crossing? The fire?" Harry had thought, in his invertedly romantic way, that his juicy girl was a buyable voter; she ends by summing him up objectively as a social calamity.

Some of the script seems politically cautious and dated now, with its veiling of McCarthyism as "Fascism," in the guise of Harry's cartel-making versus Billie's conscience, and with its care not to make the heroine more than a being of instinct. But the love of Garson Kanin and the director, George Cukor, for a certain kind of American survivalist is true and sweet. Billie is one of the best parts that Judy Holliday ever played, and typical of her style. Her comic task as a smashing-looking girl was always to cover up great boredom at having to shimmer around in lamé pajamas and pretend to be a dumb broad. There are ravishingly funny scenes in her films when she will furtively interest herself in other and cleverer things in the middle of man-made, typecast seductive circumstances—dancing expertly by herself to a radio turned on in a corner, or beating a chap on his own ground with a startling hand of gin rummy, or managing the chewing of gum at the same time as the technicalities of a long cigarette holder, or dealing a death blow to pedantry with a magnificently simple mutter of sense after some sciolist thinks she has made a crushing point.

Judy Holliday was of her time in the way she had to hide her brains from men. A girl character probably couldn't do that now without seeming coy. But maybe concealment of one kind or another characterizes a lot of American humor—W. C. Fields concealing his booze and his bank accounts, and Groucho Marx his terror of Margaret Dumont, and Laurel and Hardy their fear of being only two, and Lenny Bruce his panic at the way things in the world were going.

JULY 25, 1970

Beatrice Lillie, Elaine May

In the late 1920s, Beatrice Lillie appeared in the film *Exit Smiling* as the bottle-washer member of a tenth-rate touring company. The leading lady was inevitably laid low one day with ham's sore throat or something, and Miss Lillie got her chance. She climbed like lightning out of her usual parlor-maid's costume and into the star's seduction clothes, waylaid only for a moment by the hanger that she had left in the shoulders, and lay on a sofa onstage in her slithery black dress to be ravished by a cad in riding boots. All went as it should go in melodrama, except that she looked for a second at her watch over her lover's shoulder, which is something that people do only in real life; and she looked, moreover, at a watch made apparently for a muscle-man, worn under her evening dress around the ankle.

Enter Laughing—from the Carl Reiner book about show biz in the 1930s that was adapted by Joseph Stein into a play and has now been turned into a film, directed by Reiner—often reminded me of *Exit Smiling*, subject and title apart. Elaine May, cast as the lanky daughter of José Ferrer, who plays an actor-manager of the old school of bossy boomers, has an off-center practicality that is every bit as engrossing as Miss Lillie's. (She is also much more skilled than most strongly individualized performers at playing scenes with other actors.) Like *Luv*, *Enter*

Laughing is a tame container for her, but it is impossible not to be riveted by her funniness and her brains. Now that she has made her doubting way into two films, I hope someone will have the wit to let her write her own script for the next, instead of exploiting her to energize Broadway rehashes.

The dubiety expressed in the long, beautiful, yawning-dromedary face is part of her comic temperament. So is the intelligence, which is characteristically obdurate and out of step at a time when comedians often trade on being victimized and gormless. A lot of the acting now regarded as funny in films has been wretchedly debased by the response-begging of television performances. Elaine May asks nothing. Her personality is there to be taken or left; she does nothing to sell it. She is like a buffoon in Dostoevski—aware of her existence as profoundly ludicrous but never of her manner as funny. She seems movingly a self-creation, with idiosyncrasies rooted in her own sensible incredulity about commonly accepted states of affairs. At the simplest physical level, her point of view is expressed in the position she seems to take toward her clothes. In *Luv* and in *Enter Laughing*, she obediently dresses as women are supposed to when they want to be womanly, and keeps having a go at high heels and spangled cocktail things that have the glum glitter of those neon signs saying GAS—EAT, but she sometimes lets slip a hint of an enormous longing to wash her hands of the whole dumb endeavor. One's own strong impulse is to reprieve convention's uncomplaining hostage and put her in jeans and gum boots. Like Bea Lillie tangling with a stole, Miss May has a scene in which she contends pleasantly with a red feather boa, and you can see her quelling a small pang of worry about wearing only a slip as she welcomes a man into her dressing room. She says, though, in her typical tone of nervous reassurance, that he must come *in*, this is the *theater*.

To anyone not yet totally brainwashed by the womanliness dogma, Elaine May's alert part is a lot more sympathetic than the numb bridal prospect, played by Janet Margolin. Practically every commercial American film now seems to be stuck with some milk-drinking, self-absorbed young nullity as the marriageable heroine, even though she would obviously drive anyone up the wall after five minutes of living with her. It is a sad falling-off from the days of, say, Katharine Hepburn, and also a gross misrepresentation of the capacities of the American theatrical profession, that the young female leads now should so often be played by the most regularized, vitamin-fed, technically dull beauties available, in spite of the quantities of American actresses with more character and more uncapped teeth. The stage-struck boy friend of this particular film, who would be better off celibate, is another machine-belt product of dentistry and orange juice, played by Reni Santoni. The part represents the usual bashfully healthy hero of current American comedy, all gulping sex-starvation and afraid to ask. Again, there is a young character role in the film—played by Michael J. Pollard, a good actor with a squashed-looking face out of Hogarth—that is made to seem a hundred times more rewarding as screen company.

José Ferrer is genuinely and surprisingly funny. He calls the hero "boy" in an Olympian but worn-out roar, like God waked from sleep on the seventh day. He has to coach the lad in an unspeakable melodrama, full of prodigally spent rhetoric, which generally turns out to be addressed to the empty air since the boy nearly always misses his cue. In an audition to cast the part, Miss May has been perfectly charming to a scared and extremely short candidate who says, as if it were his last hope, that he is going to be twenty-seven. "Yes," she says, in that comforting and ventriloquial voice, "I'm *sure* you will be." Shelley Winters is rather funny as the boy's maddeningly self-effacing mother, who moans on about wanting him to be a druggist. But, oh lord, those juvenile leads who are supposed to be so appealing! There was a time when Hollywood knew that guts and peculiarities are better box office than line-toeing and a perfect little nose.

AUGUST 5, 1967

Murray Schisgal's *Luv*, now filmed by Clive Donner, is a funny and very American suppressed howl about some of the same ideas that exist in *Privilege*. Too many words chasing too little feeling, too much dulled general speech for personal things best expressed by shutting up. Mr. Schisgal stylizes a nightmare culture of oversophistication and bogus sensibility, in which bigger and bigger formulations are being used for tinier and tinier whimpers of self-pity, and in which people worn out with talk about "marriage" and "interpersonal relationships" and "a very wonderful human being" have begun to suspect themselves of retching the words "I love you" on an empty stomach. The three chief characters chat about love—Luv, as in Lux—with the brainwashed sprightliness of housewives dropping in on one another for a friendly gossip about soap powders. The hero, played by Jack Lemmon in a high tragic mood less funny than ordinariness would be, tries to make his life a statement of lovelorn passion by throwing himself off the Brooklyn Bridge. He does it with gloomy inefficiency, spurred on only by a bemused and baseless sensation of being objectively detached from his robot self, so that he can look forward keenly to admiring the probity of his suicide after it has been accomplished. The second man in the story, played by Peter Falk, is also shopping around for some acceptable hook of suffering from which to hang his life. He happens to be married to a woman who impresses you as beyond improvement in the eerie interest yielded by living with her, but in these conventional and deep-breathing times he feels duty-bound to eat his heart out for some duller other woman. The crackpot central lady is lanky, avid, and glum, and alert to hypnotically off-center things. She constantly loses track of what she is in the middle of being vehement about, and wears clothes that look like lampshade trimmings or Victorian bellpulls. She has apparently been told so often about the fractured existence of brainy women in modern society that she sees the Board of Education as her deadly foe, and regards her razor intelligence in paleontology as being forever at loggerheads with what her gender entitles her to, which she horribly calculates on a chart in terms of her diminishing sexual activity with her husband, poor overobserved man. The character is played by Elaine May, in her first film part. She has a very, very funny presence on screen, and possesses the simple but unusual movie-acting technique of making it seem that the events are happening to her now, instead of looking as if she were imitating things that really occurred long ago in a script. The woman she creates appears to be living perpetually a bit below par, as the best comic characters generally do. She is fired now and then by encouraging words like "flamenco" or "divorce" but mostly behaves with a severe and removed lugubriousness, using her quizzical fingers as if she were picking feathers off something covered with marmalade, and sometimes clenching her lips over her long teeth like a ratty horse.

JULY 29, 1967

This Unpopular Century

More good films and plays and books and paintings must have been made in distaste for the age now than at any other time in the life of mankind. Though it is rare for anyone really to want to *be* anyone but himself, it is for the moment very common—given the ritual nods to the advantages of modern egalitarianism, rock music, medicine, and plumbing—to want to have been born at some other point in history. Frank Gilroy's striking and clean-cut début as a film director with *Desperate Characters*—which he also produced and adapted, from a novel by Paula Fox—is about middle-class New Yorkers of forty-odd who hate their mistaken lives. The errors silently detested emerge in a film so truly peopled that the minor distresses are like slips of the tongue disclosing the longings of an epoch.

The characters possess a wit that runs into the sand because it is mostly self-addressed and hopes to correct nothing. They have a vivacity that is punishing to themselves because they can find no purge for it, and this often misleadingly gives them the manner of people in a rage, though all they are really doing is jousting for a target. It strikes them sometimes that the target is their own inertia. They fear boredom; nearly as much, they fear that they themselves are boring, although they would pick their own company in favor of any New York stranger, whom they would suspect of listening to nothing and of talking to himself all the time. Sometimes the four main characters of the film will hit a patch of sparkling good fortune when people pay heed to each other, but mostly they talk as if they were alone, sleep out of rhythm with each other even when their private clock of living together is the same, and take it out on answering services and hospital emergency wards.

There is a peppery tang to this movie that is entirely its own. The dialogue has a speed one hardly hears now except in revivals of movies from the 1930s, when the clever people who were in the movie industry weren't reined back by exhibitors demanding spare time for popcorn munchers who might miss half the talk between chews; they also weren't restrained by the mannered propaganda that fast talk necessarily isn't visual. Frank Gilroy makes it perfectly visual. (His cinematographer was Urs Furrer.) The characters' places always look like real houses—which they are—and the lines come out like shot. For once, we are in the middle of a New York City-baiting work that is possessed as powerfully as any Chekhov play by the sense that things needn't be so. This is one of the elements that lift the picture away from all the millions of other New York-is-impossible pieces, with their ersatz fatigue and their compensating bright jokiness for the sake of box office.

We are in the company of intimates. They take it that the rule of the city is that their lives are committed to perpetual motion, and that, like sleepwalkers, they will suffer something unknown and terrible if they stop. It is only with one another that they even contemplate coming to a halt. There is no exposition between them: no need. Shirley MacLaine, in a part that is a giant stride forward for her in its show of what she can encompass technically, plays an intelligent, subtly beleaguered woman called Sophie, wife of Kenneth Mars as Otto Bentwood, a lawyer whose big, lumpy face hides some unappeasable regret and distemper.

He can talk back as fast as she can but not as wittily; she can turn on a dime. They live in a vaguely chic brownstone near Brooklyn Heights. The classiness is no protection against the common paranoia about theft and rape and muggings. They must be paying the earth in antipopulace devices. She once had a lover, now gone; she just got into a taxi, and when she turned back to wave he was looking into a bookshop. So the world ends. Only the regret for perfidy now remains in the air, like the fumes of a gas leak.

The telephone rings. It is this that is really the chaotic intruder: the telephone—in this house, with its complicated burglar alarms and locks. She suspects, from the look of her, that it might be her lover ringing again. So does her husband. So do we. No one answers the phone for a long while. Then a dark energy suddenly floods her veins like ink, and she whips up the receiver and yells into the phone at one more New York crank. Who is deceiving whom? Maybe it *was* a burglar. Or maybe someone for her husband whom she doesn't want him to speak to. His closest friend was Charlie, his ex-partner, whom he has just split from, and who enrages him afterward by coming to pour out his story to Sophie in the middle of the night. Here, following the Ibsenist style of the film, we enter as late observers. The thing that is obvious and palpable is that they all have behind them a world of knowing one another; simply to listen to them talking to each other makes one party to that.

Sophie's best friend is Claire (Sada Thompson), who is having a long-lived, self-amused, wordlessly harrowing affair with her ex-husband, an Eng. Lit. professor (Jack Somack), who talks about the classic hallowed idiot in literature and dislikes her tradition in the making of soups. Everyone in the film seems to live on soup. The very best soup. Not tinned, entirely enlightened, and French, served in plates from some Provençal-import place, but still obviously a nightly soup, for which husbands and ex-husbands cherish a mild nightly spite. Claire has left herself go self-mockingly to seed, in an intellectual's style. She has taken to clothes that look like horse rugs bought to benefit key radical causes, and to jewelry possibly Vietnamese and, if so, definitely from the North. Her ex-husband talks painfully about their past, like a tongue that won't leave alone a hole in a tooth. "I don't like what I'm doing with my life!" cries the subtext of his lines in the exquisitely layered film, in which there is a lament for an existence under his witty rancor about the young, about his twenty-year-old complaisant son by another marriage, who thinks the world began in 1950, about students and inept theses—a rancor that sometimes pretends to be philistine, for the sake of relief or energy or simple change, but that always has the grounding of a deep care for books.

Sada Thompson is the actress who became famous in *The Effect of Gamma Rays on Man-in-the-Moon Marigolds*, but before that she had a crucial background in rep and the classics. (She was in *Tartuffe* and *The Misanthrope*, for instance, and in Beckett's *Happy Days*.) The character has settled for less, and now she asks herself "Why?" This is the steel hawser of the film. It drags the apparently eventless action along underwater. The same question is wonderfully put by Shirley MacLaine's performance. Other actresses would have been more obvious casting. Shirley MacLaine is surprising in the part, but she is working miles within her resources. The character looks forty, intelligent, unextended, fortified from within, taking refuge in sedate black clothes when she is trying hardest to deal with life, happier in jeans but immoderately strengthened by Bergdorf Goodman and a membership in the Museum of Modern Art, where she taps like a dowager on the window to get the attention of a friend (Rose Gregorio), who escapes from her with some funny fake-highbrow nullities about the children's training in a wholesome, psychoanalytic approach to tennis.

Shirley MacLaine helped to set up the film, with English financing from Sir Lew Grade—$350,000, which is about a tenth of the usual American cost of such a carefully detailed picture. The actors rehearsed together for two weeks. They spent the second week in England with the cameraman to plan the setups. The director and the stars, and even some of the crew, worked for token amounts and a piece of the possible profits. Lew Grade is also handling his own distribution to cut the costs more. If this picture makes its money back and goes on to do as well as it should, something will have been proved about the kind of film that can be made for a reasonable amount as long as people aren't greedy. Novelists and poets and painters are ready to work on spec—why not people corporately involved in films, as long as they're sure that the accountants aren't cooking the books? But how to achieve that? This is one of the first pictures we have seen that have been made on such a budget without losing the look of a lovingly made, carefully finished film. Most cheap movies propagandize the random, but not this one. One can see that this picture would have been rewarding for Shirley MacLaine to do. She must be tired of playing a pretty young kook.

The question raises itself, of course, of how pity can be aroused by the spectacle of lucky people talking in taxis about being driven to the end of their tether by small things. But you could ask the same question about *The Three Sisters*. The pity lies in the fact that everyone in the film knows powerfully well that there must be a world elsewhere. The story is without much action, on the face of it: the crank telephone call to the Bentwoods; a rock thrown through their bedroom window; a cadging visit by a con man, who sufficiently intimidates them by his straits and his color to take ten dollars off them for some invented trip to his mother in Albany; a desecration of their country place by vandals, who have left stabbed mattresses and lakes of dried ketchup. It is the arbitrariness of things, of course, that is edging the couple to their limits, and pushing a peculiar wedge of expressionlessness between them. Each one is much alarmed by passion in the other. The dilemma is really that everyone in the picture is an atheist suffering what used to be called Doubts. Given Doubts, the rest follows, as the faithful know: skepticism about the Virgin Birth, Infallibility, Damnation, Penance, Absolution, Cardinals, Incense—the lot. In the nonreligious, Doubts have to be about the good of living in such-and-such a way. Once given the rather more noble Doubts that the Bentwoods transmit about the unsupported moral lives they are living out, the well-known mayhem of life in Manhattan becomes the ethical whipping boy, even the national frenzy of packaging can seem a spiritual symptom, and garbage gets it in the neck from a character as morally intelligent as Sophie. The people in the film are very quick on the draw about the bad man stalking them down Main Street, but they aren't sure of his face; that's the poignancy of it.

SEPTEMBER 25, 1971

Cackle in Hell

A rich man on some headlong run from his life is blinded in a car accident while he is driving with his mistress. She takes him to convalesce. With them goes her doubly hidden earlier lover, whom the rich man believed to be homosexual when he could see, and whom he now can't even detect to be present. The two with eyes play pixie pranks. "Am I facing the sea?" says the blind man, settled into his villa and believing himself loved. "Yes," says his girl, having placed his chair to stare at a blank wall. In Nabokov's novel *Laughter in the Dark*, the disproportion between what we and the hero can perceive of his situation is wicked enough. In Tony Richardson's film it becomes really harrowing, for the movie piles onto this disproportion our privilege of also literally seeing. Just as we know that it is really the man's bank account that is being devoured, and that he himself is being pushed to the side of the plate, so we are privy to every physical trick that is being played on the far side of his black glasses.

Richardson's *Laughter in the Dark* is a fine film. It is piercing, intelligent, and pitying about a gulled man in ways quite different from the concerns of Nabokov's novel. It is also fairly camp, reflecting the plot, for the whole ploy of camp rests on the exhibition of something hidden and inaccessible to any aliens in the company. If the film is profoundly unlike the book, I can't see that this means a thing. The business of whether or not a movie is "faithful" to a novel generally seems a barrel-scraping question. The beautifully simple screenplay is by Edward Bond, the English playwright, who strikes me as the strongest and truest innovator to have come up in the London theater of the 1960s. It isn't surprising that his script has a tone far from Nabokov's book. Bond is a writer, not a tracer. And second, the fussed-over theory that a novelist is capable of an intellectual complexity not open to film directors hasn't much bearing on this particular movie. Some ideas are lost here, but then other ideas of great interest are gained about the way a man's vision of the knowable world is shaped.

In Nicol Williamson's acute performance as Sir Edward More, a newly blinded man bumps into bruising questions about the reality of his old structures. His doubt is harsh and poignant. While he has his sight and lives his null, grand life as an art expert with his wife—a strained beauty played by Sian Phillips—he thinks that this is the way things are, in an absolute sense. But perhaps he isn't actually seeing much when he confidently records his mandarin television talks about art appreciation, and perhaps he notices little or nothing about his wife. If he had looked at her and seen some other reality—seen the possibility that she existed distinct from him, and not as an annex of his own boredom—he might have found himself already happy. He does try, but his way of observing her has whittled both of them down. No fantasy, no fun, no license. "Shall I come in with you?" he says as they lie in their single beds. "It's late, darling," she says nicely, going on reading, wide-awake. So he falls in love with a girl way off to the side, moving into what feels more like "reality" because it stabs him. It happens on a day when he is sitting angry and alone in a cinema. The vicious joke of it is that the girl who takes him into this world of feeling—a cinema usherette at the National Film Theatre, played by Anna Karina—has obviously never had a pang or an ache in her life. The character is like some unscrupulous little monkey who has learned the gestures of humanness by copying. She moves in on him and coaxes him away from home, making the signs of loving. All mimed. She takes him on a mock-idyll, along with the young lover who is passed off as a homosexual (Jean-Claude Drouot). We can all see what's happening behind the hero's back—that he is being cuckolded, that the girl is crazy about the other man, that they are both after his money and scorn him so much that they barely trouble to hide the wild affair they are having in the hotel rooms and sailboats that he pays for. He will come to the recognition stumblingly later, in hell. "I love you," he says now, and "You are a child." It's heartbreaking, for he truly does, but she is no child. She seems eerily postmoral, and older than anyone whom any member of our present, lingering, hopeful species should ever have to cope with. After the car accident, she lifts his hospital bandages before they should have come off, and idly introduces him to a piece of knowledge that might have stopped even an SS woman in her tracks awhile.

Before he was blinded, he had begun to see—to understand—what was happening, though it is now going to have to be redeciphered. There was a brilliant scene of cruelty on a beach, with a water-skiing acquaintance gurgling through a lot of ice cubes in her mouth and choking out the giggly news that she fell over in the water because she saw a couple (his couple, his *girl*) making love in a boat. After the accident, the double-dealer's faked concern redeceives him and he has to learn the truth about her all over again, feeling it out, as he has to map the physical world in a new way with a white stick. She takes him off again to the sun, her lover softly with them. Sir Edward thinks they are two; we see they are three. The lover, dodging around the villa on bare feet and sometimes naked, sits secretly at table with them and glugs from their bottle of wine and makes signs to the girl to give Edward wrong answers to questions about the colors of the room. Edward is misled by the moving around of furniture. We get to know two villas at once: the one visible in the film and the one detectable to him, which seems to keep changing. The casual malice of the young lovers is agonizing to watch. Even when the hero could see, they managed to twitch the strings of his physical sense of things in much the same way. The film augurs that particular power over him in a frightening little silent scene on the beach, when all three are on swing-back chairs and the hero, in the middle, clicks his own backward and then forward in obedience to the movements of the gleeful pair, who savor their quick shared rhythm and the slowness of his pickup. Nicol Williamson, an unmistakable great actor, movingly plays Edward as a man who develops a stoic heroism he was not born with. By the end of the film he has learned. He is going to sit it out. "I can manage," he says near the finish, when a sympathizer offers to pour a brandy for him. He seems a very lonely hermit who once thought he had many friends.

MAY 24, 1969

LAST-DITCH WITS

Godard's Folly of Soldiers

War is stupid, says everyone, fighting and buying armament stocks the while. No, says Jean-Luc Godard's blandly insulting *Les Carabiniers*, it is soldiers who are stupid. War itself is very clever. It gets the ill-placed to do the top brass's dirty work, it sanctions acts of arson and genocide that lone criminals might jib at, and it sells the recruitable on the idea that their lives are duller in peacetime. Without great idiocy among the men who fight, says the film—which has only just got a New York run, though Godard made it in 1963—war could scarcely work so brilliantly. This startling, craggy picture is haggard with intellect, but the brains and concern are disclaimed. *Les Carabiniers* wears an off-focus callousness that is peculiar to Godard. He proposes cliff-faced paradoxes upon which familiar sympathy can obtain no purchase. They are illustrated with all the inhumanity he can muster, and he dares you to presume pity in him at the peril of your own cool. But some freezing alertness to people's suffering in the vise of modern arbitrariness seems to be there all the same, and his drive to deny that he feels affection is part of the same racking contemporary trap.

The brothers who are the chief characters are Ulysses (Albert Juross), a thin, resourceless man with a deceptive look of mastery, and Michelangelo (Marino Mase), a cream-faced loon whose tiny eyes are habitually screwed up in a hopeless mime of shrewdness.

Michelangelo's temperament finds silver linings all over the place. When the king of the film's imaginary country tells him to fight, he interprets the order as a chance to see the world. Nice of His Majesty to write, he thinks. He swallows codswallop by the carload and looks on the bright side with a fixity beyond Candide's. Neither he nor Ulysses has apparent forebears, or anything but the most barren personal context. Godard always tends to abstract characters a little from naturalism and to show them in outline against lives that are like bare walls, much as Raoul Coutard, his great cameraman, chooses to represent them physically. The brothers have their civilian being in a shack and use an old cart as a couch for reading paperbacks. Their women are rock-bottom models of womanishness whose salient quality is a gift for staying numbingly cheerful through anything. While the girls hack public crisis down to the size of a mishap to the hair dryer, the brothers feel manlier passions, and lust after a Maserati car. Soldiering presents itself to them as nothing but license. "Can I kill the innocent?" Michelangelo asks a policeman. "Yes." "Can I leave a restaurant without paying?" "Yes, yes," impatiently. "It's *war*." What a spree, the enlisted feel. There is carousel music suddenly on the sound track. "Bring back a horse and a lot of ribbons," says one of the girls, blithely putting something lyric into rapacity. The women—called Cleopatra and Venus—are entranced by the idea of their men in khaki. They encourage them in their new careers with a long appreciation of the wonderful things that can accrue from battle. This sequence balances one at the very end of the film, when the soldiers are back from the fatuous massacre with a suitcase proudly stuffed with picture postcards. The postcards are thrown onto the screen in a mishmash symbolic of the fruits of war as the brothers' dimmed minds see them. The montage of photographs—ancient architecture, cars, famous beauties, cheesecake, a Persian cat in a soppy pose, a Modigliani nude—turns into a ghastly thank-you to systematized slaughter, for the looting it allows, the sight-seeing, the ecstatic dreaming forced on lonely, frightened men in pain. The jumble of empty mementos stands for all that the brothers can retain of anything that happens to them. Nothing is assimilated. Pictures of things are accepted in place of their meanings, and civilization is melted down into a souvenir. The girls look on indifferently. "I don't want the Parthenon," says Cleopatra. "It's ruined."

Cleopatra, Venus, Michelangelo, Ulysses. *Les Carabiniers* is about insensate people carrying legendary inscriptions of which they know no more than the postcard knows of the Parthenon. It is about minds that see history as garbage; about the way the world looks when insight and the sense of consequence have been lobotomized; about being a tool. Brecht often wrote of the same things. He was obsessed and saddened by our readiness to buy life as it comes and to believe the labels. The bemused clods in *Les Carabiniers* have been sold a fake, handed out the existence of curs, but they trust the tag and obediently act out the part of fortunate men, just as the characters in *Mother Courage* truly suppose themselves to be doing well out of the war that exploits them.

The intellectual substance of the picture is compressed in the device of attaching noble official pronouncements to scenes of harrowing military muddle that they don't match at all. Soothing slogans are intoned over images of wretchedness like benedictions uttered over a Catholic peasant woman at the end of her tether. Godard is really making a humane point of linguistics. Hang on like grim death, he says, to the difference between words and meanings. Language denies the visible truth all the time in this picture. There is a shout of "*La guerre est finie!*" but the explosions continue as usual. While a voice sonorously announces triumph, civilians in a town square scatter under a low bombing raid. The womenfolk at home trot out to the mailbox for lunatically stoic letters saying that the bloodshed proceeds magnificently and that their men kiss them. On the third Christmas Day of the war, beside a stingy tree in a corner of their shack, Cleopatra and Venus experiment happily with festive ways of doing their hair.

The film is full of the vilely familiar iconography of the news photographer—shots of women waiting, of scared people running for cover with children in their arms, of shopkeepers in doors looking up at a sky full of planes. It is a system of imagery that we recognize as fully as our forerunners recognized the emblems of the saints. By pushing the terrible very slightly toward the imbecilic, Godard makes it a little worse; in one of the rare close-ups in the film, for instance, Michelangelo wearing a gas mask stares at the camera. It is a mindless, ugly sight—some napalm-age cartoon of a knight with his visor down. "We captured Santa Cruz," the buffoon announces proudly, in a handwritten title. "I went to the movies." He sits in the cinema, grinning, and then holds his arms over his eyes to protect himself from a head-on shot of a train in the film he is watching, although he has never twitched a muscle about butchering people in real life, or even shown fear for himself. Then there is a bath scene from an old silent movie. Michelangelo goes up to the screen and tries to stroke the girl in her bath, yearning for the photograph of her as he never aches for the flesh of his wife. It is as if everything in life as he knows it were now ersatz, just as all history has become incoherent and all old endeavor been canceled. But now and then, characteristically, Godard's black world will light up with an epiphanic flash of something better, so that the ground once won by the species seems not altogether lost. A Leninist girl condemned to be shot in a wood puts off the firing squad by reciting a poem of Mayakovski's. The men usually love their work, but the ideas stored in her head make them stall. It is impossible to shoot her. She is so inconveniently in the middle of something —a recitation, or her life. The white handkerchief that they have hung over her face doesn't really help. It suddenly looks like a sculptor's cloth hung over a clay head to keep it damp for work next day. "*Frères!*" says the voice beneath the handkerchief, several times, wrecking resolve even further. To make murder routine again, the squad has to count "One, two, three" and fire in unison.

Les Carabiniers is a chilling comic fable about habit. It is also about the dizzying impulse to push the atrocious always a little further. There are lines dealing with the same instinct in Godard's films about private life—moments when lovers wantonly say, "I do not love you," to test how much pain they can cause; and in *Pierrot le Fou*, when Pierrot says to a badly-off garage boy, "You'd like a car like that? Well, you'll never have one." The men in *Les Carabiniers* are inevitably less interesting than these characters, because their responses seem devised, and not their own. They are the victims, never the agents, of the obscuring of their consciousness. The film is more of a thesis film than any other that Godard has made; it is deliberately even less particularized than usual, and sometimes even more contrary. I realize that the maddeningness is a device, but occasionally it can be—well, maddening. Perhaps it is a trick he uses to shield himself. (His ex-wife, Anna Karina, once touchingly said that his reason for wearing dark glasses all the time is not that his eyes are weak but that his universe is too strong.) The shrug that one catches in his work, the self-protective guise of cool, can sometimes look very like an updating of the hallowed and facile old French game of playing the unsurprisable cynic, but it can also strike you, when his films are most expressive, as the self-defense of a uniquely troubled, rancorous, and tender intellect. Godard regularly uses affront as a style for statement, maybe to stop our gum-chewing or maybe to give himself something to hide behind. In *Les Carabiniers*, his weapon is stupidity—woodenheadedness in the soldiers, and even a surface of simplemindedness to the thesis of the picture. But after you have thought about the film for a while you haven't much doubt that what drives it is not willful flippancy but distress. In his own way, Godard belongs historically to the line of great intellectual cartoonists—the witnesses who goad by deforming the familiar and by pretending callousness, the provokers who deliberately seek to be drastic because they see themselves as the reporters of last chances.

MAY 11, 1968

In the Thick of Europe

"Poland is a fine country but badly located," a Polish film-maker said to me once, after he had been through a frightening struggle with the censors in Warsaw. The liberty won in Gomulka's revolution of 1956 was beginning to wear thin, and the director's freedom to make the films he wanted to make was dwindling. In his maneuvers to work as he pleased, he could resort for the moment only to ruses and irony. Artists are at least wittier than their watchdogs and persecutors. They have that poor compensation while the toll is taken. The film-maker was Andrzej Munk, director of *Eroica* and *Passenger*, who died in a car crash before the resolve of Gomulka's October had finally crumpled to its knees. The dryness of his remark was very like him—and rather like the character of European revolution itself, perhaps. His fellow director Andrzej Wajda is nationally summed up as Munk's temperamental opposite, but to foreigners there are things in their work that are much alike. They have the same worn energy, a humor that plays dead but always gets up for more, and a skepticism that probably has to do with geography—that "badly located" country. Wajda's great trilogy about Poland in the months during and after the Second World War, which was made in the first years of Gomulka's Poland but is still scarcely known in America, strikes me as one of the most eloquent and complex political statements in cinema. During this week of dim commercial releases, overhung by the news from Czechoslovakia, I went back to see *Ashes and Diamonds*. The picture was made in 1958–1959. It is the third film in the triptych, following *A Generation* and *Kanal*. In the light of what has since happened to Polish film-makers—purged of

Jews, robbed of work, dragooned into positions of nonalliance with the Czechoslovakians' own revolution—it is a shaking film to see.

The Poles are often accused of romanticism, as if that necessarily meant sentimentality and decorativeness. Their form of it seems to me to be something different. In Wajda's film it emerges as a hard-won gaiety, deeply bitten with a knowledge that the only other option is fear. The feeling for Poland in the trilogy is passionate but not deluded, and always tinctured with dark humor. Farther west, romanticism peters out into reverie, but in Central Europe it often ends in fierce and poetic action. Unless we have lived in a country accustomed for centuries to terror, informers, knocks at the door in the middle of the night, constant choices between the terrible and the only slightly less terrible, I'm not sure that we are equipped to criticize such romanticism. The history of Poland can make you feel that we know nothing. *Ashes and Diamonds* is a sage and brilliant statement by a film-maker from a land where for hundreds of years politics has been not an exhibition game played by the few but the common name of how to survive.

When the three films came out, they seemed what they literally are: a born film-maker's account of the experience of a young generation of Poles schooled only to kill—to kill first the Nazis and then one another, in the battle for power between the London-based government-in-exile and the Moscow-trained government waiting to move in from Lublin. If one sees it now, it has even more resonance. There is not only the echo set up by the double time scheme of a post-Stalinist film-maker recording a Stalinist period. The films also seem to contain some strange and sober knowledge of what was to happen after they were made—knowledge of how revolutions are betrayed, and of the attrition of the revolutionaries themselves—much as good portraits often prefigure what the sitter is going to look like ten years later.

Ashes and Diamonds is set on the last day of the war in Europe: May 7, 1945. Chaos, joy, exhaustion. Every aspect of life is confused and depleted. The film is about a Poland razed to the ground, about young nationalists who have had no youth but assassination, about heroes of the Uprising suddenly hunted down by the Communists as Fascists. Other heroes, who were lately their fellows in the last-ditch struggle in the Warsaw sewers, are lining up with the tank-shaped bureaucrats sent to rule by their recent ally and historic oppressor, Russia. The perversions become total. Celebration incredibly turns into new emergency. The debonair Zbigniew Cybulski plays one of two patriots of the uprising who arrive at a banquet with orders to kill a Russian-trained Pole; two wrong men are killed, and the Cybulski character is himself shot in a chase through a yard full of laundry. The figure that looks like a child playing ghost in a sheet gets a hand free to feel his own blood, and smells it with an inquisitiveness near amusement. No wonder the young of Poland responded to him. "Cool" is a more vital virtue there than here. Cybulski's way of dying makes no claims for himself. It brought back something from a Brecht play: "Unhappy the land that has no hero," and the reply, in Brecht's own voice, "Unhappy the land that needs a hero." Sometimes Wajda is called baroque, as if he created flamboyant figures that invite overblown loyalties, but in the trilogy he does exactly the opposite. He sees heroics as an ambush that has already murdered generations. Cybulski describes his famous dark glasses, which the character wears in the story because of the time he spent in the sewers, as "A souvenir of an unhappy love for my country." "Will I be a big shot?" asks a fairly sloshed old man at the victory banquet, sizing up the factions and deciding to look after himself with the likeliest side. "Poland is ours again!" says a tearful worker who has never held title to anything, and never will. It is a fine film, low-toned and charitable.

AUGUST 10, 1968

Polish Exile

Le Départ was directed, in French, by the Polish-born Jerzy Skolimowski, who collaborated on the scripts for Polanski's *Knife in the Water* and Wajda's *Innocent Sorcerers*. The film looks dazzlingly interesting, shot in grainy black and white, often with dark shapes against pale walls, like shadow play done with hands for a child. It opens with what seems to be a drowning sweater struggling to semaphore, but a face eventually emerges from the woollen neck. The owner of the face is a nineteen-year-old hairdresser's assistant, played by Jean-Pierre Léaud, who made his shattering first appearance in Truffaut's *Les Quatre Cent Coups*. His face has thinned and grown a little older, but it is not much changed. He still looks like an evacuee, alert and isolated in a very hostile territory. It is a rackingly modern face, moving, wary, expecting nothing. Léaud doesn't act, he behaves. One watches him from a distance as if he were a stranger in a newsreel, someone in the street caught up in a pressing event.

The hairdresser's assistant wants to be a racing driver. He has entered himself in a race as the owner of a Porsche that he means to swipe from his boss. He trains by night with a hairdresser friend and daily massages the scalps of rapacious chatterers who talk over him to one another between the washbasins and idly seduce him with promises of a car. The film has a peculiarly Polish monkey-on-a-stick humor, but something—exile?—has taken away its roots and made it seem only flip. The temperament of the film itself, with its shock farcical jumps and its cranky alarms, is very like the boy's own style of behavior when he suddenly shoves a safety pin up to the hilt in the muscle of his forearm or absently turns a hair-washing jet onto a grand client's false eyelashes because he is in a daydream about racing. Both the film and the character try a bit too hard to startle you, like a child jumping out from behind a curtain or putting his fingers to his eyes and mouth to stretch his face into an ogre's. The picture makes effects, and then stalls, because the hero never expands into anything more than what he literally is; he remains a boy who wants to be a racing driver, described in a not very fine-textured or detailed way. The film doesn't express whether anything more than random bravado stirs him. It reminded me of a lot of advanced work of the Polish Film School. It seems a prodigious freewheeling exercise, bent on caprice—in heroic recoil from the ensconced and the lip-serving, but at a cost.

APRIL 27, 1968

At the famous Polish State Film School in Łódź (pronounced Woodge) a clever, cannon-ball-headed young man called Jerzy Skolimowski quietly so constructed the series of short films required of him for his exams between 1960 and 1964 that they would assemble into a feature film. He later called this laziness. The film's name was *Rysopis* (*Identification Marks: None* in the English title). No one seems to have objected to his brilliant scheme for apprentice idlers, a trail he blazed so that he could skip having to become an assistant director or make more short films when he graduated. The vicious-circle logic of film-financing usually holds that you can't make a feature until you have made a feature; Skolimowski, who has always nourished a smoldering intimacy with the arguments of folly, took this one in his arms with a typical lax grin and embraced it to death. *Rysopis* did fine.

After film school, and collaborating with Wajda and Polanski on scripts, he directed two features in Poland: *Walkover*, about a hustling boxer, which is the most restlessly energetic of all his high-strung films, in spite of the apparently contradictory technical feat of containing only thirty-five cuts; and *Barrier*, which is about the chasm between the Poles who remember the Second World War and the ones who don't, and has a scornful scene of veterans singing noble war songs without anyone's noticing that they are hopelessly out of synch, like soldiers who have broken step to go across a bridge and now can't recover the knack of unison. Then he made *Le Départ*, in Brussels, with Jean-Pierre Léaud. Léaud played a hairdresser's assistant who wants to be a racing driver, planning to swipe a Porsche from his boss for a race. Then Skolimowski went back to Poland and made *Hands Up!*, long banned, about the attrition of rage in post-Stalinist Poland. It is really an attack on the concept of cool, but the attack itself has so much cool that the blade turns back on the film.

His new picture, called *Deep End*, and set mostly in a municipal bath in a seedy part of London, is a work of peculiar cock-a-hoop gifts. Jane Asher plays Susan, a sullen, beautiful red-haired bird who looks after the women's section of the public baths; it is a horribly well-observed character. Susan is absolutely modern in her nonchalance, but she is also unchangeably bourgeoise in the attentions and the engagement ring she demands of her fiancé. Eighteen months more of pop records and miniskirts, you feel, and then she will have been submerged completely in small-mindedness about paper doilies under the glasses. At the moment, though, because she has to pretend to be tougher than she yet is about fighting for small rights in a rotten job, she can't quite conceal flashes of gentleness. A fifteen-year-old called Mike, played by John Moulder Brown, his hair flopping over one eye like a spaniel's ear, has just started being a male attendant in the public baths; first time out to work, ten quid a week and seven of them to his mum. The trick of making a bit on tips in the awful place —tiled in bilious green and yellow, where the echo of voices is as mysteriously incorporeal as the surrogate sexuality that fogs the chlorine air—seems to be to exchange sections every now and then with the girl attendant. The women customers like it. They can call him into their cubicles and ask him to get them some shampoo, and then exclaim at his sauce for coming back with it when they're half undressed. Befuddled, Mike clings to Susan, whom he deifies: the rapacious housewife in the bud looks to him a glory. Their scenes together—eating plastic modern food on a diving board when the giggling schoolgirls have gone and the smell of municipal disinfectants must be thick—have something idyllic and intimate about them. Mike is so in love that he follows Susan and her fiancé to a porn movie, where they watch a grandiose lecture about frigidity, conducted by a grave lady with a riding whip, who suddenly opens a refrigerator door on a pretty girl who is hunched up like a trussed chicken and wears a look of mindless cheer while Wagner is played on the sound track. Like the middle-aged ladies in the swimming bath, Susan soon goes to theatrical lengths to protest to her fiancé that Mike is molesting her, and sends him out to fetch the manager; and then, with real sweetness, turns round and kisses the boy; and then, as soon as her fiancé is back, abuses him without batting an eyelid. The observation of cool quixotry is exact, but it becomes undercut by the film's own quixotry and by its own aspirations to airiness. Sometimes the film seems to be daring you to guess whether it is being funny on purpose or by accident, or simply absurdist in a Polish key, or nothing more than careless and off pitch, with that rather random courage which exiles often have to use if they are to function imaginatively in another language. When Skolimowski made *Le Départ*, for instance, he barely spoke a word of French, and parts of the film were as if he were challenging himself to do something supremely difficult and supremely futile, like putting together a Meccano model underwater without having read the instruction sheet and when the sea salt was scalding his eyeballs. The same sort of thing is troubling about *Deep End:* it seems defiant, admirable, gifted, gay, but almost suicidally prankish.

People often say about Conrad that his command of a foreign tongue was a miracle, but if the command were really complete it would strike no one as a miracle. It is the slight mistakes in his idioms that make the endeavor fierce and moving. The same faint sense of error hangs around *Deep End*. For lack of an English-speaking director, the actors often talk to each other with the mixture of garrulity and fuddle that makes scenes stall in improvisations at rehearsals; the words in actors' improvisations are nearly always credible and idiomatic, but the lines tend to run into the sand, because the purposes that would drive them properly are factitious or simply not there. The difficulties that beset a film director working away from the country he knows are nearly tragic, because movies rest crucially on recognizable detail. How does a foreigner know, for instance, what a particular character does when he is alone? How can he put a finger on the particular things that drive the man to despair, that make him convivial or feckless, that define his resilience, that attract him to radical change, that strike him as funny? It seems stirring that Skolimowski should have managed it at all, and that his London should seem so nearly like London when a lot of the film was actually made in Munich, with German-speaking actors in the small parts. The slightly off-note ear and the gaps in knowledge don't so much muddy the film as give it a peculiar asymmetry and lack of repose. They also make it incidentally eloquent about artists working in exile from what they know, although it is in Skolimowski's character to conceal all effort in a shrug. Like English schoolboys, Poles often serve an ethic of seeming not to try. Work must be done, but it must also not be seen to be done. Show nothing, expect nothing. Skolimowski expresses that view very simply and purely in the face and movements of the English boy whom he has cast as the hero. In spite of the director's contempt for the Polish generation that dwells on the war, Mike looks extremely like a teen-aged bomb victim. The film itself is Polish through and through: deeply bitten with irony, assuming mannerisms of the slapdash, sometimes silly on purpose, terrifyingly observant about discomfiture, comic and melodramatic, fragrantly inconsequential but furtively in praise of the indestructible.

SEPTEMBER 4, 1971

The Chaos of Cool

Rosemary's Baby, written and directed by Roman Polanski from a book by Ira Levin, is a horror film about pregnancy. The expectant father is Satan, which is supposed to be the horror part of it, and the story takes place in the Dakota apartment house on Central Park West, which I find more authentically horrific, as a matter of fact. The film is very proficient, but all the same, what's it for? If it weren't made by Polanski (*Knife in the Water*, *Cul-de-Sac*, and *Repulsion*), I suppose one mightn't ask the question. A horror film isn't *for* anything; it's just something to scare yourself with. The trouble is that *Rosemary's Baby* doesn't really scare you much, though this complaint puts one in the position of the character in an English comedy by N. F. Simpson who kept glaring irritably at a skull on the mantelpiece and saying that if it was supposed to be a *memento mori* it might as well go, because it didn't remind her of death at all.

Polanski loves making films. That's very clear in this picture, as it always has been. He has also learned a touching amount about a foreign country. He has cast the story meticulously, and directed the actors with a perfect ear (apart from a pun—"Tannis, anyone?"—that no one brought up in English could have borne). But why on earth does a major film-maker feel seduced by a piece of boo-in-the-night like this story? Perhaps it would have held together if there had been more detail of behavior and less dependence on instant belief in the existence of a New York City guild of witches, which is quite a large given, even if the headquarters are supposed to be in the Dakota. The doomed girl who comes to live there, a nice, bird-brained mooner well played by Mia Farrow, is married to an actor (John Cassavetes). Their next-door neighbors, who latch on to their wish for a baby all too cannily, are an elderly and chatty married couple, both practicing witches, whose tongues are hanging out for a newborn recruit. Satan's couple are played by Sidney Blackmer and Ruth Gordon, who is a joy. She does her fiendish work with a tireless good humor that wears her young neighbor into the ground. Gossiping and prying like Lucifer's retired nanny, she clucks around the grim brown costliness of the Dakota bearing glasses of demonic milkshakes that mature the poor fetus's character as a nasty little outrider of the Antichrist while he is still in the womb. The mother loses more and more weight, and justly complains to her obstetrician, but he is a key witch himself, as anyone but this patient could tell in a second, and he goes on forbidding vitamins in favor of Miss Gordon's tannis-root brews. The husband is also in the club, for suspiciously careerist purposes. He appears to be a fairly rotten actor. He played a minor monk in *Luther*, and something in a piece called *Nobody Loves an Albatross*. Thanks to the Evil One's throwing his influence around on Broadway, he lands a new part in place of an actor chum who suddenly loses his sight. Leaving aside the matter of the blinded friend, the chance of getting back to work seems a poorish Mephistophelian bargain in exchange for a baby with horns and the dubious fun of the witches' get-togethers, which are sticky occasions, like fund-raising cocktail parties.

Polanski is socially very funny, but he doesn't do nearly enough filling out with ordinary behavior. The amount he does is so shrewd and mischievous that you pine for more of it. He half throws away the most fruitful part of the story, which is the theme of a boring, amiable girl who can't get anyone to believe what she is saying. The situation is cast-iron. It always works, as it did in *The Lady Vanishes*, especially if each successive hope of help looks reasonable before it is dashed, but Polanski never makes her position look anything but hopeless. In the book, for chapters her husband's attitude was explicable as actor's self-absorption; in the film, she is months behind us in divining that he is up to something pretty foul. His rape to get her pregnant, when she is sloshed and comatose, has a reek of brimstone beyond the dreams of Savonarola. The scene is clever and startling. It is also deeply revolted by the flesh, and as sodden by the sense of sin as any in modern cinema. Not that Polanski means a moment of it. I take him more seriously when he is openly fooling around with us, as he does in a scary sequence in a phone booth, and in one where Mia Farrow scrapes an alarming chocolate mousse prepared by Ruth Gordon into her dinner napkin. But just as the book didn't know how to top itself at the end and culminated lamely in superstition instead of getting back to the chill, common daylight of good thrillers, Polanski hasn't solved the problem.

The film is elegantly designed by Richard Sylbert and cinematically well executed in every way, but it adds up to a rather trivial and slaphappy piece of work. Polanski is a natural filmmaker. An exercise in Gynecological Gothic like this seems a capricious expense of him. It must be hard for a hip young director from another continent to keep his bearings in the chaos of cool.

JUNE 15, 1968

Political Fables from Poland

A courageous Polish film director once told me in Warsaw that he was making a comedy about a man who chalked up subversive slogans about the government. I asked him how he had got the slogans past the censor, and he said that it was a matter of diverting the eye to the wrong thing: he had made his hero a lavatory attendant, and the censors' Ministry had been so concerned to ban any of the lewd graffiti which might involve naked plumbing that the wording got by unscathed. The Poles must be hard people to censor.

For years now a young writer called Slawomir Mrozek has been producing plays and stories whose existence behind the Curtain seems almost magically mistaken. Most of them are openly political; they are cast as fables, but they are as obviously rooted in the reality of Poland as a political cartoon is in the reality of a face.

"Why did we torture our poor poets and abstract painters?" says a character in *Police*, a short play about a totalitarian Utopia where the police have been so successful in quelling criticism that they have to take off their uniforms and behave as *agents provocateurs* in the hope of creating someone to arrest. One defrocked policeman, totally undermined by plain clothes, gets his wife to sew some official braid on to his underpants, which in a police state must be a fairly frightening idea as well as a funny one.

Mrozek is tartly undeluded about the universal authoritarian practice of giving the rebel a little harmless rope; even in prison, the insurgent is still allowed his revolutionary outlets. "He can stand on a bucket on the bed and look out of the window, which is forbidden. . . ."

Before Professor Jan Kott's Edinburgh productions of *Police* and *Out at Sea*—the first piece of directing by the witty author of *Shakespeare, Our Contemporary*—Mrozek's only available work in English was a book of short stories called *The Elephant*. The stories are short and swiftly drawn, like Japanese hieroglyphs, with a pernicious alertness to self-deception on the right and on the left. There is one story about a man so keen on the required political virtue of optimism that he paints himself in the colors of the rainbow, bends himself into a hoop on a balcony and falls to his death, but goes on spreading the correct spirit even as a corpse because he has instructed that his coffin should be covered with a flag reading "Three Cheers." It was for these stories that the Polish State Cultural Review blandly awarded Mrozek the annual literary prize in 1957.

Out at Sea is a fable about capitalism and totalitarianism in one. A fat man, a medium man, and a thin man on a raft are conducting free elections that can have only one outcome, which is that the two of them who are well endowed in flesh will eat the one made of skin and bones and brainwash him into a state of euphoric belief in his freedom of choice. Both this play and *Police* are theatrically very slight; like the stories, they are drawn really in one ribald, doodling line, and if Professor Kott's Scottish had been more fluent, instead of what he apologetically calls "Kottish," I think he would have compressed and hardened the verbal delivery out of recognition. But the bravery of Mrozek's mood is hard to resist, all the same, like his humor.

He has also written a prankish full-length play, called *Tango*, not yet produced outside Poland and Yugoslavia. It is an enormously funny piece of writing that should be staged here by someone with the wit to do it flat as a pancake. Mrozek knows himself that eccentric people are funny on stage only if they are intensely boring to one another. The verbal texture of *Tango* is wonderfully irritable, a fabric of the lectures and insults of a family of libertarians who have sent one another into a stupor with their theories.

Like *Police*, *Tango* is about a group of dejected Utopians, and the question that it sweetly asks them is why Utopia should have turned out so lousily. The freethinkers have degenerated into a coma of disgruntlement about one another's liberties; what is more, they seem to have spawned a copper-bottomed right-wing bigot for a son. Their central achievement, still rejoiced in, is that they have escaped from a convention that long ago prevented them from dancing the tango. Dad has won the freedom not to button his trousers; Mum, "in the flower of middle age," is unenthusiastically promiscuous with an exceptionally sordid freethinker called Eddie. The rebel reactionary son stages a sniffily old-fashioned wedding for himself and becomes a sort of domestic Fascist. The implications about political nostalgia and wet liberalism are as recognizable in England or America as in Poland, like the surreal rudeness of the humor.

OCTOBER 10, 1965
WARSAW; EDINBURGH

Pinter

When people say to each other, "What did he mean by that?" they don't want to know what the words meant but what you think the speaker said them for. They want to know whether you caught sight of a knife being whipped out underneath. The tramp in Pinter's *The Caretaker* is haunted by suspicions of malevolence, but he has no one to ask about them; so when he is talked to he often says "What?", not because he hasn't heard, but as a hopeless way of gaining time and puzzling out how much ground he has just lost.

The fact that people often talk like this, replying not to the meaning of speech but to what they can guess about motives, is such a simple and compassionate observation that it is hard to think how so many great writers of dialogue have managed without it for so long. For unless your characters are Jesuits, to follow a question by the answer that makes logical sense is actually a very stylized way to write lines. It is one of the things that give Shaw's plays, for instance, their rather inhuman surface.

But this is the way most dramatists have always written, even when they intended to be realistic. It is as though for thousands of years we had been drawing profiles of people with two eyes and just this moment noticed that only one eye actually shows. To most people in the past, to have followed a line like "Where were you born?" by "What do you mean?"—which is what the tramp says in *The Caretaker*—would have been pure gibberish. The stinking, obsequious old man replies like this because he thinks the brother played by Robert Shaw, who has given him a bed in his lumber room, is trying obscurely to get at him. If he could get down to his papers in Sidcup, everything would be all right. He has talismanic feelings about Sidcup, just as he has about shoes.

The Caretaker is very funny. It is also painful: Donald Pleasence's tramp is a terrible study of servility. He has a persistent gesture as though he were touching his cap, and sometimes fills in a pause with "Good luck" like a beggar. The second brother, played by Alan Bates, seems sent to plague him and to take away the puny hospitality he has won; but however much the tramp hates him, he is ready to abase himself to please him. His brain goes over and over both the brothers' words without getting anything more out of them, like a defunct carpet sweeper that has stopped picking up the dust.

Every reflex he has is secretive: he eats with his mouth open, in an elaborate mime of honesty that seems designed to show onlookers exactly what he has in there, but he instinctively waits to swallow until no one is looking. He pretends to be asleep when he is awake, and he wears his clothes as though he were hoarding them. When he sits down in his filthy overcoat he lifts the skirt like a pianist in tails.

A lot of films made from stage sources deserve the ritual snobbish abuse about photographed plays, but I hope *The Caretaker* doesn't come in for it. Every line in it involved rather delicate decisions of film-making, and Clive Donner and the cameraman —Nick Roeg—have taken them impeccably. The only things that struck me as crudities were the cut-ins of the real room during Alan Bates's fantasy about doing it up. All three actors are even better than they were on stage.

MARCH 15, 1964

The opening of Harold Pinter's *The Homecoming* was an exultant night. Quite apart from the experience of seeing a modern play produced in a style as achieved as the best we do for Shakespeare, it offered the stirring spectacle of a man in total command of his talent.

Pinter's technique is perhaps rough for him to control. In his television play *The Tea Party* he seemed to be slipping into vulgarity and hollowness. The new full-length play pulls back from the brink: its fastidiousness is exact, and the ideas in it are solid.

"It's a question of how much you can operate *on* things, not *in* things," says the character played by Michael Bryant; "I mean it's a question of keeping a balance between the two." This is one of the notions that Pinter's conflicts spring from. There are people who can operate only *in* things, like the name-character in *The Caretaker*, and people who can operate only *on* things, like the name-character in *The Servant;* in situations where they are incapable of keeping a balance, they are thrown into fear and fury. The inch-by-inch fighting that makes up the matter of Pinter's plays is never to gain the points that are openly declared. It comes out of a mutually murderous mood between a man who feels himself to be floundering in a swamp and a man who loathingly sees himself to be keeping his feet dry.

In *The Homecoming* there are five men in the family. Mum is dead. Their home is a vast open-plan North London living room, workingclass tat in epic concrete: a magnificent structure by John Bury, furnished with a Welsh dresser painted Berlin-black and a smoky armchair. The whole thing is in monotone blacks and grays, the colors of mashed newspapers and cigarette ash and old sweaters. Uncle Sam (John Normington), who holds the reins of the kitchen, is a diluted man who works as a chauffeur and has some dim sense of importance about taking his bosses to London Airport. Dad is a retired butcher, played by Paul Rogers with a perfect grasp of the fact that half of the grating comic power of the dialogue comes from speaking a line against its surface meaning, roaring hatred when demanding a hug or vilifying his puny life when his words are apparently boasting about it.

The two sons at home are a beefwitted demolition expert who boxes in his spare time and a neat lad, who turns out to be a pimp, played by Ian Holm with dapper and glinting ferocity. The visiting son is Michael Bryant, doctor of philosophy, a cut above them and equipped with a rilingly sexy wife played by Vivien Merchant. Like the pimp, their habit of character is to operate on things, and their effect on the three who operate in things is enraging and hideous.

The drama in *The Homecoming* is not the plot. In Pinter it never is. It consists in the swaying of violent people as they gain minute advantages. A man who does the washing up has the advantage over a man sitting in an armchair who thinks he can hear resentment in every swilling tea leaf. The member of a married couple who stays up late has the advantage over the one who goes to bed first. A father has the advantage over his children as long as he can make them think of their birth and not let them remind him of his own death: the sons are condemned to ruminate interminably about what happened "the night they were made in the image of those two people, *at it*."

Pinter must stylize more than any writer in England apart from Ivy Compton-Burnett, which is why Peter Hall is right to direct the play so antinaturalistically. Pinter's people are entirely creatures of maneuver, hence the peculiar freezing mood of their moments of randiness. The sexual instinct in Pinter isn't at all emotional or even physical; it is practically territorial. There is one woman in *The Homecoming*, his recurring character of a tarty bourgeoise wife who contemplates promiscuity as evenly as if she were counting the doilies; she looks on her body rather as a landlord would look on a corner site. As soon as she has apparently been exploited sexually she really has the advantage because she owns the property.

If the second half of the play seems a shade undernourished, I think this is the effect of Pinter's vision and not a fault of technique. His cold, indifferent eye is essential to the tone: without it the play could never be so funny, nor preserve itself from the crevasses of patronage and sentimentality that are on either side; but it obviously has its dangers with audiences who demand to be moved and involved. Given the prescribed limits of the play, I doubt if it could have been better achieved. The understanding of the way we use language is uniquely comic, provoking pity without expressing it, and the implicit assumption that a play is concerned only with what is disputable is a very honorable one.

JUNE 6, 1965
LONDON

The Cleared Deck

Alain Jessua's *Life Upside Down* is a first work written and directed by a young Frenchman who has worked as an assistant with Max Ophuls and Jacques Becker. It is a cool, funny account of a man in a state of mind that might variously be called madness, or Zen jesting, or simply a more open stage of a common kind of obscure self-sabotage.

The hero lives in growing silence with a chatty fashion-model girl who is engrossed in the possible prospect of mothercraft and spends most of her time cooking meals for them both to eat in bed. His way out of the havoc that she instinctively creates, which he unresentfully calls a brothel, isn't to quit but to marry her. In the same way, when he loses his job, his answer is not to look for work but to sit at a *café* table and later observe a tree.

He begins to be ambushed by objects. In the middle of his wife's eventually suicidal desperation to catch his attention, he is fascinated by the craggy detail of a loaf of bread on a piece of cloth. The more intimately he lives with her, the more she merges into an anonymity. In bed, while she thinks he is feeling sexy, his gaze is actually tracking slowly up her back like an astronomer's telescope trained on the moon. At breakfast she is crying for him to listen, and all he can hear is the explosion of his knife slicing through a boiled egg.

In the end he is in a state where he has driven both her and his mother away, emptied the room of nearly all the furniture, and reduced his life to delighted nonthought, sitting on the floor picking at a grape, having declared to himself that isolation is the only security. It is a belief that no society can allow, of course, and one that makes the doctors proclaim him undoubtedly mad:

which may or may not be right. The quizzical spirit of the film would be unbearable if it were assumed, but it is obviously genuine and as personal to the director as a sense of persecution was to Thurber.

SEPTEMBER 6, 1964

After Man

I think Stanley Kubrick's *2001: A Space Odyssey* is some sort of great film, and an unforgettable endeavor. Technically and imaginatively, what he put into it is staggering: five years of his life; his novel and screenplay, with Arthur C. Clarke; his production, his direction, his special effects; his humor and stamina and particular disquiet. The film is not only hideously funny—like *Dr. Strangelove*—about human speech and response at a point where they have begun to seem computerized, and where more and more people sound like recordings left on while the soul is out. It is also a uniquely poetic piece of sci-fi, made by a man who truly possesses the drives of both science and fiction.

Kubrick's tale of quest in the year 2001, which eventually takes us to the moon and Jupiter, begins on prehistoric Earth. Tapirs snuffle over the Valhalla landscape, and a leopard with broken-glass eyes guards the carcass of a zebra in the moonlight. Crowds of apes, scratching and ganging up, are disturbingly represented not by real animals, like the others, but by actors in costume. They are on the brink of evolving into men, and the overlap is horrible. Their stalking movements are already exactly ours: a down-and-out's, drunk, at the end of his tether and fighting mad. Brute fear has been refined into the infinitely more painful human capacity for dread. The creatures are so nearly human that they have religious impulses. A slab that they suddenly come upon sends them into panicked reverence as they touch it, and the film emits a colossal sacred din of chanting. The shock of faith boots them forward a few thousand years, and one of the apes, squatting in front of a bed of bones, picks up his first weapon. In slow motion, the hairy arm swings up into an empty frame and then down again, and the smashed bones bounce into the air. What makes him do it? Curiosity? What makes people destroy anything, or throw away the known, or set off in spaceships? To see what Nothing feels like, driven by some bedrock instinct that it is time for something else? The last bone thrown in the air is matched, in the next cut, to a spaceship at the same angle. It is now 2001. The race has survived thirty-three years more without extinction, though not with any growth of spirit. There are no Negroes in this vision of America's space program; conversation with Russian scientists is brittle with mannerly terror, and the Chinese can still be dealt with only by pretending they're not there. But technological man has advanced no end. A space way-station shaped like a Ferris wheel and housing a hotel called the Orbiter Hilton hangs off the pocked old cheek of Earth. The sound track, bless its sour heart, meanwhile thumps out "The Blue Danube," to confer a little of the courtliness of bygone years on space. The civilization that Kubrick sees coming has the brains of a nuclear physicist and the sensibility of an airline hostess smiling through an oxygen-mask demonstration.

Kubrick is a clever man. The grim joke is that life in 2001 is only faintly more gruesome in its details of sophisticated affluence than it is now. When we first meet William Sylvester as a space scientist, for instance, he is in transit to the moon, via the Orbiter Hilton, to investigate another of the mysterious slabs. The heroic man of intellect is given a nice meal on the way—a row of spacecraft foods to suck through straws out of little plastic cartons, each decorated with a picture of sweet corn or whatever to tell him that sweet corn is what he is sucking. He is really going through very much the same ersatz form of the experience of being well looked after as the foreigner who arrives at an airport now with a couple of babies, reads in five or six languages on luggage carts that he is welcome, and then finds that he has to manage his luggage and the babies without actual help from a porter. The scientist of 2001 is only more inured. He takes the inanities of space personnel on the chin. "Did you have a pleasant flight?" Smile, smile. Another smile, possibly prefilmed, from a girl on a television monitor handling voice-print identification at Immigration. The Orbiter Hilton is decorated in fresh plumbing-white, with magenta armchairs shaped like pelvic bones scattered through it. Artificial gravity is provided by centrifugal force; inside the rotating Ferris wheel people have weight. The architecture gives the white floor of the Orbiter Hilton's conversation area quite a gradient, but no one lets slip a sign of humor about the slant. The citizens of 2001 have forgotten how to joke and resist, just as they have forgotten how to chat, speculate, grow intimate, or interest one another. But otherwise everything is splendid. They lack the mind for acknowledging that they have managed to diminish outer space into the ultimate in humdrum, or for dealing with the fact that they are spent and insufficient, like the apes.

The film is hypnotically entertaining, and it is funny without once being gaggy, but it is also rather harrowing. It is as eloquent about what is missing from the people of 2001 as about what is there. The characters seem isolated almost beyond endurance. Even in the most absurd scenes, there is often a fugitive melancholy—as astronauts solemnly watch themselves on homey BBC interviews seen millions of miles from earth, for instance, or as they burn their fingers on their space meals, prepared with the utmost scientific care but a shade too hot to touch, or as they plod around a centrifuge to get some exercise, shadowboxing alone past white coffins where the rest of the crew hibernates in deep freeze. Separation from other people is total and unmentioned. Kubrick has no characters in the film who are sexually related, nor any close friends. Communication is stuffy and guarded, made at the level of men together on committees or of someone being interviewed. The space scientist telephones his daughter by television for her birthday, but he has nothing to say, and his wife is out; an astronaut on the nine-month mission to Jupiter gets a prerecorded television birthday message from his parents. That's the sum of intimacy. No enjoyment—only the mechanical celebration of the anniversaries of days when the race perpetuated itself. Again, another astronaut, played by Keir Dullea, takes a considerable risk to try to save a fellow spaceman, but you feel it hasn't anything to do with affection or with courage. He has simply been trained to save an expensive colleague by a society that has slaughtered instinct. Fortitude is a matter of programing, and companionship seems lost. There remains only longing, and this is buried under banality, for English has finally been booted to death. Even informally, people say "Will that suffice?" for "Will that do?" The computer on the Jupiter spaceship—a chatty, fussy genius called Hal, with nice manners and a rather querulous need for reassurance about being wanted—talks more like a human being than any human being does in the picture. Hal runs the craft, watches over the rotating quota of men in deep freeze, and plays chess. He gives a lot of thought to how he strikes others, and sometimes carries on about himself like a mother chattering on the telephone to keep a bored grown child hanging on. At low ebb and growing paranoid, he tells a hysterical lie about a faulty piece of equipment to recover the crew's respect, but a less emotional twin computer on Earth coolly picks him up on the judgment and degradingly defines it as a mistake. Hal, his mimic humanness perfected, detests the witnesses of his humiliation and restores his ego by vengeance. He manages to kill all the astronauts but Keir Dullea, including the hibernating crew members, who die in the most chillingly modern death scene imaginable: warning lights simply signal "Computer Malfunction," and sets of electrophysiological needles above the sleepers run amok on the graphs and then record the straight lines of extinction. The survivor of Hal's marauding self-justification, alone on the craft, has to battle his way into the computer's red-flashing brain, which is the size of your living room, to unscrew the high cerebral functions. Hal's sophisticated voice gradually slows and he loses his grip. All he can remember in the end is how to sing "Daisy"—which he was taught at the start of his training long ago—grinding down like an old phonograph. It is an upsetting image of human decay from command into senility. Kubrick makes it seem a lot worse than a berserk computer being controlled with a screw driver.

The startling metaphysics of the picture are symbolized by the slabs. It is curious that we should all still be so subconsciously trained in apparently distant imagery. Even to atheists, the slabs wouldn't look simply like girders. They immediately have to do with Mosaic tablets or druidical stones. Four million years ago, says the story, an extraterrestrial intelligence existed. The slabs are its manifest sentinels. The one we first saw on prehistoric earth is like the one discovered in 2001 on the moon. The lunar finding sends out an upper-harmonic shriek to Jupiter and puts the scientists on the trail of the forces of creation. The surviving astronaut goes on alone and Jupiter's influence pulls him into a world where time and space are relative in ways beyond Einstein. Physically almost pulped, seeing visions of the planet's surface that are like chloroform nightmares and that sometimes turn into close-ups of his own agonized eyeball and eardrum, he then suddenly lands, and he is in a tranquilly furnished reproduction Louis XVI room. The shot of it through the window of his space pod is one of the most heavily charged things in the whole picture, though its effect and its logic are hard to explain.

In the strange, fake room, which is movingly conventional, as if the most that the ill man's imagination can manage in conceiving a better world beyond the infinite is to recollect something he has once been taught to see as beautiful in a grand decorating magazine, time jumps and things disappear. The barely surviving astronaut sees an old grandee from the back, dining on the one decent meal in the film; and when the man turns around it is the astronaut himself in old age. The noise of the chair moving on the white marble in the silence is typical of the brilliantly selective sound track. The old man drops his wineglass, and then sees himself bald and dying on the bed, twenty or thirty years older still, with his hand up to another of the slabs, which has appeared in the room and stands more clearly than ever for the forces of change. Destruction and creation coexist in them. They are like Siva. The last shot of the man is totally transcendental, but in spite of resistance to mysticism one would find it stirring. It shows an X-raylike image of the dead man's skull, re-created as a baby, approaching Earth. His eyes are enormous. He looks like a mutant. Perhaps he is the first of the needed new species.

It might seem a risky notion to drive sci-fi into magic. But, as with *Strangelove*, Kubrick has gone too far and made it the poetically exact place to go. He and his collaborator have found a powerful idea to impel space conquerors whom puny times have robbed of much curiosity. The hunt for the remnant of a civilization that has been signaling the existence of its intelligence to the future for four million years, tirelessly stating the fact that it occurred, turns the shots of emptied, comic, ludicrously dehumanized men into something more poignant. There is a hidden parallel to the shot of the ape's arm swinging up into the empty frame with its first weapon, enthralled by the liberation of something new to do: the shot of the space scientist asleep in a craft with the "Weightless Conditions" sign turned on, his body fixed down by his safety belt while one arm floats free in the air.

APRIL 13, 1968

Stanley Kubrick's *Dr. Strangelove: or How I Learned to Stop Worrying and Love the Bomb*. Witty, icy title. The film is about the most devastating piece of art about the bomb I can remember; even more disturbing than *Hiroshima, Mon Amour*, because comic.

Most antibomb films and plays are awful. They always seem to be overrun by a peculiar kind of wet naïveté, which is a worse disability than usual when you're letting off about a subject as sophisticated as nuclear politics. Antibomb plays generally happen in a folksy vacuum, with abrupt dialogue going on about the large good simplicities of life between people who stand up all the time. Antibomb films are on the same lines, though they're more arty than folksy. They seem to be full of uncharacterized figures who stand for the New Generation or the Emergent Nations, and the children and Africans charged with this thankless job never, never say anything which is supposed to make them more symbolic.

This is only to sketch in the kind of work that *Dr. Strangelove* emphatically isn't. One of its virtues is that it is very, very sophisticated. Another is that it is absolutely specific, as specific as the wound of a stiletto, and so close to the facts that it makes you feel ill. It happens, not in a vacuum, but accurately in America: in a nuclear bomber, in an echoing model of the War Room at the Pentagon, and at a nuclear base camp where the hoardings say "Peace Is Our Profession" and "Keep Off the Grass." Whereas most left-wing art is concerned to emphasize that nothing is any particular nation's fault, so much so that it seems practically an act of Fascist racialism to give any of the characters a recognizable accent, all the people in this film are wickedly localized. The observation of different kinds of American male speech would satisfy Professor Higgins, and the photography seems to be almost deliberately like a reportage on wrap-it-up TV. *Strangelove* must be the most anti-American comedy ever made, and only an American would have had the experience and guts to do it.

The premise of the plot is very simple. It is the one that the professionals themselves are worried about: the danger that a single psychotic in the right place could start a nuclear war. General Ripper, played by Sterling Hayden, is a broody nutcase who has fluoridation of water on his brain. He sees fluoridation as one of your real hard-core Commie plots to sap the American people's body fluids. After years of fuming about the injustice of it he puts into operation Plan R, originally devised to appease a senator who complained that the American deterrent lacked credibility.

In the interests of greater credibility—i.e., greater risk of the deterrent going off—Plan R allows an underling to press the button, immediately seals him from contact with anyone who could stop him, protects him with a force of soldiers who proceed to defend him to the death against the intervention of the President, and prevents any of the planes from being recalled because only the ecstatic nutcase knows the code. The machine is in motion; no one can stop it, and the moment the first bomb falls annihilation of animal life on the planet will follow because no one, not even the Soviet Premier, can stop the Russian Doomsday machine from going off in response.

The key of the brilliant comic tone of the film is in the title. What makes the picture so funny, terrifying and horribly believable is that everyone in the film really *has* learned to stop worrying, as smokers do about lung cancer after living with the statistics for a bit. Disaster is half an hour away but nobody goes berserk with fear. The President—Peter Sellers, very good as a calm Adlai Stevenson figure—talks to the Soviet Premier on the telephone in the voice of an analyst trying to calm down a hysterical patient. George C. Scott as a midriff-slapping general, first discovered in Bermuda shorts and Hawaiian shirt in a bedroom with his secretary, is so proud of his boys' initiative when he gets to the War Room that he can't bear to call them back.

And meanwhile the general who started the holocaust sits in the base camp quietly chatting with Peter Sellers as an RAF officer, while the place is being besieged by his own countrymen. The general believes in an afterlife, which must be a help. What he still seems most bothered about is this fluoridation, a deadly danger that he says he discovered during the act of love. "I don't *avoid* women," he says, suddenly worried about his virility-image, which is a funny thing to want to preserve if you're about to go up in smoke, "but I do deny them my essence."

The film has a sort of running theme about this kind of priapic hauteur. At the end, with Peter Sellers in a third incarnation as a naturalized German nuclear scientist—the only place where the film's foot slips—everyone in the War Room is entranced by the scientist's suggestion that they will have to preserve the race by going down a mine shaft with ten fertile women to every man. No one quite believes in his own death. The rasping ram played by George Scott, swooping proudly about pretending to be an airplane while the President asks him questions, really does think he'll be back in bed with his secretary any minute. The Biggin Hill figure played by Peter Sellers runs up against a hardcore hetero colonel who won't let Sellers telephone the President because he thinks he's struck a mutiny of preverts [*sic*]; but what Sellers threatens him with is a Court of Inquiry, not extinction. The character of Dr. Strangelove gets more forced in the last ten minutes, and it sometimes seems a gimmick to have Peter Sellers play three parts: why? It isn't as though the three men were aspects of the same characteristics in people, which would have been an inner reason for doing it. Perhaps it was the only way of getting finance for the film, which in a timid and conventional industry is a different kind of inner reason.

The thing that is exhilarating about *Strangelove* as a piece of film-making, apart from the masterly way it is organized and the acting of all the American parts, is the wit of the screenplay. Kubrick did it himself, with Terry Southern and Peter George, and every sharp-eared line of it is a pleasure. They have caught, for instance, the plump, loping euphemisms used by nuclear strategists, and the way bureaucratic Americans don't recognize European sarcasm, and the way some busy men will use a first name in every other sentence. It was a funny idea to catch on to this mannerism in a conversation on the hot line between the President and the Soviet Premier when the world is blowing up:

> Now then, Dmitri, you know how we've always talked about the possibility of something going wrong with the Bomb. The BOMB, Dmitri. The Hydrogen Bomb. Well, he went and did a silly thing. . . . Well, I'll tell you what he did. . . . Well, how do you think I feel about it? All right then, who should we call? Where is that, Dmitri? . . . Soviet Air Command in Omsk. Listen, Dmitri, do you happen to have the number on you?

Like N. F. Simpson in the theater, Kubrick is working one of the best veins in comedy: the simple observation that our planet is inhabited by a race of eccentrics who, unlike all other animals, take practically no notice of anything that is going on outside their own heads and have absolutely no sense of priorities. *Strangelove* is a real comic achievement. It is savage, undeniable, and uniquely defiant.

FEBRUARY 2, 1964

In Praise of Cowardice

The Bleecker Street Cinema is showing a surreally funny hour of film called *No More Excuses*, which is goonish, rude, and altogether relieving. It was directed by Robert Downey and Robert Soukis, written by Downey, and edited by Soukis. In the credits Mr. Downey refers to himself in parenthesis as "a prince," for his own good reasons. He also plays a Civil War soldier. In what seems to be 1968, roughly, the soldier is still alive, thanks to refraining from courage on the battlefield, or maybe to the film's own shambling absent-mindedness, which extends a warm welcome to anachronisms as to all other deviations. Further characters include President Garfield ("1881–1881") and his nervous assassin, who has mad hidden ambitions to be a public servant; a number of real-life people who are interviewed about sex in the current crop of singles bars on the East Side; an ape that bounces up and down with an air of scholarship on a very big naked woman to the accompaniment of the Hallelujah Chorus; and a proselytizer who intermittently holds the screen to speak to us all about clothing our nude animals. The editing is very fast, with a slapping rhythm to it like the timing of a skilled sandwich-maker laminating bread and innards and mayonnaise in a drugstore at lunchtime. You have to understand that there is no narrative whatever, and certainly nothing like dramatic conflict, apart from the deadly combat of the three component subjects as they struggle to keep their ends up: (1) the newsreel of the assassination of President Garfield, with the killer glumly bungling it every time; (2) the questioning of real-life people in 1968 about stark questions of lust and smut; (3) lust and smut themselves, which keep getting elbowed out of the film by the preachings of the inflamed animal-nudity protester. He envisions a mass march down Fifth Avenue to an anthem called "Wings of Decency," and sometimes swings into dire warnings about the possibility of fifty thousand naked combat dogs' infiltrating Manhattan during some long, hot summer because we have never allowed them to share our sense of propriety and shoved them into clothes.

One could say, if pressed, that the film was in praise of cowardice, pleasure, fatness, ineptitude, and apes, and against drive, dying for one's country, and boxer shorts for dogs. Apart from the Civil War soldier, who survives a light graze and a noisy battle by feigning dead until the enemy has safely disappeared, the most affectionately seen character is probably the unemployable assassin. But the film even has a weakness for the animal-decency prophet, with his wild dreams of giving a summons to a policeman for riding a nude horse, and his one-man crusade against the army of lewd pets around him. He approaches his colossal task armed only with eloquence and a handkerchief, which he flourishes suddenly at the camera and refers to as "this little garment": it has a hole in the middle, and his point is that such a thing can easily be devised by anyone as any emergency measure to throw over a dog's tail until proper clothes can be fitted. When his ranting allows the interview-subjects to get a word in edgewise, the thing that strikes you—as with *Candid Camera*—is people's astonishing patience and goodness of heart toward intruders asking favors of them. Who would guess that so many citizens of ratty Manhattan would be indulgent to larky film-makers catechizing them about sexual license. An older man—a Negro—says carefully about young lubricity, "It's a lot better than smoking LSD." A very old lady indeed chuckles and brings up Adam and Eve.

Downey and Soukis have a long way to go to throw off the clutches of a hard-driven time when the random and the cool are modish, but for the moment they have produced a benign piece of cheek. There are a few pushed minutes, but not many. Most of the film works with easy and genial idiocy. And when the shambles is over, the makers possibly turn out to have been rather serious about a world that finds a whole body naked in bed more indecent than a smashed one in a military uniform.

MAY 25, 1968

Under Skin

Richard Lester's *Petulia* is about pain, and about two ironic life-styles devised by the two central characters to survive an age in which they are aware of so much injury around them that the only possible course is to deny its existence. The film sees it: smashed bones, accidents, bust marriages, loss, perfidy, slaughter by silence. So do the two characters—a girl (Julie Christie), married for six months to a man whom she casually ditches, and a newly separated doctor (George C. Scott), who has a grueling affair with her, with the surface manner all kidding and resilience. They receive pain, they deal it out, they observe it concealed in others and lying in wait for themselves, and there is too much of it to manage. So they cultivate systems. Flippancy, sarcasm, hipness, kookiness, angry autonomy—anything not to admit that pain is actually painful, just as the hospital staff in the film hideously treats the ill as if there were nothing wrong with them. The behavior of these two people is a trick to try to take the humanness out of themselves. It has the effect of the frame of sterile cloths lapped around an operating incision point, which allows a surgeon to forget that surgery hurts: this Mondrian square of skin obviously has nothing much in common with the body he saw in his own bathroom mirror the same morning. The cloths stylize the act of cutting so that it hardly seems related to wounding.

Lester's two characters stylize what happens to them by the

same necessity, in case it should turn out to be a gash in their own flesh. The girl redesigns reality by quirkiness and by living without a sense of consequence. She breaks up the structure constantly, so that it is smashed before she has had time to grow fond of it or to see someone else's boot destroy it. The man protects himself by a coldness that is unconvincing but unremitting. When they first go away to make love, in a deathly motel, they talk to one another as if they were telephoning room service. Their attitudes are flat and modern as hell: big deal, what's the difference, hang on to your cool. The story is laid in San Francisco, and aptly. The doctor, within a day, makes love to a beautiful body, works on a wrecked one, and eats a sandwich with a colleague in a topless restaurant where a naked girl on a swing ticks to and fro like a clock part. After a grinding breakup and absence, the lovers exchange casual hails from passing cable cars. Over. *Nada*. No, more unsaid to come.

Dick Lester has always been a visibly brilliant director. I've never thought before that he was a particularly passionate one —not even after *How I Won the War*, where he allowed nothing to accrue around character. *Petulia* is something else. He has suddenly made huge strides in his direction of actors, and the taciturnity of the film comes to seem a moving expression of his own view of people's capacity for anguish. The tension and perplexity of the technique grow more and more harrowingly true to the matter of the film. The first few scenes can take you in; they don't quite prepare you for the concern that Lester is going to express. There is a shot, for instance, of a portly woman in a neck brace going upstairs by lift to a party, dressed in a red satin evening coat, with people around her who look fresh from the taxidermist. I thought he was being prankish about the numb follies of the privileged, and nothing much more than that. As the film goes on, though, it turns out to be agonizingly observant of the devices by which a faithless generation hopes to induce a little insensitivity in skin otherwise too raw for pride or survival. The games of the two main characters playing waggish moderns aren't very deceiving. They behave like sci-fi robots, but they still bleed. There is a subtext of powerful feeling under every scene; something quite else is always going on beneath the self-protectiveness and backchat, something aching, as it does in Charlotta's lines while she is doing her magic turns in *The Cherry Orchard*.

Petulia is a fine, hard-minded film. It was written by Lawrence B. Marcus (from a novel by John Haase), photographed by Nicholas Roeg, and cut by Antony Gibbs. The look and the editing of the picture are part of its character. It has a peculiar rectitude in the reporting of the sensibility of here and now which is grieving and distinct.

JUNE 15, 1968

Czech Wave

The new Czech cinema is amazing and unforgettable; the knife is often on the bone. A group of serious and gifted people are suddenly expressing themselves through film as naturally as, say, the writers of the Spanish Civil War did through poetry. The phenomenon is moving and significant. It possesses as much energy as the Polish cinema's after Gomulka's 1956, and perhaps it will be fortunate enough to have more staying power. In some of the films there is a technical vivacity equal to the French New Wave's, though their content strikes me as a great deal more organic to the state of their country. The intimacy of purpose among the members of the group seems as powerful as Bloomsbury's was, but there is nothing cliquish about it. And there is an air of having scarcely begun.

At their best, the pictures use the cinema at full stretch, conveying the simultaneous experiences of private and outward life as film uniquely can. This isn't the familiar Western use of movies to manufacture other people's fantasies, or the equally familiar

Iron Curtain use of them to beat audiences over the head with object lessons, but an attempt to shoot into the film-maker's own dark places of poetry and violence and nostalgia for play. Czech directors and screenwriters are trying to find expression for the rock-bottom instincts that are often censored by the self long before a bureaucrat gets near them.

I was first in Prague in 1960, and at that time the movement hadn't even started to gather. Cinema people would speak affectionately of their best-known director, Jiři Weiss, and the famous puppet films of Trnka, and then turn to the satiric theater and the acts in pocket night clubs, as though forms for minority audiences were the only ones that offered any hope of carrying a man's real voice. The assumption then about film-making in Czechoslovakia was as deadened in its way as our own commercial industry's at its most hapless. There was the same despair of speaking eloquently to many people at once, and generalizations of ideology seemed as inescapable an enemy as the generalizations of profit guesswork to the particularity of good cinema. The sudden flowering is a triumph of superior nerve, humor, seriousness, cheek. A lot of good work is cheek.

The flavor of the new films is pungent and distinct. Their point of departure is not the one we are saddled with, which assumes that audiences won't understand the oblique, that they hanker after fantasy fulfillments about face-pulping and after comedies about tax-deductible adultery, and that they need to be humored with lies about their material status as if they were suffering from some shopper's form of *folie de grandeur*. The Czech films at the Museum of Modern Art seem to start from the assumption that everyone in the audience notices everything, that everyone is sick to death of public utterance that nibbles round the edges of things as they are, and that there is not a man left in the country who could honestly be deceived. It is a powerful context for film-making. I don't want to oversell all the pictures in the festival at the expense of the handful that are first-rate works of the imagination. Some of them are technically rather sedate. In one or two of them, there is a tang of the patronizing humor about eccentric "little men" which disfigured the later Ealing comedies. But all Slavs seem to possess some of Chekhov's transfiguring gift of seeing idiosyncrasy without finding it bizarre. The Czechs' ability not to diminish strangeness into quaintness is part of their natural engagement, like their absolute incapacity to shelter in banter. There are a lot of very funny things in these films, but they aren't wisecracks, and no one jokes in an adopted voice. Gags in Prague are obviously a weapon against propagandist pathos. The good boys of Stalinist art were coated with a pathos like blubber, and jokes work faster than a reinterpretation of history to scrape off the lard.

In Jiři Menzel's *A Difficult Love* (mistaken title) and in Hynek Bocan's *Nobody Laughs Last*, the bureaucrats seem to be out of Gogol. There are foppish informers, minor officials with bankrolls of fat around the neck, Philistines operating as social moralists, and two ludicrous trials conducted by small-fry potentates in an ecstasy of regulations. *A Difficult Love*, one of the near-Ealing comedies, is about a shy, whey-faced boy during the war who takes a job at a railway station as a likely opportunity for shirking, coming as he does from a long line of shirkers. His forebears include a hypnotist grandfather who once sufficiently roused himself to try to stop the oncoming German tanks by glaring at them in his professional capacity. He was not successful. His grandson, veins pulsing with the blood of ancestral duds, battles with sexual defeats on many sides while Nazi ammunition trains pass through the station almost unnoticed. The rest of the railway staff seems half-seas over with lechery. Their irritability about one another's pleasures is very funny, since they feel the utmost placidity about the flamboyance of their own. One of the underling officials is hauled to trial for stamping German State Railway signs on his girl friend's bum. The human parcel blows gently on the indelible ink to make the stamps print clearly, lying with her head on what seems to be a railway-signal chart.

Hynek Bocan describes *Nobody Laughs Last* as "a comedy with a sad subtext." The hero is a clever, self-amused young art critic whose sense of humor outstrips by miles the situations of politesse and line-toeing into which he is always being put. An abysmal essayist nags him for an opinion of a manuscript and starts whining that his career depends on the famous man's endorsement. The critic, who not only hasn't read the manuscript but has also lost it, answers him with the sort of lying fob-off that is used all over the world—"Though your essay is very interesting . . ." He lives to be clobbered with that adjective. Before judgment strikes, he retreats into larking with his girl friend, a beauty who sometimes sleeps with homemade wolf fangs stuck in her mouth, rather as more dedicated women wear eye masks. Occasionally she throws a crumb or two to the rubbernecks in the opposite building by doing a one-woman shadow drama of a seduction scene on the window blind. The dogged reference-hunter turns up at her flat and takes her for a wife, which is a cruel cut for such a swinger. The man's distressing capacity to irritate is so insistent that even his poor plastic raincoat begins to look craven and due for extinction. Bocan's particular accomplishment is to have made the hero's send-up humor seem seriously based, as the defense of a clever man against mediocrity and fawning. But then the film begins to fill in the other face of his languorous kidding, in scenes with less adroit people at his mercy and in pain. His mood is hideously out of joint in a meeting with his victim's wife, and the director's eye for her misery expands the spirit of the picture.

Prague generated its own humor of the absurd long before Ionesco was born. Painstaking local apologists accommodate it now politically by explaining it as a protest against the unmanageable logic of the bomb, or alternatively as an indictment of itself, though I'm not sure how one indicts the depravity of the absurd by being depravingly absurd. Its reason for existence may have more to do with its funniness. Though Vera Chytilova's *The Daisies* is surprisingly analyzed by herself as "a necrologue about a negative way of life," perhaps to repel hostile boarders, it struck me as a delicately balmy and freewheeling piece of slapstick, dedicated to recording the passing impulses of two ravishing teenagers with the premoral interests of infants. The heroines lead lives of hedonism and chat in a world bounded by hair curlers, men, bikini underclothes, and looming, enthralling food. They have a try at an existential conversation in the bathroom over a piece of bread, and one of them lusts unendurably for marmalade while she is being seduced. In a restaurant scene, with one girl playing a fifth wheel and the other enthusiastically enacting grown-up behavior with an understandably muted man, the redundant girl fills up a silence by remarking intelligently on the heaviness of the spoons. At the end of the film, bearing on their eyelids a good kilo each of mascara, they invade a banquet hall on an eating binge that is weirdly joyful and funny. They pummel steak tartare barehanded, and thwack cream cakes like mud pies. Lofty food in aspic goes down their gullets or onto the floor by the ton. Then they are sorry. The recantation scene is shot in remorseful black and white after the full-color blowout, and the sound track crackles with self-addressed mutters about doing better. The havoc artists are dressed now in penitential newspaper and string, trotting about quite cheerily and piling back wrecked food onto silver dishes as if it hadn't been turned into pig swill. A fable about depravity? Surely not. The first female Mack Sennett. A dainty hymn to gorging, photographed with energy and taste by the director's husband, Jaroslav Kucera, and played by dolly girls with the voice boxes of goats and the bodies of succubi.

JULY 1, 1967

A Report on the Party

Jan Němec's *A Report on the Party and the Guests* was made in Czechslovakia, from a screenplay by Němec and Ester Krumbachová, and lucky us to see it; the Czechs had to wait nearly two years, until the Dubček regime this spring lifted the ban on it that has probably now dropped again. The film is a painfully sophisticated comic fable about the happy man's ready instinct for relinguishing the good in favor of the constrained before he realizes what he is doing. It begins, under the titles, with the sound of running water in the country. A brook somewhere. People are at ease, having a picnic. They eat and joke. Life is sweet. There is a rat-squeak of danger when a girl says gaily that she could never bear to be alone. Then strangers are about in the forest: perfectly benign, it seems, but they begin to hustle the picnickers by the arm as they make friends, and edge them into a dell where they play enigmatic games that have a kindergarten character with a tinge of malignity. The picnickers queue up in front of a table, trying to question nothing. They do what they can to sustain the old mood: it is a day off, after all, and nothing has much altered, apart from the influx of cheerful enough strangers behaving on the eerily playful assumption that they are in command. Here and there, the picnickers show a chink of worry ("I thought they were guests." "So did I"). Still, the sun shines. "We'll line up here." "Perhaps alphabetically, if that's what they want." "Men on one side, women on the other." A man facing the jovial playmate behind the table finds himself offering his papers. Suddenly there is a mugging, pleasantly done. A girl says, "But that wasn't a nice welcome, beating a man up." Her tactless moment passes, and a white-costumed dictator-host comes tripping along, to lead everyone to a formal banquet in the sun beside a lake. There are candelabras, waiters, the appearance of good will; also henchmen, yes-men, and the host smiling and keeping his hands clean. The original picnickers are mixed indistinguishably with the chubby invaders. They are dragooned into enjoyment—people who might be schoolteachers or foremen, and an ordinarily obedient wife who is too keen on the party (the tacit pun seems bitterly meant) to follow her husband when he leaves to go for a walk. Without a word, the group scents an escape. Places are suddenly shuffled. No one feels himself to be sitting in the right seat. The dictator-host figure asks a clever-looking man to make a speech: "People know your name. Your word has weight." A funster who is adept at voicing the line of the moment cries merrily, "One for all, all for one!" Though no one quite says so, the husband's empty chair is troubling now in a different way, for unanimity has set in, and if one guest has left, all should go, surely? "Maybe he likes to be alone," says someone polite, visibly trying to imagine such a thing and failing in the sunny herd. The guests eat daintily, pretending that the travesty banquet in the company of unknown fellow eaters who may be informers or murderers is a lucky improvement on their picnic. At the end of the picture, the dogs are after the man who left the table; there is a sound of barking under the final frames, and the candles in the daylight are snuffed out. Oh, Prague.

SEPTEMBER 21, 1968

Dream of an Outrun Man

After the denunciation of Stalin by Khrushchev, a Czech film-maker named Jaromil Jires lost all his hair in a few weeks. Ivan Passer remembers it happening. Passer is a fine director and screenplay writer, maker of the beautiful *Intimate Lighting*, a liberal who left Czechoslovakia in 1968 to try to work in America. Jires is still in Prague. They see things differently, but Passer would understand that. "He is a very upright man. We were just on the other side," Passer said once when we were talking about Jires. "He is a romantical man, you see, the kind of romantical which can combine with that orthodoxy." And now the Grove Press International Film Festival shows us Jires' *The Joke*, a wry movie that goes to and fro between the days of Stalinism and Dubček's 1968 in the life of a character piteously trapped in that romanticism of the orthodox which permits, as time goes on, only the steel bite of disappointment on the leg of a man trying to move. Jires' complicated and touching hero, called Ludvik Jahn (Josef Somr), is prey to a vicious political melancholy that will never let go. It is nothing like, say, the melancholy of people in Chekhov, which you always feel can turn in a second into some card trick of Charlotta's or some passionate absorption in the way to pickle cucumbers. That melancholy is redeemable because Chekhov never sees it as damning, only as one passing signal of man's limits. But *The Joke* tells us in every scene that Jires himself once lent his heart to the idea that we are systematically perfectible, and his hero's compulsive memory records an unshakable and grieved obsession with the moment of discovering that we aren't. In the scenes twenty years before the Dubček spring, the young Ludvik is still a believer. He may be temperamentally remote from all the folk-dancing and programed merriment, but this doesn't stop him from being a party intellectual to the core. He is simply more sardonic and prankish than, say, his earnest girl friend, who says no to going to the country with him in favor of two weeks of party training. She sends her own kind's version of the conventional holiday postcard, full of enthusiasm about Stalin and the spirit of optimism. Ludvik stoutly writes her a card back: "Optimism is the opium of the people. A healthy spirit smells of stupidity. Long live Trotksy." The girl denounces him and delivers the card to a council of his fellows at university. There is a wonderfully detailed scene when Ludvik is first simply talking to three of these young men but already seems to know the full horror ahead—talking to these old, familiar friends in this old familiar room and laying out his socks to dry on the radiator while everything is about to change. The postcard is then read aloud in formal session, and he is unanimously condemned, even by his girl friend. She looks round at him with her dangerous chubby face, naïve, full of peasant energies, and strict. There is a cut-in flash of her with him beside a river, with cheerful folk music playing on the sound track, telling him sweetly that the party has a right to know everything. He is sentenced to six years' terror—an Army camp for "traitors," prison, the mines. His head is shaved, in shots that are even more charged and saddening when you remember Jires' reason for losing his own hair. Sentenced for what? For having a longer sense of history than a totalitarian state can ever put up with? For having a kidding sort of seriousness that is beyond the grasp of the tank-shaped dolts in power? From then on, everything that happens seems upside down to him. He sees a really orthodox prisoner being as misunderstood as he was, but for the opposite reasons: a man so far gone in conformity that he once unblinkingly boasts to the hero that he denounced his father for the sake of the party is now killed by the prison guards because he insists, deathly ill in the middle of a ludricrous relay race that the other prisoners rebelliously bungle, that he isn't anything so politically incorrect as tired. The man is already nearly dead of consumption. A puzzled, tight-faced man in steel-rimmed spectacles. He dies in bafflement.

In the course of the densely intercut film, Ludvik sees betrayal and naïveté everywhere. The long arm of blight stretches out from 1948 to touch the good Prague spring of 1968. You can see it in the way he looks at the exhilarated young, whose sense of present bounty he envies but can't hope to share. You can see it in his face as he listens to old, treacherous friends making easy amends, papering the cracks, pretending that the past never happened, and in his furious terror of women's instinct for idle melodrama, which is an instinct that once again greatly injures him by the end of the film. There is a taste of hell on his tongue, and he can't get rid of it. Even in 1968, it seems to him that the times are not so clearly all right as all that; at one minute he sees something new and wonderful, and then at the next he recognizes the old face of perfidious sunniness. His sense of ambiguity is very honestly recorded. It seems to be Jires' own. The film expresses a character that is honorable, careful not to vilify, and subtle about blame. It must be a difficult personality to have now. Jires has done something unusual and to the point in giving an account of a modern man who has been doomed to pessimism by events but who would give anything to flick the switch in his head. To Ludvik, his own biliousness makes him puny, although an audience will see him differently. A young piece of Trotsky's called "On Optimism and Pessimism, on the Twentieth Century, and on Many Other Things," written early in 1901, sometimes has the tone of Jires' hero as Ludvik tracks over and over the past and wonders whether the present can hold: "If I were one of the bodies of the universe," wrote Trotsky, then still Bronstein, "I would look with detachment on this miserable ball of dust and dirt. . . . I would shine upon the good and the evil alike. . . . But I am a *man*." Somewhere in the time span of the film there must have been a moment when the hero signaled for help, in sight of people, and no one came.

APRIL 25, 1970

PHYSICISTS

Langdon

Keaton, Chaplin, Lloyd, Langdon; and the unsung of these is Langdon. A lot of his silent films are beautifully funny.

If Harold Lloyd looks like a schoolboy who is hitting the awkward age and who is also a bit of a swot, Harry Langdon looks like a small girl with high hopes of one day being eight. The exquisite Bessie Love face is hung with panniers of puppy fat. The make-up, which weirdly manages not to seem androgynous, gives him the likeness of a child who has been mooning for hours in front of a looking glass with its mother's lipstick and mascara. The mouth looks babyish and jammy, and the eye-black has been put on in a state of trance; the whole face has then been dreamily smothered in talcum powder. When Langdon gazes into the distance in a film—when he is playing a soldier looking for his regiment in country too hard for him—his lineless, unpanicked face is the mask not of a mind hard at work, like Keaton's, but of a mind gently lolling at anchor, like a punt. He seems to be contemplating not a problem but his own reflection, with an interest too infant to be called vanity. Any intrusions of thought would be perilous, like noises that could make a sleepwalker break an ankle. The face exudes great sweetness and placidity. When cunning takes over, it is the response of someone before morality. He is very much an only child, and it has made him a duffer at games. As a 1914–1918 private in *The Strong Man*—the only private in the whole Army who might easily fail someday to absorb the fact that the war is over—he takes abstracted aim at a tin can and then at a German officer's helmet; using Army biscuits slung from a catapult. Only a girl would find such a rotten form of bullet, and only a girl would be so thrilled and surprised to get a hit: a girl with aspirations not to be a butterfingers, but doomed in the hope, and solitary. Langdon automatically goes his own way, without troubling himself to get in touch with the rest of the world. The position seems to be shared by all the great cinema comedians; the movies' double acts, the fables about alliance, derive from the stage, and never seem to be as glorious on screen as they can be in music hall.

When Langdon is in mufti—when he isn't being a soldier, or isn't dressed up in a morning coat to marry some scheming, avaricious bride—he generally wears a hat with the brim turned up all the way round, an outgrown jacket of which only the top buttons will fasten, baggy trousers, and large, amoebic boots. He stands with his feet in the first position of ballet, toes out, again like a girl without much of a clue. There can never have been such a spry comedian who gave such an impression of unathleticism. He looks as if he couldn't run for toffee. The best of his films—including some that he directed himself—reflect his schoolgirl torpor and move along with a beautiful dumbbell liquidity. He has a child's blitheness in egoism, a child's greed and hope and other-world criminality, and if the characterization ever slips into a moment of adult, this-world proneness to wounds, the film falters. Keaton is entirely grown up, stoic, decisive, ancient; Langdon seems most himself when he is unformed and seraphically naïve. He is a virtuoso of infant twitches that signal some tiny, fleeting worry, and a master of the beguilingly fatuous motions of beings who are still at the stage of experimenting to find their muscles. He can be especially splendid when he is working at a slant, trudging around the precipitous floor of a shack in a cyclone as if he had only just learned to walk.

The girls in his films are filthy grownups, treacherous and not very pretty. There is a terrible harridan in *The Strong Man* who cons him into thinking that she was the flower-faced girl who was his pen pal at the front; back home in America, she slips a stolen wad of bills into his pocket to offload detection by a dick behind her, and then faints massively outside her choice of mansion. Langdon is told severely by a servant that one can't leave one's women lying around like that. He lugs her inside as if she were a very large roll of carpet, keeling under her weight and avoiding several nasty blows from her diamanté jewelry. Her neck looks like a boxer's. Langdon staggers, sees the immense curving staircase that she wants to be carried up, and staggers some more. Starting the long haul, he gets his foot stuck in a flowerpot. There is a joyful moment when the overdressed burden, who is still pretending to be in a swoon, has to be propped on the marble banisters for an instant and then slides all the way down on her stomach. Langdon anxiously begins over again, sitting down on the stairs and carting the woman up step by step on his lap. He has indoctrinated himself so sternly into making the taxed movement that he plugs on with it, still backward, up a stepladder at the head of the stairs, right to the top of the ladder, and then beyond and over. It is a marvelous passage of mime. Maybe inflexibility, automatism, abstractedness and unsociability are great staples of funniness; Langdon's films sometimes have them all.

Unlike Chaplin and Harold Lloyd, he doesn't wheedle. We might as well not be there. He is subject to attacks of entirely private petulance, and doesn't give a damn that they're dopey. He will kick a cannon, or throw things irritably, and with a girl's aim, at a cyclone. In one celebrated set piece in, again, *The Strong Man*, he has a cold and attends devotedly to curing himself with stinking remedies in a crowded vehicle. The other passengers object, especially when he rubs his chest with Limburger cheese instead of liniment. A fusspot on his left is incensed. Langdon, hampered by feeling lousy, gives him an effete punch and also manages to spatter cough syrup over his dandyish enemy. His revenges are always serene and his movements oddly meditative. As with the business of lugging the hefty woman thief upstairs, his physical gags often come out of the old vaudeville-comedy discipline of repeating a movement mechanically after the need for it has gone. In *Tramp, Tramp, Tramp,* he somehow gets himself into and out of a prisoners' work camp in the middle of a cross-America walking race; he has grown entirely accustomed to walking with a ball and chain when he rejoins the race, and when a train happens (never mind how) to run over the chain and cut it loose he picks up the ball gamely and carries it as if it were a given of life. Sometimes he will stoop to pull up the iron links around his legs because they have drooped like sock garters. You can see that the things have given him pins and needles. He rubs the circulation back. Comedy is to swallow a camel and strain at a gnat.

Comedy is also to be tenacious in pursuit of hermetically peculiar tasks. In *Long Pants,* Langdon tries desperately to train a ventriloquist's dummy to run, doing demonstration sprints again and again, and coming back each time to see if the lesson has taken. He is fine with props, and a great punster with objects. Planning radiantly to murder his prospective bride in a wood, he drops his pistol into the undergrowth and retrieves in its stead a pistol-shaped branch, which he carries on with for a while. The historic team of the Goons used to do this sort of thing in their great days at the BBC. Spike Milligan would suddenly pick up a passing banana in the recording studio and plant it in his ear as a telephone receiver for an improvised call to Peter Sellers, blandly ignoring the fact that they were doing radio, not television.

Harry Langdon was born in 1884—child of two Salvation Army officers, which was a start. He worked as a cartoonist, a prop boy, a barber, and a performer in a patent-medicine show, and then in vaudeville for twenty years before he went to Mack Sennett. It was Frank Capra, a Sennett gag writer at the time, who invented *Tramp, Tramp, Tramp* for him. Capra apparently understood Langdon's comic personality perfectly, and begged to be allowed to work with him. (Later on, it was Capra who directed the two films that are probably Langdon's best—*The Strong Man* and *Long Pants.*) In *Tramp, Tramp, Tramp,* Capra correctly shows him coming out on top, as infants do, and winning the cross-continental marathon in spite of the ball and chain and in spite of infatuation with a girl played by Joan Crawford. The spiritual load for Langdon of loving Joan Crawford is inspired.

In Langdon's most characteristic films, the girls tend to be armor-plated. While he slips them love notes, they are likely to be immersed in some manly correspondence with other criminals about loot and dope. His attitude toward them is distant and spiked with decorum. He may sleep with a framed poster of the beloved's face in his bed, but this is as far as he will go. The strapping lady thief in *The Strong Man* tries to seduce him; though he is perfectly polite, the occasion is beyond his experience, and all he knows is that it tickles. There are some Langdon pictures in which the misogyny becomes delicately surreal. In *Three's a Crowd*, which he directed, he has a nightmare about having to fight in a brightly lit boxing ring, with his girl rooting against him, eyes hard as quartz; in the end, loopy with bloodlust, she bites her straw hat to pieces. Girls are never much help to Langdon. His best friend is providence—some fall of a stone in the nick of time, some Old Testament collapse of a saloon filled with stronger enemies. There is one cast list in which the characters include "His Bride," "His Downfall," "His Finish"; all three, predictably, are girls. Nonetheless, he is chivalrous. There are standards to be kept up. Sometimes he will explain these standards in a subtitle. They have a charming impatience and oddness: "Can't you see, Pa, when your sweetheart's in distress you can't go around marrying other women?" His love letters have the same straightforward idiosyncrasy: "I love you, I love you, I love you, I love you, and hope you are the same. Harry."

The America of his films is grounded in the 1920s. It is a world of marathons and patent medicines and bootlegging, of religion that has a thunderous edge to it, of wedding rings in hock, of keeping one's end up. There is an out-of-work strong man who wears a brocade waistcoat for bravado; he boasts, to maintain his spirits, "I lift the heaviest weights in the world, and when I shoot myself from a cannon to a trapeze it's a sensation." Sometimes Langdon's films movingly catch the desperate, squalid courage of the epoch. His father in *Tramp, Tramp, Tramp* is a small-time cobbler on his way out because of the coming of mass production. "I can't battle those big shoe manufacturers," Pop says tremulously from, of course, a wheelchair. The sentimentality about crafts and private enterprise also belongs to the times; it seems half-mock, but meant, too. The great silent comedians demonstrate a philosophy of me-against-the-world, of small-town decency against metropolitan mayhem, of the loner against the propertied. Greed whirls over the landscape in a dark cone, drawing with it everyone except the tramp comedian and his kin. But though the tramp doesn't have a bean, he has benedictive luck. In one of Langdon's famous stunt sequences, he has leaped over the fence of a yard enticingly labeled "Private, Keep Out," to be saved on the other side only by a nail from falling down a cliff face. Whoever wrote that notice had a satanic passion for property and no great feeling for the lives of natural daredevils. Langdon's belt catches on the nail, and so does his sweater. He removes the sweater from the nail carefully and starts to unbuckle the belt. Then he sees the drop below him, absorbs it gravely, and does up the buckle, going on to cover up the sight of it with his sweater, in one of my favorite hopeless moments in silent comedy. Langdon did the stunt himself. "There was no one else to do it," he told a friend later, after the talkies had come in and his career had hit bankruptcy, "so I had no alternative." He was apparently deeply worried at the time because there wasn't a titter from the crew as he hung there. He didn't allow for their being fond of him; he thought it meant the sequence wouldn't be funny.

APRIL 24, 1971

Chaplin on the Set

Buster Keaton once told me that when he and Chaplin first used the new sound cameras what they most missed in them was the noise. The old silent-picture cameras made a rhythmic racket that both of them had unconsciously taken for a beat when they were acting. Perhaps this is why Chaplin now writes his own film music; knowing that he is going to be the composer, he can direct a scene with a tempo going on in his head.

To see him work on a scene in *A Countess from Hong Kong* is rather like watching a classical ballet master teaching behind glass. The beat that he can hear is out of one's own earshot, but it is holding the work together. Comedy for Chaplin is choreography: placing, movement, the intricate classical disciplining of vulgar energy. His urge to make his teaching concrete and physical is like the nostalgia of a great old dancer taking his thousandth *Swan Lake* class from a chair, unconsciously mimicking a *pas de deux* in a sort of muscular mumble, and exploding onto the set to dance the *corps de ballet* steps himself when some wretched cygnet misses a cue. The dancers in the *pas de deux*, whom he obviously greatly admires, are Sophia Loren and Marlon Brando. The cygnet one day was a ship's steward in the film who had to make an entrance during a scene with Brando and offer a double brandy. With so little to do he fluffed it altogether; Chaplin catapulted onto the set and mimed it himself, and it was like Pavlova with a napkin over her arm.

A Countess from Hong Kong was made at Pinewood Studios, which in their time have produced some of the most deathly conventional films ever made. To Chaplin, then seventy-seven, who had made eighty-one films, this isn't of the faintest consequence. As with most of the great classicists of comedy, conventionalism is really just what his work springs from. Rules, propriety, order, loyalty, romanticism, and a sweet decorum are the elements of his style; anarchy suggests nothing to him. A studio that had been the home of other people's technical revolts would have little to offer Chaplin. His needs are simple, oddly formal, and entirely his own.

Buster Keaton told me that to his mind the most enviable place to work was a broom cupboard. Chaplin's broom cupboard is obviously a studio. I think he would be happy enough in any studio at all, provided it were professionally competent to do what he wanted; and if it weren't he could undoubtedly teach it to be, because he knows every trade of his craft backwards. The freedom that other directors find in working on location means nothing to him. The intrusions of commonplace life are not an inspiration to him but a distraction. If he works outside a studio he finds his ideas and concentration "blowing away on the wind."

The conditions at Pinewood are what he needs. They are a familiar focus for work, and everything extraneous to that seems to be invisible to him. The mock-Tudor front offices obviously don't jar on him, the crew has learned how to do what he wants, and the huge sound-stages scattered with sets of a liner are a convention that only make him imagine the reality of his film more fiercely, like the genteel flower-curtained caravan on the set that is Brando's dressing room, and the tea-stall where the technicians stand in line for currant buns and a black brew of tea that lays a coating of tannin inside the mouth like an animal's pelt.

Chaplin in his old age seems to feel physically forty-five. Anyone watching him at first is bound to have an undercurrent of worry at the sight of a man nearing eighty who not only keeps the ruthless hours of film-making but also demonstrates practically every take himself; but after a while any concern seems a patronage. The outstripped crew have given it up long since. The only thing that bothers some of them is that they can't quite recognize him as he is now. I saw one of them holding up a finger against the sight of his distant face to blot out his upper lip and try to imagine him with the old Hitler mustache. With his present white hair he looks almost like the negative of his silent-film self. The wide mouth, stretched like a child's eating a slice of watermelon, isn't quite as one remembers it; perhaps it was always changed by the mustache.

He seems to feel the cold, but then he has lived out of England long enough to grow unused to the conditions that the locals dourly call livable. The studio is what fellow citizens think of as living-room temperature, which is like March out of doors. He wears a thick sweater under a thicker jacket. Usually he has a hat on against the glare of the lights. When he feels debonair he tips the hat over his eyes; when he is growling at the stupidity of his extras, or at the unwieldiness of conventional modern film lighting, he pushes it impatiently to the back of his head. During holdups he will often suddenly wheel away from the stage to find his wife, Oona, a shy, beautiful woman who generally effaces herself behind a pillar. He seems to look to her not so much for advice as for some sort of confirmation. When he speaks to her about a scene between takes, he does it almost as if he were talking to himself. Her constant presence on the set, even and affectionate, seems to have some trick of pulling the knot of his mood.

He keeps the technicians at a distance. They call him "sir," and if he jokes with them they watch carefully to make sure that they are right to joke back. "OK, print that," he says once at the end of a take, and then he hears an airplane overhead that will probably have wrecked it. "Dammit," he says; not his furious version of the oath, which is an American-accented "Goddammit," but an atavistic curse out of his English youth which is practically a pleasantry. The crew notices the inflection and deduce from it that they can freewheel with him for a minute. "There's a humming. Why didn't you tell me?" he goes on to the sound technician with the headphones, giving the start of his wide grin. "Because you were talking, sir," says the soundman daringly, because he is suddenly licensed to. The atmosphere in the set is at its warmest, sunny and trustful. But one take later Chaplin says "Oko" instead of "OK": he often pronounces words wrongly when he is in a hurry, sometimes even trying to force them into other meanings—and when the crew tentatively kid him about it he ignores them, with an implied rebuke for diverting his attention.

The immediately endearing thing about watching Chaplin work on this picture is the way he goes on laughing at it. He doesn't laugh at the lines in themselves; he laughs at the way they are executed. One has the feeling that when he wrote them he probably wasn't even yet amused. The chuckles must have come later, when the actors had gone through the lines mechanically, overemoted, lost their confidence, learned their moves backward, broken through some sort of actors' sound barrier, and eventually found the work as easy as breathing.

It is ease that always makes him laugh. He keeps saying that this is a *romantic* film, not a comedy. He wants to make a film about love that simply happens to be funny, without anyone in the picture knowing it. "Play for absolute realism, not for comedy," he says again and again. One can see the details of Brando's performance becoming daily smaller and more meticulous, like the movement of a watch. His attention to Chaplin is total. I found it technically enthralling, and often moving.

Brando plays a stuffy American ambassador to Saudi Arabia, traveling from Hong Kong with Sophia Loren embarrassingly stowed away in his stateroom as a dispossessed Russian countess. The ambassador's wife, played by Tippi Hedren, is an amused lounger who has been separated from him for two years. She discovers Sophia Loren's bra in his cabin with nothing more than elegant glee that he should have so undiplomatically been an ass. His Excellency is traveling with his valet Hudson, played by a stone-faced English actor called Patrick Cargill; the valet has to be induced to marry Sophia Loren in order to give her his nationality as a way of getting her through American Immigration. The valet's resistance to marrying the most nubile woman imaginable is very funny on the set. When the subject is broached, he behaves as though he has been offered the wrong wine with the fish.

Most of the action happens on the ship. The sniffy valet is

given his orders in the sundeck lounge. Before shooting, Chaplin sits on the edge of one of the chairs in the set and listens to Brando and Cargill running through their lines. He mouths most of the dialogue with them unconsciously and makes tiny replicas of their movements. When he is rehearsing actors his muscles often seem to twitch like a dog having a dream.

"You are an American citizen, aren't you?" says the ambassador to his valet.

"I've been an American citizen for the last sixteen years," says the valet stiffly, in the most English voice possible. Chaplin laughs at the way he does it. Then the valet is told that he must marry Sophia Loren.

"I'd like you to marry her," says Brando, so disarmingly that Cargill laughs, but also so lightly that he makes it seem like kidding.

"Don't denote anything on your face. Keep your voice up. Insist on the action." The ambassador does the line again, bland and clear.

The valet pauses, and then replies, "If I may say so, sir, this is rather sudden."

Chaplin: "More polite. You're disguising your feelings by being very polite."

Cargill says it again.

"But before you close up, just a shade of shock on that line of Marlon's. 'I'd like you to marry her.' It lays an egg a little bit." He laughs. "So long as you're not suave. A suavity here would kill the whole scene." This is real comic shrewdness; most people directing these lines would have thought that unruffled suavity was their basis. Chaplin turns out to be quite right, of course. It is like the funniness of P. G. Wodehouse's Jeeves. The comic point about the godly servant isn't that he is totally impassive, but that across the immortal calm there is an intermittent flicker of ordinary humanity. The crack in the Olympian surface has to be microscopic, but it can be gigantically expressive. It is a difficult thing for an actor to do without oversignaling. Lazy American comedians now would tend to make the crack a large crevasse; lazy English comedians would leave it out and settle for unbroken haughtiness. Chaplin is patiently insistent about the point. Finally the lines make him laugh.

The extras have to walk across in the background. They have been told exactly where to go and how fast, but everything is fumbled and Chaplin watches in agony. Some of the extras are old trouts who habitually go to sleep in the armchairs on the set although one of the masters of the cinema is working under their noses. Some of them are bored young hacks who aren't even alert enough to be nervous. They import an atmosphere of crassness and laziness that is sniffed by the members of the crew with instant dislike. The fact that they have turned up in the wrong clothes is one of the common absurdities of big-budget film making, but it is enough to upset a perfectionist like Chaplin for the morning. "They should be in lovely summery clothes—lovely pale shoes . . ." I hear him saying to himself unhappily between takes. "They look as if they've just got off the 8:17 at Victoria Station," says the amiable cameraman with an edge of irritability.

"Remember your tempos," Chaplin calls out to the extras, who do their jobs again. One group has to saunter, the other to scurry. They manage it eventually, looking as awkward and unreal as any extras in any big studio in the world, which is one of the penalties that Chaplin pays for working under conventional conditions. The rehearsals for this scene take a long time. Chaplin himself demonstrates a steward's entrance twice, arriving and pivoting exactly on cue, saying "So-so-so-*so;* so-so-so-so-so-*so,*" as dummy dialogue. It is rather like Toscanini giving an entrance to the triangle-player after a hundred and fifty bars of silence.

Eventually the moves harden and become mechanical, which is what he wants. Once the routine is fixed and has started to bore the actors, the comedy begins to emerge. He works from the outside inward: first the mechanics, then familiarity and physical skill, and after that the right emotions will come. It is the diametric opposite of the Stanislavskian style that has become accepted modern dogma.

"Do that line again, Marlon. 'Oh, in about ten minutes.' Quickly. Take off the fat." The working atmosphere between them is relaxed and easy. Brando is one of the greatest screen actors in the world and he has been trained in exactly the opposite tradition, but he listens and absorbs with an attention that seems unflawed.

He is doing a close-up shot of the scene now, with the cues given to him by the producer, Jerry Epstein. Brando fluffs twice, saying "husband" instead of "Hudson," and the producer starts to get the giggles. He finds himself infected and starts saying words upside down. At the end of the final take Brando squints at Chaplin, laughs, and says to the producer, "Do you want to get some Scotch tape and sew yourself together?"

Epstein is an old associate of Chaplin, and an obvious contributor to the mood of fun that Brando and Loren both sense on the set. His way of giving Chaplin a prompt when the director is signaling for it looks like the result of years, rather like an operating-theater sister shoving the right instrument into a surgeon's hand. To an outsider Chaplin's "So-so-so" and grabbing fingers aren't at all explicit, but Epstein obviously feels that he should know by instinct the line that he wants, and when his concentration is absorbed enough he does.

The attention that Chaplin demands, and gets, is fierce and total. Where other directors become most inventive by allowing energy to fly outwards, with Chaplin the pull is always towards the center. He knows exactly what he is doing. When he is shooting a scene he seems to be gently chivvying the actors towards something that is already complete in his head. Like a tug edging a liner away from a quay, he has coaxed the incomparable Brando into a manner that is just faintly at odds with the one he is known by. The sumptuous, time-taking style, spaciously intelligent behind an opiate gaze, has become smaller, quicker, and sometimes comically testy, just as the histrionics of Sophia Loren's abundant comic temperament have been converted into a very funny stoicism. In her work before *A Countess from Hong Kong*, she made people laugh by Latin fluster; in the scenes that I saw, she does it by phlegm. "He had made me quite different," she says. "When I see rushes I don't recognize myself. He doesn't like me to use my hands much, especially near my face. We're trying to do everything as naturally as possible. . . ."

Directors and actors always say now that they are working for realism, of course; it is one of the modern pieties of the profession, but in Chaplin's case it is precisely true. Again and again when he is directing a scene he will cut out some gesture or response that reveals itself the moment it has gone as a hamstrung comic mannerism. His laughs in this picture nearly always come from doing apparently as little as possible very fast. "Lots of lift, lots of tempo" . . . he often says. The takes that he decides to print are always the ones with the most dash and lightness; sometimes when he is talking under pressure he makes a bouncing movement upward with his hand as though he were keeping a ball in the air.

"It wants a beat," he says to Tippi Hedren, after she has been working on a scene where she enters with the identifiably outsize bra that she has discovered in her husband's cabin. "This is all a great comedy to you. No malice. You haven't lived with your husband for two years. You come in with great gusto. You're kidding him." Through the next take he looks worried. "There was no tempo." He gets up from his chair by the camera, wrinkles his nose and prances through the moves himself, saying "So-so-so," like a groom sedating a horse. "So-so-so *Your Excellency*," he says, pivoting on the words. "Your're mocking him. You're glib. That's it. Can we come in with a bigger spread? I would burst in here. It's sort of breezy. One—two—" he gives her the time, and catches his breath on the upbeat as she enters. "Can we keep that lovely movement?" In a previous take she had turned on one of her lines and practically flowed on to a sofa; he does it himself to fix the move in his mind, looking comically grand in an imaginary tea gown, and makes sure that the camera movement fits it.

For Chaplin, the pacing of a camera articulates a scene. On the whole he doesn't seem to like camera-movement very much. ("The actors should be the performers, not the lens.") He doesn't care for trick angles and he hates the laziness of cryptically significant shots that show nothing but door-opening. "Orientation" is an important idea to him. He believes that an audience must always know where they are in a room, and that actors must know exactly where to stop, where to turn, where to stand, whether to talk directly or indirectly.

I had expected his physical business to be graphic and hilarious, but I hadn't been quite prepared for the precision of his sense of words. To talk about Chaplin's mime is rather like praising the height of Everest; it is his pin-fall ear for dialogue that is technically so absorbing to anyone fortunate enough to see him working. "There's something woolly in that word, Sophia," he says; the fuzz is there, an emphasis that is faintly implausible and faltering, but a lot of good directors would have let it go. "Most films are just in and out," said the chippie (the film carpenter). "Not this one. He's definitely got something on his mind."

When he is coming back from the lunch break or inspecting the sets in the morning he carries his script against his chest as if it were a buckler. Like Keaton, he stands and walks with the arched back of a small boy, perhaps because of the ferocious physical training that both of them had as tiny children in vaudeville. "He's a perfectionist," says the director of photography, Arthur Ibbetson. "When he did his own bit it was rather a day." (Chaplin appears in the film in a tiny part as a steward who gets seasick.) "All he really did was sweep the deck with his head down. Other people would have made a production out of it." Ibbetson does a mime of someone milking laughs. "There's one passenger asleep on the whole deck and when he's finished he sweeps the muck very neatly behind his feet. That's all he does, see?"

SEPTEMBER 1, 1966

A Countess from Hong Kong on Screen

Chaplin apparently once told Eisenstein that the reason why he scattered food to the poor children in *Easy Street* as though they were chickens was that he despised them. Eisenstein took him literally and felt shocked, missing the fact that Chaplin loves kids to the point of sentiment and could only have been deriding the idea of anyone accepting slops from society's soup kitchen, in which he would always include swallowing society's conventions.

The tramp of the early films is Chaplin's ideal man. He is totally practical, created by acts, not rules, and responding always to what is really there. The incompetent cops and addled factory workers and crazy bank presidents of the silent pictures are retarded by comparison, because they react theoretically. In his new film, *A Countess from Hong Kong*, the ambassador-hero and his manservant are both so screwed up by protocol that they are practically deficient. Shut up in a ship's stateroom with Sophia Loren, her dolphin hips slithering around mesmerizingly in a man's silk dressing gown, the men avoid the irregular fact of her existence and behave as if she were something untoward that had been brought in on a salver.

The ambassador is played by Marlon Brando with a neat, tight voice and spasms of silent-comedy spryness. It is a disciplined and generous performance. He often plays the feed to the manservant, an implacable celibate called Hudson, done by Patrick Cargill with the sort of sniffy wit that one seems to be able to get only in England. It has something to do with physical stance, as well as the security of five hundred years of lawn-rolling: a look of hanging from the collarbone as if it were a coat hanger, like Gielgud in *The Importance of Being Earnest*.

His Excellency, steaming away from a night out in Hong Kong spent with a bunch of White Russian titled gold diggers, wakes up with a skull full of hangover and a shirt-front scrawled with telephone numbers in lipstick, which the depressing Hudson efficiently notes down before laundering. Sex never exists in itself in this film; it is only signified—by the blur of a headache, the rape of a nice clean shirt, the implication of a girl stowaway. The escaping countess, played by Sophia Loren, obediently playing patience and chess with herself all day and ordering huge amounts of food from room service, doesn't even present any danger so authentic as a possible source of pain to the ambassador's wife, who turns out to be nothing more than unpleasantly amused.

In His Excellency's eyes the stowaway is simply a blunder who could get him the sack from the diplomatic service, and in Hudson's she is a call of duty, since the poor starched nit is told to marry her. He wakes up chaste and practically lying to attention in bed, still calling her "madam" in front of the startled waiter, and later muttering troubled things about consummated soup.

Sometimes this distressingly heavy film is funny: Chaplin himself opening the door as a steward and looking unprofessionally upset by sea-roll, Sophia and Brando leaping for cover with their legs flashing like the blades of a bacon-slicer, the eerie courtesies of Hudson when he is ethereally sloshed. Margaret Rutherford is an engaging invalid, especially when she is in bed with a toy panda whom she refers to as "my Russian friend." Sophia Loren has a new comic style, small-gestured and swift, with a sumptuous long stride in low-heeled slippers that is like an oiled version of Groucho's. But the jokes about the size of her bra are fairly ponderous, like the ambassador's three belches, and the stateroom doorbell that has the sound of a raspberry. Like a lot of intensely decorous people, Chaplin off the lead can suddenly seem pixie and coarse.

Long passages in the dialogue go dead, partly because the lines usually make exactly the same point as the shots, with the music chiming in third. I am afraid the film sometimes weighs like lead, as well as seeming mysteriously committed to repeating the most trite and bourgeois old Hollywood bedroom gags about girls wearing men's pajamas. Yet the buoyancy of the scenes that work best, and the passion of the film against conventionalism, makes it obvious that Chaplin dearly wanted exactly the opposite.

He calls his film a romantic comedy. You have to wait until very near the end for the romanticism, but when it comes it is genuine and rather serious. Brando and Loren play a love scene in which they connect for the first time instead of being the hermits of farce. They are sitting together at a horrible gala dinner on the ship, under the eye of his chilly wife, who is watching from the dance floor. He talks fast, looking elsewhere, saying things about the hell with his career and appearances; and she weeps, because she knows perfectly well he doesn't mean a word of it.

The happy ending after that is a fib twist, a formula. This is the real ending, a declaration of strength by a character too accustomed to failing himself to sustain it. Chaplin has always celebrated indomitability; it is rather moving that in his old age he should assert that failure is also worth committing.

JANUARY 8, 1967

Funny in Need of Help

As Freud says in *Jokes and Their Relation to the Unconscious*, a solemn tome which can do much to release one from the Freudian thrall, "We should bear in mind the peculiar and even fascinating charm exercised by jokes in our society." A careful study of the literature, however, enables him to make the good point that "It is quite impracticable to deal with jokes otherwise than in connection with the comic." In his dissection of joke-mechanics he therefore always distinguishes meticulously between *funny* jokes, of which this is an admired example:

> Two Jews met in the neighbourhood of the bath-house. "Have you taken a bath?" asked one of them. "What?" asked the other in return, "is there one missing?" This example calls for a graphic presentation:
>
> The first Jew asks: "Have you taken a bath?" The emphasis is on the element of "bath."
>
> The second replies as though the question had been: "Have you *taken* a bath?"
>
> The shifting of the emphasis is only made possible by the wording "taken a bath." If it had run "have you bathed?" no displacement would have been possible. The non-joking answer would then have been: "Bathed? What d'you mean? I don't know what that is." But the technique of the joke lies in the displacement of the accent from "bath" to "taken."
>
> Let us go back to the "Salmon Mayonnaise," since this is the most straightforward example. . . .

—and jokes that, as he puts it, though they may be undeniably in the *nature* of a joke, do not give the *impression* of a joke. He offers examples of these, too.

Mae West's autobiography, *Goodness Had Nothing to Do with It,* certainly has the structure and character of a joke, but there may be those who feel that in the end it fails to have a joke's effect. The character of Diamond Lil is energetically enacted on every page, but the lush self-regard and curiously muscular sexuality that are still so funny in *She Done Him Wrong* have acquired something resistibly mechanical over the years. The quoted letters signed "sin-sationally yours" begin to cause a chill. Even a joke-hound like Freud might find the book chiefly rewarding not as entertainment but as a case history; she interestingly confesses, for instance, that she has a "driving, fiery compulsion toward lion-taming," and that she wrote a scene into *The Lady and the Lions* to indulge it. Alone with the beasts in their cage:

> Excitement began to take hold of me . . . charging me with electric voltage until I could see nothing, hear nothing, feel nothing but an overpowering sense of increasing mastery that mounted higher and higher. . . . I discovered I was smiling and couldn't close my mouth to stop it. . . .

One also learns that she dislikes vulgarity and drunkenness, is harsh in her relations to tobacco-smokers, and would like to see every teen-ager learn the benefits to the figure of a nightly massage with cocoa butter. The total effect is so far from ironic that one begins to wonder whether the self-mockery associated with her performances was really an accidental implication of that swaggering sea-lion walk. It may be that, like Freud, she is handicapped as a jokester by lacking a sense of humor. The funniest line in the book is W. C. Field's casual insult at a passing fire engine while they were working on *My Little Chickadee*—"Damn drunken house painters"—which she cites without amusement as evidence that he must have been tipsy at the time.

In *Goodness Had Nothing to Do with It* Mae West follows a familiar pattern of show-business memoir-writers in expressing a great deal more insight about her work than about herself. As usual, it is the precise and technical notes that are fascinating: for example, the way she instinctively overruled the director of her first film and made him hold the camera on her to milk a laugh when he wanted to cut on the line. In Charles Chaplin, Jr.'s, book, *My Father, Charlie Chaplin,* there is the same disparity. When he is recalling his father at work—making up, struggling with a music track, developing a piece of mime—the book becomes momentarily direct and absorbing. He seems perceptive about the nature of Chaplin's horrified mirror-image relationship with Hitler in making *The Great Dictator*. But other elements in the book, more to do with the implied strain between the author and his subject than with the not very likable exposition of Chaplin's private affairs, make it painful to read and almost impossible to write about. One senses distance and unease in their relationship, a difficult mixture of competitiveness and enthrallment in the son, and possibly some suspicion of filial cashing-in underlying the stiff quoted letters from the father.

SEPTEMBER 23, 1960

Harold Lloyd

Whereas Buster Keaton looks like some poetic widower, and Harry Langdon looks like an infant dope fiend, Harold Lloyd really only found his comic character when he saw a film about a fighting priest in glasses. According to James Agee in *On Film*, he thought about the spectacles day and night; and once he had adopted them as his own he must have discovered how very like a young cleric he is. He has an anxious, evangelizing stance, and the teeth of the true curate.

The World of Comedy is an American anthology of the best of his films. It is put together in a way that is a glum piece of evidence of the decline in the film industry's opinion of public literacy, with a voice as declamatory as *The March of Time's* painstakingly reading aloud redundant linking passages that are printed on the screen anyway; but the hour and a half of Lloyd himself is ravishingly funny.

There is a marvelous sequence about a nine-foot man with toothache whose incisor the hero sympathetically lassos with a rope before scaling his chest like a mountaineer, looking as though he is about to sink an ice ax in his breastbone. When this fails, he tries sprinting up the street to get a purchase on the rope but the mammoth patient, foggily aware that he has found a friend, undermines the plan by bounding trustfully after him.

Harold Lloyd deals in this sort of delicate letdown. He never does anything that is as beautiful or moving as Keaton, but he does a lot that is technically brilliant: there is nothing in film comedy to better the sheer theatrical adroitness of the twenty-minute danger sequence in *Feet First*, when he has survived every crisis on the face of the skyscraper and only gives in to panic when his feet are two inches from the ground. This is the real flowering of Mack Sennett. But there are other things that are more like germinal Goonery: during a chase, for instance, a very young baby played by a midget suddenly clambers around a pram hood and gives a weird thuggish roar.

JUNE 24, 1962

The Vaudeville Infant

While I was watching Charlie Drake in *The Cracksman* I kept thinking how much he would have enjoyed making a silent for Mack Sennett. It isn't really his voice that is funny: his accent, a kind of landlady's front-parlor English, is in fact rather ogling. The spirit of his comic personality is better expressed without words, because it is the spirit of a toddler.

With his heavy, troubled head and kewpie-doll limbs, Charlie Drake has the odd look of anxiety that you see in babies up to the age of two. Sometimes he gives a furious yell, or moves his hands as though he were thinking of throwing everything out of his pram. In a physical discipline like the one that must have been in the Sennett studios, where almost everyone had been trained in the circus or vaudeville, his childishness could have developed into a comic style as distinct as Harry Langdon's, whom James Agee once described as looking as though he wore diapers under his trousers.

In *The Cracksman*—directed by Peter Graham Scott and

scripted by Charlie Drake with Lew Schwarz—he plays a master locksmith who is innocently used as the vital technician in a series of robberies. Thrilled to be asked to show off, he fiddles the locks of Bentleys, safes, and rich men's houses with no more insight into what he is doing than a tin opener. When a gangster has parked him in an opulent drawing room and left the chump happily alone with the cigars while the place is rifled around him, Charlie Drake is still eyeless in the world of Chubb and Mortice locks. He finds himself looking at a television play in which an actor is blowing up a safe. The risks that the man takes give him a pain. He is harshly critical of his technique, but at the same time obviously bothered about being hard on an amateur.

Intensely partisan on two sides at once, he is in the sort of split-minded fighting mood that silent comedians used to be able to milk laughs from for five minutes. It is typical of the change in screen comedy that it goes by for a tenth of what it might be worth. I think writers and directors now are frightened to make detours from the narrative in case the audience forgets where it is. But most comedy consists of just that: of living inside the skull of a man who is constantly distracted from his objective and who will spend ten minutes picking fluff off his suit when he is standing in the wake of an avalanche.

The trouble with *The Cracksman*, like most British comedies, is that the screen clown now has so little to support him. The characters played by Chaplin and Keaton and Harold Lloyd and Harry Langdon lived in a world that was full of comic paraphernalia, including their erotic and exquisitely dismissive heroines: vamps in motorcars, lofty girls whose long drawers kept showing, great strapping Valkyries with ripe thighs and prim little bangs on their foreheads. Their only contemporary equal is the girl whom Joan Littlewood has defined, the chirpy bird who wears a skirt as taut as a balloon and amiably tells men to keep their hands off it. The girls in *The Cracksman* are like the nonentities in every other British comedy: brassy, antierotic, impossible either to dote on or to send up.

Nor is there any help from the sets. What is a comedian to do if he is put down against a background that has about as much character and fantasy as a display of three-piece suites? Apart from the charming set for the hero's shop, most of the rooms in the film don't work with any comic style; there is a lot of the humorless opulence that I associate with James Bond, a sort of Thug's Luxe that isn't parodied enough to be funny. In the Sennett comedies, the screen seemed to fizz with baroque bedsteads and wallpapers, and eccentric, beautiful props. And the cluttered country parlors in some of Chaplin's films are eloquent about a whole kind of American frontier life. The only person who does the same sort of thing now is Jacques Tati.

JULY 7, 1963

$9-Million-Worth of Scrap-Yard Comedy

Mad World has been sold hard as an exuberant throwback to Mack Sennett. It isn't any such thing. The world it is about isn't mad at all: it is the world that is so bleakly summarized by Los Angeles, grim, greedy, and casually destructive. At the beginning of the picture, after a spectacular car crash, Jimmy Durante dies with a message on his lips about a hidden stolen haul; the rest of the plot is a scrambling race between the motorists who overhear his last words. If it had been filmed by another director, William and Tania Rose's witty script might have had the tone of, say, *The Ladykillers;* but Stanley Kramer has made it abrasive and bilious.

Technically the film is very skillful. The new one-camera Cinerama process is now better. No tremble, no joins. Some of the panning shots make you feel like Bertie Wooster moving his eyes too quickly with a hang-over, but Kramer has discovered a lot about how to edit deftly on the elephantine Cinerama scale. It is the rancorous character of the picture that is going to give the United Artists salespeople trouble: this is no romp, however much Kramer has tried to placate audiences by the trick of casting likable comedians in utterly disagreeable straight parts.

The characters played by Ethel Merman, Milton Berle, Sid Caesar, Buddy Hackett, Mickey Rooney, Phil Silvers, Terry-Thomas, Jonathan Winters, and Edie Adams are vile, ill-tempered, and avaricious. A honeymooning wife is prepared to let her husband electrocute himself without stirring an inch. A child refuses to help someone unless he gets three bucks. Ethel Merman plays a vicious caricature of what Kramer obviously hates in American women, a squawking mom who will be sitting under the hair dryer enjoying Mother's Day when her husband dies of a coronary. Even Spencer Tracy as a policeman, the actor who embodies niceness if ever there was one, turns out to be a twister.

It's a Mad, Mad, Mad, Mad World is about greed and feminine hysteria, and about how people behave in a panic, which in this picture is always badly. Every comic convention has been turned sour. Slipping on a banana skin breaks bones, and it is the pain of their enemies that makes the characters laugh. The title is a hoax. It should be *We're Lousy, Lousy, Lousy, Lousy People*. At first the plot (and the casting) makes it sound like a modern silent comedy, since it is about this chase through America by a bunch of neurotic motorists in search of the thieves' haul that Durante told them about when he was dying after his car crashed. But the movie is actually a grim new variant of the old knockabout form, a comedy that deliberately brutalizes every convention that makes people laugh. What it becomes, not surprisingly, is a comedy that makes people feel battered and bleak.

The fantasized conventions of clowning have gone down the sink. The exaggerations here have the character of the oversize statements of hoardings along a freeway. The innocence of comedy has disappeared, and so has the invitation to participate. You have no wish for anyone to win the chase in this film because everyone in it, including the children, is greedy, opportunist and vicious.

The violence that is done to cars and buildings and human beings doesn't seem to belong any longer to the painless and immortal world of slapstick; it has the spirit of the scrap yards where they pound two-year-old obsolescent Chevrolets into hunks of metal worth a few bucks. This isn't a mad world at all. It's poisonously practical.

Obviously there is nothing wrong with savagery in art: Picasso's "Guernica" is savage, so is Swift, so is Evelyn Waugh. To say that something in art is alienating isn't an insult, except in the soft fibbing language of film salesmanship. It could be a bold device to turn slapstick comedy inside out and use it to express hatred, and to make audiences feel that in laughing at people slipping on banana skins all these years they may have been laughing less benignly than they thought they were. At the root of Stanley Kramer's picture and of William and Tania Rose's script, there seems to be an accusation about the whole disguised nature of comedy; they imply that what we really split our sides about is always the sight of someone else's humiliation. The parallel-running theme is about specifically American kinds of competitiveness and brassiness, and it looks as though the spirit behind this must originally have been Kramer's, since the first idea of the authors was to set the story in England.

So far, then, it sounds like a fine, strong, unpopular film. The weakness is that the picture is decked out with the trappings of entertainment, that it goes down on its knees to make you laugh, that it is cast with the biggest list of funny men in the business, souped up with jolly music and made for $9 million with a colossal apparatus of cheerfulness. You can't at the same time make a sour picture and also hope to con people into thinking they're having a ball so as to bump up the box-office takings. The film aspires to offend you, but it also passionately hopes to placate you. It is the ha-ha jokes in the film that are uneasy, not the spleen.

NOVEMBER 10, 1963
DECEMBER 8, 1963

Norman Wisdom

The latest Norman Wisdom film, *A Stitch in Time*, is the second comedy in a fortnight that ends up in a hospital ward with the leading characters encased in plaster. (The other is *Mad, Mad World*.)

In this new department of dread holiday humor, the joke is to see the patients falling about with merriment at someone else's pain—either at the sight of yet another bone going, or at the sight of a leg in plaster being agonizingly jacked up to the ceiling and then dropped crash onto someone's precious watch. "When their ribs break, you'll laugh till your ribs ache!" (*Sunday Sadist*): "Warner Bros., the greatest name in family entertainment, has done it again! Take the kiddies!" (*The New Brutalist*).

I can just see, squinting, the humor to be wrung out of bedpans—the Rank Organisation has been wringing it ever since I can remember—but broken bones really aren't the biggest laugh in the world. Nor are the perfectly healthy teeth that Norman Wisdom jerks out by mistake in a glum riot in a dentist's clinic, nor the spastic gait that he puts on as a disguise, nor the patient on crutches who is knocked down by our hero while he is driving a motorized stretcher like a maniac around the hospital corridors. Nor indeed are the brutal swallowing mishaps that seem to be a running theme in *A Stitch in Time*. A head butcher swallows a presentation watch, a dental patient swallows a whole roll of cotton wool that he has had shoved down his throat by Norman Idiocy, and then a St. John Ambulance man in a brass band swallows his flute.

After watching the film for a while you begin to think that the thing that should have been swallowed is the star's pride. Norman Wisdom's films usually include a character who is planted to tell us how lovable he is, but I've never known the line to be advertised quite so hard before. In between knocking ill people down and driving his best friend's unconscious head like a battering ram into an ambulance, he keeps getting told about his lovability by a soppy nurse. He is the only man in the film who cares enough about a little orphan in hospital to give her back the will to live, and he is also the only man at a charity ball who understands what real charity is. What spinach.

A Stitch in Time is a nauseating combination; it is very heartless, and also so sentimental that it sticks in your fingers like flypaper.

As a relief from Wisdom I went to see George Stevens' *Talk of the Town*. It was made in 1942, with Cary Grant, Ronald Colman, and Jean Arthur. Cary Grant plays a liberal-hearted jail-breaker unjustly accused of murder and arson in a corrupt town. Ronald Colman, who harbors the fugitive without knowing it, is a distinguished and spinsterish professor of law (Hollywood directors always seem to cast Englishmen when they want integrity without sexuality). Jean Arthur plays a witty scatterbrain who has the ritual old-time sex-comedy scene dressed in men's pajamas. The script is by Irwin Shaw and Sidney Buchman. The messages about justice seem a bit ponderous and simple-minded perhaps because the film was made at the height of the war, but the comedy is marvelously handled. Ronald Colman's performance is dapper and immaculate. He is the only actor I can think of who could make a toothbrush look as though it were a cigarette holder.

DECEMBER 15, 1963

The new Norman Wisdom picture is called *Press for Time*, a pun that must mean that he plays either a dry cleaner or, as it turns out, a reporter. He is supposed to be the by-blow grandson of a Tory Prime Minister, born of the PM's suffragette daughter by a sewerman who chanced to be near the railings of the Houses of Parliament, and the boy has been hidden away on a provincial paper to keep the scandal quiet.

Norman Wisdom specializes in a bashfulness verging on mental deficiency. The reporter he plays reminded me of Shirley Temple, though not so bold. Her sentimentality was a straight to the jaw, whereas his slides around the ear. He is gormless through and through, and alert only to the possibility of getting the boot. Passing help comes from a girl reporter who knows more than he does and manages life better, as the women in Norman Wisdom's films generally do; their competence always seems to intimidate him almost as much as their sexiness.

In their presence he is a pygmy. His view of them is very like the outmatched awe depicted on prewar seaside postcards, where starveling young men with nervous shoulder blades crept around confident feminine rumps on the beach. In one sequence he dances with himself in a winsome fantasy about girls, clutching his square-shouldered jacket around him and sticking out his bum like a bustle; the scene hasn't much fun or blood about it, but everything else about it is an astonishing throwback to thirty years ago, even the dance steps and the furniture in the stuffy room.

Maybe the reason why Norman Wisdom can have such a melancholy effect on the people who don't respond to him is that he tugs desperately at strings of social pathos that aren't connected any longer to a context. Sometimes he seems to be begging sympathy on false terms for a folk hero of the Depression. A lot of the elements in his style and look are pure period; the underfed physique, the Brylcreem, the clothes that sadly try to ape a fashion patented by a remote boss class, the nervy upward squints with his face pressed against the chests of policemen and battle-axes, the scampers for safety and the leaps on to the tops of lamp-posts.

It is all very much as it used to be, except that the hero's troubles seem fabricated now that he hasn't the backbone of a time. Instead of cheek he possesses only coyness, and his double-takes are more shaming than funny. In the impossible situations where

Max Miller would have blown a raspberry, or where Eric Morecambe would turn away his head with a lofty peck and think of something else, Norman Wisdom turns in his toes and sucks a finger.

I suppose the real source of embarrassment about his performances is that he doesn't seem to have very much affection for the period errand-boy characters that he plays. If he had, he couldn't make them seem such pipsqueaks when they are obviously meant to be seen as engaging victims. His 1930-ish re-creations feel like a trick, with the vague drabness clinging to them that often seems to be present in pastiche. Their class consciousness and rather affected fear of the sack can have a lonely effect, like the fake bonhomie and tankard-bashing of mock Victorian music hall.

DECEMBER 11, 1966

Demolishing Comedy

There seems to be a vein in Hollywood comedy now that might be called the comedy of demolition. *It's a Mad, Mad, Mad, Mad World* was one long junk yard. *Robin and the Seven Hoods* is in an ecstasy about breakage. I suppose this is natural in a society that is up to here with bilge about consumer goods, but the trouble is that the people who make the films have forgotten what the silent comedians knew you had to do to make destruction funny.

In itself it isn't funny at all. There's nothing hilarious about an electric drill. There might be about the man working it—if, say, he were deaf to the noise that was driving everyone else crazy, and were quietly doing algebra in his head—but the drill on its own is just brutal. To make smithereens comic you have to lock some human personality inside the chaos who objects to it, either by ignoring it or by placidly putting some useless square inch of it into his own private kind of order, like a man making an alarm clock out of the spare parts of a lot of old cars that are about to be pulped.

Seven Hoods is a spoof gangster-picture about the prohibition era in the United States. It is full of sequences like the one in which Sammy Davis, Jr., kicks a cash register to bits and machine-guns the bottles in a bar: the orgies of smashing are obviously meant to be funny, but they make you laugh about as much as the work of a bulldozer. There are only two things in the picture that really come off as they're meant to, and I think it's because they have an instinct for the old rule that violence is funny only if there is someone who succeeds in making his own kind of sweet eccentric sense in the middle of it.

One of them is the thug with a face like a beat-up old cauliflower who sits knitting something in baby blue wool in the midst of gangster conferences. The other is the sequence when Sinatra's gaming club is raided and the gun molls and murderers serenely convert the place in ten seconds into a revivalist mission hall. The jazzy walls revolve, and turn into dingy expanses lettered with mottoes about writing to mother and the evil of drink. Tables ready laid with meager soup-kitchen meals flip out of the walls like ironing boards to cover up the gambling tables, and Bing Crosby sings a teetotal number called "Mister Booze" that the sozzled gangsters in revivalist disguise swing to as though it were a hymn in Harlem.

Otherwise there are long stretches where there is nothing pleasurable to do but watch Sinatra. I wish musicals were a bit more skillful about getting from dialogue into song. Every now and then in this exceptionally talky picture there is a moment when people who have been speaking to each other quite normally suddenly seem to be going mad, repeating each other, not listening to each other, edging near each other for no reason, and getting glazed looks like goldfish or old waiters. You can't think what's up with them. And then you realize, of course: they're about to sing a number.

JULY 26, 1964

The Trouble with Dither

After Danny Kaye's frenetic new film, *The Man from the Diners' Club*, I happened to come on the familiar London sight of a telephone man sitting in a canvas tent quietly ringing up his mates in the middle of traffic. It seemed much funnier than anything in the film.

I suppose it's a question of temperament whether you laugh more at someone behaving like a dervish or at someone being placid at the center of chaos. There are really two great classes of comedy, the comedy of dither and the comedy of phlegm. Danny Kaye belongs to the first, like Jerry Lewis and Norman Wisdom and *It's a Mad, Mad, Mad, Mad World:* the telephone engineer belonged to the second, like Bea Lillie, Buster Keaton, Tony Hancock, and Jacques Tati.

The physical characteristics of the first are a flailing arm, a twitching face, a rubbery bounding action, and a flustered instinct for flight. The physical characteristics of the second are a stoic body, a face stonily alert for the worst, a look as though objects are advancing like storm troops, and a dogged instinct to stay put and fight it out. Think of Keaton, boiling an egg with majestic complication in *The Navigator* when a difficult kitchen had almost thwarted him; or of Bea Lillie arguing in the middle of a Noël Coward song about whether a robin would really sing "Ho."

The trouble with the dithering kind of comedy is that it is more likely to be sentimental. It also seems to me that it is harder to make it funny. A comedian can't afford to get into too much of a flap, because total hysteria isn't comic. You have to stay just this side of the brink, like Jack Lemmon. He makes you laugh in *Some Like It Hot* when he is lying on the bed saying "I'm a girl, I'm a girl" because, even though he is the neurotic of all time, he is still having a go. Great comedy never gives up.

Frankie Howerd has a patent in neuroticism, but under the garrulous woman with persecution mania whom he plays most of the time there always seems to be a grumbling old ox who is suddenly going to stick his hooves in. The voice goes higher and higher, like the Mothers' Union whipping itself up over a grievance, and then it drops an octave and says something dead rude.

But in *The Man from the Diners' Club*, the life of the Danny Kaye character seems to be right out of control. His job alone sends him crackers, quite apart from his girl, who is trying to get him to the altar, and the thuggish Diners' Club member who wants to bump him off and scoot to Mexico. The hero is supposed to have a trauma about winking lights, and the flashing computer behind his desk sends him into a spasm every time the operator does a bit of filing. If the routine were gone through with about a tenth of the energy it might be rather funny.

Like all the films Frank Tashlin makes—he does the Jerry Lewis comedies—*The Man from the Diners' Club* is disastrously maladroit in its physical sense of humor. I don't think it was just the brutal context of the news from Dallas that made the press-show audience sit in horrified silence through a scene in which Danny Kaye pretends to be a German masseuse and nearly beats his patient's brains out. It was about as funny as a pileup on a freeway. The script is as crude as the direction; the best thing in it is an endearingly hard-working prewedding Spoonerism about it being bad luck for the grime to see the brood.

DECEMBER 1, 1963

Telling It Like It Isn't

Don't Raise the Bridge, Lower the River, Jerry Lewis's thirty-seventh picture, is the best he has made outside Hollywood. It was produced in England. Something around must have calmed him down. His style is much less hectic than usual, though one can still be blind to the quality in him that millions of people find winning. He makes the oddities of his comic heroes seem very feigned. His wildly rolling eyes don't strike me as eccentric or beset; they look more like the expression of a tryhard man out of his element and saddled forever with the role of being funny to a backslapping carful on a commuter train. There is something obscurely bullying under his self-deprecation, as there is under Norman Wisdom's. Keaton, W. C. Fields, Fred Allen, Sid Field, and the beloved and haunted Tony Hancock, who has just died, had more dignity. The funniest men always seem independent of your opinion. You take them or leave them. Sometimes Jerry Lewis appears to beg, like the bad patches of Chaplin, except that Lewis does it with the hypomania that so often characterizes current show biz when it has no real fuel to run on. One sees the same ersatz energy in a lot of musicals, and on television all the time.

In *Don't Raise the Bridge*, Jerry Lewis plays an American businessman in England married to a prissy English girl, who predictably throws in the sponge after three years of his harebrained get-rich schemes. You know at once, from the opening scene, which shows his wedding, the sort of comic character the man is going to be. A zebra suddenly crops up from nowhere, led by a man in a fez, and Jerry Lewis says, "Not now." I'm not sure why he doesn't make this funny. If Robert Dhéry had done it in a scene with Colette Brosset, waving the zebra aside and getting on intently with something more commonplace—as one of his troupe once doggedly got on with fitting washers on taps backstage at a strip show—it would have broken me up. I think the difference has something to do with the way Lewis so deliberately sets up his gags to be zany. All the same, there is a good idea in the situation of a man who is trying to reconcile the roles of a bridegroom out of this world with a dewy new wife and a compulsive telephone-answerer strenuously in this world to woo fast bucks. The hero of *Don't Raise the Bridge* is the kind of guilt-stricken, divided go-getter who might well wreck a honeymoon by giving a promotional interview to the local newspaper while his wife fretted around in her negligee. There is, in fact, a scene in which Jerry Lewis is dining by candlelight with his dumb cluck of a bride yet can't resist any interrupter who knocks on the hotel-bedroom door. One is an Indian snake charmer, who barges in with speechless melancholy and takes a place at the table. "Is your head any better?" Jerry Lewis asks him, solicitously and inscrutably. The wife's back finally breaks under the weight of her husband's genius for spreading himself thin among improbable overseas contacts, and she starts to get a divorce. Her globe-trotter rather endearingly puts his failure down to having given her no permanent home, and makes hopeless amends by turning her own house into a discothèque. It doesn't work, of course. Something then occurs that has to do with smuggling to Portugal the oil-drill designs of his wife's posh engineer lover (Nicholas Parsons). The plans are hidden in the tooth filling of a free-lance airline steward, agreeably played by Bernard Cribbins. A crooked money raiser is played by Terry-Thomas, dressed in a green smoking jacket and full of his usual appalling cheer. The screenplay is by Max Wilk, an American who seems to have absorbed some of the kinds of music-hall humor that are assumed to make only the English laugh. The verbal constructions often strike the ear as pure Blackpool-vaudeville, and blissful. (There are some fine lines about dentistry, for instance. "What? Tinker with an occlusion?" says a cross man who feels seriously about teeth.) Mr. Wilk has cottoned on to something huffy that is central to the style of a lot of English comedy, from Lady Bracknell to the *Carry On* films, which are always full of Kenneth Williams climbing onto his high horse. The best comes last—an appealingly odd performance by an English actress called Patricia Routledge as a Girl Guide den mother who could all too easily have been guyed as a stock English hearty. Miss Routledge makes her individual, funny, and rather nice. When Jerry Lewis shelters from derring-do behind the excuse of mumps, she says firmly, "Mumps? Is that any reason for showing the white feather?"

JULY 20, 1968

Nether Villainy

Any film character who is introduced with only the bottom fourteen inches of his trousers showing is going to be a bad lot. The unidentified ends of leg in the new James Bond picture, *You Only Live Twice*, which are eventually attached to the face of Donald Pleasence, do indeed turn out to belong to a wholesale rotter. 007's current enemy, who lives grandly in a converted volcano under the crust of the Far East, has developed a caddish mechanism for swallowing other people's astronauts so as to provoke a Soviet-American war and seize the earth. His foreigner's speech has the accent of an upper-class Englishman, which is no longer the sign it was in Imperial days of having learned manners and cricket, and he has a scar that must have meant a wretchedly early make-up call for Mr. Pleasence in the mornings. The ambitious despot also carries a white Persian cat in his arms, and he seems to have no secretary. In this sort of power-fantasy movie, having no secretary signifies a political villain on a big scale. The way the film framed the shots of the tyrant's trousers might have signaled the entry of any old burglar, but our beast is recognizable as a sadist at the top of the tree as soon as it is established that he does no desk work. This is one of the conventions of the form, which isn't wedded to reality—no important dictators have come to power by unplugging the telephone and stroking a cat.

James Bond himself emerges crisply from a plaster mummy coffin after burial at sea, unpacked from an oxygenated cellophane container in which he lies like frozen food. The influence that he exerts over the picture is as nonchalant as usual. He is still emphatic about things like serving *sake* at 98.4 degrees Fahrenheit. But he seems even less than ever a man to care about; unlike most bang-bang movies, *You Only Live Twice* incites an audience to mind much less about the winner than about winning. Where the heroes of chase pictures and Westerns are people victorious through character, the idol of this picture is really victory itself. It isn't 007 you cheer so much as his success and the brilliant superiority of his hardware. In the same way, the sexuality of the film exists not so much in the girls themselves as in Bond's achievement of getting through as many of them as possible without a pang. His numb leading ladies in the picture, affable sexpots who are killed off at a rate of knots and who could surely be told apart only by their mothers, are subsumed into one long, cool act of painless ditching. One of them is eaten alive, dropped into a private pool of man-eaters through a trick floor that is operated by the villain's foot on a long-distance clutch. Another dies of a drop of poison that slides evilly down a piece of black thread into her sleeping mouth.

Practically every point in the film seems to have to do with gaping jaws, or openings in the earth, or gadgets with trick cavities. Floors suddenly yawn, and the jaws of the villain's whalelike spaceship snap on the rockets of the Cold War as if they were Jonahs. A desk opens up to show an X-ray machine detecting a gun in 007's pocket, a booby trap shoots him down a gullet of stainless steel, and the tyrant's open-plan living area is reached through a hole in the earth-face. The satanic drawing room is in the Bond-baronial style, with a huge fireplace, expensive modern furniture, and the religious Old Masters that murderers like. Hi-fi equipment is apparently somewhere, since the seating arrangements have the particular marooned look of chairs and sofas that are sited the right distance in both directions from hidden speakers. This enlightened room scheme for entertaining and listening, comically wasted on a nutcase who lives alone with a cat in a constant racket of slaughter, is buried deep in the volcano. A cavernous launching pad and sliding roof adjoin it and carry out the lip-and-orifice motif, which is certainly both Freudian and intentional in a Bond picture. Ken Adam's sets for the series are celebrated and deserve it. The launching-pad scene makes a use of scale that gives it a look of one of the Romantic movement's prison engravings, turning the human figure into a pygmy in a towering dungeon of mechanisms.

If one identifies with anyone during the colossal onslaught of neocomic barbarisms, I suppose it is with the cat. The Sean Connery character seems deflated. Once dashing in himself, he has become the instrument of dashing production ideas. Some of the inventions are knockouts, but it would never occur to you that the hero's more stunning technical escapes from trouble could have originated in the head of the character. They obviously come from the director, Lewis Gilbert, and from the Saltzman-Broccoli production alliance that has always given the series its rollicking tone and squashed 007 when he got above himself. The man in the film is beginning to seem oddly inert, his eyes glazed with gadgets, as if this were Christmas morning in a millionaire's house and he a spoiled and lonely child with little flair for fun.

The feat of the series has always been its element of cheery self-parody, which managed to envelop Ian Fleming's brutish fantasizing in something more benign and secretly sensible. The gaggy screenplay for this installment coarsens the style. The earlier films had something genuinely blithe about them, unlike the grinding exhibitionism of the books, and in spite of their own surface sadism; but in *You Only Live Twice* the sense of play keeps getting lost. The most beguiling thing about it is the simple energy expended on bumper surprises.

JUNE 24, 1967

The Silents' Code

If you can bear to be reminded any more of how much funnier and more poetic screen comedy once was, go and see *Thirty Years of Fun*, which is an American anthology job put together by Robert Youngson and including some ravishing Chaplin, Keaton, Harry Langdon, and Charlie Chase. The huckster's commentary is an offense, but never mind. The film excerpts are defiantly stylized, recklessly personal, and marvelously funny. They embody, as instinctively as breathing, the simple principles of how to make people laugh. For instance:

1/Brutality can be funny if it is directed at someone whom we all really agree we must protect, such as children and animals. A covert swipe at a horrible child or someone else's lap dog makes people laugh because we have often only just managed to stop ourselves doing the same thing. Harry Langdon, the chalk-faced, grape-lipped comedian whose cheeks always seemed to be full of boiled sweets and whose eyes were made up like a girl who has been crying, appears here in a very satisfying extract from *Smile, Please* in which a sadistic toddler gets unknowingly thwacked by his own besotted mother.

2/Disproportion is funny: for instance, making an effort that is out of scale with the task, such as a strong man losing his temper with a flea, or Einstein training all his intellect on boiling an egg. In the same way, it is funny when a man behaves stoically in a situation that would throw most people into a fit. Buster Keaton, the most fastidious comedian there has ever been, appears in a sequence in which he is escaping from a horde of policemen and gets stuck on a paddle-steamer wheel that starts to turn. The thing is that, as he walks rapidly round the inside of the wheel, he looks more like a dapper clerk striding to the station, and what he seems mostly bothered about is his hat.

3/Blindness to commonly perceived restrictions is funny. Everyone else knows that a telephone receiver is firmly a telephone receiver; Chaplin thinks it is within an ace of being a trumpet. The alarm clock in the excerpt from *The Pawn Shop* strays off into being a failing heart, a yard of drapery ribbon, and a can of niffy fish. No one has ever made puns with objects like Chaplin.

JULY 7, 1963

FARCE-MAKERS

A Comic Master

I have worshiped Ben Travers' farces ever since I was a schoolgirl. This is a stumbling love note, slipped across the desks under cover of a not very good revival of *Thark*.

Mr. Travers, hero of the prewar Aldwych Theatre, is a comic master. *Thark* itself is a title of genius: better than *Henry IV, Part I*, when it comes down to brass tacks. The world of archetypes that Mr. Travers creates, the browbeaten husbands and dithering fiancés and suspicious, critical matriarchs called Bone or Twine, is mysteriously ripe and timeless. He has an instinctively radical spirit, and his beautiful style can often make you agog with laughter even in bad weekly repertory productions. I wish the National Theatre would do *Rookery Nook*, with Olivier and Robert Stephens; Edith Evans would be stunning as Mrs. Leverett, who is one of the most imperious of Ben Travers' decided servants.

The great thing about his characters is that they have exceptionally fast brains. The lower orders in the Aldwych farces put up with murder very alertly. When Mrs. Leverett is identified by vague young men as "Mrs. Flannelfoot" or "Mrs. Thunderguts" it seems a petrifying impertinence. A butler in *Thark*, a morbid visionary quite properly called Death, has to change his name to Jones to oblige a nervous mistress, but the amendment is obviously as absurd as rechristening Jehovah.

Faced though they are by wage-paying battle-axes and living in an atmosphere of bedroom fluster that they find very offensive, the employees preserve a stoic isolation and tend to become the umpires. They make their positions darkly plain and speak with the tongue of convention. Their verbal mannerisms are elliptical, to put it mildly, but they never have the patronized oddity of, say, chars in West End conventional comedy or Danish *au pair* girls in mechanical Broadway shows. The quirks of Ben Travers' characters are more high-flying than that. Mrs. Leverett, who is given to shooing away an imaginary cat, has some inversions that catch like German measles. "Earlier than that I cannot be," for instance. Or "No." "Yes." "Nein." "Ten." "Finish": this is a typical Ben Travers exchange, with monosyllables bouncing off the sides of meaning like a ball in a squash court.

His typical beset young hero is always very sweet to girls. He calls their dresses "frocks," and worries when the bottom of their satin pajama trousers get wet with dew or when they sit by mistake on a loofah. Sometimes, in a way that is rather like N. F. Simpson, he will get absorbed by the loved one's inner works. Gerald in *Rookery Nook* is suddenly enchanted by the way his girl friend's fingers flop back when he plays with them, "like a piano."

"You dare to come here, crawling upstairs like a balloon. . . ." When they have their backs to the wall, pinned there generally by a middle-aged woman, the male characters talk very strangely. They speak before they think, which is a characteristic of people in farce, and the reason why farce can be played faster than any other form of theater. Speech propels speech, almost without mind intervening. Told reprovingly by a landlady that he doesn't write very clear, Peter in *Cuckoo in the Nest* instantly provides the excuse that he has just had some very thick soup.

Ben Travers men are always floundering suspiciously. The only reason why the women ever neglect to follow up the suspicions is that they regard floundering as man's estate. Whether they are booming dowagers or girls with laughs like cuckoos, the women have minds evilly bent on sexual rumor. Their view is that man was born sinful, even though he may have spent a wretchedly innocent night wrapped around the plumbing of a hotel handbasin. Ralph Lynn has some racked business in a film of *Cuckoo* when he tries like a little dog to scratch a place for himself to sleep. "You call yourself a couch," he says furiously at last. "You're nothing but a *sofa*." When women round on men, men have no one to blame but things.

Ralph Lynn was the great improviser of the original Tom Walls-Robertson Hare company at the Aldwych Theatre before the Second World War. In later revivals he would often direct the cast in the midst of acting, turning away from the audience to clutch the forearm of an actor who had got a laugh to show him how to get another. "Wait for it," he would say; "wait for it; wait for it; *now*." Like all good farce actors, he was exceptionally spry and used to spar round a joke like a boxer. At seventy, he told a young actor in a revival of *Rookery Nook* to go out and buy a skipping rope. He thought it was a good idea to be able to tap-dance; he believed that if an actor gets his footwork right in farce, the rest follows.

Ben Travers made the matching technical discovery about writing. In 1925, he suddenly found that if the words are right, a dramatist can get laughs where a paraphrase with a different rhythm will produce silence. *Cuckoo in the Nest* was written first in 1922 as a not very successful novel; the situations are much the same as in the play, but the style is literary and the comic engine sputters. The fascinating thing about the work at this stage is that it was a vehement tract about middle-class hypocrisy. It is acid about young women who are afraid of public opinion, and murderous about the overbearing Mrs. Bone. ("Waterloo . . . was won at the childbed of a large number of big, haughty, rather contemptuous and absolutely indomitable women.") Three years later, stripped of fury and written like a metronome, the novel became a play and tamed a whole audience of Mrs. Bones at a blow.

Stripped of fury: that was part of it. The disciplines of farce are classical, and the romantic emotions are ruinous to it. The present revival of *Thark* makes the modern mistake of smudging the outlines with neurosis. An Actors Studio version of Ben

Travers doesn't work. The characters have to be absolutely stable and indestructible, or else their situations are too painful to be funny. Ray Cooney, the director, compounds the sentimentality by casting the sarcastic Lady Benbow as a mild charmer; Alec McCowen even tugs the points of her waistcoat, which should be as unthinkable as goosing the Gorgon.

JULY 25, 1965
GUILDFORD, ENGLAND

The Funniest Schoolmaster

George Devine, director of the Royal Court, the theater that mounted N. F. Simpson's two unforgettably titled comedies, *A Resounding Tinkle* and *One Way Pendulum*, speaks with some relish of a Sunday newspaper reporter who recently rang him up and asked for details of Mr. Simpson's eccentricities. Hobbies, clothes, for instance? A quiet schoolmaster who lives in Battersea, not given to hobbies and dressing very like a Battersea schoolmaster, Simpson is not particularly good fuel for this kind of journalism, and the telephone conversation had reached something of a deadlock when George Devine suddenly said, "I'll tell you something that is very eccentric about him." "What?" asked the reporter, alerted. "His plays," said Mr. Devine.

Reporters are ever-hopeful in expecting authors to behave like their characters, and this man was understandably let down to find that Mr. Simpson had no hobby parallel to that of his most recent hero, who attempts to teach speak-your-weight machines to sing. But in Simpson's case the link between the creator and his product is even more tenuous than usual. There can scarcely ever have been a writer more dissociated from his writing. He views it quizzically, sometimes even with suspicion: and when he puts down a funny line he admits that it can make him laugh for hours, as though it had appeared quite autonomously. A yawning chasm separates the man from his work, and the yawn is an apt expression of his cool detachment. His style is the most unheated in the repertory of farce.

Of the many precedents that are to be laid at Mr. Simpson's door, one of the most revolutionary is that he allows his characters to admit the strain involved in being entertaining. They speak often of the silence that has to be held at bay, the curtain that somehow has to be brought down, the audience that incessantly requires placating. The program of the first production of *A Resounding Tinkle* contains a dejected reference to the vista of the centuries ahead, ravenous for entertainment—the author believing himself, "rightly or wrongly, to have heard it said that the earth can support life for another twelve hundred thousand million years. It is the vision of these years (and they will have to be got through somehow) that determines the form and content of his work." This frank declaration of the difficulties that face the playwright is not at all what we are accustomed to. It is also rather un-English, forming one of the differences (there are, er, others) between Simpson and, say, William Douglas Home, who keeps a stiff upper lip throughout the whole exhausting process and sportingly ignores the strain that an audience imposes.

The author's reference in this note to the form of his plays raises a vexing subject. He has struck some critics as being a supplier of the kind of writing that comes by the yard: the piece-goods of comedy rather than the made-up garments, lacking what reviewers generally speak of as "shape." Mr. Simpson has this well in mind. In another program note he gives due warning: "From time to time parts of the play may seem about to become detached from the main body. No attempt, well-intentioned or not, should be made from the auditorium to nudge these back into position while the play is in motion. They will eventually drop off and are quite harmless."

Indeed, far from being oblivious to the question of form, he might even be said to be preoccupied with it, merely avoiding a decision for the moment because he feels that there is so much to be said on both sides. "Sometimes," he told me once, "I'm afraid that form distorts what's essentially amorphous. One's breaking faith with chaos. . . ."

However, shooting a characteristically baleful look at the auditorium, N. F. Simpson has given his next play a stolidly consistent thread. The theme is a rope, and it will hang there throughout the proceedings.

Logic is the essence of Simpson's comedy. Anyone who speaks of nonsequiturs must have a tin ear. What makes it eccentric, if you like, is that logical courses are pursued without the faintest reference to external events. His characters are pre-Dewey creatures, slaves to habits that have never been modified by interaction with their environment. When Simpson read Bergson's line suggesting that "We laugh every time a person gives us the impression of being a thing," he sprang upon it and recognized the voice of an ally. It is funny, in *A Resounding Tinkle*, when Bro Paradock talks like an electronic computer and later apologizes for his deficiencies as a machine by explaining that he was shorting; and funny, in *Pendulum*, when people talk impatiently about an aunt as though she were a piece of furniture ("great old-fashioned thing in the living room"). But N. F. Simpson's characters are also capable of giving devastating imitations of human beings. Bro and Middie Paradock, a married couple who know one another inside out and have long since stopped listening to one another, come dangerously close to expressing an essence of husbands and wives.

The author is wary about people who try to read significance into his plays. "When they start coming to a theater looking for a meaning," he said, dolefully, "you can't tell *what* they'll find." He looks upon meaning as an incidental: as something that may or may not occur as a by-product of seeing a play. (Pressed by a literal-minded theater executive to explain what the title of *One Way Pendulum* meant, he told him that it was just a name, like Simpson, or London. "No, but what does it *mean?*" "Well, it means a pendulum that only goes one way.")

When people start to investigate their reactions in front of Mr. Simpson they are apt to sound like his own parody in *A Resounding Tinkle* of the BBC Critics program. On TV's *Monitor* recently, during some earnest self-analysis by a number of producers who had been to see *One Way Pendulum* as part of a seminar, one of them said to him accusingly, "I laughed nearly all the way through. Was I meant to? Because I also found myself feeling—oddly—yes, disturbed all the way through. Now," triumphantly, "was I meant to do that?"

Ducking the question of meaning and holding on like grim death to the data, perhaps one could say that the root of N. F. Simpson's comic style is the excessive difficulty any two people have in engaging one another. Talking to a whole audience is bad enough, he suggests, but a public of one is almost unmanageable, immediately reducing communication to mere communion. Any duologue might equally well be a handshake, or gibberish: the need for contact is what impels it, nothing more.

To an intellectual, which is what Mr. Simpson is, this is a very funny and rather desperate state of affairs. And to the extent that he inclines his audience to see it this way, too, his unique and intense brand of farce makes intellectuals of us all. As he says, there is nothing particular about being an intellectual: it is just that it happens to be the only way out. After banging away at all those locked doors you are simply relieved when you find that one of them opens.

APRIL 14, 1960
LONDON AND CAMBRIDGE

Feydeau

People who dislike farce will often say that their reason for hating it is that the characters are inhuman, making the form unfunny and frivolous. I think "inhuman" is the wrong word. The people in classic farce—such as Feydeau's *A Flea in Her Ear*, produced with great brilliance by the Comédie-

Française's immaculately witty Jacques Charon—are not so much inhuman as partially human, men with half their characteristics cut away.

Characters in farce undergo the most severe moral stylization in all drama, because everything admirable about humanity is absent in them and everything superficial is uncompromisingly isolated. Far from being responsible for making the form unfunny or frivolous, it seems to me that it is exactly this process that can make farce hilarious and serious.

The character in the middle of the appallingly funny action of *A Flea in Her Ear* is a brisk Parisian bourgeois who has suddenly grown impotent in bed with his wife. If he were a fully described man—if he weren't stylized, but existed instead in something like a drawing-room comedy—this wouldn't be much of a joke. It becomes more tempting to laugh, but no more permissible, when Feydeau establishes that the thing that has put the poor man off is a customs officer, of all sure erotic extinguishers—a figure in a play that he thinks of constantly, in which a seduction scene was wrecked by an official who burst in saying, "Anything to declare?"

But the fact that really makes it possible to laugh is that the character's violent feelings are not about sex but about etiquette and face. Albert Finney gives a very funny account of the man, with everything but brisk expediency disciplined out of it. He also doubles as a slow-witted hotel houseboy who gets intricately mistaken for the anxious bourgeois; facing an English theater full of born class-experts, it is a difficult thing to bring off.

The houseboy is incessantly victimized and bawled at, but nothing shakes him. Like all figures in farce his self-esteem is impregnable. In the stylizing process his capacity for pain has been cut away. Another character achieves the unlikely task of making a cleft palate hysterically funny for exactly the same reason; unlike many afflicted men, he luckily has no idea of the way other people see him. To his own loving mind he is a perfect enunciator and it is other people's ears that need cleaning out. "I' a bi' thi' " he complains sourly, in circumstances that are indeed a bit thick.

In the meantime the world tells him, with vintage heartlessness, not to talk with his mouth full.

Edward Hardwicke plays the mumbler with great charm and no neurosis at all. When he suddenly loses his false teeth he dives after them in a mood of mere pooh-poohing irritability, like a man chasing a lost bowler in a high wind. He is never mortified by his affliction; he is only huffy. Seventy-five per cent of the action of farce springs from huffiness. The rest comes from panic and architecture. The architecture in this particular farce, designed by André Levasseur with a pristine sense of the taste of the square but doggish in the 1900s, has an alibi hotel bed that can be swung round in crisis to present an identical bed on the other side of the wall with a bitterly nonadulterous old man in it.

Someone in the play says that men and women are the only two of God's creatures who lie. As far as farce is concerned, an even more crucial characteristic about us is that we are the only two of God's creatures who possess the evil gift of suspecting lying in others. The agent of the action of this play, which is mechanically perfect, is the sniffy nose for fibs possessed by the hero's wife, a redhead in a tabby boa played with electric attack and funniness by Geraldine McEwan. I think she may have based some of her performance on Groucho Marx. She has the same "aha!" head movement, describing an arc like a lobbed tennis ball; her eyes swivel lewdly from side to side, sometimes narrowing as though over a particularly rough cigar. The effect in a pretty woman is very funny. It is the best female performance in farce that I have seen in England.

It isn't really lechery that gets the characters into trouble, because they never feel any emotion so conscious as lechery is of anyone else. Their undoing is their disastrous mixture of rock-hard vanity and jelly fluster. The two vainest lovers in the play are non-French, perhaps because Feydeau anticipated the difficulty of getting a French audience to see anything funny in Frenchmen's being sexually proud of themselves. One of the butts is German, naturally; the other is a jealous husband called Carlos Homenides de Histuanga, who is played by Frank Wylie with an exquisite Spanish lisp, sucking in lurid cheeks below lilac-rimmed eyes and dragging his toes as though to the applause of a crowd in a bullring when threatening *crimes passionnels*. He is suspicious on principle, even about a doctor who has only carried out a test on him: "Why did he make me pith?" he yells, ready to kill.

The passions in the play are all like this. They are the passions of throwing down dueling-cards, steaming open letters, snubbing invitations; the play is like a deckle-edged Greek tragedy with an R.S.V.P. at the end of it, and this is exactly the note that John Mortimer's social ear catches so funnily in the translation. "I am ready to commit a folly," writes a lady character graciously on scented paper. "Will you join me?"

FEBRUARY 13, 1966
LONDON

There is a verb that should perhaps exist in English and French: the verb "to trouse," meaning to set into action a farce. That which so acts is a trouser. *Le drame trousera:* they are about to be let down by their trousers. *Il se trousa:* he went and trousled himself. One of Feydeau's nippiest works about the bottom half of men's clothing, *The Birdwatcher* (1892), is now to be seen in a good English translation by the director, Richard Cottrell. You should go and see it not only for the incomparable trousing, but also for a blissfully funny performance by Michael Bates as a doctor who writes swelling verse in his spare time and shouldn't be caught in his long underwear, which he is, in a hundred years. Sometimes he leans against an invisible tree like a horse rubbing flies off itself, or quotes a dreadful line while he is on his way out of the door to get some champagne for an irredeemably prosaic married woman. "Oh, poetry," says Prunella Scales, "that is nice"; like "Oh, cocoa."

Physically Mr. Bates's performance is spruce and bouncing. When his wretchedly wronged and debagged frame has been used to propel a new bout of plot, it bounds up into position again like the figure of a footballer in a pinball machine. In emergencies, which is to say in underclothes, he dances as though the world were scalding the soles of his feet. He expresses an exquisite confusion between the proprieties of a brisk GP and the proprieties of a rotten poet, having hygienic principles for other people about not making a fuss but also upholding his own right to a good wallow in self-pity.

Such an overriding sense of propriety is the key of farce. Where tragic characters feel pain, farcical characters in very much the same extremities will merely feel offense. Often they have to endure professional ruin as final as the Macbeths'; they may well also be cursed with the family of a Lear and the ill-luck of an Oedipus, whose life-long capacity to be in the wrong place with the wrong information at the wrong moment would have equipped him to do very well in farce. But in spite of all this, farcical characters suffer nothing. Like the heroes of antique tragedy, they submit to a hostile fate; but they submit without insight, and it is a fate at the level of etiquette. The characters in *The Birdwatcher* feel only social humiliation, not a sense of damage to life, and when the long arm of coincidence smites them it is only the leg of an incriminating pair of trousers.

JANUARY 16, 1966
LONDON

When Farce Boils Over

Farce traditionally depends upon order and the existence of a set of widely shared assumptions. French bedroom farce came out of an attitude to wives and mistresses that was as systematized as a theology. English farce before the war was rooted in a middle class which agreed that the Church of England was serious (making a parson without his trousers funny), and that any decent Englishman locked in a hotel bedroom with a girl would keep in his monocle and sleep under the washstand.

Since then the atom has been split, but conventional farce still assumes cohesion. The archetypal Whitehall Theatre farces, for instance, take it for granted their audiences are firm in agreeing that modern art and homosexuals are funny. The new genre of expense-account farce represented by *Diplomatic Baggage*, which distills a carefully judged mixture of saloon-bar bragging about sex and the most intimidated conventionalism about it, is addressed to the standard that infidelity doesn't count as long as it's on a trip for the firm.

Henry Livings' *Eh?* is the first anarchistic farce. It is a bold, wild attempt to reflect our disorder and stop pretending that anything is stable in the flux; the result is turbulently funny. The only conventional element of farce that the author has allowed himself is a door. He said on the radio last week that farce is impossible without doors: in an earlier play called *Nil Carborundum* he wrested more out of a lavatory door than Feydeau could have dreamed of. The device in *Eh?* has been pared down, which is to say that the door has no walls round it. It has a comic function rather like a recurring gag about a man who can never get beyond the first sentence of a story: it emits a cut-off burst of industrial bottled music every time it opens.

The room it gives on to is not a bedroom but a boiler room, which John Bury has filled with a grunting brontosaural structure of ovens and funnels and sprockets. The monster needs a keeper, to sit in front of it on a green swivel chair and turn a knob every four hours; the man who applies for the job, marvelously played by David Warner, is a hunched, combative, apprehensive eccentric who wears a brown swallow-tail coat and chestnut-colored boots with black Cuban heels. Mr. Warner in this play looks vaguely eight feet tall, with a length of arm that seems curiously arbitrary, and he has apparently left the wardrobe-rail inside his coat shoulders. He is constantly surprised by the turns he takes, and blows sometimes into his checks so that they pulse like the throat of a frog.

Conventional farce depends on nonstop activity. What happens in a society that is trying to *eliminate* activity? Valentine Brose in *Eh?*, fighting off the horrors of lethargy in a world fit for boilers, attempts to people the void by growing mushrooms in the throbbing cellar and then by moving his new wife covertly into the bottom bunk, which very nearly ends in boiled bride. The scene when she is hiding from the works manager and hopping shoeless across the sizzling boiler is as funny as Keaton's *The Navigator;* there are a lot of things in Peter Hall's production that are very like a film.

The works manager, who is played with a hissing head of steam by Donald Sinden, is a hysteric driven mad by the way life cannot be contained. He is a man fixed at the moment of infant fury when we discover that the external world exists and can defeat us. It is no good trying to interpret the character as anything so generalized and definable as an archetype of trade unionism, any more than the Brenda Bruce character can be made to symbolize psychiatry just because she tells Valentine Brose he is a schizophrenic: people's speech and uniforms in this farce belie their nature.

Nicholas Selby plays a clergyman but he has the most incongruous relationship with his dog collar, dissolving often into a Rugger blue or a visionary atheist. In the second act, he has a colossal pagan speech about dragons that is the center of gravity around which the flying chips of the play revolve. Men invented dragons where reality provided nothing worse than lizards; by the same process, the machines made for mankind's ease by our clever and constructive talents are turned by our insensible and chaotic genius into objects of mythic fear.

Eh? is about a world of Protean men who are possessed by maverick impulses and sometimes almost obliterated by their own surprising vocabulary. The play makes the entirely modern observation that words can often precede meanings and touch off feelings instead of following them; the arguments in it follow a pattern as formal as a fugue with people getting engrossed by someone else's keynote and taking it over so that the lines of the quarrel merge and change sides. The confusing action reflects the combats pent up in our skulls, where we are simultaneously lords and convicts in solitary. I'm not surprised that the gallery booed for something more comforting.

NOVEMBER 1, 1964
LONDON

Power-Cut Laughter

There must be somewhere dark backstage at Chichester, an airing cupboard or a coal hole perhaps, where the actors withdraw for five minutes to train their eyes before they come on. They play the opening of Peter Shaffer's *Black Comedy* in what seems to be total murk, commenting cheerfully on colors and skimming invisibly around an arena that we know to be clogged with furniture; it must take very well-adjusted irises to do it.

Then the lights snap on, and the characters are immediately floundering in a power cut. The idea is an alert swipe from a Peking Opera sketch in which a duel is fought in a dark room that we see as brightly lit; it is a brilliant supposition for a farce, a plotful of mistaken identities at a stroke. Derek Jacobi, as a sculptor expecting a visit from a millionaire collector, tests the floor with little pats of his outstretched leg like a crab on a rock. Louise Purnell as his debbie girl, who keeps her high heels on—isn't one's first instinct in the dark to take them off?—walks about with her wrists braced against the air as though it were the door of a strong room.

Children have a repertory of horrible games based on the situation of watching the deluded displays of people who can't see: making someone jump off a stool that he thinks to be ten feet high, for instance, or guiding his finger into a tomato and telling him it is Nelson's eyeball, or getting him to follow their finger movements and methodically transform his own face with a make-up of soot. John Dexter's production goes out of its way not to indulge the mirthless savagery of childhood, and thank goodness for that. But there is something else in all games with darkness that might have been developed here, something hallucinatory and out of joint that could have made the play much more startling and touching than it is about people whose usual links with one another have suddenly become damaged and suspect. *Black Comedy* would have lost no comedy if it had had the nerve to be more black; as it is, the play seems a blinding idea not very boldly pursued.

There is a sign of its bland temperament in the fact that the physical techniques eliminate the sick fear implicit in moving in the dark. Graham Crowden, as the deb's father, sits down in a chair that he expects to be steady but which has been replaced for plot reasons by a rocker that pitches him backward onto his skull: he doesn't huddle on the ground trying to reorder a world gone mad, he gets up again.

As one watches the actors resourcefully chugging and reversing around Alan Tagg's set, which is full of a mixture of the sculptor's own orange-box furniture and some camp tat lifted from a neighbor's flat, the spectacle is as affable as those electronic robots that are trained to draw back when they hit something and then to compute where to go next. The characters very seldom do anything arrestingly human in the dark; they don't yawn in a lover's face, for instance, or smell themselves, or stroke their own limbs for reassurance, or say something with an expression that they haven't bothered to match to the remark.

It is visibly a production that could do with months of improvising rehearsal. The actor who has driven furthest so far is Albert Finney as the queer neighbor. His movements and expressions elaborate a reaction to the dark that is absolutely particular. The power cut doesn't befuddle him, as it does the mild old body played by Doris Hare, who mopily takes to the gin in her blindness; it doesn't sting him into risky truth games, like the ex-mistress played by Maggie Smith: it simply makes him cross. Another of life's charming little tricks, he thinks acidly, blinking at people a foot off target, one hand indenting his lovely waist and one knee bridling against the other leg. His limbs are very funny, and furious. So are Maggie Smith's curling gorilla toes before she swings into an inspired bitch's invention in the voice of an imaginary daily who reports that the deb, Maggie Smith's replacement, is at the bottom of the young master's heap. The engine of the plot is at its best here. The opportunity to cause chaos and the awry mood to do it both zoom beautifully out of the given situation of being in the dark. Doris Hare has a sloshed outburst similarly born, a very funny explosion generated by ten minutes of lonely brooding about the assistants who won't assist in supermarkets.

AUGUST 1, 1965
CHICHESTER

Birth-Pill Farce

In *Prudence and the Pill*, Deborah Kerr and David Niven play one of those stylized English couples who dine in full evening dress every night even when alone, meeting without a word at the top of a socking great circular stairway to go down to a dinner served by a maid who belongs to some pre-1914 *Punch* cartoon. I think she may have said "Lawks!" at some moment between courses when I had passed out. She is, of course, in tears, and pregnant. By the chauffeur. The chauffeur tells the Master about it in a blissfully foreign idea of Cockney servitude while they are driving somewhere green in the Rolls. The Master's mistress also gets pregnant, by the Master. So does his wife, by a racy Harley Street specialist, played by Keith Michell. So does Joyce Redman, as the nice middle-class mother of a nasty libertarian daughter, who doesn't. This layabout is the *only* one who doesn't. Pregnancy is the total joke of the film. It is achieved by a fearfully complicated web of viciousness in which everyone in turn secretly substitutes vitamins or aspirin for other people's supply of the Pill, for varying gormless or Machiavellian purposes.

I suppose *Prudence and the Pill*—I am afraid Prudence is the name of the heroine—is classifiable as a farce depended on two givens: (1) a period of manners that regarded adultery as beyond the Pale, and (2) a period of architecture that provided a lot of doors. In our time, the Anglo-Saxon's bedroom film-farce apparently rests on (1) a period of conventionalism when adultery is suddenly quite OK as long as it is blessed by children and consummated by previous divorce and remarriage, and (2) a period of medicine that provides a lot of different pills. By a hairsbreadth, *Prudence* is even more retarded and leery than *Yours, Mine and Ours*, and having inadvertent babies is again the single recurring plot twist. This may be a trend. The evidence is starting to pile up. I remember at least two awful stage comedies in the last couple of years that had the same central deadening comic idea, about birth-control slip-ups among the privileged and middle-aged. Leaving aside their sentiments, their lack of humor can be concussing. The experience of *Prudence and the Pill* is like being kicked in the forehead by a cart horse.

Commercial English-speaking sex comedies have never been exactly truthful in their notions of human intimacy, let alone open-spirited, but at least there was a time when they were funny. In the present dog days of coyness and vacuity it is hard to remember it, but television revivals bring back the lost period. Those were the days when "hostess" still meant someone you visited, not a paid dolly on a plane or a high-class manageress controlling a restaurant queue. The films I'm thinking of generally had a key scene in which the heroine wore the top half of the hero's pajamas and the hero the bottom half. The circumstances were always entirely chaste, but the dialogue was often rather sophisticated, and there was a sense that everyone involved, including the audience, understood everyone else to know a lot more than he let on. All this has changed. For one thing, the equivalent films now aren't funny. For another, they emit the strongest impression that they regard the mass sitting there in the theater as doltish. Most contemporary sex comedies seem to have grown up with their heads inside Beverly Hills shopping bags.

Some insane interest made me go to see a thing called *Yours, Mine and Ours*. Apart from being so maudlin that it sticks to your fingers, this object labeled a sex comedy reaches peaks previously unscaled in nonsexiness and noncomedy. I took it to be an aberration. Nothing like it could ever happen again, I thought, coming out into the comparative cheer and sensuality of the Times Square of cut-price radio shops. The gag of the picture was about having a colossal number of children and then making another gurgling little mistake in blue or pink, I forget which, at an age that is supposed to be hysterical. Lucille Ball and Henry Fonda played characters with about a hundred and seven kids between them, and then they adopted one another's children, and then they jointly produced a wee surprise. This was the whole thing. I had a moment when I wondered if it could possibly imply that unplanned parenthood in the age of the birth-control pill was going to be Hollywood's new genius stroke of farce about sex. But then the fear passed and I buried the hatchet, and went back to remembering Katharine Hepburn and Cary Grant.

JANUARY 22, 1968

Feydeau, Move Over

Farce is on its back and groaning. And in the meantime some pretender is up there instead, getting obedient audiences to laugh as if it were the real thing. One used to have a fine, silly time watching complicated troubles and strategies developing from small events among people whose wits were keenly bent on survival with honor—watching men skidding in and out through hotel-bedroom doors, and pretty girls skedaddling up chimneys, and highly intelligent people in minute but knotty social situations where they would invent brilliant solutions to do with, say, the whereabouts of a dowager aunt's prize heifer, or improvise alibis as eternally useful as Oscar Wilde's Bunbury. The attention to detail mattered. In the new farces, the casualness of the characters is a great hurdle. It is hard now to find a hero with his mind on things. The director simply cuts away at the height of any dilemma, and the laughs peter out.

In the old, strict sense, farce was the obverse of tragedy. In the new sense—the sense of Robert Downey's *Pound* and Theodore J. Flicker's *Up in the Cellar*—farce actually *depends* on an aura of public calamity. If one were to remove from these two new films the underlying apocalyptic assumptions that America has gone to the dogs and is about to blow up—the same received idea that foreign newspapers habitually gloat over when there is a cloud of U.S. air pollution, or a prison riot—both would collapse. They rest on an expectation of catastrophe, and they look for custom to an audience that will laugh at the mere sight of President Nixon's face. They rely on a joky complicity between film and audience—no persuading is ever done—and on the instant, thoughtless, and so not even truly pessimistic notion that society is beyond redeeming: that modern universities have regressed to a new Dark Age of computers, that all talk is now mechanized into cliché, and that all human beings are dehumanized. This is push-button Swift. It lacks the rancor to ask for better, because it has no idea of things as they might be otherwise. I take it that an implicit insistence on the existence of an option is satire's force. What we have here instead is something determinist and flaccid. When George Grosz drew the people of Berlin between the wars and gave them the looks and mannerisms of the monstrous—drew overfed magnates with backs of the neck like wads of rolled chequebooks, and skunk-snouted women carrying pampered little dogs that look more fragile and more sympathetic than their owners—there would have been no great moral weight in the monstrousness unless the style of the draftsmanship had powerfully convinced you that Grosz could easily have evoked the sweeter order from which his avid grotesques had strayed. The brutality shown in Picasso's "Guernica" is a picture of grace withdrawn that simultaneously states, as clearly as the line in *Coriolanus*, that there is a world elsewhere. In the same way, a Hogarth drawing of languid, unread nobs showing off in a library in front of more alert-looking maids tells us that the wrong people sometimes have the leisure and that they don't necessarily, as their underdogs might, use it to find anything out.

If one is going to raise gasps and laughs from disproportion or aberration, one needs a strong hold on what things have wandered from. Robert Downey's *Pound* is about a lot of animals who are played by people and who represent the bestial pass that people have come to. They are waiting passively in a pound for rescue or for extinction. The trouble is that the film gives you the feeling that these animal sketches reach about to the limit of Downey's ability to evoke the recognizably human. The cast includes a Sheepdog, an Airedale, a Mexican Hairless, a Pointer, a Setter, a Mutt Bitch; none of them much remind you either of people or of animals you might know. Their keeper is a large Negro policewoman in a miniskirted uniform who welcomes them to the pound with a curtsy. The film—plotless, as anything with satiric intent now conventionally is—goes in fits and starts, like a walker spasmodically halted by an attack of sneezing. There is a parody of a Noël Coward love scene, a parody of some bygone type of soprano warbling "That Old Black Magic" to a listening black, a gag about potheads who are on McLuhan ("Nobody's into words any more, you fool"), and even, typically, a jibe about the film itself, when a Chinese complains to thin air that there isn't an original thinker in the whole joint.

The film's theme, it begins to seem, is not so much the moral hideousness of our species as the sorry lag of most of us behind the physical standards of a Miss Rheingold. For instance, a song will tell us that "lonely people are the ugliest in the world," in Downey's particular tone of a man who is about to knock you over and crack up with laughter, and the idle dislike of human rack and ruin will even begin to seem more or less meant when we have so often been shown the characters' faces craning up at us through distorting lenses that vilely squash and widen their features, like silk stockings pulled over the faces of criminals. The only apparent reason the proper murder of the lonely and the ugly hasn't come to pass is that the supply of gas to eliminate them isn't working. (There is a visual reference to showers producing jets of gas which couldn't have been made, I think, if anyone to do with the film cared much about Hitler.)

But now and again—and this is where Robert Downey's throwaway films are always booby-trapped—there is a ten-second spurt of plain, far-gone, inspired funniness. There is a pleasing character played by Elsie Downey, a helpful, Naugahyde-faced woman in a hat, who will graciously introduce herself as a Socialist and ask if there is anything she can do for anyone; she speaks like a hospital's lady almoner, though from behind bars. And one grows fond of a character played by Harry Rigby, a gentle-faced chevalier who seems rather at odds in the bestiary and who asks what he's doing here, since he's a penguin? He has, in fact, a little of a penguin's temperament, trotting about to white-tie parties in a sad, sweet-natured way and trying mildly to smooth things out. But in another mood *Pound* has a scene about a black character in prison who is having a nightmare of not being able to get through to the New York telephone operator; this is the sort of lapse when the film gets very close to the most knowing and middlebrow and numb sort of old revue, even if it has come up from underground. Most of the other things about the movie that are not good have to do with lack of rhythm. The director doesn't seem to be able to pace jokes, or shots, or pauses. The wrong moments are allowed to run on, and the wrong moments clipped. The picture is sometimes like a tune on a harmonium that is being pumped by a drunken toddler.

To be fair, it is exactly this atmosphere of jolly, energetic, pie-eyed muddle that sometimes makes the picture funny, but it does sabotage any sense that the director has things under control. One gets the feeling, as one often does watching these straining, punch-drunk new farcical satires, that the film is somehow muscle-bound and too big for the furniture. The new film surrealists (the outasight ones) can make you suddenly think of a very large, strong, cheery wrestler, with thumbs the size of most people's wrists, trying with all his might to thread a needle. The biceps bulge; the effort is visible, massive, Atlas's; but the thread doesn't go through the eye. Flicker's *Up in the Cellar* is like this. It is one of those campus farces that are just as common now, and just as deeply absorbed in a nourished sort of schoolboyish blackguardism, as shocking melodramas about prostitution were in the Victorian Nineties. The hero of the film, a flop-spined lad, is furious because a computer has decided that he doesn't deserve a poetry scholarship. There seems no reason for us not to agree with the computer, but these are dissident days, so we dissent for the sake of peace. The hero himself dissents so much that he climbs up a radio tower dedicated to the ambitious college president so as to throw himself off it and kill himself (kill himself "relevantly," I expect). He has already tried to commit suicide once, but he took a laxative instead of sleeping pills. The mistake has given a wealthy fellow student the idea of creating a martyr out of him. This leads us, as you foresaw, to satirical jokes about the media making capital out of student protest, which is quite a dicey position for a commercial film to be in, but still. We also get Nixon-family jokes—the college president makes television appearances supported by a wife-and-daughter team whose nearly identical clothes and stately come-ons would probably be funny enough in revue—and there is a rather dim theme about myths of black sexuality, with the college president's black mistress turning out not to be able to cope with the hero because "three hundred years of black love have made people expect too much." The president's wife (Joan Collins) is an astrology nut who likewise lands up in bed with the hero. She is dazed with the high excitement of horoscopes and not greatly moved by the boy, who is characterized as the overmothered, glassy-eyed trudger who seems to have been at the center of sophisticated film, stage, and literary farce for ages. Nicely played by Wes Stern, the character has a career of unexampled disgruntledness, masked by the opiate face and the mock-schoolboy, aghast grin that have been worn uniformly by the young heroes of protest movies for quite a while. Farces like these specialize in "going too far," and they invite people to call them too much, but perhaps they're nothing like enough.

AUGUST 29, 1970

SCAMPS

Leading Back to Renoir

Arthur Penn's *Alice's Restaurant*, with Arlo Guthrie playing himself, comes from Guthrie's beautiful best-selling ballad, the talking-blues story called "The Alice's Restaurant Massacree." The film has the comic mood of the song, which is wry, light, staunch, and sweetly ironic about an America that rains blows on the heads of its dissenting young and also says that they can have the world. (Song: "You can get anything you want, at Alice's Restaurant. Exceptin' Alice.") The Arlo of the film is one of the gentle middle-class radicals who seem to be changing America. To avoid the draft, he first thumbs a ride to "an institution of higher learning." But higher learning disappoints him—or the institution does, maybe—and he leaves it, staring the draft in the eye, for a cheerful communal life led by Alice (Pat Quinn), which is going on mostly in a deconsecrated church. Perhaps only people living in America now will be able to recognize his precise social background. It is rather important. His hippie clothes and his swinging locks of hair might give the wrong clues. Arlo's peculiar mood, mixing an imperishable sense of farce and a docile obduracy, is moving because it is a matter of choice. When he says no, he has other options. He has the money to take himself off to his institution of higher learning, and he leaves it again in the full knowledge of what will happen next. He comes not from a ghetto full of rats but from a middling-well-off family with its own private troubles. His father is ill with a disease that Arlo, in a single line spoken through a car window, shows himself to be very frightened of inheriting. Earlier, after seeing the fine-faced old man in hospital, he has spoken alone to his mother: "He's got a lot worse since I saw him." "Well, let's say no better," she answers. The incident is unemphatic, as the ballad would have made it. It comes piercingly in the narrative line of the film, which continues with a hippie gathering in the deconsecrated church on Thanksgiving Day and a feast with Alice, a soft-voiced woman who dispenses a welcome to anyone coming up the aisle. Ray (James Broderick), her older, coachman-faced husband, likes dressing up as a squire of other times and has a core of secret fierce nostalgias, like a Russian.

The Thanksgiving gang do what they can to say thank you for Alice's trouble, in a mood of comic housewifery. ("We decided it would be a friendly gesture to take the garbage to the city dump.") Her garbage. But from then on officialdom is more and more befuddling. The dump pompously says of itself that it is "Closed on Thanksgiving Day." ("We had never heard of a dump closed on Thanksgivin' before, and with tears in our eyes we drove off into the sunset.") The gang carts the garbage to another possible place and offloads it onto a suggestive-looking small start of a pile of junk, casually including an envelope addressed to Arlo. The merry slip of identification brings revenge, and the law descends. A charmingly portrayed cop called Officer Obie (William Obanhein) goes doggedly after a conviction for littering. He behaves as if he were on to a major crime. The stinking dell of old cans begins to buzz with solemn doings. Aerial photographs are taken. Police dogs snoop. Cubic areas of garbage are measured, and Arlo is hauled off to the night clink. ("I don't think I can pick up the garbage with these handcuffs on.") Officer Obie finally fails to get the conviction he has trudged after. There is a shot of a blind judge walking out of the courtroom with his dog after imposing a minimal fine, and following it the sight of Obie's dignity, crumbled. I can't think of a more endearingly shown cop-enemy in the American cinema.

Then the foreseen happens and Arlo has to go for his physical.

The draft-board scenes are a slapstick routine of cheated urine tests and hollow psychiatric catechisms. Because of his littering offense, Arlo is clapped into a room of inductees labeled Group W—benches of father-murderers and mother-rapers, fingering jackknives and despising a mere garbage offender. After this farce sequence—the film has been very beautifully cut, by Dede Allen—the picture goes into its last stages, which are full of a pagan sobriety that seems to belong uniquely to the hippies. There is a strange funeral scene for one of the gang, held in a snowstorm while a girl whose nose is red with cold sings "Songs to Aging Children." And then Alice and Ray marry again, at a better, hippie wedding, with flowers and festivity, unlike their previous one, which was dull and at a JP's office; and when the young hippies decently leave them alone together they get sad, because they wanted to live in a family free of departures, like the people on some huge, warring Russian estate where old friends might quarrel over pickled cucumbers and at the same time find one another indispensable. *Alice's Restaurant* is a purely conceived film, clownish and sad, beautifully put together, with a haunting affection for the American face which reminded me of the shot of the Midwestern mother's expression in Penn's *Bonnie and Clyde* as she stood in the middle of the dust bowl after a picnic and told the two romantics that they weren't going to be seeing her soon at all, that they were going to have to keep running.

SEPTEMBER 6, 1969

Bedbound

A man who stays in bed because he can't for the life of him construct a convincing argument for getting up is a natural comic character. The prone hero of *Oblomov*, on stage between the sheets in a halting adaptation by Riccardo Aragno of Goncharov's novel, is a tsarist absentee landlord who belongs as much to the bothered world of the great clowns as he does to mid-nineteenth-century Russia.

Comic heroes are always being ambushed by the kind of primary questions that everyone else negotiates without trouble. Most of the world successfully get dressed every morning, for instance, but these men are people quite liable to be fatally waylaid by the ambiguities of a hook and eye. Oblomov is beset by a kind of self-tripping mechanism that our period understands very well: it is sometimes much like the difficulties of the men in Kingsley Amis's novels. He has tried getting up in the past but sees no reason to go on with it. He lies instead under a fur rug, visited by racked sophisticated friends who rightly strike him as no testimonial for the life of those on their feet, and twitches with awkward thoughts that Spike Milligan delivers in a mild and roving mutter, like a child talking to itself in a cot. Why go out? Why, in particular, go abroad? Why be polite, when being rude might save you from having to listen to a rotten pianist? Why get married, when marriage brings not one woman into the house but a whole trade union of them, housekeepers and hairdressers and *relations?* Why stand a servant who is a reeking idiot?

The performance hasn't, of course, anything remotely to do with Russia. The only one that has in the whole production is Bill Owen's as the reeking idiot, wearing a distraught Neptune wig and a soldier's coat that looks as though it had trudged here from the Napoleonic wars. He keeps the house scrupulously undusted, and pays no attention when Spike Milligan softly complains out of nowhere that last night there were "mices galloping around upstairs." When the bearded Goon has to switch off and play anything like the love sequences with Joan Greenwood, there is a collision of styles because the nearest he can get to acting —unlike her—is a swift cod of an emotion as though he were posing it for a tableau or a joke period-photograph. He also, because he can't help it, eliminates one of the most powerful and serious elements of Goncharov's original character, which is the fear that a genuinely apathetic man can strike in other people.

But I don't think that any of this would have mattered if the adaptation and the production had had a firmer hand on what is satiric and theatrical in the book.

The implications of a man who has decided not to get up aren't only funny. They are also naturally scathing, because it is quite a privileged decision to be able to make. Goncharov was not a radical man politically; all the same, his hero still embodies the sharp comment that only the best-heeled neurotic is able to feel about indulgent torment. The author apparently sensed that his book would have little chance of publication during the reign of a man like Nicholas I, who controlled a regime that, in the words of an unusually liberal censor, "transformed the censorship department into a police station where ideas were treated like thieves and drunkards," for he delayed finishing it until Alexander II came to the throne.

After all, it isn't every hero who has the income and the servant necessary to allow him not to have to get up, not even a servant as hopeless and abusive as Oblomov's Zakhar, who squats absently on his master's bed with the coal scuttle and habitually insults him when he is asleep. Zakhar is a kind of servant who seems to be peculiar to Russian nineteenth-century literature, a grumbling blood brother of Chekhov's Firs, exploited and exhausted, but at the same time immovably embedded into his employer's life and uniquely outspoken about it. The relationship between him and Oblomov loses 90 per cent of its force here; the scenes between them still work better than anything else in the play, though, partly because they consist not of duologues, which the adapter can't write, but of dialogue more like two monologues laminated. Frank Dunlop's production is frail and tripping, hopelessly at odds with the rogue genius of Milligan and not seizing on much of the natural theatrical imagery of the book.

OCTOBER 11, 1964
LONDON

When the curtain went up on *Son of Oblomov* there were mutinous mutterings from under the great fur rug. "Same old bed," said Spike Milligan faintly. Well, not quite the same: not if you saw *Oblomov* as it started. In Milligan's transfiguring wreck of the original the bed has moved over a bit to the prompt side in the first scene. "Same old audience," the grumbler under the bedclothes goes on, bracing himself to be an actor and start the play.

Son of Oblomov takes a rebellious technical decision. It acknowledges freely that an audience is present, lodged in a different time scale to the play and with a limitless capacity for boredom smoldering below its hungry belt; it also states that the actor is not the character but a paid workman trying to look natural under a load of someone else's lines. By this dazzling flash of the obvious, the evening becomes helplessly funny and the most liberating theatrical experience in London.

The candor is all Milligan's. Acknowledging the obvious is the art of his comedy. He does it because he isn't capable of anything else, and the trouble with his original Oblomov was that he tried too hard, lying down obediently in the satin-lined casket of Riccardo Aragno's adaptation and attempting to pretend it was natural to be embalmed.

In *Son of Oblomov* they have let him rip. The *Son* springs not really from Goncharov's near-masterpiece of a novel, and certainly not from the Aragno adaptation, but from Spike Milligan's perpetual awareness that here are the three of us in our three corners: the actor, the play, and the audience. He points out implicitly that we have three quite separate kinds of existence: a man at work, much more observant of play and audience that anyone thinks; a work of art; and a body of wary ostriches who believe themselves to be invisible. It is out of this battling triangle that theater emerges, and the important thing about *Son of Oblomov* is that it gooses all three into a much more dynamic life, including the ostriches.

In a commercial theater now this is something of a revolution, in spite of Brecht influences outside it. The usual pretense is still that the audience doesn't exist and that the actor and his role are one, making total identification the most generally admired kind of acting. (This is what Ionesco once said exasperated him about the theater. He found the sight of an actor weeping real tears unbearable.) Pretense has nothing to do with the theater's useful apparatus of illusions; it has more to do with prudery, and we passionately need to be rid of it. We have drifted further than we think from the mainstream of the theater, Greek and Shakespearean and Restoration, in which it was natural for actors to detach themselves from their roles and recognize the audience. Watching most plays now is like watching TV. It happens behind glass. Have a choc, they can't hear. Try a toffee crunch.

Spike Milligan *can* hear. He practically puts the audience through an audition. He can also hear all too clearly that a lot of the dialogue in the original script sounds about as human as a mouthful of grinning orange peel. Joan Greenwood has to mime-play a harpsichord, the audience as usual secretly watching like a hawk to see how well she matches her hands to the record in the wings: "I don't know why, Olga, but you played tonight as you never played before," says an admirer. On the opening night, this line hit the Goon like a ripe plum. "With the lid up," he commented softly.

The original *Oblomov* was dubiously asserted to be happening in Russia; *Son of Oblomov* states firmly that it is set in Russia and the Comedy Theatre. Milligan/Oblomov lives in bed in a house where the windows are washed on the inside only, "so that we can see out, folks, and they can't see in." He is attended by Bill Owen as his servant Zakhar, a loving dolt so lazy that he does the master's hair by holding the comb in a rock-still stupor while Milligan leaps up and down against it.

Russian friends periodically come in to try to persuade the idler to get up; or, if you see it the other way, actors come on to tussle with the lines and lock horns with the rearing Goon imagination, which spies double meanings and two kinds of reality going on day and night. "Why do you waste your time with that financial leech?" says an actor in character. "Well," says Spike, out of one, "he's in the play, and he's cheap."

Only a man racked by the real self-questioning genius of a great comic actor could throw so much into doubt, boot through so much fabric, and make you feel sure that his kind of chaos is closer to the truth than the ordered literary quadrilles that often pass for serious theater. The feat of Milligan in *Son of Oblomov* is that he constantly makes it possible to admit things that are usually covered up. A lot of the mincing production-clichés and spinsterish writing that still clutter our stage survive only because we don't care to call them hollow: but what are we protecting? Ourselves? What from? The embarrassment of the frank? Isn't it really more embarrassing to watch inhibited stagehands dressed up as flunkies moving the scenery, which was the convention of the original production, than to see Milligan solicitously leaping to a gauze in trouble? The theater is full of hiatuses that everyone politely ignores, but he can see a hiatus coming and seize it like a weapon, converting it with the same punning inspiration as the minute when he is offered two French rolls and says eagerly, holding them to his eyes: "Ah! Roast binoculars!"

DECEMBER 6, 1964
LONDON

The Divan Comedy

Only Two Can Play is based on Kingsley Amis's *That Uncertain Feeling* and scripted by Bryan Forbes in solid sympathy with the idiom of the book. It has the funniest script since the heyday of Ealing. In the opening shot the hero, John Lewis, a Welsh assistant librarian played by Peter Sellers, is lying awake in bed. The room is in the grip of the last hush before the alarm; the geyser is quiet, and the stags on the living-room wallpaper are out of sight, smothered under three coats of

House and Garden Pink but still rampant. Modestly, the librarian begins to assault his sleeping wife. She rebuffs him affectionately out of her torpor and he turns back to the ceiling.

Like all true comic heroes, John Lewis is full of gloomy self-knowledge. He understands, for instance, that sex for him is something to be contended with rather than enjoyed; sometimes his world seems to be awash with breasts in the bus and girls playing tennis, but the energy they arouse in him always gives out at the post. He habitually evolves situations that demand a man capable of guiltless promiscuity and vast sexual optimism, but his temperament remains monogamous and given to unhappy self-inspection. His character is farcically unsuited to the work he loads on to it, like a hammer made of Plasticine.

After he has collared the local Mrs. Thrale at a literary party, where the sanctification of posturing Welsh-speaking nits has buoyed him up on a wave of rage, he quickly loses his nerve and asks her carefully what she would do if he kissed her. The anxiety of his question is obviously well founded. In his melancholy obsession with women ("You know. Women in general. Women *apart from men*") he is aware of an inborn tendency to muff it. "From the Old Welsh verb, to muff from a great height."

John Lewis is hot on Old Welsh, or "things Welsh," as the enemy would probably put it. Welsh characteristics are all right: he has a good deal of them himself, carrying on a war with his landlady that is marked by the same engrossed contempt as the gaze of the conductor who daily gives hard attention to his efforts to leap onto a moving bus. It is Welsh culture that does him in. Even more than his own moodiness, caution, and hypochondria, he loathes the charlatanism and pomposity that the game of Welshness supports. When his Mrs. Thrale comes into the library looking for a book on national costume, he blackly offers her a choice of *Memoirs of a Welsh Hatter* (signed by the hatter), *A Concise History of Codpieces*, and *Expediency and Morality in Welsh Dress*. The scene of his fatal refusal to endorse literature like this, in the presence of a Library Selection Committee manned by a claque of touchy bigots, is one of the cornerstones of his character.

Like most comic-heroic figures since 1950, John Lewis is not as arrogant as he looks. He is rather a timid man: his spurts of impossible behavior come out of a deep and often self-sacrificial resolve to earn the scorn of people he knows to be phony. In the film the springs of his revolt are much less clear than in the book. This is partly because of Peter Sellers, whose comic genius lies in suggesting slow-churning instincts, not outraged ideas, but chiefly because of the script, which gives the moral direction of the book a dog's-leg by pretending that the hero never actually made love to his mistress. The evasion turns him into a jocular figure, and it makes something frivolous of his guilt. The film also supplies an obsequious penitential ending that does violence to the whole idea of marriage in the story, which is otherwise tenderly honest. The screenplay shows his wife forcing a conversion out of him; the book knows that fidelity is offered, not extracted, and that it is something he will go on finding difficult to the end of his days.

The real comic triumph of *Only Two Can Play*—directed by Sidney Gilliat—is in the dialogue. For the first time that I can think of in the history of British film comedy, a screen marriage is as grown-up and as rich in private jokes as the relationship between Katharine Hepburn and Cary Grant in *Bringing up Baby*. The vocabulary is the one we all use about the house, but we had despaired of ever hearing it in the cinema. Virginia Maskell as the pretty, exhausted wife gives a very good performance: during the final row in the kitchen she is marvelously observant about the self-protectiveness of a betrayed woman who is still irritably in love with her husband. Some of the small parts are beautifully done, and there is an exquisite glimpse of a man at a party caught scooping his host's cigarettes into his own case.

JANUARY 14, 1962

Four Sharp Men

In such standard revue talents as how to sing a sentimental number called "Under the Juniper Tree," how to write sketches about the impoverished nobility, and how to dance in tight gray flannel trousers while carrying a chair by its back legs, the four members of the *Beyond the Fringe* company are admittedly deficient. They cannot cavort, nor can they warble; they are merely eruptively funny. When they burst upon the stately Edinburgh Festival one rainy midnight last August, it was instantly clear that they were the sharpest thing that had happened in their field since the debut of the alert Miss Lillie, and the most avidly satiric entertainers in revuegoing memory. If we still value comic genius with a radical edge, their theater should be full to the roof.

Though the national talent for rude and stinging wit continues to thrive in private and in cartoons, it has virtually disappeared off the British stage. The young generation takes it for granted that *diseurs* with bite are to be found only on American gramophone records, and that the function of London revue is to provide nondyspeptic entertainment for rather trickily compounded expense-account parties or family outings. The traditions within which it works are two: the vein of Right-wing badinage that derives from Coward, and the vein of fantasy that derives from *Cranks:* both are debased forms of their originals, and neither of them harbor any attitudes that could be remotely perturbing to the psyches of a sales-manager or a reactionary relative.

The four performers and progenitors of *Beyond the Fringe* knock the ancient formulae on the head. They assume as naturally as Mort Sahl that politics are the proper province of revue entertainment, and would agree eagerly that their show is likely to be combustibly offensive to, among others, Right-wing Tories, V.C.'s, transcendentalists, Empire Loyalists, Lord Beaverbrook, and Civil Defence workers. This partisan approach will take some getting used to, for revue has been dogged for decades by its fair-mindedness. It was not really surprising, though absurd, that one silver-haired critic after the Edinburgh opening should have complained that the revue was rather hard on Mr. Macmillan and that the fun would have been more gracious if the shafts had been aimed at "politicians in general." Unlike the Boulting Brothers, the cast of *Beyond the Fringe* are flagrantly biased: they distinguish between political parties.

Of the company, all male and all well under thirty, only one —Peter Cook—has anything to do with the theater professionally. A tall, bonily good-looking man responsible for most of a memorable Cambridge Footlights two or three years ago, he first streaked into the West End with *Pieces of Eight*, and must be credited with nearly everything that is good in its limper successor, *One Over the Eight*. Like many successful revue-writers, he is obsessed by circular conversations and by married duologues in which husband and wife have long ceased listening to one another. We begin to grow resistant to assumptions that cliché-ridden characters are automatically poignant, but Peter Cook is often steelier than that, suggesting they are equally likely to be hypocritical or grotesquely prejudiced. He is a very funny solo performer, and can develop a single wild thought—such as the idea that Constable was really a secret painter of nudes, covering them up with loads of hay merely for the sake of Victorian propriety—with sustained expository skill.

Jonathan Miller, the second Cambridge member of the all-Oxbridge cast, whetted managers' appetites five years ago with his now-legendary appearances at the Footlights and in cabaret, and then firmly refused all offers and disappeared into his serious career in neuropathology. His style on stage is conspiratorial, beaky, and swooping: in the sketches when he is left to himself, he will stride hugely about musing curiously on some such theme as the piles of perfectly *new* London Passenger Transport Board trousers in the Lost Property Office, and will then suddenly dive downstage to lie full length, one lone eye glaring at the audience above the footlights while he hisses some paralyzing query. He belongs to the 75 per cent of the company that is over six feet tall, and seems to have an instinctive recourse to nonhuman movements. During lulls in rehearsal he may be seen in a corner muttering to himself and strutting strangely, like a Nazi pelican. He is a rare man among physicians in thinking of medicine as abutting onto sociology, psychology, and even the arts; and besides being a passionately interested observer of the cinema he is very well read.

If Jonathan Miller is the natural writer of the four, Alan Bennett is the natural academic. Now a junior lecturer in history at Magdalen, he is still teaching three hours a week, commuting at the expense of the management in a chauffeur-driven Rolls with a speaking tube, which gives his modest and mordant temperament a good deal of quiet pleasure. He is writing a thesis on the retinue of Richard II, and a friend admiringly comments that the paper, which will cover a ten-year period, has already taken him seven years of research. Much the most introverted of the four, he is also the most worried, obdurate, and quietly savage; the political points in his material are barbed and poison-tipped.

Most of his monologues take exegetic forms—lectures or broadcasts or sermons, based on years of chilly observation of platform techniques—and the result so perfectly reproduces the blandness, intellectual patronage, and inappropriate joviality of the originals that some lulled spectators can even miss the irony. Several enthusiastic members of the Edinburgh audience, for instance, clearly took his parody of a television chat by Dr. Verwoerd as a rather persuasive and moderate argument for apartheid; and during a sermon delivered on the classically fruitless text of "My brother Esau is an hairy man, but I am a smooth man," inured churchgoers found nothing to startle them. The pious handclasp and the concerned way of taking off his spectacles are a precise pastiche; so are the uncomfortable attempts at man-in-the-street metaphors: "Life, you know, is rather like a tin of sardines. But don't you sometimes feel—I know I do—that you are not really getting everything out? That in the corner of the tin, a little bit of sardine is always lurking?" Believers in Britain's Civil Defence booklet will find an equally acceptable sort of common sense in his new lecture on what to do in case of nuclear attack. "Now, I know you're probably sick to death of all this but it's not the Government's fault if you're bored with the H-Bomb, is it? It's the fault of the demonstrators. The issue is a simple one, after all. Kill—or be killed." (Another speaker on the platform, interjecting with a laugh, "Or both." Appreciative chuckles.) "The golden rule about nuclear attack is—*be right out of the area where the attack occurs*."

The fourth member of the cast, proportioned so differently from the lanky others as to seem almost another species, is Dudley Moore. He is professionally a serious composer and jazz musician, and in this context a brilliant parodist-pianist and a mimic with an absorbing range of tics, twitches, and verbal impediments. In one sketch he plays a thick-tongued teddy-boy trying to communicate with a rock-and-roll vicar. The parson, ingratiatingly robust, is bent on getting violence "off the streets and into the churches, where it belongs"; Dudley Moore's struggles to explain that the reason why he doesn't like church is that "it's all dark and stuffy, not like the cinema, where they show you to your seat in a civil manner, wiv a torch," may well be crippling to future British television religious programmes for teen-agers.

Physically he finds it very easy to look like Myra Hess, playing a sublime parody of "Jesu, Joy of Man's Desiring" in the manner of the National Gallery concerts in the war. ("The music you're listening to, Timothy, is German music," says Jonathan Miller aside, quoting a passage from Humphrey Jennings' *A Diary for Timothy* that was ripe for destruction: "We're—fighting—the Germans. That's something you'll have to—work out—later.") He also readily converts into a Shakespearean fool, being jester-shaped; and into a bounceable-looking Russian, which is the way he opens the show, playing the National Anthem with deep fascination and strange uncontrollable modulations. The three others, Englishmen listening hard behind their newspapers, accept with the merest shrug that it is natural enough for a Russian to have this recurrent urge to play "God Save the Queen." "I suppose it's because they get so little of it over there."

Like most of their generation, the cast of *Beyond the Fringe* is sardonic about national loyalties, sees no great moral difference between bombing Manchester and bombing Murmansk, and finds it absolutely impossible to take a film like *In Which We Serve* seriously. It is quite likely that anyone over thirty will want to give the young puppies a good hiding; the rest will merely offer them an ovation.

MAY 10, 1961
EDINBURGH

Beatles in Their Own Right

When some unsuspecting plodder asked why N. F. Simpson's play was called *A Resounding Tinkle*, the author said politely, "Because that's its name." In the same way, when a reporter in *A Hard Day's Night* asks one of the Beatles what he would call that hairstyle he's wearing, he replies blandly, "Arthur." Comedy never explains. Who knows why Robert Dhéry calls his brother-in-law "Amsterdam," or why Beatrice Lillie in *Exit Smiling* wears a man's wrist watch on her ankle?

Like the slipped vowel in their own name, the way the Beatles go on is just there, and that's it. In an age that is clogged with self-explanation this makes them very welcome. It also makes them naturally comic. They accept one another with the stoicism of clowns. None of them tries to tell you that his peculiarities are a sign of the traumas of modern man or because Mum did the wrong thing at six weeks. In Alun Owen's script, which has such a lynx ear for their own real speech that their ad libs are indistinguishable in it, they behave to one another with the kind of unbothered rudeness that is usually possible only between brothers and sisters.

I think it is really this feeling that you are looking at an enviable garrison of a family that is at the root of the Beatles' charm. I don't believe it is just the Lennon-McCartney numbers, good and sweetly odd as they are; when Richard Lester was shooting the numbers in this film the kids in the Scala Theatre were yelling so loud that they didn't even realize they were listening to six new hits months before anyone else. The only thing that would probably finish the Beatles with the fans would be if they split up as a family.

A Hard Day's Night has no plot. What it has instead, which is plenty, is invention, good looks, and a lot of larky character. The narrative is simply a day in the Beatles' lives, and their situation when you think about it is pure comedy: four highly characterized people caught in a series of intensely public dilemmas but always remaining untouched by them, like Keaton, because they carry their private world around everywhere. Whether they are in a train carriage or at a press conference or in a television studio, the Beatles are always really living in a capsule of Liverpool.

As a piece of grit in the narrative Alun Owen has given Paul a scratchy old granddad (Wilfrid Brambell), about whom the nicest thing that anyone can say, and even this seems doubtful, is that he is clean. Granddad resents their unity and manages to create a fair amount of chaos. His gibes slide off Paul, John, and George, but they find a victim in Ringo, who is already worried enough about his shortness and the size of his nose. They are also the last straw for the boys' distraught manager (Norman Rossington), who is conducting a war of nerves with John that is lost from the start because John hasn't *got* any nerves.

Like Lennon's book, *In His Own Write*, and like Richard Lester's own *The Running, Jumping, Standing Still Film*, *A Hard Day's Night* is full of slightly out-of-focus puns, both verbal and visual. For instance, a Beatle will make a dive for someone's square tie and ask vaguely, "I say, did you go to Harrods? I was there in 1958." Or John Lennon in a bubble bath will suddenly see a hand-shower as a submarine periscope and start playing war films. One of the best sequences, as in *The Running, Jumping, Standing Still Film,* is a fantasy in a field. Lester obviously adores fields. This one inspires a jump-cut speeded-up sequence mostly shot from a helicopter in which the boys horse around, do a square dance, and lie down with their heads together in close-up as though they were swimmers in an old Esther Williams picture. There is a feeling of liberation about this sequence, like some of the dances in *West Side Story*. When the film sags, which it does a bit in places, there is a small part wittily played by Victor Spinetti as a television director, neurotic, queer, and implacably contemptuous: this is a new subdivision of social war, the camp against the hip.

The lighting cameraman on the picture was Gilbert Taylor, and the grainy blacks and glowing whites and freewheeling camera work are a minor revolution in a British pop film. *A Hard Day's Night* technically lifts a lot from *cinéma vérité:* in the use of hidden mikes, throat mikes, and hand-held cameras, for instance. But if you compare it with a real piece of camera truth-telling like Granada's Beatle film, *Yeah, Yeah, Yeah,* made by the Maysles Brothers in America, it's clear that Dick Lester's film hasn't very much to do with *cinéma vérité* in its character.

A Hard Day's Night is better described, perhaps, as a piece of feature journalism: this is the first film in England that has anything like the urgency and dash of an English popular daily at its best. Like a news feature, it was produced under pressure, and the head of steam behind it has generated something expressive and alive. If this is personality-mongering, which of course it is, it is also very responsive to temperament and eloquent about it. Ringo emerges as a born actor. He is like a silent comedian, speechless and chronically underprivileged, a boy who is already ageless with a mournful, loose mouth, like a Labrador's carrying a bird.

JULY 12, 1964

A Pox on Dying

Hugs and Kisses (what a title) is a Swedish picture about a disrupter who comically effects convulsive change without seeming to do anything at all. Hakan Serner plays a tongue-tied, agreeable writer called John. At the beginning of the picture his girl friend abruptly accuses him of being a baboon and throws him out. She uses the excuse that she needs peace to practice Bartók on her piano. She is obviously under stress, but it doesn't seem at first that there is much justice in the accusation about the baboon. Though sloppily dressed by the standards of store managers, I suppose, the man looks hygienic and strikes you as being above the average human being in perceptiveness. But you begin to see that he has a presence that can bore into other people's lives in a peculiar way.

Having been hoofed out of his girl's pad, with the girl benignly hurling her typewriter at him from the window as an expulsion present, he goes to a crony called Max, a sedate and rather interesting man who runs a haberdashery and lives with a fashion-model wife called Eva (Agneta Ekmanner). Eva is ravishing, and even bright. John trades a place in their house for a surreal sinecure as their amateur housekeeper. He brings them breakfast in bed, proudly bearing it on a servant's tray, but he is in his underclothes, and he proceeds to crouch on the bottom of their bed and eat more than a third of the food. For all his silence, and his absorption in problems entirely his own (such as how to release his foot from a door handle that he was trying to open by toe without putting down a tray, or how to import the true, easy utopia of Buenos Aires into pernickety Sweden, which he reviles from a bike in the park for its obsession with carrying out obligations and keeping up life-insurance premiums)—for all his hermeticism, John is far from being one of those third figures who can sometimes enigmatically bolster a marriage by their friendship and their company as witnesses. With his arrival, things between the couple start to fall apart. Eva begins to see her constrained husband as ice-cold. She also resents and envies his boisterousness with John.

The picture could very easily have been one of the current exploitations of a rather studied kind of kookiness, but it isn't. The director, Jonas Cornell, who also wrote the screenplay, fills it with something more attentive and composed than that. The comedy is beautifully shot in black and white, and it gives itself time. There seems to be air around the characters. The eccentricities of the hero are his own and genuine, and they impart a tone to the film that is both cheerful and sad. His fixation on Buenos Aires as fun and as the way out for Sweden, and his odd uprightness in eventually directing the laser beam of his attention away from Eva onto a blowzy and rather dull girl who runs a typing school, express a tenacious spirit that is somehow always going to triumph on its own terms and at its own tacit expense. Friends half recognize him as a pest, but he also commands great loyalty. The squeezed-out, nearly severed couple, taking refuge in a bar from his noisy affair with the typing expert in their own flat, simply say helplessly to one another, "John must play. John lives with us." The singular man is victorious, and Max begins to go to the wall. The film has a mood a little like *Les Jeux de l'Amour*, but with interludes of a strange and droll melancholy—for instance, a scene in which Max comes into his wife's dressing room at work while she is taking off her false eyelashes. He is not alive at once to her impatience with him but feels only a sense of something missing, and he talks laconically to her about having once imitated Gary Cooper. "He's dead now. There was a picture of him with Hemingway. Hemingway's dead, too. They're all dead, or dying."

AUGUST 24, 1968

A Fairy Tale of New York

We are on Fifth Avenue, in the cavernous dawn light that fashion photographers have made their own, and a skinny girl in full evening clothes gets out of a cab. From her backview—a black dress that looks like a vague gesture with an evening glove, and a bib of pearls loping around her shoulder blades—one would think that she was a model. She wears dark glasses, perhaps on the grounds that it is not yet daytime. Staring at the rocks in Tiffany's windows, she shows herself to be Audrey Hepburn and dunks a doughnut into a beaker of coffee.

Blake Edwards' *Breakfast at Tiffany's*, glowingly adapted by George Axelrod from Truman Capote's far more acerbic story, is about a ravishing, scared girl called Holly Golightly who reserves for jewels and money the steady passion that most girls feel only for a man when they are in love. The achievement of the film, as well as its hedging flaw, is that one leaves this unquestioned at the time. *Breakfast at Tiffany's* is a fable that silences carping, written with the same desperate lonely wit as Elaine Dundy's *The Dud Avocado*, and acted in a mood of guileless sympathy with the characters' quirks. It is only afterwards that the pea under the mattress begins to bore into one's bones.

Holly Golightly, married at fourteen to a doting disused husband, lives in suspended chaos in a brownstone apartment with a cat whom she refers to, in a spirit of steely fraternity, as "no-name slob." Above her lives Mr. Yunioshi, a Japanese photographer, played by Mickey Rooney with a heavily upholstered top lip, who endearingly chooses to sleep bang in the middle of a barish room immediately under a lamp that concusses him every time he wakes up. The tenant below is Paul Varjak (George Peppard), a promising short-story writer of 1956 who has had no ribbon in his typewriter for some years and who lives off a sourly predatory interior decorator.

From the moment when Varjak first sees Holly peering with opiate eyes around the edge of her front door, hot out of bed wearing a man's boiled evening shirt, a sleeping-mask with gold false eyelashes, and a pair of earplugs like flapped earrings, the stymied author finds her frenzied and raffish life irresistibly poetic. She keeps her ballet slippers in the icebox and her scent in the mailbox, and once a week goes off to see a friend in Sing Sing—which should, she feels, be an opera house—wearing Givenchy clothes to stave off "the mean reds." (This is not an insult hissed through the Iron Curtain; it is her name for a brand of *Angst.*) The convict keeps tabs on her accounts, in which the only incomings are the fifty-dollar perks that her escorts give her for the powder room. The outgoings are on repairs to the dresses they rip, and food for the cat.

The prettiest passage in *Breakfast at Tiffany's* is a rapturous spree when Holly and the writer enter into a pact not to do anything they have ever done before. Their day includes a cool shoplifting sprint around Woolworth's, and a sedate discussion with an assistant in Tiffany's about a present that is not to cost more than $10.

The happy ending of the film is as true to its scampering spirits as Capote's fade out was true to his own much more stinging original. The speciousness lies in sweetening the character of the heroine so that she can be played by Audrey Hepburn without in any way changing her motives or actions, which remain monstrously avaricious. Truman Capote noticed, for instance, that her eyes sometimes had "an assessing squint like a jeweler's," that she could wear "a tough, tiny smile that advanced her age immeasurably," and that she was capable of vague-seeming well-placed bitchery. The book observes the streak of cold brutality that is often present in the romantic; the film merely sees the vivacity and sweetness of Audrey Hepburn.

OCTOBER 22, 1961

In the Best Bedrooms

If *L'Amant de Cinq Jours* had been made in English, a course that keeps suggesting itself as one listens to Jean Seberg speaking French, it would have been a very different kettle of fish. Miss Seberg's role would have been that of a luminous innocent, skipping away from the camera in backview at the end of the film instead of continuing on her imperturbable deceiving path. Her husband, played by François Perier, would have been defeated by a mews flat the moment she went away instead of accepting her protracted *cinq-à-sept* with quizzical indifference and saying companionably to his year-old twins, babbling softly over their boiled eggs: "You're wondering why Mummy's late. It's because she wears high heels and can't hurry." And in an English film her lover, the quill-nosed Jean-Pierre Cassel, would have given her up in a spirit of sacrifice, not because he wanted to; and her friend (Micheline Presle) would never have been running a secret affair with the same man; not if the film was intended to be funny.

What is more, of course, the film would not have *been* funny. *L'Amant de Cinq Jours* takes its style from a class of people who are now about as agile or pungent as pillows. The eroticism to be wrung from, say, the stock type of an expensively educated London insurance broker who calls his mistress "old thing" is fairly slight. Laughter about sex used to be an upper-class domain: it is now Lucky Jim's or Billy Liar's, and therefore no longer high comedy or farce in the old sense, rooted as those forms are in a rigidly codified and privileged society like Feydeau's or Congreve's.

In America it is possible to make a sex-comedy by setting it in suburbia, as in *The Facts of Life;* the owner of the ranch-type home has the necessary standard of living, the necessary conventionality, and maybe the necessary sexiness and speed of riposte. But with English works like *The Grass Is Greener* and *Roar Like a Dove* we move into a world where, though the characters abundantly possess the first two qualifications, they lack the last. For the moment a witty film like *Infidelity* seems to be beyond the English.

L'Amant de Cinq Jours was directed by Philippe de Broca, who made *Les Jeux de l'Amour*. Like the earlier picture it moves at a breakneck, mocking pace. Even *in extremis*, or bed, the characters maintain an insulated self-amusement. "*Qu'est-ce que tu bois?*" says a woman to her lover, when he is scarcely inside the door; "*Tes lèvres*," he says, bounding on her with a thrilling guttural. Most of the dialogue is beadily funny, and the scarcely remarked enthusiasms that possess the characters are intriguingly odd: there is a passing sequence, for instance, which establishes that Jean-Pierre Cassel is keen on country-dancing in clogs. Moments like this, and the scene in which Micheline Presle importantly mows a square yard of lawn while her miserable lover reads bad verse to her, remind one a little of *Mon Oncle*. The difference is that de Broca has none of Tati's lonely poetic eye, and his characters, unlike the citizens of Hulot's world, are supremely self-aware.

The tone has its sags, and some of the laughs seem not so much evoked as extracted: the audience's guffaws over a bursting-collar gag at a grand party, for instance, sound like the gasp of men in a half nelson. "The critic," said Shaw with a glare, "soon gets cured of the public's delusion that everything that makes it laugh amuses it." But the film would justify itself if only by the moment when, standing in a frigid group of deceiving wife, discovered lover, and treacherous friend, François Perier sweetly says into a silence choked with vitriol that an angel must be passing. Both the male performances are eccentrically good.

AUGUST 6, 1961

Philippe de Broca was the director of a fond and quirky comedy called *Les Jeux de l'Amour*, about a wary trio of people plugging on with the necessities of their love lives in a hostile clutter of Victorian claptrap in an antique shop. His new English-language film, *King of Hearts*, takes on a comic subject that sounds everything that Anglo-Saxons nervously mean by "Gallic" when they speak of humor, having in the backs of their heads the caperings of the Comédie-Française at its worst. The story, set near the end of the First World War, is about a Scottish soldier who is ordered to dismantle a bomb in a French village deserted by everyone except the inhabitants of a lunatic asylum and a zoo. One would expect the combination of French-fanciful and Scots-twee to be hard to surmount, and it is. Alan Bates—good, good actor and electric listener—is the wrong man to ask to leap winsomely in the air and chat to carrier pigeons. Producers and directors tend to see him as typecasting for born victims and go-betweens; they should try thinking of him for something more resolute. But all the same, a quality in the film makes it work. It looks beautiful, with easy dissolves from shots of frightened villagers fleeing the wet, field-gray streets to choreographed groups of the insane gently at liberty. The lunatics are dressed like generals and courtesans and acrobats, some of them raptly riding around in a coach drawn by a fluffy camel. De Broca must have real sweetness and force of character to turn the film into what it often is: a dream of a carnival respite from caution and death.

JUNE 24, 1967

I have admired and loved Philippe de Broca's earlier films, but *Le Diable par la Queue*, his new crime-comedy, seems over the line between genuine quirkiness and affectation. A cast that includes Madeleine Renaud, the ever-smiling Maria Schell, and Yves Montand—funny and agile as a bank robber with a talent for dandy living—is afflicted by the sort of twitter that is the non-fan's nightmare of a company playing farce. But there is a nice minute with an exploding hamburger, and with a nattily dressed thug rapt by Wagner; and I was fond of a true de Broca moment when Yves Montand, in sylvan rapist mood, with a rather middle-class-looking cow wandering across the background of the shot as a girl seducingly asks him to snap up the bodice of her dress, tells her with dignity, "I *unsnap* snaps, I don't snap them."

JULY 5, 1969

A Movie, a Jug of Wine, a Loaf of Bread and What Was the Other Thing?

Sequences of prankish shopping in Paris. Sequences of rich American sixteen-year-olds licking the salt off each other on the beach. With the release of *Tu Seras Terriblement Gentille* timed to lend feelings of surrogate fun and company in the emptying hot city, the New York film-distribution process suddenly seems dedicated to the Lady Bountiful business of bringing a little color into our drab lives. You get whisked into another world as long as you respect that charity, although you may react the other way to films that treat you like —well, a Victorian between-maid on the yearly staff outing to a countryside she has never known, or an indigent visited by the gentry with baskets of nourishing potato peelings. "It's cool inside!" promise the theaters themselves, as if some halcyon picnic weather reigned there, although the smog within is actually the same as the smog without, but freezing. And "Take a break from yourself!" say these summer movies. "See how the fortunate live, and come out feeling that you're as well off as they are!" Dirk Sanders' *Tu Seras Terriblement Gentille* is a French love-comedy about a sage little girl who brings together her fashion-model mother and her film-director father after years estranged. The picture is, as you see, cheerful. It is gaily made, and sad in the same instantly mendable way as *Un Homme et une Femme*, and terrifically well dressed. There are scenes set somewhere that looks like Cardin, snazzily shot, with jump-cuts and a general air of democratic breeziness that is light-years away from any technique used long ago to shoot similar scenes at, say, Worth. This isn't one of your snooty movies. There's nothing to make you feel you couldn't look just as wonderful as the fashion-model mother on your scullery-maid wages. Your own little life, you think (huddling into your air-conditioned upholstered seat, using the *Times* to cover your icy arms, and catching a snorter), is within an ace of being as enviable as the life of this fashion-model character and this film-director character. That's the sort of good-natured movie it is. It also hands out the consoling thoughts that people only love once, that shopping plugs the gaps, and that the ancient talent of movie children for putting together shattered marriages remains intact. The little girl—Leslie Bedos—is gravely competent. Worn out by a short lifetime of being yanked around photographers' studios, she starts to cry and then recovers herself by making a necklace of chewing gum. She tells her mother, with misleading saintliness, that Mummy must be tired. Mummy: "How did you know I was tired?" Child: "Because you made me cry. When you make me cry, it means you're tired." The small counselor—who is appallingly admirable, though she has some nice resilient lines and engaging bounce—is polite to Mummy's lovers but hankers privately after her father, just as Mummy does. (It may say something about Mummy that the trouble between the adults is repaired only when Daddy has leaped from being an unrecognized photographer into a film director one hears about.) Anyway, when both a lover and

Daddy turn up to take Mummy, the child, and their recognizable Vuitton luggage to Orly Airport, Mummy and child and their Vuittons are instantly accommodated in Daddy's car. One of the most comforting things about this entirely amiable, cloud-cuckooland picture is that it takes no account of the changes that happen between people with the passing of time. The film would be hard to enter into if anyone you knew well were sitting beside you, because it is blatantly such a fairy tale about behavior and loss. Look, it says—see how much a few boutiques can buck you up; see how difficult things are, even for this pretty girl, and how happily they can end; and just see the balm of good luggage.

JUNE 28, 1969

Back to the Trees

Hi, Mom! is about—well, what's happening. That's its bag, and this is what it's really into, and this is where it's at, and right on. A white boy back from Vietnam and dully crazed by New York capitalism takes first to making blue films and then to acting in the modish theater of revolt with a troupe called Be Black, Baby. Liberal white playgoers, eager to keep up, submit to participating in psychodramas of rape and theft played out by blacks in whiteface. One of the enacted rapes nearly comes off; the whites, blacked up, riot; the hero, playing the role of a cop, has to side with the blacks; and soon afterward the blacks are shown raiding a co-op apartment building. They are led by a youngish white revolutionary and eventually mown down by a middle-class white with a handy machine gun. After this crammed parable about everything and nothing, the hero gets married, becomes an insurance salesman and suddenly blows up his own apartment house by putting sticks of dynamite in one of the washing machines in the laundry room. Passersby are interviewed about the explosion. They say that there's obviously going to be a lot of this, and that it makes room for dog-walking.

The inanities in the film are sometimes funny, sometimes pretty forced. Brian De Palma, who wrote and directed it, obviously has his own view of life and a load of scamp's energy. Many a lumbering flight of fancy is helped into the air nowadays by people's general longing to dignify the random as the surreal; the period will turn out, I think, to have been wistfully kind to pieces of work like this. No harm in it, as long as the notion of real satire doesn't get fogged and lost. *Hi, Mom!* is the ersatz form, ruled by the times. Its mockery of contemporary voices is exact but also eerily complaisant, and the weight of the parody seems to land equally on everything in hearing. Of picking up sounds out of the general earshot this sort of work knows nothing. Common currency is obligatory, and the satirist's impulse to spit in the face of his century—that loneliness, that high-handed anger—is replaced by the instinct of hunger for company, producing lines that deride the age in a voice that is the age's very voice.

MAY 9, 1970

THE DANDIES, THE BUNGLERS OF CASTE

Gogol

When members of the Russian upper class voyaged in Europe in the nineteenth century they were often scandalized by the lack of corruption. In 1897 a nobleman who had had to wait his turn in a German post office, instead of paying the usual Russian bribe to be served first, wrote a letter home saying loftily that the country would never progress until it learned graft. This is very much the background of Gogol's *The Government Inspector*.

The one-eyed town that the play depicts is deeply impressed by corruption as a political system. The mayor, judge, and civil officers sixth-class practice it rather humbly, as though only the *ton* of Saint Petersburg really knew how to do it. The muffin-faced officials in Peter Hall's very funny production seem to think of graft as an accomplishment that properly belongs to the classy, something they are liable to make crashing mistakes about. Their efforts at slipping silence-money to the ravenous young clerk whom they take to be a high-bred tsarist inspector are made in a mood of thrilled servility. It is the clodhopping heaviness of their attempts to be silky that makes the production so engaging. Edward Marsh and Jeremy Brooks's version of the Russian gives them a comically impossible language to be sycophantic in, uncontrollably robust, and about as blasé as a gum boot.

I imagine the town of the play to be rather like Gogol's own birthplace, near Poltava, in the Ukraine. It is a community that has never before entered anyone's calculations, being a good three years' gallop from any frontier. The Mayor's room (sets by John Bury and Elizabeth Duffield) is a cluttered place and probably loaded with bugs. The contents include an upright piano, a stray stirrup, a vase of sunflowers, and a string of onions. The floor is raked, and when Paul Scofield as the imagined high official (Khlestakov) is most enthralling to the citizens they will come downstage and close up into a tiny space like a crowd down at the rails at the Derby.

Scofield wears a willow-green suit and a blond wig with a beautiful kiss-curl. The inn where he is first seen, trying to get some food out of the landlord without having to flog his ravishing trousers to pay for it, is a stinking hole that makes his vowels skid about in agonies of genteelism. When he says "Niaouw," the negative gets as many diphthongs as Eliza Doolittle's. The influences on the accent seem to include Weybridge, Birmingham, a lot of sermons, and the girl who recorded the speaking-clock on the telephone.

In Khlestakov's room, where he grandly says that the bedbugs bite like wolfhounds, the hungry dandy bolts unspeakable food and complains about it as if he weren't getting down a mouthful. As soon as he cottons onto the role that the town has invented for him, his gift for patronizing finds a task. "I suppose you've always lived round heah?" he says royally to David Warner, cast as a myopic postmaster who has obviously never set a galosh anywhere else in his life. Transplanted to the Mayor's house, the hero gets slowly and radiantly drunk. "Shall I compare thee . . . ti tum ti tum. . . . One of my sonnets." He also claims *Romeo and Juliet*, *Don Juan*, and *The Marriage of Figaro*. The town swoons.

Khlestakov tells them about a four at bridge in Saint Petersburg: "The English Ambassador, the Foreign Minister, the French Ambassador, the German Ambassador and . . . me." After miscalculations like this he tends to leave his mouth ajar for a while. (It would have been a wonderful part for Sid Field or Tony Hancock.) Scofield is helplessly funny physically. He gives the man a genius for making movements that furniture prevents him from finishing. Patience Collier as the Mayor's wife, wearing blue eyeshadow and a hair-do like a peroxided geisha girl, finds the impostor quite flawless. After he has made a spinning sloshed exit, yelling "Salted cod!" in the cracked voice of Lear, she says after a polite pause, "Wha' a fescineh'ing man."

The characters are dressed and played rather as though they were heavy animals dolled up for a dinner dance. In a state of later religious mania Gogol interpreted his work as a Christian fable, with the town representing the state of men's souls and the final announcement of a real inspector a Day of Judgment; but Peter Hall ignores all that and produces it as a Ben Jonson comedy of humors. The small parts are exquisitely well rehearsed.

JANUARY 23, 1966
LONDON

Like nearly every other Russian play, Gogol's *Marriage* includes one character who is unmentioned in the cast list, and that is Russia herself. As Turgenev wrote once, Russians think about their country as obsessionally as Englishmen are supposed to about sport and Frenchmen about women. In Robert Gillner's meddling rehash of the play, retitled *The Marriage Brokers*, the delicate Russianness of the way Gogol writes somehow seeps through even Mr. Gillner's brutish style.

The Russia of *Marriage* is the Saint Petersburg of the 1830s, a decrepit middle-class structure that would collapse if any of the middle classes had the energy to blow on it, which they haven't. They prefer to stay in bed, like the hero of Goncharov's *Oblomov*, or to arrange academic marriages for themselves with a limp determination to see that the project peters out before they reach the altar, like the jibbing wooer in *Marriage*. They worry poetically about their beloved Russia, but their anxiety is totally inert, a sensibility that is almost submerged in an unstirring pool of Slav warm temperament, like the one emergent eye of a hippopotamus cooling off underwater.

When the production lets it appear, this temperament that Gogol so loved and understood is perfectly expressed in the play. It is prodigal, prone to swoops of quite unliverish depression, dartingly comic, and delicately greedy. Three avid suitors have been found by the matchmaker for the nubile heroine. The greed of the first is fixed upon her property: he is a delousing expert and he bangs the walls of her house for soundness as though the place needed a thorough going-over with a spray gun before a husband could be expected to lie down in it. The greed of the second suitor, a minute naval officer, is sighted mostly on plumpness. The third suitor, Podkolyassin, a tall prevaricator all surplus spine and dither, has been conned into courting by a marriage-making chum; what his mouth really waters for is a continuation of blessed, undutiful bachelordom.

The only scenes that are played with much reality or grace are the ones between Robert Eddison as Podkolyassin and John Moffat as his friend. Physically they are very funny together. Robert Eddison makes himself look a nervous ten foot tall, braced for instant flight, with something deeply alarmed about the knee; John Moffat is erect and elegant, with a stylish chest and the crisply bossy movements of a balletmistress.

These scenes are admittedly exercises in the highest kind of Restoration camp, and they therefore have nothing at all to do with Russia, which arguably has the most noncamp national character in the world, with the possible exception of South Africa or Iceland. But this couldn't be said to be damaging when the whole production has about as much relation to the spirit of the Russian original as a Mothers' Union meeting. The writing seems to have been done with the blunt end of a ham bone, and most of the acting matches it; this is the sort of tenth-hand, bawling stage behavior that makes so many film-lovers hate the theater. And why on earth the wedding-bells happy-ending—which could only actually strike anyone as happy who had spent his life in an incubator alone with the silliest kind of musical—instead of the caustic flight from the altar imagined by Gogol?

FEBRUARY 7, 1965
LONDON

Anouilh

The theme to which Jean Anouilh incessantly returns, like a tongue to a broken tooth, is the willful destruction of innocence by the jaded and corrupt. What raises his thesis above the trite is the antithesis he pits against it: that the innocent, in this encounter, wreak equal damage. In Anouilh's work the disillusionment of last love is every bit as distressing as the first.

Of his many variations on this theme, *The Rehearsal* is one of the most sourly adept. Long a star-piece of the Barraults, and at one time thought of for the Oliviers, it is now tardily brought to London in a knife-edged production by John Hale, of the Bristol Old Vic. (The translation, by Pamela Hansford-Johnson and Kitty Black, is also sharp and steely; the glinting exactness of the language seems miraculously gallic.) The scene of the drama is a château, and the costume is Louis Quatorze, for we are in a house-party of people rehearsing Marivaux's *La Double Inconstance;* but though the sexual situation is a cunning mirror image of the eighteenth-century play-within-the-play, the barbed, wary mode in which it is conducted is tartly modern. The Count, who is directing the amusement, observed by his quizzical wife and his openly accommodated mistress, casts as the ingénue a chaste young beauty with whom he proceeds to fall vindictively in love. Wife and mistress develop in complicity against the common threat, and finally commission the Count's hard-drinking friend to seduce the girl and send her shamefully fleeing. The action, layer upon layer of subterfuge and void revenge, is conducted in a cold and stylish repartee that mingles almost indistinguishably with snatches of Marivaux's play, rather as the first act of Strauss's *Ariadne* flickers with themes from the inner opera to come.

Of all races, the French are the most accomplished spectators of themselves; they often tend to talk about their deepest affairs as though they were observing themselves in a play, and Anouilh's exquisitely painful stroke of making this literally true has the effect of twisting out of them some of the most wry and mordant comments on sexual strategy that can ever have been made, even on the French stage. (It also produces, in the second act, an equally typical and paradoxical speech in celebration of sexual pleasures. If Anouilh identifies sensuality as a villain in human relationships, he is equally ready to recognize it—unlike any English playwright—as a solemn and sufficient form of love.) Robert Hardy, Phyllis Calvert, and Diana Churchill, respectively the Count, his wife, and his mistress, give performances of the most delicate acrimony, and Alan Badel as the soaker friend is in his element: he plays a particular kind of witty, self-loathing debauchee better than anyone on our stage.

APRIL 26, 1961
LONDON

Most of Wolf Mankowitz's screenplay for *The Waltz of the Toreadors* teaches us that sex is comic, cheerful, consoling, and everlasting. The last part suggests that it is tragic, ferocious, biliously lonely, and a brief way of fighting off the dark.

The film is adapted from Anouilh, but the change of mood, which makes the film seem broken-backed, is not really his: Anouilh's view is consistent enough. Sex in his plays is always tinctured with a sophisticated sort of melancholy, and poisoned with remorse about a vanished innocence that few people in the real world ever regret losing.

The film, however, is as different from the play as Blenheim from Versailles. General Fitzjohn, the rollicking buffer played by Peter Sellers, has become an absolutely English figure, one of our long line of lecherous nobs: staring enraptured at the back views of a lot of schoolgirls picking his flowers, shaking down into the saddle like a sack of wheat as he gallops through his parklands, tweaking the between-maids in the pantry, and warming his hands at a shop-assistant's skirt.

Rude as only the upper classes can be about their families ("Oh, my god, they're ugly!" he exclaims about his two daughters to his adjutant), he has the imperiousness and the wacky turn of speech of the copper-bottomed eccentric. There is also something comically English about his mechanistic view of sex, which he shares with a friend who talks about women as though they were cars going in for service. "Well," says the General to him agreeably, "you'd better go up and lubricate my old heap."

It is the old heap, a nagging hypochondriac wife played with humor and pity by Margaret Leighton, who breaks the spine of the film. The scene when she cycles grimly to a threatened suicide, crouched over the handle bars with the tails of her nightshirt flying, is pure hard-hearted farce; and then she wheels on her husband in a murderous fight, the water turns black with blood, and one wonders how one ever laughed.

Peter Sellers' randy, tender old General, his eyes clenched as though he were used to wearing a monocle in both of them, and his stomach stony with corset, is played with such talent that he could carry the whole film on his own. If *The Waltz of the Toreadors* were in the current tradition of English comedy, he would have to; but the director, John Guillermin, is obviously a director with a sense of humor. In a recent interview by phone it sounded as though he needed it. Apparently his producers—Rank—snipered his efforts to bridge the awkward change of mood by hacking Margaret Leighton's scene to a fraction of its proper length and cutting in their own farcical passages. It seems to be a classic piece of wrong-headed interference. But in spite of the fifth columnists, this is still one of the more skillful entertainments that has come out of a British studio for a long time.

APRIL 15, 1962

Bosses and Their Judges

Like Wodehouse, Brecht . . . No, begin again. *Puntila and His Servant Matti* is hardly as funny as the great Wooster chronicle, mostly because it isn't easy for Brecht to be comically imperturbable. All the same, they have something in common beyond the obvious shared element of the master-servant theme that is one of the six or seven historic situations of European literature. The link is in the notion of what separates the master's temperament from the servant's. Puntila and Bertie Wooster are dangerously variable, Matti and Jeeves are fixed; the privilege of changeability belongs to the bosses, and the sackable have to be implacable.

Matti, played by Patrick Magee in a caressing drone that I am beginning not to be able to disentangle from all his performances in Beckett, is hired by Puntila as a chauffeur. What he dislikes about his employer is not his surliness when sober but his pleasantness when drunk: Matti has a Jeevesian sense of place, and Puntila's boozy mateyness offends it.

The part of the boss, who is a rude Finnish landowner, is played with poetic physical wit by Roy Dotrice, dressed in a checked tan suit pregnantly padded and speaking in a North Country accent through a cigar. He moves with the lightness that is common in the very fat, flapping and buckling when drunk like a turbot walking on its tail, and hurling himself at the austere landscape in a vintage car, commanding the bends in the road to straighten themselves out.

In Brecht's *Galileo* there is a scene in which a man is robed from his underclothes outwards, changing under scrutiny from a puny man into His Holiness the Pope. In *Puntila* there is a scene rather like it and just as theatrical, with the benevolent drunk undressing, going into a sauna bath, having cold water thrown over him and becoming with each bucketful a more sober and ungenerous man. In the second half of the play the process is run backwards and an overbearing brute is transmuted by alcohol into someone quite likable, roaring vows about going on the wagon and meanwhile, after drawing a corkscrew from his hip like a Westerner pulling a gun, getting slowly and benignly sloshed. He is not a bad master; the Brechtian question put at the end is whether it is possible to be a good one.

Michel Saint-Denis's production, using an adaptation by Jeremy Brooks that is full of ripe slang, has the jolliness that often gets lost in staging Brecht. The comedy was explicitly written in the form of revue, which builds in the difficulty that there is no carryover of tone to be credited from one scene to another; some passages bite on bullets, some merely grind their gums.

The best performances are in the bourgeois scenes, which have the sort of obstreperous and noisy spirit that Brecht clamored for, enacted under white top-lighting like the glare over a boxing ring. Glenda Jackson plays Puntila's flouncing daughter looking like a girl in a Gainsborough film from the late 1940s, heavily lipsticked and huffy, and there is a funny performance by Ian Richardson as her diplomat fiancé, a guffawing twit with a genius for ruining jokes who walks as though he were gripping something between his knees. The only maladroit gag is the playing of the peasant women, who guy themselves clumsily and should have the straw taken out of their hair.

JULY 18, 1965
LONDON

The Outclassed Husband

Without the appallingly expert European sense of class distinctions, a good half of post-antique European comedy would scarcely exist. Robbed of the endlessly investigated theme of the master-servant relationship, for instance, or the situation of the bourgeois upstart, or the poignancy of the last gasps of gentry in decline, the drama of France, Russia, Italy, and England would be ruinously depleted.

Molière's *George Dandin* is a poisonously funny tale of war between a middle-class climber and an indolent old family into which he has rashly married. In the same bill there is Edward Albee's *The Zoo Story*, which makes a skin-crawlingly well-matched pair for it; the modern American theater may be free of the geiger-counter European class-sense, but in its obsession with the social shame of homosexuality and the importance of an exhibited pure-bred virility it has developed a fair equivalent.

To degenerate Europeans, worries about whether the wife's family suspects you of being effeminate are apt to seem not much larger scale than a neurosis because a dowager caught you saying "pardon." It struck me while I was watching *Zoo Story* that it would be possible now for an American wit to write a scathing high-comedy parallel to *The Importance of Being Earnest* about sexual snobberies in America, with a lunch-club Lady Bracknell wearing mirror-fronted royal-blue sunglasses investigating John Worthing for cracks in the he-man fiber: I suppose his Bunbury alibi would have to be an affair with a famous mistress.

The double-bill is very well done. The Molière is set outside the climber's house, not in the country, as the text states, but in what looks more like a suburb of Glasgow in the 1890s, with a view of a villa larded with chips of Victorian stained glass like designs in cheap bath salts. Dandin himself, played by Ewan Hooper, wears the traditional badge of the upstart, a tweed in a loud check: and the tweed is cut, what is more, into a pair of plus-fours that are both far too new and also quite wrong off a macadamized road, which in an old European nation signals social volumes.

As his accent is Scottish, and as one of the few facts that every Englishman knows about Scotland is that the Scots have very little class-sense, it is therefore made to seem perfectly credible that he should have taken on the otherwise unthinkably difficult task of marrying a woman who is not only a scorpion but also streets above him socially, and supported by inviolably snobbish parents who assume automatically that suspicions of adultery can apply only to the lower classes and that in their offspring's case they would be unthinkable, as though a vulgar mini-car breakdown were to happen to the engine of a Bentley. It is a family in which "chastity is as hereditary to the women as valor to the men." The husband, vilely unlikable himself, hasn't a hope; for him to try to convince anyone of his wife's promiscuity is a task as clearly doomed as complaining in the wrong accent at Fortnum's that there is margarine in the sandwiches.

It isn't the fault of David Thompson's translation that the text reads more bitingly than it plays. On stage the cavorting of the characters begins to seem exhaustingly thin, like watching singers go through the libretto of an opera without the music. The real point of the evening is to see *Zoo Story*, a clear arc of modern dramatic writing that is every bit as formalized as Molière and the most fully achieved and honestly framed play that Albee has written. Beside it, *Who's Afraid of Virginia Woolf?* seems a clever boulevard mock-up; for in *Zoo Story* there is no audience pap, only a stiffened and hideous resentment of exactly the same kind of benign married couples who watch the exhibition-fighting in *Virginia Woolf* from such an intrigued and unthreatened distance.

Zoo Story is written for two characters; one of them is a family man called Peter (Ewan Hooper), the play's representative of the sexual bourgeoisie, a publisher sitting on a park seat comfortable in the knowledge of a planned family of two daughters and two parakeets. The other is a clamorously egocentric homosexual called Jerry (Stephen Berkoff), steeped in a messianism not far from Salinger's and dyed in unbudging resentment of the man he has buttonholed. He resents Peter's daughters, and even more he resents the parakeets. Recoiling with typical fastidiousness from the details of a heterosexual's private life, he suspects the birds of having lice.

Jerry envies Peter his social invulnerability, but at the same time he profoundly despises any man who can be so impervious to his own spry lunges of irony, as Peter is to the question about whether Baudelaire and J. P. Marquand aren't his favorite writers: "Baudelaire, of course," says Peter, "—uh—is by far the finer of the two, but Marquand has a place—in our—uh—national . . ." To Jerry, national is for the birds, because the national ideas are accommodating exclusively to men like Peter and also because they make the assumption that life is workable, which to him is a sorry lie. He can't make any contact that he trusts to be honest, even with a dog. The character's mixture of mawkishness, self-pity, acuity, and real despair is untricked and sometimes singeing; the style of the prose is a piece of sustained histrionics that is a remarkable feat of modern English.

FEBRUARY 14, 1965
LONDON

Could-Haves

"I could've been educated. Worked in a hairdressing salon. Learnt myself to speak well." "I could've sued. All the legal advisers say I'm in the right." "I could've married him. A doctor. I could've bettered myself, except I didn't choose to." The spoken language of England, especially working-class England, is full of sad, vengeful could-haves, miles from the possible. Encouragement given to oneself while stationary. English writers of the last fifteen years have caught and recorded the note, but it would be a piece of pride in period to believe they were the first. Oscar Wilde heard it, for instance. So did the Restoration. So did Jane Austen and Dickens. Any age alert to the class system—which brings with it that bracing, painful scholarship in the overtones of the spoken word which every Englishman inherits—will be eloquent about people's notion of their unspent possibilities. Because in England the notion belongs to a formalized society, it is usually expressed through formal things: dreams of education, of knowing as much as someone on the BBC, of broken-off engagements to an invented man in one of the professions, of unknown authority figures in medicine or the law who are invoked in monologues about revenges that will never actually be carried out or self-justifications that can never be begun because the fantasist can't write a letter. In America, where the same notion belongs to a society without contour, it is differently expressed: "I could've been a contender" (from the famous scene in *On the Waterfront* between Brando and Rod Steiger).

Perhaps one could define a man's class—and also one of the cruelest things about the class system—by the ceiling he puts upon expectation. Joe Orton's *Entertaining Mr. Sloane*, an English stage play now filmed by Douglas Hickox, is about four English working-class people whose expectations are wildly fantasized but, all the same, bitterly low in reach. While the slumberous savagery of the action goes on the characters chat to each other in a mixture of genteelisms, crime journalese, pub-brawl insults and desperately repeated pieties lifted from advice columns. Their cautious, orderly little house is actually a defrocked chapel, standing in the middle of rubbish-damp tat—much like their lives, though no one is going to say that. Looking out of the window at the pesthole they live in, they will make polite conversation about the view. The oldest and rudest of them is Kemp (Alan Webb, harrowingly good). Kemp is a furious, chirrupy sage whose main hope is to get by and to steal a bit of boiled ham from his middle-aged children, who are twice his size, anyway, and as plump as kiwis. His instinct is to take the locks off the insides of doors in case anyone might plan to get up to mischief. He survives by the rule of don't-just-stand-there, hit-him-first, and the energy to do it is supplied by his terror that his daughter is going to leave him on his own or put him in an old people's home. He creeps about the place behind pebble lenses that look like the headlights of a car driving into a night storm. Grousing, half gaga, but wholly there in knowing how the deck is stacked, he hasn't spoken to his wide-boy son Ed for years. They are walled up in one of those famous Anglo-Saxon domestic silences that would probably be beyond the tolerance of most other nationalities, and who is to say whether the thing that sustains them in their immurement is a matter of endurance or of having left themselves no option? Ed—played by Harry Andrews, magnificent in quite a different sort of part from the military buffers he often gets—is a bluff queer with a posh pink car who shows off about imaginary business associates. He has borne down jealously on his sister's sex life from the beginning. The sister, Kath, given to euphemism, religion, and nymphomania, is played by Beryl Reid. The character often talks about herself in the third person, as if to a baby. She can sound like Mrs. Bowdler even in the very middle of seducing her young lodger, Mr. Sloane, whom she calls "Mr. Sloane, dear," and she habitually burbles to him about housekeeping standards with a grandness that doesn't quite come off. "One does like to keep the smells down to a modicum," she says stylishly on the stairs one day, waving an aerosol spray about and wearing a hairpiece and a broken-down white housecoat with ostrich feathers. Peter McEnery plays Mr. Sloane. He looks like a crash-helmet Billy Budd, and he has no morality or heart at all. The other characters live on habit, on expecting nothing much further of life in spite of prattling in silver-lining proverbs, and on the tensity of speaking in a tone of voice that is totally at odds with the situation; but Mr. Sloane lives on his wits, and he expects better than this, thanks very much. Kath pines for him. She also manages, poignantly, to put him off from the start with her woman's-magazine chatter about love and mothering; if ever there was a boy who demanded that people shut up, this is one, but she can't stop for the life of her. Like Mary Musgrove in *Persuasion*, she suffers volubly and her minor ailments are always worse than anyone else's. She has terrible migraines, and nobody feels for her poor nerves, just as nobody knows what she goes through when she remembers the young man, now among the dear departed, whom she says she nearly married. She would claim for her sex as its highest virtue that it loves longest when hope is gone. This is far outside the ken of Mr. Sloane, who lives in the present and from hand-to-mouth on principle.

The language of the text is like parquet over a volcano. Kemp is eventually kicked to death by Mr. Sloane because he was a witness to an earlier, idly committed murder of his. Kath, perky transparent dresses to the last, remains entranced by Mr. Sloane and thinks of polishing the lino upstairs to make it look as if the old man slipped. Mr. Sloane insures Ed's and Kath's silence by agreeing to marry both of them, going through a grotesque double-marriage service in the stuffy, murderous little house. Six months of life ahead with each of them in turn. Half the time with Kath (bosom heaving with excitement under her artificial pearls and her little gold crucifix), half the time with Ed (who employs him as a chauffeur, dressed all in guaranteed-non-imitation leather).

The film script, by Clive Exton, is skillful enough to hide a lot of the difficulty of making such a theatrical piece of writing into a movie. All the performances are wonderful. As to Orton's text, it would be possible (but not exact, I think) to argue that this is actually a highly moral piece. If it shows us people with a knee-high view of life, barbarous infants in genteel grownups' carcasses, there could be said to be an implication that the world should have done a lot better by them. Voltaire also wrote about people who are totally disreputable but issues that are absolutely serious. The young Joe Orton, though (now dead—clubbed to death in awful imitation of art by his boy friend, who then killed himself), was understandably not yet so sure of what he was doing. Voltaire could shock; so could Firbank, whom Orton admired. But it takes genius to shock. In this text, perhaps, there is only talent, and a strain of the professionally outrageous. There may attach to it, in our heads, the notion that outrageous things ill-done have courage because they repel, but the truth may be that they repel because they are ill-done and not very brave. All the same, the piece is by a young master of artificial diction and ribaldry, a writer whom other writers recognized. Sean O'Casey said cheerfully to me that this was a play to make a man pull his trousers up.

Its trouble is the time's, not Orton's in particular. It can't quite find its own voice. Not only the characters but also the text itself seem to be speaking in quotation marks. Nothing is said directly; everything is on the bias, spoken at a tangent to mock suspect "sincerity." This may be one of the few specifically modern characteristics (cool, for instance, is nothing new; nor is gallows humor). It can impose a terrible load of mannerism on writing, even though one of its causes, paradoxically, is the modern horror of indulging the phony. I believe Orton was a serious-minded man; it is this contemporary problem of utterance that belies his work, this problem of his not seeming to mean a word he says. He would probably have got round it by some technique of his own if life had been halfway forbearing with him. Instead, along with his plays, he has now posthumously left us this film: a revenge tragedy going on among the antimacassars and the doilies and the ketchup; an analogy of *The Cenci*, but one that has no comprehension of the blasphemous.

AUGUST 1, 1970

Coward Revived

Noël Coward's *Hay Fever*, immaculately revived by the author, has been called a comedy of situation; but it isn't really that at all. It is a comedy of characters who are absolutely impervious to situation. This is one of the clear natural differences between farce and comedy. Farce is about people who are preternaturally alert to the outside world, to the dangers behind bedroom doors or the dragons in boilers; comedy is about people with such massively engrossing and indestructible characteristics that the outside world bounces off them like grapeshot off elephant hide. *Oedipus Rex* would be a comedy if, with the plague of Thebes running through the drawing room, the royal family remained blind to their people's agony and thought only about being attractive to each other.

This is pretty much the situation in *Hay Fever*. The Bliss family have invited four wretches for the weekend whom they proceed to wrack with inattention, starting with no introductions, going on to no explanations of a party game at which the theatrical Blisses shine, and ending by leaving them coldly alone with some unpleasant haddock at Sunday breakfast from which the outsiders tiptoe back to London, worn out with histrionics. The Blisses don't notice; they have the survival power of drunks and the hermetic family infatuation of the Greeks.

Edith Evans plays Judith Bliss with a dimension of tenderness that no one else could give it. When she yells "October is such a mournful month," she is unforgettably funny; she is the only actress alive who can yell so slowly and beautifully. It doesn't matter a damn that she is logically too old for the part. Nearly all the performances are impeccable, especially Maggie Smith's as a fastidiously frigid lounge-lizardess, Robert Lang's as an idiot diplomat, and Lynn Redgrave's as a flapper, humping her beads on to her lap like a carrier-bag. The work of the Master, writer and producer, is clean and sharp.

NOVEMBER 1, 1965
LONDON

Bergman as a Comedian of Manners

Just as an Irish playwright finds it all too easy to have the Little People wandering in and out of his work, so a Scandinavian can quite naturally make a film about devils. In Ingmar Bergman's elegant comedy-morality *The Devil's Eye*, half the characters are on the staff of Satan. Quite apart from the fact that the film is based on an ancient bit of Celtic folklore holding that chastity is a sty in the eye of the Devil, the tone of it makes you feel that the Swedes are sometimes very Irish. They put baleful magic into ordinary clothes in an attempt to pretend they are not scared silly of it.

The Devil himself looks like a foul-tempered executive, wearing a lounge suit with box-shaped corners and leering horribly because of his sty. Outside the french windows, hellfire churns as monotonously as a washing machine. His chief advisers, a count and marquis preserved from the randy eighteenth century, who are described as "men of such noble blood that their perversions sent voluptuous shudders right up into the Archangel's pinion," know that the boss has to be appeased. Shaking their periwigs like naughty-minded sheep, they trace the sty to the virginity of a parson's engaged daughter and Don Juan is dispatched with his repressed manservant to seduce her.

It is typical of a Bergman film that Don Juan should have no luck at all, while the servant finds a market in the parson's invalid wife. The hierarchic distinctions are always very strict in Bergman's movies: the employers are tormented and ascetic because they have intellects, the employees are blissfully amoral because they are mindless. Wage-earners, he implies, are happy animals, but management and monks have a tougher time in the sight of the Lord because they should know better. In a serious Christian film it seems a doubtful ethic to pursue, but in a sophisticated comedy it works with funny irony, which is one of the many reasons why Ingmar Bergman's entertainments have so far seemed to me better than larded pieces of metaphysics like *The Seventh Seal.*

The Devil's Eye is not as good as *Smiles of a Summer Night,* but it is wonderfully witty and enjoyable. As usual, Bergman has done the script himself. The dialogue, subtitled for once by someone who can write, is peppered with those abrupt, musing rudenesses that crop up in Chekhov. "You have an unusually ugly nose," says the vicar's sickly wife ungratefully to the satanic valet who has crept into her bed. The performances by the Brueghel-faced Bergman repertory company are wry, peculiar, and comic. Free will, says the Devil, is seriously practiced only in Hell; by falling in love, Don Juan has forfeited it and joined the determinists who inhabit the earth. Bergman has never delivered his perpetual message so mockingly.

JANUARY 13, 1963

The Bungling Detective

Inspector Clouseau is an incredibly bad film, but Alan Arkin is sometimes very funny in it, especially when he doesn't try to be. I can't say "Don't be put off by the beginning" —which is a scene showing Arkin getting soaked on the tarmac of London Airport without his shoes and wagging his big toe at the rain through a hole in his sock, heavily establishing (a) funniness and (b) English weather—for there is a lot more of the same to come. But there are a few bonuses to pick up along the way, like the tips that might enliven an evening in the fixed-grin job of a Playboy Bunny. Arkin has the part of an unemployably inefficient French detective. He is called in by Patrick Cargill, as the Commissioner of Scotland Yard, to help about a big robbery case. The Commissioner takes the step under duress from the Prime Minister and clearly loathes doing it. A sniffy man with a knighthood, he obviously feels a great deal better without blasted foreigners around his neck. The narrative twists of the film go on with remorseless dopey invention, and the physical gags are so full of effort that I started getting twinges of sympathetic rheumatism, but Arkin finds some good things to do. Dropped among the weary, clever, and perfidious English—any one of whom would run rings around him even if only trying to beat him to an ice-cream cone instead of being involved in a high-powered bank robbery—the Inspector is imperturbably confident that he has Albion taped. He knows the idioms inside out, sometimes literally. To a suspect Cockney who says "I don't know nuffink," Monsieur Holmes replies keenly, "He who knows nothing knows something, eh?"

A lot of fine things in film comedy have happened just out of earshot, like some of the great moments in Jacques Tati. Arkin has a beautiful outburst of broken-English muttering in a prison barbershop. The writers—Tom and Frank Waldman—have given him a funny characteristic of overexplanatoriness, and he develops it by the way he phrases his lines. He will appear to have finished some supremely self-evident sentence, and then muster himself for a whole fresh clause of fatuousness. Much of the best rescue work he does for the film is the result of his ear for change of volume. For instance, he has a laborious comic scene in which he is outfitted by the Yard with a tape recorder, gets shy of speaking into it, and then bawls an unabashed song, which I suspect is the place where the film-makers thought the joke was. The funny part actually comes when he has finished yelling and says, very softly, "Song."

Inspector Clouseau is the sort of thriller that you can come in on or out of at any time, since the plot seems to have been concocted of used typewriter ribbons and old sweaters, but I do find the Inspector's character endearing. He has a habit of talking in severe and quite meaningless apothegms. Some of his wisdom sounds like the Book of Ecclesiastes set up by a compositor with drunken creative urges. "There is a time for laughing, and a time for not laughing, and this is not one of them," he says sagely. He is insanely confident with machines, chatting confidingly about "drowning" a bomb as he dips it in water, in the style of some television cooking demonstrator saying that now she is cutting up our onion as she cuts it. A girl driver has had a car breakdown on the road, and he helps her, looking as much like an expert as possible. "When this is connected in *one of two places*," he says emphatically, waving a wire from God knows where, "it makes the motorcar move." I won't go into the story of the picture, partly because anyone who describes in print even the first ten minutes of a thriller gets so many murder threats from readers, partly because giving an account of it would be about as interesting as describing an egg-and-spoon race. But though it makes you sorry to see such good actors as Frank Finlay and Barry Foster playing unrewarding parts in garbage like this, there are things that make you laugh—the plain daftness of the film, sometimes, and Patrick Cargill (the Englishman who played Brando's valet in Chaplin's *A Countess from Hong Kong*, and an actor of real wit who always looks as though he had bitten on a lemon), and the lugubrious Arkin himself. Whenever Arkin cools down, his style is technically as delicate as any other comedian's in America.

JULY 27, 1968

Underling Spies

The Spy with a Cold Nose, which is an original about a bugged bulldog, cost several billion less than *Casino Royale* a warred-over adaptation from Ian Fleming. And it had four fewer directors, being made by only one. It is also simply better. It is funnier, less fanciful, more attentive to its loopy story, more agreeable. *Casino Royale* has had all this time and money spent on it, and ended up spoiled: what a nanny once used to dismiss as "ex and shoff," which meant excited and showing-off.

The Spy with a Cold Nose was written by Ray Galton and Alan Simpson, who have the gift of being able to root even a dopey spy fantasy in something recognizable and local. Their hero, played by the dear egg-faced Lionel Jeffries, belongs heart and soul to a cautious, testy commuting belt of Greater London. He has a bullying wife, three vile children, humiliating long underwear, twenty-three years of unrevealing experience in the Secret Service, and no self-confidence at all. He refers to his children, with a jauntiness quite wretchedly assumed, as his spawn. "I will not have my spawn ashamed of me," he says. His wife, draggy creature, says that he should never have become a spy in the first place and that she doesn't know how other spies' wives manage.

Away from what is supposed to be home, he works in a basement where his name is listed somewhere above the broom closet's and below the boiler's, in an atmosphere of irritable expertise where sharp-eyed officials are quick as lightning to spot the difference between Budapest and Bucharest and get deeply fed up when they can't find any visible ink. The Lionel Jeffries character is easily charmed by spies' gadgets and natty bits of agents' apparatus made by the Nipponese, who are, as he says, very clever, and have *tiny* fingers.

Sheer pleasure in the job gets him somewhere in the end, or maybe simply misery at home, and Laurence Harvey as a worn-out-looking vet (who is said to be the third-best-dressed man in the world) supplies him under pressure with a bulldog that transmits information out of Russia from a radio buried in its surly guts. There is rather a funny scene when Eric Portman as the British Ambassador is trapped in his own Embassy in midconference under a sound-proof globe, steaming up like chicken *sous cloche* until the butler brings the breakfast. The film is mild and small stuff, but it knows its own scale, whereas *Casino Royale* seems to be under the impression that it is *Cleopatra*, or the party of the year, or something. People keep on arriving, and making entrances that stun them to smithereens, and then never even meeting the host, let alone taking any notice of one another. Peter O'Toole, Peter Sellers, Belmondo, David Niven, Ursula Andress, Deborah Kerr, Orson Welles, Woody Allen . . . If only someone had been asked whom no one had ever heard of. The inexhaustibly self-hypnotized series of guest appearances that are made with no gift but aplomb makes the experience of the film exactly like being in the company of some gang of social nits at a costume ball, all of them quite deaf because they are so engrossed by the sight of themselves in periwigs. I don't think I remember a film that so bore out the popular cant about what the company of actors is like. Nobody concentrates on the story for more than a second. Every scene is ambushed by some preening gag or egomaniacal bit of business. When it penetrates even this bemused film's skull that the movie may be suffocating under the weight of the awful guest list, then it turns out to be only time for yet another hair-raising piece of producer's folly. Let's interest them with a flying saucer in Trafalgar Square; let's have a parachute drop of Cowboys and Indians; oh, yes, I know, let's have somebody *famous*.

Better not to list the directors and writers whose work was presumably travestied in the familiar misguided processes that led to this flailing mishmash. It was risky of the picture, I should have thought, to spend such a lot of its time elaborately bitching the rival Sean Connery Bond series, which have a lot more popular sense, grasp of movies, and circus flair. Woody Allen is sometimes rather sweet. He has a line about people under four feet six inches that makes him sound rather as if he sees himself as a mascot without an owner: a penknife, perhaps, with hopes of being tucked into the belt of Ursula Andress's bikini.

APRIL 16, 1967

Unemployable Maigret

Blake Edwards' *The Pink Panther* has a very endearing set of opening titles. They are mostly occupied by a sugar-almond-colored panther in a huge state of good humor about himself, who keeps trying to take the credit and messing up the lettering. The arrangement of the title that he seems to like best is *The Pink Pant.*

The picture has a performance by Peter Sellers that is one of the most delicate studies in accident-proneness since the silents. He plays a kind of hopelessly inefficient Maigret, a small French police inspector who is sublimely self-confident about his capacities as (a) a detective and (b) a seducer of his beautiful beanpole wife, in neither case with any basis at all. When he throws open a door to detect eavesdroppers, for instance, there is never anyone there and the door bangs back on his behind. Objects seem to wait in ambush for him, his dressing-gown cord goes into a Gordian knot just as he is climbing besottedly into the marriage bed, and he misses every clue that is staring him in the face.

His wife, well played by the over-criticized Capucine, is secretly in league with David Niven as a titled rotter who is planning to steal the biggest diamond in the world; but the inspector suspects nothing, and happily trots off to get her some hot milk while she slips through an adjoining door to make some criminal arrangements. Sellers' part is played with a flawless sense of mistiming. Every move the poor man makes seems doomed to end fatuously, like the moment when he grandly spins a globe to show the scope of his dragnet and then rashly leans on the whirling surface. He speaks English fluently but wrongly, with a perfect grasp of a slang that no Englishman ever quite spoke, like an Indian.

Capucine here shows a lot of elegant and grown-up humor. It was a funny idea physically to cast her opposite Peter Sellers; she looks worlds too sophisticated for him, quite apart from the fact the he only reaches up to her kneecaps. The long bedroom scene they have together, with two lovers hiding under the bed or under the bubbles in a bubble bath, is as funny as *Rookery Nook*. So is most of the big set piece at the end, a fancy-dress party with the inspector tracking down clues in an unhelpful suit of armor and the house filled with policemen in awkward disguises. The best things in the film are all farcical. It's a pity the rest isn't exaggerated in the same way. David Niven's character has the basis of being a marvelous send-up of all the classy cads in fiction, but neither the star nor the director seems to have quite the energy to do it. Claudia Cardinale's part is another near-miss. She plays the princess who owns the diamond: a frosty-mannered royal virgin patently bursting with sexuality is a good farcical start, but it doesn't come to anything much. The dialogue is flabby as soon as Sellers isn't there to speak it. It is the sight gags that work best. Blake Edwards follows Robert Dhéry and a great silent tradition by letting some of them flower just off-screen, with pregnant sound effects.

The other two comedies of the week are dire. They are both about sex, though not as we know it, and they both seem to have been made by some know-all child with ambitions to grow up into a Legion of Decency inspector. Sometimes I think there must be a sex-film comedy-kit now that is sent to every big studio at Christmas. The component parts seem to be exactly the same from film to film, and the assembly uses about as much creative talent as cleaning your teeth. The parts in the How-to-Make-Your-Own-Exciting-Comedy Set include:

1/One virgin who does everything the beauty ads tell her to do to attract men, but spends the whole film screaming about hanging on to her virginity.

2/One man destined for marriage, who is as dull as ditchwater.

3/One Lothario character.

4/One room with brown walls, white carpets and gold lampshades.

5/One cocktail bar where the Lothario character mixes himself hangover breakfasts.
6/One skeptically brainy girl friend of the heroine. (In the old days the character sometimes *was* the heroine; not any longer.)
7/One standing joke about all men hating marriage and all women thinking about nothing but.
8/One stately happy ending.

JANUARY 12, 1961

Snub by Computer

Hot Millions is an entirely goofy English comedy, directed by Eric Till and written by Ira Wallach and Peter Ustinov. Ustinov plays a butterfly expert with a Cockney accent that you could cut with a knife. In professional life the character is a con man, an embezzler, and a computer expert—self-taught, which is a blow for our side, considering the intimidating air of patronage that computers exude toward mankind. Maggie Smith plays a gutsy, lonely girl who tries job after job, including one as Ustinov's secretary, glumly bashing a beautiful office typewriter on the tab key and saying, "Oh, I'm not going to like it here" when the carriage jumps at her. Maggie Smith is quite an actress. The parts she played in *The Honey Pot* and *The V.I.P.s* didn't begin to use her, and even this immensely funny performance is only one aspect of what she has done on stage. In *Hot Millions*, which is agreeably rude to all machinery, she plays a very characteristic comic part. It has a surface that is peculiarly hers, both grumpy and blithe. There is a scene in which she walks around her lodgings in a trance of love and a fog of burning sausages. Her relationship with the Ustinov character is endearing, the essence of their skepticism and insulting horse sense being that they are secretly sweet to each other, though they would kill anyone who said so.

Hot Millions is an enjoyable, affectionate film, full of pleasantly anarchic impulses, such as a victorious scene about how to drive a computer to distraction by hitting it with a bucket. Sometimes the camera movements themselves express the heroine's caustic mistrust of modern life: there is a nice half-realized zoom shot when a lens moves in on a modern office building crammed with identical non-see-through glass windows, grasps that it is never going to get anything more out of the shot, and gives it up, with a faltering shudder, two thirds of the way through.

SEPTEMBER 21, 1968

Feeling in the Wrong Is Wrong

Somewhere, sometime, feeling guilty suggested that one might be to blame. Now it shows only that some beastly person, probably Mother, is in the act of trying to make one feel rotten. The psychoanalytically healthy will resist this new twist in the caste-system. Philip Roth, whose *Goodbye, Columbus* has just been filmed, knows the process backwards. He has cottoned on to one of the great inspiring whoppers of the post-Freudian West: that one's own guilt is the fault of *other people*. As we now see it, Oedipus took a self-destructive decision about his eyes. It made him a *victim*. "Look here, Ma," he should have said. "Quit trying to make me feel bad, will you?" Dictionaries are out of date. The ancient sense of sin and the modern sense of guilt have nothing to do with each other. The sense of sin is harbored; the sense of guilt is thrown back at the guilt-instigator as fast as possible, like a ball under the three-second rule in netball. Guilt is to be interpreted now as a signal for revenge, not for apology. If a woman cooks bacon and eggs and a man doesn't eat them, then the cooking of the bacon and eggs should be read as a sly device on her part to make him feel guilt, and the guilt should be hurled in her face. The comic new view of shame that has been codified by Roth, among many other funny writers, is that the immemorial uneasy feelings are not incurred but inflicted. It is beautifully mechanistic like the outrage of an old woman I know who complains bitterly about the ugliness of the clothes she buys, as though they happened to her out of the blue while she was having a nice quiet read. If a man trained in the new ethic fails to telephone someone back, he will not blame himself for putting things off but concentrate instead on hating the one unphoned. Or if he kicks his girl where it hurts, then he will stare resentfully at his toecap and lam into her for leaving her blood on his jackboot. The energy needed to lay one's guilt at someone else's door is majestic, although the result in peace of mind seems peanuts. There is something immortally funny about the sight of people putting a disproportionate amount of effort into the pursuit of a prize that they're too spent to want when they've got it. They are like the characters in Feydeau who are much too worn out by the logistics of adultery to feel up to committing it.

In Roth's *Goodbye, Columbus*, as in *Portnoy's Complaint*, the heroes are so busy suspecting others of practicing victimization-by-guilt on them that they become the victims of suspiciousness itself, exhausted by wariness and by jumping on poisonous motives that turn out to be earthworms. It is a classically farcical sight, and faintly harrowing. At the end of the film, a nice Jewish middle-class college girl (Ali MacGraw) has got herself into trouble with her parents by leaving a contraceptive in her drawer at home. In a hotel room with her boy friend (Richard Benjamin), she gets distraught about the letters from her viciously jealous mother and father, but the boy turns on her at once, with only one interpretation in his head. Another man in love might have a dozen understandings of the situation, and tend to shut up while he thought about them; but this kindly, edgy boy, armored by habit against the ploys of his own family, doesn't believe that she might have left the thing behind by accident, or wanted a child, or needed his support against malevolent parents. He detects only an impulse to make him feel guilty of letting her fly in the face of a heritage of savage priggishness that she secretly upholds. And so he wades into her. Benjamin plays the scene with such power of sad distaste that he makes the judgment seem less arbitrary than it probably is—speaking as he lies back on the bed, and nerving himself to a course of leaving her that is going to be hard for him to carry out.

Benjamin is obviously intelligent, like all the funniest actors (W. C. Fields applying his mind to running rings around spiteful toddlers, or Keaton alertly solving the problem of boiling two eggs in the kitchen of a luxury liner equipped to deal only with hundreds). You can see the hero's mind whirring in *Goodbye, Columbus*. He seems a hundred times as bright as his reproachful Aunt Gladys, who slaves to make the members of her household feel guilty by cooking food that they are forced to eat in phased solitude, alone in turn at the table, and naturally falling into her trap by having no hunger for grub so blatantly prepared in the somber half-hope of rebuff that has become comedy's standard style for older Jewish women. In his girl friend's family house, the blood-related obstacles include Jack Klugman as the stylized American Jewish father, horribly henpecked but sometimes mustering the authority to say a frenzied word for peace, and Nan Martin as the mother, a woman with clenched standards for sex and patterned silverware. The girl friend also has an exquisite dolt of a brother, played by Michael Meyers. He is a football major with a dreamy taste for André Kostelanetz, and he goes into an engaging trance when he hears a radio commentary on his own game. And there is a ten-year-old sister who is the classic guilt-giver in the bud. Naturally, it is she who catches Benjamin at the fridge. Ravenous, as people are in other people's houses, he has secretly pocketed a few cherries. Only this severe child could make him then feel so stricken that he squashes them to jam, just as only this child could so accurately prefigure her maturity by yelling housewifely things at adults about not keeping the front door open when the air conditioning is on. There is something a bit banal in the story, but perhaps that is because there is something banal in a society that has distorted guilt into a technique for comic reprisal. Benjamin's scenes with Ali MacGraw are finely detailed and nice to watch; the reactions of the two mesh as if the characters were really in love—at least for a summer. Larry Peerce directs the best performances with Philip Roth's tone.

My impression of Roth is that he is freer of obsessive comic Jewishness—more critical of it, less up to his neck in it—than his public sometimes seems to think. "Look," he says. "This is what it's like to be on the boat, but I'm on the shore. And look. This is the real, wound-picking Jewish joke—to be a man like the men in my books, who knows the joke but still can't help being part of it." His heroes are exhibitionist masochists like their mothers: Hey, thinks the reader sometimes, why are you trying to put me in the same position that your mother put you in? OK, let that pass, but there also exist good-and-evil, love-and-cruelty, rich-and-poor—there are polarities apart from Jewishness and non-Jewishness, aren't there? *Goodbye, Columbus* is about a crew of people who don't see it that way, and about a boy who finally begins to. Only very witty Jews could have written, directed, and played the appallingly funny wedding party in this film, which is pushed as far as some farce of collapsing group-hilarity in Gogol. It is grotesque, lewd, limping, and endless—like most ritual parties, in fact, only more so, because it is exaggeratedly possessed by this Jewish/non-Jewish bewitchment. When the hero recoils from the spectacle, he is made to seem a saved man, off the couch and out of the door.

APRIL 12, 1969

DISRUPTERS

To W. C. Fields, Dyspeptic Mumbler, Who Invented His Own Way Out

"The time has come," W. C. Fields would moan, with his usual all-seeing, alcoholic meditativeness, "to take the bull by the tail and face the situation." Well, to grasp a tail, the new films around at the moment are nothing to write about (not even to write home about, which Fields would have thought a pretty rotten fate even for a bad movie, since home left him to his own resources at the age of eleven). *The Maltese Bippy*, directed by Norman Panama, with Dan Rowan and Dick Martin, tries earnestly hard to be zany, but that's its trouble. The muscles bulge. I suppose the comedy isn't that bad, unless you have been seeing something actually funny. There are also not more than about two minutes of horror when you might want to look away, which counts as a record at the moment. They happen when the heroes are trying to nerve themselves to operate on a naked stomach with a meat knife to get out a diamond. ("Godfrey Daniel!" as Fields used to say in the quiet caw he used for homemade curses, flummoxing the Hays Office.)

One can draw a veil over two other films, *The Fool Killer* and *The Tree*. Good acting has gone into both pictures so there's no call to hammer the poor misbegotten things into the ground, except that both contain a rough *sixty* minutes when you might want to look away, which is a high proportion of time to be turning your back on a medium primarily meant to be faced. There is now a preview audience's appreciation machine that registers the sweatiness of people's palms. Sweatiness in this case counts as good, so by that standard these two films would have to be called terrific. In each of them, you are offered the sight of a child looking plainly cognizant of what's going on during scenes about adult psychoses, beatings up, insult-matches, and art-movie killings, which are now much more brutal than they are in films for the big markets. W. C. Fields himself might have had a hidden qualm about those kids. He was known to have been furtively kind even to Baby LeRoy. And he would have had more than a qualm about *The Maltese Bippy*, because he knew what was funny. I would say he was one of the four or five funniest men we have lately had in the world.

Not everyone responds to Fields, but the people who do love him recognize a blood brother. He is one of life's losers, and the hell with it. He is not in the race. Fields is truly stylish and his own man, a covert friend to mongrels and a brilliant enemy to privilege, hiding affliction under a far-off and sulphurous view all his own. He is Chaplin's diametric opposite. Chaplin's little man can seem to be on his knees and cringing for sympathy with his bravely managed suffering, but Fields is on his feet and thinking. ("It is much more easy to have sympathy with suffering than it is to have sympathy with thought," wrote Oscar Wilde in an essay on socialism.) Fields is a smoldering independent who asks no pity and who saves himself with eccentrically conceived and harmless vengeances. In *It's a Gift*—which has been turning up regularly in the art houses, along with the other Fields works—he tries hard to run a grocery store that is eventually flooded with molasses by Baby LeRoy. Fields lets the little saboteur go unscathed. The incident merely adds a baleful new jot to his analysis of the human condition, and the notice that he hangs on the door of his wrecked shop mildly reads "Closed on Account of Molasses."

Surrounded by virago wives, soppy girls and overblessed children, he deals unexceptionably with the immediate situations, walks away with a skeptical expression somewhere around the hips, and implies that the better part of his considerable brain is disreputably engaged with other things. His battleship wife, Mrs. Bisonette ("pronounced Bissonay," he writes loyally on a placard, obeying her haywire snob teachings), makes him halve a sandwich that he then has to eat in the middle of a storm of cushion feathers. She yells, never satisfied, that these were her *mother's* feathers. But Fields has secretly won, all the same, for even if he is getting hell for obligingly eating a stingy half sandwich full of feathers, he is also eating the half sandwich that contains the complete sandwich's ration of meat, which he has neatly swiped from his own greedy child during the forced act of partition. Fields often has a bad time, but he is no victim. He is fortified because he always holds an opinion, even if the opinion isn't exactly communicated in speech as we know it. Fields doesn't so much speak as amuse himself with self-addressed soliloquies. The to-and-fro of less doughty men is not for him. His is only the fro. In his great films he is always the reactor. He plays the muttering straight man to Life, the counterblow to a punch in the stomach. His retorts are conceived for himself alone, like his endearments and his curses.

In *Million Dollar Legs*, as the weight-lifting President of an otherwise rather weedily athletic state called Klopstokia, he tries to do something about the economy and simultaneously deal with his dopey daughter's suitors. One of them is visible out of his window. "What's his name, Angela?" he says, with his native distaste for his own offspring's name, though his hungover Richard Tauber voice suggests that the seraphic fib committed at her christening is only the way of the world and scarcely worth reacting against. "I call him 'sweetheart,'" says Angela. "Hey, sweetheart!" yells Fields vaguely out the window, and thereafter he is so beguiled by the wooziness of the word that he applies it to various sports trainers and members of his Cabinet throughout the film.

No one can use endearments more dangerously than Fields. "*Please sit down, honey!*" he bawls at a blind and deaf man who is in the process of exploding a pile of electric light bulbs by feeling around him with a white stick. If this sounds a particle cruel, the next sequence shows Fields covering his eyes with terror at the sight of the same man weaving his way through traffic. Secretly alert to everything, he pretends to a protective callousness. His kindnesses are clandestine; his open and implacable hostility is beamed at the unfortunate, the armor-plated and the prissy. This axis includes Deanna Durbin-like stars, mayors, milk, gambling laws, literal-minded listeners, and soupy women, among whom I think he would have put the nurses who tried once, in real life, to look after his own broken neck and were waved away ("It's only a flesh wound") with stories about far worse calamities that had befallen him and that he had survived with the help of "Doctor Buckhalter's Kidney Reviver."

In extremity, which was where he lived from toddling age, Fields took refuge in improvisation, in wild names, in veiled ripostes to child stars whom he sensed to be looking after Number One far better than he had ever managed to, and in a huge ration of carefully selected booze. When a friend of mine once met him, he was drinking three Martinis for breakfast and looking at a rose garden. He preferred Martinis to anything else. He told her carefully (she was about eight) that Scotch could begin to taste like medicine and that bourbon led to drunkenness. He genuinely hated drunks for their vehemence and mawkishness, two things that this calmly out-of-step and stoic man despised. As his biographer, Robert Lewis Taylor, has recorded, he always used to take a Martini shaker to the studio. He would say that it was filled with pineapple juice. Somebody mischievously once put actual pineapple juice into it. "Somebody's been putting pineapple juice into my pineapple juice!" he yelled. But he never failed to turn up for shooting, and he generally finished days ahead of schedule.

One of the many reasons he drank seems to have been that he was frightened of making the subtly understood technical miscalculation of speaking his lines too fast, which he never did when he wasn't cold sober. He had an outlaw's gift that was matched by no other comedian. Faced by the conventional breakfast, he would suddenly ad-lib an inviting burble suggesting that ordinary food might as well go out of the window. "How'd you like to hide the egg and gurgitate a few saucers of mochajava?" he mutters convivially in one film. He liked words very much. "Sars' parilla" engaged him. So did "my little plum," and "kumquats," and a game he called "squidgalum," and an uncle called "Effingham Hoofnickel," and foggy snatches of descriptive narrative out of the blue: "She dips her mitt down into this mélange. . . ." He can make gracious sentences to the dignitaries who are his natural enemy. "I am Dr. Eustace P. McGargle," he says, elegantly switching from gambling to preaching in the presence of a mayor. "Perhaps you've read my book on the evils of wagering. . . . I was a victim of this awful scourge. A helpless pawn in the coils of Beelzebub. Beelzebub . . . Beel-zee-bub . . . Lucifer."

His famous puffy nose was a source of distress to him. Most people believed the misshapenness to be due to drink, but it was really because of the bashing and pounding it had taken when he was a child living in ditches. He slips in a revealing line somewhere: "The man had a rather prominent proboscis, after the fashion of eminent men." Fields allowed himself no sympathy and he joined no one. He was the author of his own life, and he behaved as though he had no kin. It isn't surprising that our generation has loved him, and that a record of clips from his sound tracks is on the hit parade. The fact that it is No. 41 on the list is something he would probably have quite relished. He never wanted anyone's favors. He had the wiser trick of extending a license to himself, and he died an agnostic, without help, as he promised he would. "I'll go without knuckling under," he droned once, about believing in God.

JUNE 21, 1969

There is a myth that women don't really like W. C. Fields, the most prejudiced, unruly and sloshed comedian in cinema history. I think it is about as true as the one about women preferring white wine to red. It arises, I suppose, because he loathed kids and felt genial to disorder, and the male sex, which chiefly invents myths, along with slang, war, symphonic music, and obscenities, obviously has an interest in assuming that women will love children come what may, and that they will always elect to make life work. Once start admitting that women frequently cherish quite urgent desires to bonk infants on the head, and that they may well have the same fellow feeling as any other human for W. C. Fields's dogged anarchy, and I suppose that civilization as we know it would come to an end.

Fields is a moving man. The pseudonyms he used when he wrote scripts—Mahatma Kane Jeeves, Otis Criblecoblis—are not only funny but also obviously devised in an authentic moment of instinct for flight. They are part of his system of bolt-holes, like the elaborate chain of bank accounts that he instituted under a score of names. His early life was appalling; but instead of turning into a victim, he became a fifth-columnist. Where other kids grow strong on orange juice and the love of relations, he lived on resentment and solitary sniping operations. By eleven he had left home. He obviously had the deepest sense of grievance about ever being a child, at the mercy of a father who sold fruit and vegetables from a cart and sang maudlin songs. Fields hated "Annie Laurie" and the human voice in general until the end of his life, and he seems to have become sulphurously bored by the time he could talk.

Required as a minute infant to trail round after his father when he was selling greengroceries, he immediately satirized the parental sales-cry. This led to trouble. He also yelled commercials for nonavailable commodities like calabashes and rutabagas because he liked the names. In *It's a Gift*, which enshrines some of his very best languid loathing of family life, there is a scene in a grocery store about kumquats, inserted for no obvious reason but euphony. It is interrupted by a totally blind and deaf man, whom Fields holds to be the house detective over at the Grand Hotel, and by a small son sitting on the meat-chopping block, whom Pop shoves off it muttering something dark about blood poison. It seems to be the meat's blood he fears for, not the child's.

He drank prodigiously; but it was early beatings, not booze, that made his face look like a decomposing sponge. His life, like his work, held very little comfort. What they both abounded in was flair and cheek. He approached sentimentalists, dogs, preachers, bossy women and overprivileged tots from the position that they were his native enemies, and he a born loser who could win an inch off them here and there only by effrontery and cheating.

No other Hollywood personality can ever have emanated such steady contempt of the Hollywood idols who were in the same picture. His relationship to the thinly disguised Deanna Durbin warbler in *Never Give a Sucker an Even Break* seems to be one of longing to get her as intoxicated as possible and to use her vocal cords as a catapult. The Bing Crosby slush that goes on in Mississippi must have steeled him into much cunning and a good extra pint of liquor a day.

His fatigued voice sounds as if he has been defending himself against creditors and prigs and line-ups of the commonplace all his life. The famous drawl, which he can throw ventriloquially, like a cat, is never going to win him a point but never going to surrender one either. A lot of other comedians are frantic but inert: W. C. Fields is the opposite, stoic and energetic. His rudeness is afflictingly lonely, blissfully funny, and a spit in the eye of an often craven business.

FEBRUARY 26, 1967

Billy Wilder's Thin Ice

Billy Wilder's *Irma La Douce* is about a world of tarts, but they have been beautifully cleaned up. Played by girls with scrupulous underclothes and nice unsmudged lipstick, they have the charm and unreality of the co-eds who are written about in career articles in magazines; the ones who get jobs because their stocking-seams are straight.

Of course, this is what makes it funny. *Irma* is brilliantly devised as a bourgeois fairy tale that just happens to be set in the underworld. It is full of people whose worries about ethics and appearances are comically unrelated to the fact that they live by whoring and pimping. The crisis in the story is not about cruelty or drink or murder, but about the hero's deeply embedded male feelings that he shouldn't be kept by a career girl. When he grumbles that he never sees Irma because she is out on the streets earning money all night and asleep all day, he sounds like any husband on the dole with an irritatingly busy night-nurse wife. The situations in the film are always violent, but the things people are bothered about are rather gentle; it's as though the action of *The Bacchae* should suddenly stop for a committee tea about waifs and strays.

Irma, played by Shirley MacLaine, is a quizzical girl who lives with a small poodle and a lot of beautifully ironed green lingerie. Her room, she says vaguely, was first occupied by a painter called Schwarz, who cut his ear off. Nestor is played by Jack Lemmon, who does the same sort of whitewashing job on the character as he did on the hero of *The Apartment*. There is such a bomb crater where his confidence should be that it is hard to blame him for anything. Before he lives with Irma he is a gendarme, unjustifiably confident about his capacity as a one-man vice squad on account of his previous experience, which was in guarding a children's pond.

Jack Lemmon is one of the best waverers alive. There is something about the way his sentences ambush one another and fall dead of heart failure half-way through that is almost an equivalent of a high-wire comic's stymied movements. To the society you might call Neurotics Anonymous, which includes most of us, there is something very appealing about his mixture of belligerence and nerves. He looks the kind of cop who wouldn't quite like to stop the traffic.

He has at least three very funny scenes in this picture: one when he is suspected of murder and dresses up in his old policeman's uniform in an attempt to mingle unnoticed with the policemen who are searching a very small room; another when he is sleepily lugging fish around the market all night, earning money secretly to keep Irma off the streets; and another when he is trying to bribe her very hostile poodle with some champagne sloshed into an ashtray. It's a pity his set piece as an English lord in disguise isn't better. It would have been nice if it had been as impeccable as Tony Curtis's impersonation of Cary Grant in *Some Like It Hot*.

Otherwise the film is mostly enjoyable for Shirley MacLaine's sculptured schoolgirl's legs, which are clad always in green stockings, and the very pretty set designs. The script, by Billy Wilder and I. A. L. Diamond, is immaculate, but the film is miles too long. Two hours twenty minutes puts an impossible weight on a fairy tale. Billy Wilder might have used more of his famous bad taste; there are a few fine flickers of it, as in the scene when Irma is in her wedding dress at the altar, counting the minutes between her labor pains; but not enough to make you feel he was at anything like full stretch.

FEBRUARY 16, 1964

The Most Dangerous Ground

There is a kind of censorable funniness that only Americans seem to be able to bring off: W. C. Fields about milk-drinking toddlers, Groucho about Margaret Dumont, Mort Sahl and Lenny Bruce about politics. It has to do with cheek, stamina, and certainty of the comic's being at the bottom of the heap. Its voice is the voice of down-and-outs, vagrants, the stateless, the bank-accountless, the fighting born-victims who know themselves outnumbered the moment they are in the company of one, the furiously lovelorn who repine only in secret and publicly grumble blue murder about their woman as they brace themselves for another thwack on the head from the handbag of the beloved. It is the sound of the man with nothing more to lose, a yell from the last ditch, the resort of the persecuted, the humor of any citizen who sees the joke of his being welcomed as an immigrant by the Statue of Liberty with a gracious reference to him as "wretched refuse." Most other countries have nothing approaching this particular baleful, disruptive funniness. France hasn't a notion of it, with her serenity in Frenchness, her imperturbable syntax, and her limited understanding of humiliation. The wit institutes of France—farce at the Comédie-Française, say—possess nothing so raw and socially unhousable as Woody Allen's frantic confidences about being Jewish and about chasing girls. Poland's famous bad-taste wit is specifically political, a form of gallows humor that comes from being overrun, a policy of going too far personally when your country has been allowed to go nowhere for centuries. England certainly has fine bad jokes (and takes a pleasure in them that baffles practically everyone else), but the badness of its taste doesn't really hold a candle to American bad taste about being black, and now here it is, in Melvin Van Peebles' *Watermelon Man*.

The movie is a fairly lousy piece of film-making, and it is hopelessly constructed, but it is quite a feat of off-key funniness. Godfrey Cambridge, who is black, appears in it first as a bigoted Northern white. The make-up job—it is impossible to look at this film without its giving you a share in its insane bad taste, which is rather companionable of it—is elaborate and interesting. The bigot is called Jeff. He thinks he is popular, but nobody really likes him at all except his wife and children, and the children just barely. He is actually a beast. He enjoys irritating the black driver of his usual morning bus by racing the bus on foot, and he enjoys needling the black counterman at the drugstore where he daily orders some lunatic health juice to his own recipe. He fancies himself as a humorist. When he finally climbs onto the bus, he says merrily to the long-suffering driver, "If you were in the South, you'd have to drive in the back of the bus."

But then Jeff, to his horror, turns black overnight. He puts it down to his sun lamp. He then goes on being exactly the same sort of beast, and the familiar victims of his racism go on taking it on the chin, because they are so used to it. His wife (Estelle Parsons), a quiet and liberal woman of great patience, implies somehow in her manner that his blackness is simply a trouble he is going to have to be babied through, constituting only one more of the eccentric tasks she took on by marrying him. After shrieking briefly about the change in him, she becomes solicitous and practical. Jeff takes baths in milk, the bathroom floor littered with rather small milk cartons. He buys skin-whiteners by the ton from stores in the Black section of town. "These creams don't work," he says desperately. "No wonder Negroes riot." His wife is soothing. "I don't think any intelligent Negro expects it to be immediate. Don't be militant," she says. "I'm not militant, I'm *white!*" he yells, hopping mad. Worried to death about himself, racing to embarrassed doctors, he keeps up his spirits by roaring at other Blacks as usual. They look at him carefully, wondering why on earth they should stand this any longer, and put the change of skin down to a trick of light. Beginning to be defeated, Jeff retreats to the shower to pray for whiteness. Not that he believes in God, but still, God can be bullied and whined to, presumably. "Please, Lord, you will see a *nice* person coming out of this shower?" A white person, he means. Pause. "There are no *atheists* in this shower." Sob. Godfrey Cambridge is a funny actor, going miles too far in a direction that no other Black I know of has tried, and good luck to him. He takes the bile out of an impossible joke.

JUNE 6, 1970

Mukel Swink

Robert Downey's *Putney Swope* has a good title. For some reason it made me think of "mukel swink," words that come up in the Middle English Mystery Plays. "A man of mukel swink." A man of much toil. The wretched Putney Swope, played by Arnold Johnson, is a worn-out-looking Black expected to be an energizing force because of his color. He gets elected head of an advertising agency, called Truth & Soul, Inc., by the sort of mistake that can hoist nonentities to high political office. Black or white, everyone at the board table votes for him because everyone thinks no one else will. An even more worn-out-looking white, called Nathan, drooping like a highbred rose in a smoke-filled room, tells him hopelessly that it's a terrible job. Other men at the table say patronizingly that he'll make a great chairman if he stays in line. "The changes I'm going to make will be minimal," Putney says honestly, flushed with a version of the modern statesman's special sense of powerfulness when he is going to do as little as possible. "I'm not going to rock this boat."

Some phantasmic revolutionary spirit then kicks in him for a second, and he says wildly that he's going to *sink* the boat. He is seen next in African robes, elocuting a rhetorical slogan that goes, "You can't change nothing with rhetoric and slogans." Growingly muddled but clinging to spryness, he throws his weight around in the agency. Blackboards seen in the background at meetings show the way his mind is working. He will do his exhausted damnedest to keep things exactly as they are by giving them more calming labels if the public shows signs of fret. With Worth-It Life Insurance and Lucky Airlines, he seems on to something.

"Mr. Swope," says a white yes-man, playing bravely with Mr. Swope's own pencil to show strength of character, "I do exactly the same job as everyone else, and I don't get paid as much. That doesn't seem fair." "If I gave you a raise," says Swope, "I'd have to give everybody else a raise and we'd be back where we started." The white says he hadn't ever thought of it that way. "And *that*," says Swope, clinching it, "is why you get less money. Because you don't *think*." There are one or two sweet passages of false logic in the film—scraps of dialogue that might have caught the ear of Waugh, who knew as much as any wit of our century about both the ancient, sanctioned skills of casuistry and the modern forms of success-with-the-boss by voluntary missings of the point. Swope's effect on his employees is like the effect of Waugh's Lord Copper, the newspaper magnate who surrounded himself with voices to say "Definitely, Lord Copper" when they meant "Yes," and "Up to a point, Lord Copper" when they meant "No," the difference being that Swope's air of freebooting command is slightly cockeyed and seems bluffed. You feel he probably stays awake a lot at night worrying in secret. Seen occasionally in the film in revolutionary circumstances, with fellow Blacks gunning for change by this man who has simply been landed in a very staid seat, he fumbles along in the same old way and grasps sometimes at a spot of radical farce to cheer himself up. He makes a commercial that shows a black girl in a gold lamé minidress prancing around a tenement. "You can't eat an air-conditioner," says the ad gaily before plugging "a new experience in 'lectric fans." Miss Redneck of New Jersey ("Five foot four, with blond hair and matching collar and cuffs"), who works in a restaurant and majored in philosophy, is asked to tell television audiences in twenty-five words or less what her philosophy is. The distraught girl, thinking strenuously, forgets she is in a pie commercial and says, "Confidentially"—I like "confidentially"—"I think that every person of all race, color, and creed should get a piece of the action." After a lot of prompts she says "a piece of the pie."

Putney Swope jibs at form. Wild jokes come up and disappear without a trace, like the arms of jocular swimmers signaling "hello" far, far out from the beach. Some of the cock-a-hoop inventions work; some don't. Downey has a very special sense of humor, but it wouldn't be anywhere near right to say that he is funny only when he knows where to stop. Sometimes, though not always, he is funniest exactly when he does go too far and piles it on insanely. In one of his earlier films, for instance, there was a brief scene with a big naked lady, a gorilla, and Beethoven's Ninth Symphony; any two of them, one thinks solemnly, wouldn't have been up to much, but the fact that Downey did pile all three on top of one another went too far in a fine way. There are things in this new film that do the same, and others that go too far in a wan way. (I don't necessarily mean the cheeky bits or the lewd bits. A startled reply that a Black in a breakfast-cereal commercial makes to the sales gobbledygook on the commentary cracks me up. Downey anticipates trouble from quibblers, anyway. "*Gourmet* magazine calls Putney's ads tasteless," says the film. One of Swope's own aides says severely that he is confusing obscenity with originality. "Your mother had a creative idea when she bore you and you had to go and blow that," he says witheringly.) The scenes that one withdraws from aren't even exactly definable as the moments when Downey falls into the surrealists' old trap of trying too hard, for he doesn't seem to be trying particularly hard at all. The feeling of the film is more like being in the company of a crackerjack talker who makes way-out lunges and puns—some deadening, some brilliant, with a germ of fool's sageness here and there, and also with the very special appeal of buffoonery. The buffoon is a man who hasn't a notion what you're thinking of him. In the context of two much penny-in-the-slot comedy writing, trained for so long by Broadway and by television laugh shows to fit in with audience response like man and wife, there is a liberating sort of funniness about a humor that is unlivable with, that stays quite deaf to others, and drops its old socks all over the floor. When I was seeing the film for a second time, at an afternoon show, mid-week in the rain, with an audience nearly all of Blacks who seemed enraptured by the kicks at cant whenever they worked, it was like being at a party invaded by a cheerful, impossible boozer who alternately bores offended people into the ground and revives them by the sheer intentness of his ambition to swipe enough of the nobs' cocktail canapés to see him through another starving week. Some of Downey's film is lousy. Some of it has a peculiar half-pretended opportunism and a rudeness to his hosts—to the party, to the payers, to the American economy—that work blissfully. The film comes out politically as a nit's mishmash of elitist-Communist-nihilist, which probably suits the mood of a good many audiences in America at the moment. It is sophisticated, anticapitalist, heedless, distractible, with a Geiger-counter ear for cruelties hallowed by custom (a man carrying a huge metal object is sent down thirty-odd stories to take the freight elevator—the innovation being that he is white and the order comes from a black.) Downey's quixotic humor, paced to a new upper crust of the quick-witted but noncompetitive, and inaccessible to anyone not in the know, expresses something specific about Manhattan's mood now. "Things are Changing," says a placard in Swope's office. No, holds the film, things aren't, and they won't, not by a long chalk—not if we only shuffle places and keep the armchairs the same. And, along with saying that, the film sends itself up for saying anything at all, and simply enjoys—for instance—its idea of a character called Sister Basilica, a nice chain-smoking nun who is eager to impress the agency by introducing a child orphan called Billy. "If you want to be his pal," she announces, "all you have to do is fill in the necessary papers." "Why don't you just adopt me and get it over with?"

says the awful, scathing child to the fawning grownups, going on to leave them with a line of advice aimed at the hearts of all of them and shooting home the film's underlying thought about how to sort out the mayhem of bigotry and phony dissent it describes: "Whatever you do," says the kid, with nasty shrewdness, "don't do it out of guilt."

AUGUST 2, 1969

And We'll Be Back after This Message

For the last three or four years, the silent minority of England has been awash in passion for a BBC-TV series called *Monty Python's Flying Circus*, just turned into a battily funny film called *And Now for Something Completely Different*. The passion has equalled the earlier cult that followed the radio version of *The Goon Show* (Peter Sellers, Spike Milligan, Harry Secombe, *et al.*). The film, directed by Ian Macnaughton, is compiled—well, piled together, perhaps—from the wilder explosions of the great talents of a group of writer-actors, mostly drawn from Oxford and Cambridge, who have grown up together in the jungle of their inanely witty television show. Otherwise they have little in common with each other, apart from their sense of humor, and nothing whatever in common with anyone else.

In one bit of the film, for instance, we are watching Army physical-training practice overseen by a martinet who has a vein of unadmitted nervousness. The practice teaches protection against assault by fresh fruit. Homicidal attack by loganberries comes up. When dealing with a banana fiend, advises the instructor (John Cleese), looking military but clearly harboring alarm, one should eat the banana. Suppose the fiend has a pointed stick, a lily-liver in the Army class keeps saying, being as obsessed by the question of pointed sticks as others are by marauding fruit. It is at junctures like these that a conventional-looking Army officer with a breastful of medals (Graham Chapman) is apt to step in to say severely that this film is displaying a distinct tendency to become silly.

The world of *And Now for Something Completely Different* is all on the side of liberty, and notes with a basilisk eye any incursions of English authoritarianism. There is a good deal of material about the sort of people who are always seeing burglars and other dangerous party-groupists (foreigners, the young, and so on) under the bed. One singular sketch is about the peril to the public of mad forays by grannies on the prowl. Grannies are said to be no respecters of race, creed, or sex. You see hordes of flower-faced, gentle-looking old ladies in morning-church hats running riot and doing improbably athletic anti-social things like carting away telephone booths. "Make Tea, Not Love," reads a graffito on a wall, obviously chalked up by a granny on the rampage. All right; if that's their tune, the country must deal with the threat in its midst. You feel that the officer-in-command of the film is in constant and justifiable fear that it is running off the rails. Not that he truly believes that he is on the rails himself, any more than anyone else in the movie.

In an inchoate episode, John Cleese plays an iron-voiced mountaineer sternly interviewing an alertly intrepid recruit who thinks he wants to join an expedition. The leader plans to climb Kilimanjaro. The trouble is that he sees two of everything, which is a handicap in a mountaineer. He talks about going via Dovers, and strongly asserts that Kilimanjaro has two peaks, dismissing airily any climbing difficulties by saying that he means to build a bridge between the two. To the consternation of applicants coming in one by one in the usual way, he addresses them always in duplicate, often asking the person not sitting there what he thinks, and regularly talking about "both of you" to the man on the other side of the desk. Sometimes, vaguely aware that things are awry, he will cover one eye with his hand, but his demeanor and mode of address remain stiffly unchanged. No one quite likes to bring up his crucial misapprehension; the bifocal mission proceeds undeterred, with the merest suggestion from some muscular recruit who is sitting alone on the edge of a chair that there is only one of him. Tact about idiocy is everything, and politesse prevails.

A lot of the movie rests on this system of insanely sustained manners, and the form of the interview is key. A vocational-guidance adviser, for one, guiding an accountant who wants to be a lion-tamer, points out in the most kindly and practical way that the accountant is an appallingly *dull* person, *terrible* company, *depressing*, and beautifully *fitted* to be an accountant, but that he might work his way up to lion-taming through banking. There is a temporary spot of bother because the man being interviewed turns out to have confused lions with anteaters and holds stoutly that lions look pretty tame to start with.

The picture chooses to progress by fits and starts—sneezing fits and false starts, you could say—but the hell with that. One sees a nice restaurant customer (Graham Chapman) involved in a mild upset about "a bit of a dirty fork." The benignly put incident suddenly develops into Italian melodrama and a near breakdown of the manager (Eric Idle), a pugilistic but easily collapsible man. There is another fine scene in a pet shop, in which John Cleese complains with some reason to Michael Palin that the parrot he bought that day was a *dead* parrot. The pet-seller holds, against all logic of the eye—and of the ear, which can hear the body of the undoubtedly long defunct parrot being banged on the counter with a sound like the bashing of a rubber sausage in a Punch-and-Judy show—that it only looks like that because it's a Norwegian parrot and pining for the fjords. "It's bleeding demised!" says the maddened customer, trying to get his point through. "This is an *ex*-parrot." If you want to get anything done in England, he mutters, you've got to complain till you're blue in the face. Bureaucratic sloth is one of the continuing butts of the film. So is the propaganda style used in the Second World War, which the writers and actors (who cheerfully overlap and seem to do everything—including the sound effects, you suspect, which often sound like experiments in a school lab when the master in charge has quit the room because he is in a weak position) take to be so much garbage. There is a flash of sober official advice about how to kill enemy Germans with jokes. The Allied side's members have been taught the jokes word by word, for safety's sake; they then lob them at the Huns, who receive the words strung together and are massacred by being doubled up in schoolgirl hysterics. These *new* jokes, reports the commentator in the voice of wartime British newsreels, are over ten thousand times as powerful as the prewar jokes used at Munich. Nothing is sacrosanct in *And Now for Something Completely Different* (the full list of the component anarchists is Graham Chapman, John Cleese, Terry Gilliam, Eric Idle, Terry Jones, Michael Palin, Carol Cleveland, and Connie Booth)—least of all patriotism and any sort of bigotry.

AUGUST 26, 1972

ROTTEN-JOKERS

The English Joke

For all its pessimism and mournful drinking laws, England has a deep dedication to jokes. Other countries may have a town devoted to gambling, like Las Vegas, or to diplomacy, like Canberra, or to the colonic tract, like Baden-Baden, but England has Blackpool, which has given up its maudlin Victorian heart to the form of the feeble pun.

The image of Blackpool to me is of a huge, glum toddler sitting in a collapsible plastic pushchair and blowing on a hot chip. In the meantime his parents, frozen out of inhospitable digs as soon as the ketchup has been cleared away, will talk soberly about the joke-level of the season like fishermen assessing the sardine harvest.

The ocean around the island must be alive with gags. Every few miles along the coastline an old pier barnacled with *double-entendres* sticks into the sea, a long, silvery arm of jokes encrusted with lights like the sequins of drag queens in pantomimes, with bright little booths selling unimaginably censorable beach postcards and at the end of it a theater that is a shrine of the most terrible jokes in the world ("Paris, city of madness, where only the river is Seine. . . .").

I'm afraid perhaps you have to have been an English child to stomach it, reared on riddles in Christmas crackers and double-meanings in *Puss in Boots*. I don't know how else to explain the success of the *Carry On* pictures, which are made like old socks, or the Whitehall farces, which might be directed by traffic-meter wardens, or the Palladium, where one waits for the funny man as people in sane countries wait for the nudes; we must have a very great passion for jokes to do it.

Music hall may be dead, but its gags are inextinguishable. There still remain fewer jokes about politics than any other comparably sophisticated setting. The temperament remains what it has been since Hogarth: ribald, brutal, incautious, domestic. Harsh laughs still go in harness with Victorian sentimentality, "Ramona" is still sung, and even the buoyant Ken Dodd will belie his nature and silence a house with the penny-in-the-slot melancholy of a number called "Tears." The fact that fewer couples have to live with their parents now has enfeebled the mother-in-law joke, but the telly-commercial joke that has replaced it perpetuates very much the same comic impulse, a mood of sat-on derisiveness about bossy homemakers covertly lusted after. "What is a mum?" "A mum is someone who has something hot waiting for her husband." A mum is a dope, thinking in obedience to television advertising that what he wants is a beef cube, toiling over a hot fish-stick without an idea of any double meaning in his head.

The butts of the jokes are male and historic: honeymoons, cuckolded mates, paternity suits, queers, and women most of all, who are funny because they are gullible, kind, long-suffering, child-bearing, without insight into themselves, unable to tell Stork margarine from butter, intent on an irritable life-task of gnawing at the plumpness that men love them for, and never, never aware that their desirability is comic.

Comedians' acts and funny films are full of a tender hilarity about the way a girl in a job will brush away the fact of her sexiness, like a lecturer vaguely swatting a fly on his pate in mid-flow. They show us a secretary typing a balance sheet behind a sweater that forbids our meditating about anything else, or a nurse severely taking temperatures in the presence of thoughts that need a good slap. A girl in a music-hall act stands about on the edges of the joke much like the lady-helpers who move the tables for trapeze artists. She looks gracious about it, as though opening a fête, and quite unaware of her astounding, unmissable ripeness.

Morecambe and Wise, the great music-hall partners, have a doctor-and-patient act involving a nurse. She has no idea how sexy she looks, but Eric Morecambe can think of nothing else. Experimentally, he calls her "Sid." She doesn't notice, of course. They never do. ("Poor thing," as Frankie Howerd says behind his hand about Blanchie Moore, his ill-used accompanist on the piano.)

I suppose that women are most of all funny because of the very thing that prevents them from being comedians—because of their vocational pretense that life works, when men can so clearly see that it doesn't and that it is an impossibly ropy engine with most of its crucial parts lying on the ground. It is only a very few geniuses, like Beatrice Lillie, who have had the detachment to seize on this feminine tendency to boil eggs for everyone in the middle of Armageddon and see it to be funny. I remember she did a mime once about having dinner alone in a grand restaurant. Her clothes played her up, as usual; her boa behaved like a cross alleycat and her evening coat was her implacable enemy. Added to that, the waiters were nasty to her, and the lobster they brought her was locked inside a shell that no stiletto heel could crack. Ravenous but making the best of it, she started to manicure its claws.

The most profoundly comic jokes I know about Englishwomen are embodied in Mrs. Shufflewick, who is played by a man. It is the most delicate drag act in the whole range of ambiguous pop humor. The character is dogged and unshockable to a point that has made me cry. She enters wearing red gloves, a damson velvet coat, drop-pearl earrings, and a dusty flower hat much like one of the pot-plants that are put carefully *behind* the net curtains for the sake of the neighbors. Her fur, as she says, you won't see the like of again. "It is known in the trade," she remarks, in a voice worn out with booze and the double meanings seen by lecherous men, "as untouched pussy."

To Mrs. Shufflewick lewdness isn't a pleasure but a condition of life, and she has no objection herself to meeting anyone's demands, except that barmen sometimes victimize her for it. She lives in Wimbledon—"all cut glass and tennis balls"—and you feel that the people there probably patronize her. She drinks green chartreuse, and she was married once, lonely centuries ago, to a pheasant-plucker. There is something about her doctrine of getting on with it that distills half England. This is the best of English joking. At its worst it can create a foul mob, boisterous and beef-witted, but the good comedians do something different. They don't make crowds; they divide them, asserting that not much of life can be shared and turning a joke into a sort of undercover contact, as though the country were composed of men in prison flashing mirrors at one another or tapping the pipes.

That is the great charm of Morecambe and Wise—the implication that Eric Morecambe is so obviously unfitted to cope with life among the hordes of the adjusted. He is a mild, eager man who might just have emerged from some affable Tibetan monastery. Even his best friend, Ernie Wise, can't help him for more than a second at a time to concentrate on relevant things as a successful citizen must. Ken Dodd, a brilliant misfit with forgetful pre-Raphaelite hair and teeth like eaves, has rather the same habit of being ambushed by his own thoughts. Sometimes his speech pattern can sound like a short-wave radio on three stations at once. He will say something about using a cat in a sack as a hot-water bottle, and then be distracted by the idea of getting Granny's legs insulated for the winter. People confuse him because they keep striking him as objects, just as his hand will suddenly take his eye as though it were a trafficator. "Granddad used to stand with his back to the fire," he confides suddenly. "We had to have him swept." Girls alarm him rather. "I woke up in the morning with misgivings" is a line that sometimes comes up in his act, and both the idea and the pun seem to startle him.

The traditional English way to activate a terrible pun on stage is to set it into a dialogue-rhythm like a tap dance, with the joke exploding as if it were a stamp of the foot. The metres of music hall have survived the buildings:

"If you succeed with Cynthia, you'll go back to your missus with a tidy sum."

"With what?"

"A tidy sum."

"I thought you said a tiny son."

This old piece of craftsmanship comes from the Whitehall, where the jokes are more primitive, trad, and square than at any other joke-pocket in the country. "He's called Jerry." "Why?" "Because he comes from Po-land."

Next to Slav-speakers, who are considered to be funny because of their consonants, and Germans, best-known for their sausages, the most intrinsically comic foreigners seem to be Arabs, on account of the yashmak. Vicars are also good, and philistine remarks about art are winners. "The Laughing Cavalier" is endlessly profitable, like the "Mona Lisa," and the holes-in-modern-art avant-garde joke never seems to fail. Any avant-garde painting will be a portrait with two noses, and artists will always walk with the swift, knee-scraping gait that identifies homosexuals in English comedy.

"Go on, Julian, show him your swatch." The BBC Home Service has been broadcasting for years the most cheerfully off-color dramatic material in the country in *Beyond Our Ken* and its successor, *Round the Horne*. The blueness of the jokes, and their patent inoffensiveness to millions who were appalled by *That Was the Week That Was*, are made possible by a peculiar property of the English language: the fact that any word can be forced into a temporary new meaning simply by its context. It is like the story of the Irish priest who died of shock when two students said they had matriculated together after the girl had seen the boy's thesis. People in England enjoy supplying the points of jokes in the privacy of their own skulls. The English are indeed a very private race, a nation of do-it-yourself and pigeon-fanciers and collectors of things that nobody else wants.

I suppose it must be indoctrination by *Beano* and other childhood comics that makes the English feel so affectionately toward hard-working word-jokes. "I'm Forster Stand," says a character in *Simple Spymen*, merely to allow the next man to say: "What's he done to himself?" Or "Do you play the trumpet voluntary?" says the straight man at the Brighton pier show. "Oh no, I charge a few bob." Perfectly bright people adore dim puns: the more labored the better, as in the question about "What-is-the-inverted-proverb-about-a-lot-of-provincial-Frenchmen-caught-in a-revolving-door?" which comes out dazzlingly as "Having all your Basques in one exit."

Jokes like these are obviously arrived at backward, with toil. Hard plotting in the bath is rather admired. The English constitute the only civilized race I can think of that doesn't insist that jokes should seem effortless. The taste goes back, perhaps, to training in riddles, which are the pure biceps of humor: all muscles and no laugh, mechanisms which children respect for their complication and which they study in comics as seriously as stockbrokers study *The Financial Times*. What other national sense of humor would nourish the phenomenon of the items at the bottom of the front page in the *Evening News*, which exist entirely as excuses for joke headlines? " 'The meal unfortunately ended in an exchange of blows'—Essex solicitor," for instance, is titled "Slap-Up Dinner." Are they *real* news items? Apart from a work-worn woman subeditor who proofreads knitting patterns by knitting them, whoever writes these paragraphs has the strangest job in Fleet Street. I imagine some solitary and impassioned man going over the news tapes in a trance of punning, looking dreamily for the fodder for his jokes like an elephant moving its trunk over a tray of buns.

NOVEMBER 14, 1965
BLACKPOOL, BRIGHTON, MARGATE
EASTBOURNE, NEWCASTLE-ON-TYNE, LONDON

Carrying-On

The usual charge to make against the *Carry On* films is to say that they could be so much better done. This is true enough. They look dreadful, they seem to be edited with a bacon-slicer, the effects are perfunctory, and the comic rhythm jerks along like a car on a cold morning. But if all these things were more elegant I don't really think the films would be more enjoyable: the badness is part of the funniness.

Perhaps the charm of the bad needs a theory. Why do people enjoy Joan Crawford? Or Vincent Price in horror movies? And what about the pleasure of lousy jokes? No critic in his right mind devotes himself to writing about *Beyond Our Ken*, the radio program that unites a huge secret brotherhood in a binge of terrible puns every weekend. The *Carry On* films are often excruciatingly funny, but they regularly get booted down to the bottom of newspaper columns with nothing more than a worried three-line admission that they wring a reluctant grin now and then.

Most of the English-speaking world—including music-hall audiences, children, and presumably Shakespeare's public at the Globe—has always accepted without any trouble that it is quite possible for a feeble joke to be that much funnier than a good one. The only people whom this idea bothers are the ones who have trained themselves to try to explain things. There has never been any respected method in aesthetics for allowing for the pleasure of groaning, so the *Carry Ons* go down the plughole.

Anyone can see the difficulty. The *Carry Ons* flout every respectable rule of wit that has ever been formulated. A good joke, for instance, is supposed to be effortless: but in these films the jokes take as much effort as the building of the Pyramids. A comic plot should be a perfect piece of engineering; these plots are more like a tangle of defunct spare parts. Gags are supposed to come naturally out of situations, but here the situations build up to the gags, with five or ten characters happily downing tools and indulging in a great lasso of plot for the sake of a single pun at the end of it.

In Peter Rogers' and Gerald Thomas's *Carry On Spying*, Kenneth Williams as a British agent gets himself to a Viennese night club in a hat and false beard, and forgetfully hands over the beard with the hat to the cloakroom attendant; the point of all this is that he can then say, "Hair today, gone tomorrow." If you respond to this kind of travesty at all, the flagrant determination to get it in is part of the joy of it, like the contortion of riddles for six-year-olds. It doesn't matter how forced the build-up is. Lines like this are obviously born pure in someone's head one long dawn, and the convulsive plot-making that is necessary to support them comes later. If a gag is exhausted and limp with overwork, that doesn't matter either.

Perhaps the unswallowable fault on the *Carry Ons* from the intellectual's point of view is that their irresistible badness contradicts all the lessons of the crusaders who try so hard to improve pop culture. Even song lyrics now seem to be surrounded by a cloud of ethic, and the center of the teaching is always that unless a vulgar form tries to be first rate of its kind, it hasn't a hope of giving people any experience more vivid than a panel session. So it has begun to seem almost socially immoral to suggest that there can ever be a real appeal about the hammy. But the *Carry On* films visibly aren't anything like first rate of their kind; and they are still enormously enjoyable. The comedy is appallingly laborious and planted, but it makes more millions of people laugh than a first-rate, free-wheeling wit like the Goons' or a first-rate piece of plot-making like Feydeau's. It is enough to make high-minded reformers want to give up.

There is only one obvious point for them, to the *Carry Ons*, and that is that, unlike most English comedies, they don't carry any particular class tags. They seem, therefore, to appeal to an unselfconsciously large range of people—blimps, children, factory-workers, housewives, soldiers, actors. The only solid opposition that I've noticed seems to come from (a) passionate Francophiles, who often really get a pain from them, and (b) people who themselves make good puns and understandably react with the horror of master craftsmen faced with a ham-fisted lunatic running amok in the workshop.

Luckily, no one working on the films seems to have decided whether they are supposed to be with-it or not. This makes them strangely timeless, a dream-mixture of periods, like the language of Wodehouse; they incorporate without difficulty a lot of the prewar flavor of beach-postcard humor, but they are also full of the 1960s.

In *Carry On Spying* the characters are not only square enough to wear braces (partly so that they can be caught on door handles); they are also camp enough to send up the colossal bull of a woman who is the film's heavy parody of Ian Fleming's M, in charge of an organization called Stench. To put it another way, the range is so vast that it comfortably includes both Kenneth Williams and Richard Wattis. There is also Charles Hawtrey, playing an aged schoolboy as usual, with bared kneecaps as big as a cart horse's. Bernard Cribbins vaguely tries to turn Barbara Windsor into a male spy, but he can't find a place on her to hang her holster. Then he shows her how he draws his gun, which gives her a chance to say blissfully, "Oh, Mr. Simpkins, I'm sure I'll never get my draws off as quickly as that." If this leaves you in misery, don't go.

AUGUST 19, 1964

I'm beginning to feel that there is no reason —apart from reason, perhaps—why the *Carry On* series shouldn't go on beyond the vanishing point. On an American plane lately my hand-luggage label read "Carry On Baggage Permit." The film version seemed bound to come.

In the meantime there is *Carry On Screaming*, an installment that messes about with the conventions of the series and lays an egg. The essence of the *Carry Ons* is their rottenness, but it is a rottenness that needs careful achieving. Harry Corbett is a newcomer, cast as a nervously inefficient Sherlock Holmes, and he makes the distraught mistake of trying to act. If you have a go at making the *Carry On* dialogue seem in character, you only make it clear that it is enough to make any real actor go away and die. The lines can't possibly be acted. I don't know what it is quite that the old hands in the cast do with them: stamp on them, throw them down the studio drains, mash them up with old paper bags: at any rate, disown them. The dialogue can only be said as if by a mutinous voice box for which the speaker admits no responsibility and that he considers to be hell-bent beyond recall on a course of lame retorts and blue puns.

Fenella Fielding and Kenneth Williams know how to do it exactly. In this picture, Miss Fielding plays a vampire dressed a little like a lady cellist, in a jammy-colored velvet evening gown that she wears during the daytime. Kenneth Williams is her dead brother, who can be resurrected by plugging him into an electric power socket. The picture is a spoof horror film, full of the characteristic *Macbeth*-type forest scenes made to look foggy with a dry-ice machine; the plot is vaguely about a Neanderthal-looking monster called Oddbod, his hairy pelt mercifully concealed most of the time inside something that is rather like an inflated version of Winston Churchill's siren suit. There is also a junior Oddbod who gets created, very foully, out of a hirsute finger that his dad has left lying around.

I'm not sure that it's a good idea for a *Carry On* picture to do anything so deliberate as a send-up of anything, let alone of a form that is already as silly as a horror film. The progress is mostly slothful and worried when it should be cheerfully cavalier and pointless. Exchanges like "We appear to be at loggerheads"; "No, no, this is Bide-a-Wee" offer their moments of ghastly pleasure, but the film needs a lot more aplomb with them. Most of the cast seem to have lost their grip on the style of besieged overacting that has often made the series funny.

Fenella Fielding still epitomizes it. She transmits somehow that she is embattled in a daft situation with lines that no self-respecting pro can do anything to improve, and her beautiful sniffy face establishes a distance from the material that makes it work. She is signaling that she knows it to be unspeakable, and at the same time what the hell. Most of the other actors seem anxious and listless. The takes on Harry Corbett's face exude a fatal atmosphere of actor's staleness. It doesn't help, of course, that the film is edited like half a pound of sliced stale ham, with cut after cut made relentlessly on a dialogue-change and laborious establishing shots about ha-ha accidents that are going to happen in three minutes' time. The *Carry Ons* have always flourished on their badness, but it is a badness that needs a lot more boldness than this.

AUGUST 21, 1966

Bad to Worse

The film techniques of the *Carry On* ensemble have got better in their new film and the jokes, thank heaven, worse. *Don't Lose Your Head* is ninety minutes of joy.

The time is the French Revolution, with Kenneth Williams as Citizen Camembert wincing daintily at the guillotine as each new nobleman perishes and his fresh-sliced loaf rolls into the executioner's basket. Across the Channel, Sir Rodney Ffing—pronounced effing, of course, and played by Sidney James—pursues a traditional English existence of no politics, an immense amount of sex, and a cover-life of hugely boring and decorous social occasions. Same old tea parties, same old concerts, same old balls: George Robey made that joke fifty years ago, dressed in drag as Queen Victoria.

An underfed-looking duke played by Charles Hawtrey tells Joan Sims as Desirée Dubarry that he knows a little arbor. Stricken by loss of aitches but behaving with dignity, she replies cordially, "Oh, really? I 'ad no idea we were so near the sea." This is one of the hallowed devices of English pop humor: to pull the rug from under a toff by using a grand accent that suddenly folds up, so that the actor becomes the voice of ordinary horse-sense making a comment on the character. In a costume film the effect is especially startling. One doesn't normally expect to see a man in a periwig being ornately courteous to a rather snooty courtesan and then suddenly complaining in rude cockney about a discarded banana skin in her bodice, bawling at her that when she undresses it's like unpacking a wastebasket.

The photography of *Don't Lose Your Head* is in color and rather good, and the double meanings are dazzling. The women are butts, suffering humor and randiness that they incite without at all caring for them, and most of the men behave like homosexuals whether they are or not. The posh-voiced characters pretend that sex doesn't exist, and the lower orders rightly suspect them of having enviable orgies. The reflection that the film offers of the oddities of English sexual attitudes in the mid-1960s is graphic and instructive enough for it to be practically worth sealing up a print in a vault for posterity.

MARCH 12, 1967

A Nation of Farce-Drinkers

There are many, many things that astonish an American about the English theater. To begin with, there is the amazing possibility of being able to see a play on the night one thinks of it, instead of booking three months in advance; and the unfamiliar sensation of going to a theater at seven-fifteen on an overenthusiastic English crumpet tea, swiftly followed by the unprecedented kick of being able to fight for a small warm gin in the interval instead of quaffing ice-cold fresh-up jiffy-orange out of a cardboard beaker. Then there is the quixotic docility of the English in shelling out quite a lot of small cash for a programme that carries nothing but advertising, when Broadway equivalents are full of information and free; and the startling group of indigenous entertainments that are not so much plays as horseplays, such as Christmas pantomimes and the Crazy Gang, which the natives seem curiously to regard as family treats but which any sensitive visitor is bound to look upon as a rough assault-course in transvestism.

Most novel of all, there is the phenomenon of the West End long run. On Broadway a show with a long run will nearly always be a musical, and it will absolutely always have good notices; in London it will nearly always be a thriller or a farce, and a critic who has slashed it will have plenty of time to bring up a family and die before it comes off. Agatha Christie's *The Mousetrap*, for instance, is now in its tenth year at the Ambassadors, so a whole generation of reviewers is writing at the moment that has never been to an opening at the Ambassadors in its life. Every few seasons I creep in to see how things are going: the country house in which the action takes place is kept up very well, the chintz covers are regularly spring-cleaned, and one can tell which year it is by the way the actresses' hemlines go up and down.

Farces in England run almost as long as thrillers, with which they in fact have a good deal in common. They too always take place in reception rooms, as distinct from French farces, which occur in bedrooms; as the manager of the Whitehall Theatre, home of farce, reprovingly writes, "We don't have sex. That's not our style." When trousers come down in English farce, it is because they *fall* down.

Like *The Mousetrap*, an evening at the Whitehall draws its public partly because it offers an absolutely reliable world, a code of values that is never questioned, and a set of characters who are never troubled by an adult ambition or desire. Class distinctions are accepted as inalienably right, constables wipe their boots before coming in for a cup of tea, and no one in the play would dream of being found with anything but the most unchallenging cliché on his lips. (As in how to make tea: "One teaspoon each, and one for the teapot.") The title of the new Whitehall farce, *One for the Pot*, could hardly be better: not only is it a cliché, it also offers the warm security of being a cliché about tea-drinking. The fact that it has nothing to do with the play is not really the point.

There are only two courses that are considered acceptable for reviewers writing about the Whitehall. Either one is to drag in some rather shifty mention of the *Commedia dell' Arte*, which is a way of saying that the acting is awful but one doesn't like to demur because the piece may turn out to be a key expression of popular culture; or else one says that one left one's critical faculties behind and rolled about in the aisles. Both these conventions are so much spinach. *One for the Pot* has nothing whatever to do with the *Commedia dell' Arte;* there is about as much improvisation in it, or reflection of popular life, as there is the Changing of the Guard. And anyone who thinks that he can be parted from his critical faculties makes no sense. It is as though a pianist were to say that, having lopped off his hands, he gave a lovely performance.

Not that any of this matters a jot to the box office. The Whitehall is a monument to the element in theater business that is called word-of-mouth: *Worm's Eye View* and *Simple Spymen* ran not on their notices, nor even on any star names, but simply because ten thousand people told a hundred thousand other people that the evening gave you a good laugh. In the teapot-shaped program of *One for the Pot*, the successor to these two record-breakers, the actor-manager Brian Rix publishes a note to say that he once set a man to counting during a performance to make sure that there were still 585 laughs—a lugubriously funny thought in itself, in the same mechanistic vein as the revelation once made by the director of the play (Henry Kendall) that he used to blow a police whistle in the stalls during rehearsal when he felt that an actor's performance needed improvement.

Farce is generally rich in laughs of situation, provoking surrender to misunderstandings so complex that the author must have had to work them out with little flags on a war map. The plot of *One for the Pot* is comparatively simple going. Ten thousand pounds are to be given to one Hickory Wood by a roaring Northern patriarch in a wheel chair, and rival claimants turn up, all played by Brian Rix. In most fortune-hunting drama the procedure is that different men claim to have the same identity, but in *One for the Pot* this is reversed: we are offered instead a number of different identities that are all conspicuously the same man. The dilemmas that agonize the audience in this play center on the most actual question of how an actor can get to the door in time for his entrance when he has not yet made his exit out of the french windows.

Apart from this sort of physical comedy and an exuberant philistine sequence in which Brian Rix sloshes paint around in pursuit of modern art, there is also a great deal of play made with soda-siphons, with drawers that hit people from behind, and with senseless bodies that keep slipping out of cupboards. Most of this is stiflingly noncomic, but a good many dreadful laughs are winkled out of you by the excruciating puns: e.g., "Ah, you must be Cohen." "No I'm not, I've only just arrived."

I append a small manual of conventions that seem obligatory for anyone who hopes to write a farce that will run five years. (On previous Whitehall Theatre form, this would seem to mean the actors in the current Whitehall production, who customarily while away the mummifying years of the run by scribbling in their dressing rooms. Those who cannot write farces are said, dismally, to read Shakespeare.)

1/There must be a butler/valet/other underling who, like Jeeves, is much cooler and better educated than his employer, and who has a courtly way of putting vulgar things, such as "The greyhounds have been most unobliging."

2 / There must be a scene in which a man loses his temper, preferably in a wheel chair, and shouts furiously, "I'm not getting excited!"

3 / There must be an antihomosexual joke.

4 / There must be several antiart jokes. ("It's a new movement." "Well, the sooner it gets going the better.")

5 / There must be several misuses of highbrow-sounding, i.e., intrinsically funny, words. ("There seems to be a certain confliction of style," or "Any more nonsense out of you and you'll finish up in a glockenspiel for Glyndebourne.")

6 / There should be as many possible conversational references to goods that are advertised on television, thus setting up a comforting illusion that one has not come to the theater at all.

SEPTEMBER 13, 1961
LONDON

The Lure of William the Unwashable

At the age when most of the girls I knew were in love with ponies, I was in secret league with William. I admired everything about him. He was a boy, his age had got into double figures, and he floated around the world supported by a gang of bosom friends instead of jockeying for the favors of a clique of faithless schoolgirls. He was blessedly free of nerves; with grownups easily worn out and prone to attacks of the grumps, his tirelessness and euphoria were magnetic. True, he sometimes scowled, but this was a device of argument, not a sign of unhappiness. It was a fill-in to replace the shaft of logic that always eluded him. In lectures about the necessity of wearing sock-garters, say, or of being nice to a repulsively clean little girl with a lisp, called Violet Elizabeth Bott, William could never put his finger on the right retort and instead had to retreat into a hastily assumed huff, brooding Napoleonically and implying that he hadn't long to live. I think it was during a dispute about chocolate biscuits, or perhaps caramels, that his mother told him he had had enough and William replied crushingly, having forgotten the statistics, that he had only had hardly any.

The awesome thing about him was the way he coped. Nothing got him down—not even his grievous burden of soppy relations. He had a bossy grown-up sister called Ethel, whom he could shame by giving away the dated secret that her curls weren't natural, and a lovelorn elder brother called Robert, whose sonnets William kept as ammunition.

On one of his periodic days of self-improvement, when he would see himself as an entrancingly licensed sort of saint ("helpin' people and fightin' "), he armed himself with a sonnet addressed to a girl called Marion and proposed on Robert's behalf to a girl who turned out to be another Marion altogether. William responded with his usual rhetorical mutter and said, "Why don't they put *surnames* in pomes?"

He was cursed, too, with a huge and horrible godmother, described somewhere as "magisterial," which still sounds to me ruder than it is, and a flotilla of aunts, some of them not bad. There was one sporting aunt at a funfair who persevered at a coconut-shy and kindly told the Fat Woman she should see a doctor about her weight; William mastered his embarrassment about women who couldn't throw things and benignly encouraged her. He was always nice to anyone who had a go, and outlaws and eccentrics had his heart. Working-class children spelled liberation, and so indeed did anything else outside his prewar middle-class approved life, including an ecstatic first experience of washing-up.

He melted at once toward people who broke rules, and even countenanced the lisping Violet Elizabeth as soon as she got muddy, in spite of the way she held up her face and demanded to be kithed in the presence of his chum Ginger. It was the first time that William's spirit was ever broken on the boulder of a woman's love. The people who got him down included censorious vicars, overbearing women, organizers of all kinds, confectioners who overcharged, anyone hostile to Jumble (his mongrel dog), and every sort of snob. He disliked Violet Elizabeth Bott's mother, a period new-rich figure who had married Bott's Sauce and upset the neighborhood by talking about Botty "making 'is pile": but he even more disliked the neighborhood for being upset.

William was a natural anarchist. He believed in no rule but the rule of dirt. Unlike Arthur Ransome's books, which are careful adult propaganda, encouraging the cold-bath sort of public-school initiative and well-planned explorers' diets, Richmal Crompton's William stories are pure revolutionary documents, preaching sedition and licorice all-sorts. The only thing that ever made me feel alien to William was that he preferred sweets to milk chocolate. I modelled myself passionately on him until I was ten or eleven: there was a reference somewhere in the books to his horny hands, and I used to rub mine for hours on the bark of a tree to make them look tougher. I also admired him for not minding about his freckles, instead of lying out secretly in the sun and getting redhead's sunstroke in the hope that the freckles would eventually join up and make a tan.

At twelve, when I thought I had forgotten him, I read a grow-taller advertisement in a book of stamps that I found in my father's desk while I was doing homework. I longed to be tall like Sherlock Holmes instead of a runt, and by selling my children's books at a secondhand shop in Marylebone High Street, I eventually saved five guineas and sent it off for the course. The parcel that arrived back contained a brick, and a note saying, "To be four inches taller, stand on this." In shyness, my mind fled not to Holmes but to William, and I wondered what he would have done, before realizing that he would never have bothered about what he looked like in the first place. He once defended his face unbudgingly to Robert and Ethel when they were falling about at some studio portraits that were taken by an archetypal prewar cissy photographer. "It's a perfectly *ornery* face," he said, or something like it. His mother backed him up. "It's a very nice face, dear." He must have got a lot of his vagueness from his mother, and his staunchness.

My sister and I never discussed William, and I had always thought her hero was a horse until, when she was fifteen and I grown-up, I recognized a fellow worshipper: I went to take her out at boarding school and suddenly noticed that, instead of stockings, she was wearing boys' long socks with a garter deliberately missing so that the sock could subside round her ankle like one of William's. People tend to keep their heroes secret, but the *Just William* books have been going since 1921. By now I suppose there must be quite a large blood-brotherhood of English adults who were as moulded by William as we were.

JULY 4, 1965

PRODIGALS

Ophuls Restored

We are in the circus of Max Ophuls' great *Lola Montès*. Chandeliers with new candles are lowered softly for the start of a spectacle. There are caparisoned horses. Dwarfs. Trapeze artists up in the rigging. Stagehands dressed like Napoleonic soldiers, running as if they were trundling cannon into battle. (It will be a battle, of another sort, circling and complicated.) Peter Ustinov, speaking French, struts around as a ringmaster with something disturbing him under his bombast. There are low sounds of children chattering, and circus pomp from the band. The camera tracks sometimes follow movement but more often gently counter it, without disturbance, like limbs crossing in deep water. Every frame of the Cinemascope screen is crammed. Much motion; deep browns and reds and purples; subdued points of light; the Ophuls wealth of detail in the Ophuls flux. The ringmaster is putting on a show: "The truth in pantomime," he says. The "true" story of the scandalous Lola Montès, "Countess of Landsfeld, in the flesh." We are to see a story of "broken hearts, lost fortunes, threatened crowns, and a real revolution." Lola (Martine Carol) is brought on—a doll princess in a carriage, but also a real romantic sovereign deposed, who is about to feed the historic thumbs-down instinct of people at circuses. "She will answer the most scandalous questions!" shouts the ringmaster. The perfect, immobile idol, placed in the middle of the ring, is set for mauling. The audience will adore her beauty, envy her for her lovers, and wish for her downfall. "The proceeds will go to the Association of Fallen Women," says the ringmaster cannily. Martine Carol's eyes click upward. "Where did she dance without her tights?" someone yells from the audience. "In Paris," she says, answering like a weight machine. Ophuls was wonderful with actors, and he could use the inexpressiveness of his star for his own purposes.

The "true" story. The audience, salivating, knows the end in advance: that the courtesan of a king in now a circus exhibit. Lola will be miming for them a form of the truth, for she is indeed at the end of her tether, but it is not the truth as she knows it. The film whirls. There is vertigo for us from camera movement, and from midgets dangling off high wires as if they were on butchers' hooks, and dizziness for Lola, because of the difference between the stinking morsels of gossip that the public is badgering her for and the past that is still alive in her. The film, Ophuls' masterpiece, which is being shown in New York publicly for the first time in the complete version, constantly pits two things against each other. Low words from the ringmaster to Lola alone sometimes interrupt his hyperbole to crowd. In the ring, now sitting on a display table in her crinoline, she answers questions in a voice of porcelain; offstage, she clamors for a shawl and medicine and says that she must give up smoking and drinking.

Some directors make film authorship seem very difficult. Others, like Jean Renoir and Ophuls, make it look like play—something they do to enjoy themselves. The fluency of Ophuls' style is balm. The story of his Lola, the famous courtesan who had affairs with Liszt and with the King of Bavaria before ending up as an ailing exhibit in a New Orleans circus, is transformed by his easy command into something quite at odds with the fan-magazine facts of the narrative. Because of Ophuls' beneficent style, *Lola Montès* is majestic and complex. There is a sense that something unique is being glimpsed in the apparently commonplace, and this is nearly as reviving and moving as the response of Mozart to da Ponte's *Così Fan Tutte*. It is like the way some people can make a puppet show a great piece of theater, or the way some artists can make a pessimistic statement exhilarating because their very genius contradicts it. The content of Beckett, say, is concerned with endings, and with the most difficult and minute resumptions made with small hope, but the effect of his own presence—maybe it should be called his company—has exactly the opposite effect; this great technical original of our age, this peculiarly convivial stoic, is perpetually starting again on giant undertakings as if he had all the time in the world. The victorious retort of style to material in Ophuls' best work is something comparable. The sense of detail in *Lola Montès* and the vivacity of the technique—sound tracks of voices overlapping in life's muddle of statements and burble and cries not meant to be replied to; camera movements taking in scenes that flicker with comic asides—deny the doomy simplicities of Lola's outward luck and turn the show-biz image of decline into a wiser and happier tale.

Through Ophuls' dense structure of flashback, Lola is slowly established not as a gaudy object for voyeurs but as a being whose fortunes have been dictated by a lifelong feeling that she is on the run. Her childhood as a little creature prancing around with red balloons develops into a claustrophobic girlhood. We see her crossing the Atlantic with her mother and her mother's lover. She looks penned in. She is shoved into a cabin with chaperons she scorns. It grows clear that the sumptuously furnished carriages of her later life were her ways of not being cornered. They were the *salons* of a truant, boudoirs with fast feet. The circus coach, which is a prop, begins to refer sadly to the beautiful carriages of her heyday, which she took for her rightful property.

Things shown in the circus look different after each flashback. The memories are brought to her mind at the command of the ringmaster, whose jealous voice overlays her real versions of past episodes with orders to enact them for the circus. The ringmaster himself is an ambiguous character. He thinks he is running the show, but he is also in love with Lola. At the end, just as he has oratorically announced that she is about to risk her neck on the trapeze with a spectacular jump guarded by no safety net, a message comes from an underling that the doctors order the net to be there. The ringmaster ad-libs, and meanwhile seems to be arguing in his head. Loss of face by complying. But danger to Lola. On the other hand . . . And yet . . . Well, her disdain of risk is the very thing that draws him to her, and he himself is not a man of authority, only of bluster. He mutters to the messenger an order for a drink. To the audience he maintains his histrionic calm, though secretly cliff-hanging, and announces that Lola will decide. In the circus ring he may relish symbolic power, but a crisis makes real power more than he can manage. The underling, arriving back with the drink, whispers a demand for the cash for it. Ophuls' counterpoint is his own, and comic. High up, Lola sways. Don't jump, we think. Stand there. Refuse. No need. This is a trumpery version of the boldness you have built your character upon. But she leaps, and she survives. The ringmaster sees her restored to him, along with his ersatz authority. And next he can offer her to the crowd as a freak in a cage, to be kissed by any man in the mob: "An unforgettable memory for the price of only one dollar."

Lola lived in the nineteenth century. Ophuls was not born until 1902. "What I love is the past," says the master of ceremonies in Ophuls' *La Ronde*, and so did the film's director. Poetically, it was a past beyond Ophuls' memory; his hankerings were not for anything he had ever known, and his life makes that understandable. He was born a German Jew, called Max Oppenheimer, in the Saar. He eventually moved to France, and in 1938 he became a French citizen. He was also rather Viennese in tone, and he did some work in Vienna, though never as much as his work sometimes suggests. The temper of the late Hapsburg Empire was more real to him in his head than the facts of his life account for. His work as a young man began in the German theater, first as an actor, then as a director. "Ophuls" was his stage pseudonym. His début in successful film-directing was made with *Liebelei*, produced in Germany in 1932, but his name was taken off it because he was a Jew. A Europe with Hitler coming to power in it made him a vagabond, like Lola. He worked in Holland, France, Italy, Hollywood. The roaming dispersed his talent and cost him much time, though perhaps he would never have made *Lola Montès* without that expense of spirit in random exiles. He managed some characteristic work in the limbo, but not much. It was not until 1950, with *La Ronde*, that the nomad came back to his native material. He had only seven years then before he was to die of a heart attack. He never witnessed a public showing of *Lola Montès* in his own form of it. Its great cost for the time it was made—about a million and a half dollars, in 1955—and its trashy source in a book by Cécil Saint-Laurent, a sensational pop historical novelist, led both backers and public to expect something quite different from Ophuls' film, which is in no state of swoon about Lola. It is infinitely more interested in the characters of the ringmaster and the King of Bavaria (Anton Walbrook), and in the dialectic of notoriety. Without the director's consent, the nearly two-hour film was hacked to ninety minutes. Not surprisingly, this failed to make it a blockbuster.

In 1957, while the fight was going on, Ophuls bravely went to Hamburg to direct Beaumarchais' *The Marriage of Figaro*. A new start, in the year of his death. The production seemed close to the *Lola Montès* he had really made. It was played before and behind the proscenium and on a revolve. Figaro stood at the center of a whirling theatrical accomplishment that suggested a way to produce Mozart. Ophuls must have had a great feeling for opera. There is a passage of background conversation in *Lola Montès*—when Lola and the King are being urged to flee the palace at the beginning of a rising—that has the same busy, consultative tonality as a Mozart recitative when somebody has to be hidden. Ophuls liked the strictures of the operatic form; pigeonholers tend to imply the opposite when they clap him into some category of the displaced baroque, but baroque doesn't mean uncontrolled. The circling that is structurally the essence of *Lola* is built into it with beautiful discipline and range. The camera often moves through three hundred and sixty degrees. Lola's struggling sense of a wrongly re-enacted past and an awry present helps to shape her consciousness of things as a series of loops.

The action itself is set physically in a ring, and the heroine is constantly placed at the middle of a turning scene, upright on a stool or in a carriage, wheeling on display or viewed by a wheeling camera. In the King's palace, where she gets furious at having failed an audition ("You didn't have an audition to become king!" she yells at the royal ears, which are hard of hearing), she has a time of sitting on a stool in her hoopskirt, adrift in the center of the room. She looks as if she were concealing something; she looks, in fact, like one of those old-fashioned needlework crinoline-lady covers for telephones. The thing she is concealing turns out to be a great tantrum in the bud. Working herself into a magnificent rage—as we said, Ophuls can get fire out of even a stolid performer—she starts to rip open her bodice to show His Majesty that she has a figure beyond auditioning. There is a quick cut to a pair of dozing flunkies outside, more or less awakened by the unkingly sound of tearing fabric. The monarch within calls for needle and thread. What we see then is not him and Lola, whom few directors could have stayed away from, but a stately piece of graphic design expressing hubbub, with panicked servants swirling around inner balconies of the palace, and a culminating view that picks out a crippled soldier standing amazed on crutches at the middle of the funny formalization of lackey fluster. Anton Walbrook's grave performance as the deaf King whom Lola loved brings the film around to a point of elegy that Lola touches long before, in a scene at the opera, when she sits still in her seat at the start of an interval and says—as much about her life as about the music, it seems—"It's odd. I think it's going to end sadly." And now the King, much later, when her life at last seems good, reads *Hamlet* aloud to the two of them and repeats, "That it should come to this." It seems a circle she is not prepared for. *Lola Montès* is about Hell waiting down there, seen from up here—in the palace or on the trapeze wire.

It is Ophuls' technique that transports the film. Soap-opera becomes opera. His technique with actors is witty. Like those few opera directors who ever manage to get performances out of singers, he knows that one of the ways to make second-rate actors do well is to keep them moving. It is hard to be hammy or implausible if you are doing something physically practical, just as it helps a self-conscious actor transcend himself if he has something concrete to combat between him and the camera. Ophuls constantly photographs actors through foreground decoration, or half hidden behind a stove or a column. Some of the performers in *Lola* are good by nature, but all of them, if you watch carefully, seem to have been made better by Ophuls. And the performances are not even the real substance of the film. The performances and the plot amount only to the libretto; the great matter of the score lies in the way Ophuls assembles pictures and organizes two hours of rhythms. It turns a small, garish, anxious history with an unhappy ending into a work that is expansive and immortally pacifying. Ophuls may have missed and loved the past, but his last film wonderfully celebrates the present. The style catches life as it flies.

MAY 3, 1969

Renoir: Le Meneur de Jeu

"Look at this," said Jean Renoir in his Paris apartment, bending over an art book. "It is the Annunciation to the Virgin Mary, and the angel is just shaking hands. It is an interesting way to tell someone she is pregnant." He had been speaking French, and now he switched to English and repeated the last sentence with characteristic absorption, substituting for "interesting" the word "funny," which he pronounces "fonny." The ideas of what is comic and what is interesting truly overlap for him. He looked out of the window and said that the roofs of Paris houses go at angles that always remind him of theater wings. A child was playing somewhere below in this offstage life, and a wife was shouting while her husband strolled away from her, pulling on his cap at a nonlistening slant and then putting his hands in his pockets. "The first films I made were very rotten," Renoir said. "Then I started to make a sort of study of French gesture, and maybe they improved, with the help of my accomplices." The sight of his own gestures as he was talking made me remember one of those fugitive shots which can break through his films so piercingly—a shot in his 1939 picture *La Règle du Jeu* of the plump character played by Renoir himself, the fortunate, poignant stooge, who has just idly let loose the fact that he would have loved to be a conductor. In a shot late at night, on the terrace steps of a grand country house, he can be seen for a second from the back in an image of the clown sobered, conducting the invisible house party inside to the beat of some imagined musical triumph. His big shoulders droop like the withers of a black pig rooting in the dark. Recently, after I had spent some time with Renoir, it struck me that the character perhaps embodies a little of the way he thinks of himself, and that this great, great master of the cinema, who has an amplitude of spirit beyond our thanks, actually sees himself as a buffoon.

Renoir walks with a limp bequeathed by a wound from the First World War. He has a blanched, large face, very attentive, which turns pink as if he were in bracing air when he is interested or having a good time. At the beginning of the 1914 war, he was twenty. Nothing in our benighted century seems to have undercut his sense that life is sweet. He makes films full of feeling for picnics, cafés, rivers, barges, friends, tramps, daily noises from the other side of a courtyard. It is singular and moving that a man whose talent imparts such idyllic congeniality should also have such a tart and sophisticated understanding of caste. In his 1935 film *The Crime of Monsieur Lange*, for instance, the hero's world of the badly off and hungrily gregarious is pitted against a boss class of steely, swindling fops. The heroic Lange, who murders with our sympathy, is a young man who writes thrillers in the time left over from a dull job in a printing plant. Renoir's murderers are always strange to crime: an unhappy clerk, a down-at-heel, derided lover, a gamekeeper—people near the bottom of the heap who take desperate action because they have been driven beyond their limits. The limits usually have to do with what a man will take in punishment to his dignity and his seriousness about how to live, and his gestures state everything. There is the essence of ache and hesitancy in Dalio's double turn near the end of *La Grande Illusion* (1937) at the door of a woman who has sheltered him while he was on the run from a prisoner-of-war camp and whom he cannot quite declare his feelings to. Renoir's own way of standing reminded me sometimes of a shot of Michel Simon in *La Chienne* (1931), his big head bent in watch over a murdered woman. The tonic passion and lightness of the dissolving shot would be recognizable as Renoir's in a thousand miles of film. So would a special kind of cheerful misrule that sometimes runs amok in a scene, like the time his tramp Boudu, in *Boudu Saved from Drowning* (1932), lustily wrecks a room in the process of merely cleaning his boots, carousing around the world with a prodigal and abstracted serenity in mayhem.

When Renoir is in France—he spends a lot of time in America, at a house he and his wife, Dido, have in Beverly Hills—he lives in an apartment close to the Place Pigalle, on a *rue privée* with a black iron gate that is guarded, not very vigilantly, by a caretaker. The little curved street inside is lined with plane trees, and moss grows through cracks in the pavement. There are elegant iron lampstands, and gray shutters on the beautiful, rundown old houses. His apartment is on the second floor of a house with ivy spilling over the front foot. The stairwell is painted in a peeling burnt sienna with a turquoise design. It is all very dilapidated and very nice. "I think it's better when things aren't brand-new," Renoir said. "It's less tiring for the eyes." He sometimes speaks of the apartment as if it were an obstreperous old friend with long-familiar attributes, many of them a bit grating but all indispensable. "I like the proportions," he said one day, looking around at the place. "It's not entirely convenient. When it rains, it rains in here." He showed me drip trails at various points, accusingly. "But I like the proportions. If you want to make me happy, you should feel absolutely at home."

In the drawing room, where he works, there are an old-fashioned telephone, paintings by child relatives, comfortable armchairs with springs gone haywire, ancient white-and-gray plasterwork on the walls, records of Mozart and Vivaldi and Offenbach. During the days we spent together talking, Renoir usually wore a tweed jacket and old leather moccasins—with a tweed cap when we went out—and he always had a pen clipped in his jacket pocket. We seemed to spend a lot of time in the kitchen. It has two tall windows, and between them a splendid freehand drawing in brown paint of a window with curtains looped back and a bowl on the sill. He did it himself. He said, "A mirror fell down and broke, and it left a patch, so I put up that piece of paper." I said that it wasn't a piece of paper—that it was a drawing and looked rather like a Matisse. This so embarrassed him that I had to say quickly, "Matisse on an off day, with a headache." The drawing made a third window to look through, so to speak, when we were having lunch opposite it every day at his scrubbed kitchen table. Renoir's doctor recently gave him a choice of whisky or wine, and he chose wine. We drank rather a lot of it, and cooked gigot. I mentioned Céline at one point, and he lowered his head and looked pleased. "Greater than Camus," he said. "He was entirely hidden for twenty years. He was not the fashion." Renoir was genuinely unable to think it right that I should have come all the way from New York to see him, and in the end I had to put it as if I were using him as a way-station on a journey to England. "I rather hate planes," he said. "We should be able to part the Atlantic like the Red Sea and drive across it in a bus. I'm fond of buses." We swapped bus stories.

We caught ourselves in a mirror one day as we were coming into the apartment, talking mostly about actors, whom he distinguishes from stars as though a star were to be removed from the matter with a long-handled pair of tongs. He made a face at our reflections and said, "To be a star and play yourself all the time—a beautiful doll imitating yourself . . ." Ingratiation is one of the few flaws that really seem to scrape on his nerves. He picks up any hint of it fast. He once remarked to a film-maker whom we both know that there is something that bothers him in Chaplin's films, which in general he admires. He called it "an anxiety to displease nobody." Though Renoir's own films seem expansively charitable, they are altogether uncompromising. For instance, just before the Second World War, when he was making *La Grande Illusion*, the pacifism in it and the affectionate respect for the German commandant played by Erich von Stroheim were unpopular attitudes in France. Renoir said in 1938, in an interview in *The New York Times* of October 23, that Hitler "in no way modifies my opinion of the Germans." He described the film to me as "a re-enacted documentary, like *La Règle du Jeu*," and went on to say, "They are documentaries on the condition of society at a given moment. I made *La Grande Illusion* because I was a pacifist, I suppose. And am. At the time, the usual idea of a pacifist was of a coward with long hair yelling from a soapbox and getting hysterical at the sight of a uniform. So I made a pacifist film that is full of admiration for uniforms. I hope it is clear. The idea came to me when an old friend of mine, named Pinsard, turned up in command of some nearby airfield while I was shooting a scene—for another film—that was driving me mad. This old friend had saved my life in 1915. He had flown so near to me that I could see his impressive whiskers."

Not that Renoir is politically soft. In *La Marseillaise* (1938), he shows Louis XVI coming back from a hard day of pleasure at a hunt and asking about the taking of the Bastille. "Is it a revolt?" he asks. "No, Sire, it is a revolution," says someone with a less limp grasp of the moment. While the revolutionaries prepare to storm the palace, the King worries about his stomach. "I believe in the Tower of Babel, I suppose," said Renoir. "Not in the story, exactly, but in the meaning. The tendency of human beings to come together. My first attempts at film-making probably didn't find this point. But one gets into practice. When things go badly on a film, I think I will go and raise dogs, and then the crisis blows over. At one moment I feel that a story is terrible and at the next that it's wonderful, and in rare flashes of lucidity I feel that it's neither good nor bad. And so, indeed, quite like everything else. I am very much in favor of intelligence, but when you are at work on a film or a story or a painting I think you have to go on instinct. In *La Règle du Jeu*, for instance, I knew only very roughly where I was going. I knew mostly the ailment of the time we were living in. That isn't to say that I had any notion of how to show evil in the film. But perhaps the pure terror of the danger around us gave me a compass. The compass of disquiet. You know, there is a sense in which artists have to be sorcerers twenty years ahead of their period. I don't mean that they are wiser than anyone else—only that they have more time. And, well, though it is much harder for an artist to do this in the cinema, because the cinema insists on being an industry twenty years behind the public, it can sometimes be done."

He turned out to be thinking now of many young film-makers whom he admires, and to have left altogether the topics of his own pictures and of his own shocking and lifelong difficulties in raising money for them. At this moment, he has virtually had to give up the prospect of making a movie from a very funny script, written by him, which Jeanne Moreau wants to play in. No financing can be found for it. The situation seems commercially unintelligent. It is also an offense, as if Mozart were to be deprived of music paper. A short while ago, another script—a comedy about revolt, which Simone Signoret wanted to do—similarly fell through. In the meantime, Renoir remains not at all bilious and works on other things. He is writing his second novel—his first was called *The Notebooks of Captain Georges* and was published in 1966—and directing a series of sketches, also by him, for French and Italian television. He always declines to fuss. I had the impression that he doesn't like weightiness of any sort. In 1938, when he was abused by some people for making a film of *La Bête Humaine* that wasn't slavishly true to Zola, he stoutly said that he hadn't particularly wanted to serve Zola, he'd wanted to play trains. "You have to remain an amateur," he said to me one day about directing. "The big problem is not to stop at being a voyeur. Not to look on at people's predicaments as if you were a tourist on a balcony. You have to take part. With any luck, this saves you from being a professional. You know, there are a thousand ways of being a creator. One can grow apples or discover a planet. What makes it easier is that one isn't alone. One doesn't change or evolve alone. However great the distance between them, civilizations move a little toward one another. And the worlds we know, the directions to which interest bends us in our knowledge or our affection, incline to be one in the same way."

A French television unit came one day to direct Renoir in part of the shooting for a long program about him and his father, the painter Auguste Renoir. He needed a companion for a walking scene in Montmartre, and I was the obvious person, although I told him that the only acting I had ever done had been on account of having red hair.

"Lady Macbeth," he said.

"Yes," I said.

He told me what it had been like at school for him because he had had red hair, as his father painted him in the famous childhood portrait. "And who else did they make of you?" he asked, stroking his head unconsciously. "The Pre-Raphaelites?"

"Agave in *The Bacchae*," I said. "For the same reason." And he laughed.

The French sound man said politely, after a long time, that he was getting only a moan from me on his earphones, and could I talk more loudly.

"Her diction in English is excellent," said Renoir.

"Now a new setup," the TV director said, after another long time.

"Which side do you prefer?" Renoir asked me.

I said that the next part might go better from the other side, because of my nose. Renoir took me by the shoulders and had a look at me.

"A girl ran into me in a corridor at school and bent it," I said.

"It's true," he said, nicely, and put me on his other side, and we moved around a lamppost. He held my wrist, perhaps to help himself travel a slope, and then slipped his hand up to my elbow to support me through the prospect of having a seven-word line to say, while he improvised a monologue of incomparable invention and warmth.

Some time later, I asked him about an actor I liked very much in *Monsieur Lange*. Renoir beamed, and said something incidental about his own way of working. "I'm pleased you pick him out. He was excellent, exciting, subdued. However—not that it mattered—it happened that he couldn't remember his lines easily. So the thing was to give him a situation where he had to say what he had to say. Where he couldn't say anything else."

And the same day—"He is the most French director," said the actress Sylvia Bataille, who worked with him on the 1936 film *Une Partie de Campagne* and on *Monsieur Lange*. "The most cultured. He has a sense of history like no one else's. He was the precursor of everything in French cinema now. You know, when he is directing you, he has a trick. Well, not a trick, because that sounds like something deliberate. A way of doing it—a habit, the result of his nature. He will say, 'That's very good, but don't you think it's perhaps a bit boring to do the next take exactly the same way?' He will never say that the next take is to be totally different because in the first one you were terrible. I think the reason he is a great director is that he knows all there is to know of the resolves that people keep to themselves. He knows the human reaction to anything. I'm not very good, but he made me magnificent."

There exists an affectionate French documentary of Renoir directing some actors. He listens to them as if through a stethoscope. Then he may talk of other times, the times of "Monsieur" Shakespeare, "Monsieur" Molière—speaking without sarcasm. Again and again he says, "*Trop d'expression.*" He tries to get a highly charged actress to speak "like a telephone operator." There is a big moment, and he tells her not to be sweet. "*Soyons pas mignons.*" It is always "us." "*Soyons secs.*"

"If actors look for feeling at the beginning of a reading, the chances are it will be a cliché," he said to me. "When they learn the lines alone or when we learn them together—the second being the better—in either case I beg them to read as if they were reading the telephone directory. What we do is to read a few lines that can help the actors to find the part. Pick a few lines that are symptomatic. Now, what happens then is that, in spite of himself, the actor begins to find a little sparkle, provided he forbids it. Whereas if you begin to play with feeling, it will always be a generality. For instance, suppose an actress playing a mother has to speak of 'my son' when he is dead. For most actresses, it is the devil's job for this not to be a cliché if they begin with the sadness of it. And if you start with an idea of how to say it, then it is very difficult to remove it. You should start with the lines quite bare. You see, even in our day everyone is different from her neighbor, or his. We must help an actress to find a 'my son' that will be hers and only hers."

This strong feeling that people are different is obviously part of Renoir's great gift for friendship. I said something about disbelieving and fearing the icy comfort that everyone is replaceable and no one indispensable. He said securely, "*Everyone* is indispensable." We talked about Brecht, whom he was very fond of. They had fun together, loping along the streets by the Seine with some friends in a gang. "He was a very modest man, you know," Renoir said. "Well, perhaps he was, like many modest men, proud inside. He was a child. It's not so easy to remain a child. And he was also sarcastic, which people never understand. He was romantic but also sharp, and sharp people are not well understood. We had many adventures. We wanted to make films. I remember once we went for money to Berlin, to the king of German cinema. We suggested a subject. He said no. He said, 'You don't belong to the movies.' You see, he was right. On the way home, Brecht said, 'Look, Jean, don't let's make movies. We should call what we want to do something else. Let's call it *pilm*.' "

When we were back in Renoir's living room after the television shooting, he said to me, "In directing, I don't follow a script very closely. And I think it works best to choose a camera angle only after the actors have rehearsed. I suppose that between my way of working and the one of following a script closely there is possibly the same difference as between Indian music and Western music since the tempered scale. In Indian music, there is a general melody, and this general melody is ancient and must be held to, and then there is also a general note played on a particular instrument, and this note is repeated all the time and keeps the other instruments up to pitch. And so there is a melody and a pitch, and the musicians are free to move around these fixed points. I think it is a magnificent method, and I try to imitate it with actors and film-making, up to a point."

We drifted into talking about Stanislavsky. Renoir said that he had learned endlessly from Stanislavsky but that Stanislavsky had "a big problem." He explained, "Often the Moscow Art Company had to speak in front of an audience that didn't know Russian at all—or, if so, not good Russian. It forced the company to make too many clear signals. To shout inner things, so to speak."

We sat in the drawing room on another day. "Excuse me," said Renoir. "My maid is here today and I want to know how she feels. She has a bad eye." He went out and stood talking with her, his head hanging down as he listened, like a fisherman's watching a river. She was insisting that she was all right and could work, making gestures with a dustpan—a short, alert woman, one eye covered with a patch of bright pink sticking plaster. They stood there for a time, visible through two doorways and faintly audible, like people photographed in the unemphatic style of his films.

"She won't go home," said Renoir, coming back into the room. "She's very strong. She doesn't look it. She's built like a French soldier. Frederick the Great was amazed by how small we were. Just before a battle, he said, 'How can they fight?' " Renoir limped around and got some wine and said, "We lost, I believe." And then he sat down again and went on watching the woman for a while through the doorways. I looked at a photograph pinned up over his desk. It showed a cluster of men in cloth caps sitting on the ground and laughing. The scene looked rather like a factory picnic, but not quite. Renoir said that the picture was by his friend Henri Cartier-Bresson and that the men were convicts. "When their sentences were over, they didn't want to leave the labor camp, so they just stayed. They had their friends, et cetera, et cetera. And also, you see"—he spoke seriously—"I think they'd come to like the work."

We talked about a London prison where I had once lectured and shown *La Règle du Jeu*. He asked a lot of questions, often using the words "interesting" and "interested," which sprinkle his talk, like "et cetera." "I quite enjoy lecturing when I'm doing it," he said. "Not so much when it's over. Doing it is generally the only thing, isn't it? One sees that even with banking, which God knows is a stupid occupation. But when a banker is actually making the money he thinks he needs to retire with, then he is happy, and with luck the retirement never arrives. I suppose I really believe work and life are one, as the Hindus do. When I'm making a film, for instance, I don't know where the divisions are in the job. When I'm writing, I'm cutting the film in my head. And when I'm cutting I'm doing more of the screenplay. You understand, this isn't to say that there aren't terrible days before we start, when nothing is possible." He paused, then went on, "But Hollywood, because it has this genius for departments, has found the perfect way to make pictures that have no sense. A producer has a wonderful screenplay, by wonderful authors—plural—and he puts wonderful actors in it, and then he hires a wonderful director, who says 'That's a little slow,' or 'Please be more warm.' And so—well, it is most efficient, and what it reminds me of is a perfect express train racing along perfect steel tracks without having any idea that one of its compartments contains a beautiful girl leaning against beautiful red plush with a most interesting story to tell. A lot of people who are quite sincerely critical of Hollywood say that the trouble is that the people there worship money, but I believe them to be worshiping something much worse, and that is the ideal of physical perfection. They double-check the sound, so that you get perfect sound, which is good. Then they double-check the lighting, so that you get perfect lighting, which is also fairly good. But they also double-check the director's idea, which is not so good. It brings us straight to another god—or perhaps I should say devil—that is very dangerous in the movies, and that is the fear that the public won't understand. This fear of 'I don't understand' is terrible. I don't see how you can ever understand something you love. You would not say that you understood a woman you love. You feel her and like her. It has to do with contact. Something many people ignore is that there is no such thing as interesting work without the contact of the public—the collaboration, perhaps. When you are listening to great music, what you are really doing is enjoying a good conversation with a great man, and this is bound to be fascinating. We watch a film to know the film-maker. It's his company we're after, not his skill. And in the case of the physically perfect—the perfectly intelligible—the public has nothing to add and there is no collaboration. Now I am going to be very trite and say that it is easier to make a silent film than a talkie, because there is something missing. In the talkies, therefore, we have to reproduce this missing something in another way. We have to ask the actors not to be like an open book. To keep some inner feeling, some secret."

Renoir's feeling for ambiguity is powerful. He clings to doubt as if it were a raft. I told him about a playwright friend of mine called N. F. Simpson, the author of *One-Way Pendulum* and *A Resounding Tinkle*—wonderfully funny plays that some humorless drama expert in London once lammed into for having no form, though this is a great part of their funniness. "This question of perfection," said Renoir. "Bogus symmetry. It is one of the reasons modern objects are so ugly. Plates, dresses, colors. If you take the blue of faïence, the blue of delft, it is never absolutely pure, you see. There is nothing quite pure in nature. In the Army, with the cavalry, I learned that there are no white horses and no black horses. They always have a number of hairs that are another color. If the horses were plastic, that would be an unforgivable fault. My father used to talk about this idea. Not about plastic, of course. . . . He had, for example, a small piece of advice for young architects. He said to them that they might think of destroying their perfect tools and replacing the symmetry produced by their instruments with the symmetry produced by their own eye. When he was asked about a school for artists, he said he would like to see inns—inns with the temperament of English pubs—where people would be fed and where they would live and where nobody would teach them a single thing. He said that he didn't want the spirits of young artists to be tidied up. His talk was terribly interesting. Toward the end of his life, he would think deeply, perhaps because he couldn't walk. I believe sitting in a wheelchair helped him to think as he did. Often I would suppose he was working, and then just find him sitting, and we would have a conversation much like the one I am having with you. A certain spectrum of life would interest him."

Renoir's cast of mind often seems very much like his father's. "As the years went by, I found he was becoming rather a marble bust instead of a man," Renoir recalled. "I wanted to stop that. It was why I wrote a book about him, I think." He spoke about Auguste Renoir's attitude toward prowess, and it defined his own. He said that his father "didn't care for *tours de force*"—that "to his way of thinking, the beauty of, say, a weight-lifter was at its greatest when the young man was lifting only something very light." The film-maker son does that. The world he created in *La Règle du Jeu* spins on his forefinger. We talked about the biography. It is called *Renoir, My Father*, and he published it in 1958. I had the impression that he misses his father daily. We also talked about his novels. "I like writing," he said. "Because it doesn't matter."

Another day, we went to see a film. The feature was preceded by a short about the Olympics. Renoir was tenderly amused by a sequence showing the back view of a girl in a tunic running in a grandiose way with the lighted Olympic torch. The screenplay of the film—Truffaut's *Stolen Kisses*—he found "very interesting." He said, "It has no suspense. I hate the sanctity of suspense. It's left over from nineteenth-century romanticism. The film is to the point and comic. It is a sort of synopsis of the times, this humor. It is not so much something to laugh at as an attitude toward life that you can share. At least, in *this* film you are permitted to share it. So the film must be good, I think. I like it very much."

We walked out into the cool sun. Renoir inspected the streets, and said, "It seems to me that the people of Paris are gayer than usual. Perhaps it's the weather? [*"Il a une telle correspondance avec la nature,"* Sylvia Bataille had said a few days before.] Or perhaps it's the effect of the events of May." He looked closely at everything, as if he were going to draw it from memory later.

The taxi we took had a postcard of a Picasso stuck in the dashboard—inevitably, in Renoir's company, it seemed. He instantly leaned forward and started to talk about it. The driver, who chatted with hair-raising responsiveness in the Paris traffic, turned out to be a spare-time painter. "Only to amuse myself, you understand," he said.

"Why not?" said Renoir. "Everything interesting is only to amuse yourself."

The driver, making the taxi lurch horribly, produced a magazine called *Science & Art*. We nearly hit something because he was finding a page to show Renoir and then stabbing a forefinger at the place, leaning over to the back seat with his eyes on the magazine. "Paintings by madmen," the driver explained during a feat with the clutch and the accelerator.

Renoir looked at the page and exclaimed. It showed a schizophrenic's painting—a gilded dream of a Madonna and Child that also had something carnal and pagan about it, like a Bonnard, and something quite free, as things tend to be in Renoir's presence.

The two men talk with passionate absorption about, in turn, madmen, the Madonna, and paintbrushes. As we get out, the driver gives Renoir the magazine, shakes his hand, and offers his name.

"Renoir," responds Renoir, and he thanks the driver for the present as he climbs out, his bad leg slowing him a little.

"You are of the family Renoir?" says the driver, amazed, moved, something dawning on him, looking at Renoir's face.

"Yes."

"Of the painter Renoir?"

"Yes. He was my father."

The driver goes on looking. "You are yourself, then . . .

There was a famous man of the theater and the cinema. . ."

"That's my nephew Claude. A cameraman. Or my brother Pierre, perhaps. The actor."

"No, someone some time ago, a most famous man of the theater and the cinema, I believe."

"Yes, I think you are right, I believe there was once another Renoir who worked in the theater. Not related."

When we were pottering about the kitchen one day at lunchtime, Renoir said severely, "We will not have much. You don't eat, and now I don't eat, either. You must have been easy to ration," and he started talking about the Second World War. He was very kind to the English—even to the food. "Without the English, we should now all be under the jackboot. Yorkshire pudding, Lancashire hot pot. Exactly how is shepherd's pie made?" Just before the fall of Paris, Renoir and Dido joined the flight to the Midi. He took with him some of the most deeply treasured paintings in the world. His own car was in the country, far away. "I didn't know what to do," he said. "At last, it occurred to me: Perhaps one can still hire a car. Perhaps the Peugeot people are still working. So we went to the Peugeot factory, and there is every clerk at work as usual, still filling out forms, with the Germans ten miles away. I have to fill out all these forms, and then we have a car, and we drive to the Midi, very slowly, with the canvases of Monsieur Cézanne, et cetera, in the back. A big trek to the south—everyone who could find a cart or a wheelbarrow. It was a very bad sight."

La Grande Illusion was being shown in Vienna the day the Nazis entered the city. It was stopped in mid-reel. The story gives Renoir a certain amount of satisfaction. "We had wanted to make the film for three years, but nobody would put up the money," he said. "French, Italian, American, British producers saw nothing in the project. They wanted a villain. They said the German to be played by von Stroheim was not sufficiently a villain. I said the villain was the war. "The public won't understand that," they said. Well, finally a group of businessmen risked forty thousand dollars, and at the end of the first year I believe the profit was ten times the investment. You know, years and years before that, in his *Foolish Wives*, von Stroheim pointed out something to me that I hadn't known at all. I saw that film twelve times. It changed things. Something very simple I hadn't known—only that a Frenchman who drinks red wine, and eats Brie, with Paris roofs in front of him, can't do anything worthwhile except by drawing on the tradition of people who have lived like him. After *Foolish Wives*, I began to look. I mean, the movements of a woman washing her hair that we might see through this window, or of that man with the broom—I found that they were terrifically valuable plastically."

Renoir has his father's strong respect for touch, and for a kind of conviviality that is unmistakable and moving when he creates it in any of his films. He is a fine friend to spend time with. "One of the things I like about Shakespeare, very much, is that the characters have a great variety of intimacy," he said to me. "They are different according to whom they are speaking to. Of course, Shakespeare had a great advantage over cinema directors—one that interests me very much. He shares it with, you could say, Simenon. You could call it the advantage of a harness. Elizabethan plays and also thrillers are constricted, and that is very liberating. In the cinema, you can do all too much. For example, when the hero of a modern film has a phobia, you are obliged to explain it by flashbacks—I mean, to go back to the time when he was beaten by his father, or whatever thing is supposed to have had such a result. This freedom can be quite enfeebling. It makes one very literal, very anxious to make everything clear, get everything taped. You know, I believe one has to have only a rough idea when one is making a film or writing a story, or whatever—a rough scheme, like a salmon going upstream. No more than that. It's no true help—is it?—to know already where one is going to arrive. In fact, I think targets have done a great deal of harm. This nineteenth-century idea in Europe, and now in America—this idea of targets—has caused terrible damage. Rewards in the future, and so on. Those never come. Pensions. I thought about this a good deal in India when I was making *The River*, in 1949 and 1950. India was a revelation. I suppose I'd been looking for such a place and thinking it was all past, and there it was. Suppose you are interested in Aristophanes, and suppose you go down the street and suddenly see people who are exactly his contemporaries, who know the same things, have the same view. That's what India was like for me. I had been starting to fall off to sleep. In India, you could make a full-length picture just by following someone through the day. A grandmother, say, getting up in the morning, cooking, washing clothes. Everything noble. Among poor people in India, you're surrounded by an aristocracy and a nobility. The trouble now is that the advanced countries are trying desperately to grow better by the mistake of removing the ordinary. We're trying to reach greatness by reading classics in houses that have no cold in the winter and no heat in the summer, and where everything can be done without the natural waste of time. One of the things I liked about India is that the people have the secret of loitering." This brought up Los Angeles, the city famous for picking up as a vagrant anyone who is merely strolling along the street. Renoir was very firm. "All great civilizations have been based on loitering," he said.

Much later, coming back to this point after a loop of talk about food and operetta, Renoir said, "Think of the Greeks, for instance. One of the most interesting adventures in our history. What were the Greeks doing in the agora? Loitering. Not getting agoraphobia. The result is Plato. My film *Boudu* is the story of a man who is just loitering."

Renoir spoke of Satyajit Ray, his assistant on *The River*, whose Indian films are much like the ones that Renoir had just envisioned for me, and who feels Renoir and *The River* to be vital inspirations of his own work. "He is quite alone, of course. Most other Indian films are—Well, I suppose they would be called uninteresting, though I have to say that they quite often interest me very much. There is sometimes a wonderful mixture of fairy tales and daily life and the religious, and no one thinks of it as at all comic, because no one is conscious of incongruity. I saw this in an Italian theater once. A little theater not much bigger than this room. At the front of the stage, a man threatening to kill his mother. In the back, by some trick, a locomotive rushing. It was wonderful. Hamlet and railway stations. Genuinely popular. You know what I mean. Every now and then, one gets this in Indian films. In the middle of a story about Siva and a film star and dancing and so on, there will suddenly be a god with a mustache who looks like a cop. It is practically the only question of the age, this question of primitivism and how it can be sustained in the face of sophistication. It is the question of Vietnam."

This question is much on his mind, and he came back to it another day by another route. "You know, I have a theory about the decay of art in advanced civilizations," he said. "Perhaps it's a joke, but I believe it may be serious. It is that people *want* to make ugly things, but at the beginning their tools don't allow them to. When you find figures or vases in Mycenae or Guatemala or Peru, every one is a masterpiece. But when the perfection of technique allows men to do what they want, it is bad. Perfection of technique—sophistication—has nearly destroyed the movies. In the beginning, every movie was good. When we see the old silents at the Cinémathèque, they are all good. This isn't nostalgia. They are. And, believe me, I know some of the directors who made them and they aren't geniuses. It also has something to do with puritanism. I'm in favor of puritanism, I think. Not for me. But for a nation it can be very good, and for art. Those early movies in Hollywood reflected the decorum of the people, a kind of thinking that I could not abide for myself. We would demonstrate against it now, I daresay, including me. You know what I think about all this? I believe that Creation has a considerable sense of humor. Of farce. The closer we are to perfection, the farther away from it we are. This makes me think about Hollywood, of course. The interesting thing about Hollywood, Beverly Hills, Los Angeles is that it isn't really materialist at all—not in the true sense, because it obviously doesn't care for the material in the slightest. In fact, that's the big advantage of Hollywood—the fact that the buildings don't count. It is therefore a place in the abstract. You are there—no, I should say that *one* is there, and I suppose I must mean myself—only for one's friends. When Clifford Odets died, I thought I wanted to leave Hollywood. He was a prince. Every gesture, every way of thinking was noble. Although I love Hollywood, I have to say that it is without nobility. But I stayed, of course. You know what I like about America? Among other things, the obvious. The generosity. There is a great desire to share. To share feelings, to share friends. Of course, this can be a travesty and ridiculous. It can be reduced to 'togetherness' and the vocabulary that could find such a word for such a thing. But it also has to be said that there exists in America a stout attempt to do in language exactly the opposite, to make things noble. For instance, calling tea a beverage, calling a barber a hairdresser. It doesn't work, but the attempt, in the face of the obstacles—well, it's interesting and nice, isn't it? It is very much harder to live nobly in America than in India. One of the things that are helpful to Indians is the concept of privacy. It is so strong there that to have spiritual privacy they do not even need physical privacy. In America, this concept is not so easy to have, partly because of the ethic of sharing, perhaps, and partly because of the ethic of proselytizing and persuading other people, which Hinduism is entirely free of, and which has arrived so dreadfully at Vietnam for America. The problem of caste—of Western caste, of paternalism, et cetera—has led us into this proselytizing. I suppose caste is what all my films are about. Still, any big society is a melting pot, as they say. Take Rome. And the banal melting pot of America that is so much in question at the moment really works pretty well except at one point. The point of the Negro. One forgets that the slaves weren't originally brought by the Americans. They were brought by the French, the Spanish, the Portuguese. The really difficult thing to explain is that the slave-owners pretended to be Christians. All men are brothers, and in the meantime the brothers on your estate are slaves. I suppose it has to be recognized that much of the truth about Christianity is about money, and most of the truth about subjection and propaganda is about money. Outside Paris now, there are Arabs living in shacks built out of gasoline cans who make a great deal of money for Paris businessmen. Americans make money out of Negroes, and Frenchmen make money out of Arabs. Every country has a worm in the apple, and the worm in the apple of America is a very tough one."

We went out into the Place Pigalle. "Much changed since the days of my father and Monsieur Cézanne," Renoir said, perfectly cheerfully. There was a night club on the corner which had the present special tattiness of the recently new. "Sensass!" a placard said of a stripper. The whole place was plastered with the words of some arid new Esperanto. "Chinese," Renoir said firmly. "A Chinese dialect that is understood only on this side of the square."

He talked about his new novel. It is about a murder, and based on a real crime that he heard of as a small child from Gabrielle, his father's famous model. It happened in a village between Burgundy and Champagne. "Two murderers," he said. "One with a big nose, the leader, and the other the weak one. At the time of the murder, which was very terrible, the villagers heard the sound of the ax blows on the earth to bury the corpse. The earth was very cold. The sound seemed to them to be coming from under the earth. That was the way Gabrielle remembered them. They came from the private cemetery. Somebody seemed to be trying to escape from the ground, everyone thought. The cemetery had been made for a man in the French Revolution who didn't want to be buried in a religious place." A while later, considering what the story might be like as a film, he said, "Too violent. I'm an admirer of violent films, but I can't make them. Also, I am scared of them." He was about to spend five days or a week in the country where the murder happened. The name of the village—very near his own family region—is Gloire-Dieu. Someone had sent him a browned clipping of a local song about the crime, which he said had deeply wounded the villagers' sense of blessedness in their name:

COMPLAINTE SUR LE CRIME DE LA GLOIRE-DIEU
Écoutez la triste histoire
Désolant notre pays.
En faisant le récit,

Vraiment on ne peut y croire,
Car le pays bourguignon
N'a pas un mauvais roman . . .

Renoir talked about a lot of other plans. Some that had been scotched seemed no particular cue for regret. The ideas continued to interest him, and it was sometimes quite hard to be sure whether he was describing a plan of his own or the plot of some favorite already achieved—the *Satyricon* of Petronius, for one. He recited the stories of classics in the present tense, and they acquired his own tang. "There is this matron who lost her husband, and she is so much in love she can't bear the thought of being alone," he said, limping along the cobbles and helping me. "She stays in the cemetery near the corpse of her husband. There is a soldier nearby who is watching thieves—the crucified bodies of thieves. The authorities have to have a soldier there, because one thief's family wants to steal the body. The soldier says to the woman, 'Don't cry so loud,' and he comforts her so well that after two or three days he makes love, and the family can steal the corpse, and so everyone is happier, except that the soldier has failed in his official task and what on earth can he do?"

Without changing his tone, Renoir went on from Petronius to describe his unmade film about revolt. He had written it in two parts. At no time did he speak of it in the past. "One is a revolt against an electric waxing machine. The other is about war. Two corporals from two armies hide between enemy lines beneath the roof of a kind of cellar. We start with a very polite fight about who will be the prisoner of the other one. In the end, they decide there is only one decent position in the modern world and that is to be a prisoner. But each doesn't like the enemy food. Oh, and now I have suddenly found the ending, in talking to you. I think this is the ending. They change uniforms, and then each can be the prisoner of the other and have the food he likes."

The television show he is doing is "like a revue." He continues, "Some of the sketches are very short—no more than a sentence. There is one sketch of the Armistice, and a burglar breaks a vein in his neck and wakes a sleepwalker and they are the first victims of the peace. Before this, there is a soldier who is told by a sergeant that if he dies before the Armistice he will be right and if he dies after the Armistice he will be wrong. You know what has happened? Patriotism is really quite a new idea to the ordinary citizen. It happens to be useful in politics to pretend that it is a powerful emotion, but it isn't—not widely. Most people have never thought first of their country; they've thought first of their family. You know, I adore England. I have English relatives. I'd like to live there. People live there very agreeably." (Though I should think he could live anywhere, given friends, just as he can make enjoyable work for himself in strange countries or in atrocious circumstances.)

"The trouble is that techniques change and the actors' style of playing changes," he said. "Just as fashions vanish, so our films go into oblivion to join others that once moved us."

The greatest of Renoir's will never do this, but he doesn't seem to know it. It makes you pause to see a man with such a powerful sense of the continuity of the general life engaged with the form that most deals in quick deaths. He eludes that blow by understanding film-making another way, as play. He will sometimes describe a director as "*le meneur de jeu*," and he calls his friends and collaborators his accomplices. "The cinema uses things up very fast. That's the point," he says. "It uses up ideas and people and kinds of stories, and all the time it thinks it wants to be new. It has no idea that film people themselves change and are new all the time. Producers want me to make the pictures I made twenty years ago. Now I am someone else. I have gone away from where they think I am."

AUGUST 23, 1969
PARIS

Renoir: Games Without Umpires

No wonder Goebbels banned Renoir's *La Grande Illusion* in Germany, and put pressure on Mussolini to prevent its being awarded a prize at the Venice Film Festival. The film was about the First World War, but the ideas in it were dangerously appropriate to the next. Wars, it said, are run for an élite. They will always be against the interests of most of the men who fight them. The flag is a remote symbol, and military honor is punk; it is class, not honor, that unites the French and German officers in the film.

Renoir's new picture, *Le Caporal Epinglé*, goes even further. Where the conventional antiwar film simply says that killing people is wrong, this one makes the statement that killing *me* is wrong. It is rather like Joseph Heller's savage satirical novel *Catch-22*, in which all the hero's rage and cunning are directed against the people who are trying to prevent him staying alive, most of whom are on his own side. War-film-makers are often behind the mood of their period: it has taken a long time for anyone to see the heroic comic possibilities of this kind of ferocious self-interest.

Like *La Grande Illusion*, *Le Caporal Epinglé* is set in a prison camp. The hero's driving force is simply that he wants to get out of it. Now and again there are scraps of newsreel about the atrocities that are happening outside, but they haven't very much to do with the reality of his own life. All that he knows is that he is young, and intent on existing if possible; and the enemy guards seem to be in much the same mood. The most obvious advantage that the Germans have in this film is that they have first call on the *pissoir*. The prisoners in Renoir's film spend a lot of time emptying the cesspool, and the impulse that makes one of them disappear to add to it in the interest of making the job more his own is a very funny comment on the dignity of working for oneself.

Le Caporal Epinglé is a sage and touching film. There is a moment of typical compassion when the corporal, beautifully played by Jean-Pierre Cassel, is given a bowl of beans by a friend after his umpteenth escape and a spell in solitary: all he can say, weeping, is that the beans are too hot. Renoir somehow communicates that his comic hero is a man of great virtue, by which he means nothing at all to do with the qualities taught by War Offices. The soldier's code, he implies, is a counterfeit; togetherness under the flag cannot console anyone for killing or being killed. The film takes for granted the fundamental truth, ignored by most people who make battle movies, that the catastrophes of war do not happen to men in platoons; they happen to a man in isolation.

OCTOBER 21, 1962

Renoir's *Le Règle du Jeu* is a work to be put with *Così Fan Tutte* and *The Marriage of Figaro*. Society is satirized in it with Mozart's own mixture of biting good sense and blithe, transforming acceptance. Like the operas, the film has a prodigality that is moving in itself. Fugitive moments of genius pass unstressed because there is always infinitely more to draw upon, in the way of those Mozart tunes that disappear after one statement instead of spinning themselves out into the classic a-b-a aria form. The serene amplitude of Renoir's view floods the sophisticated plot and turns it into something else. He thought at the time—in 1939—that he was simply making a film about a contemporary house party. Mozart probably had an equivalent feeling when he was setting da Ponte's librettos. The script of the film—by Renoir himself, with Carl Koch—was written with actual memories of eighteenth-century plays in mind, and it opens with a quotation from Beaumarchais. After this single New York performance, it will be a shame if this glory of the classical spirit transformed isn't shown at bigger public performances all over the country. It seems not to have been around much in America.

Even for a masterpiece (masterpieces generally have savage voyages), the film has had a hard and strange history. It was made in the conditions following Munich. The opening in Paris, during the summer of 1939, was received with fury. Renoir saw one man in the audience start to burn a newspaper in the hope of setting fire to the cinema. Because of the presence in the cast of the Jewish actor Marcel Dalio and the Austrian refugee actress Nora Gregor, the film was attacked by both the anti-Semitic and the chauvinist press. Butcher cuts were made. In October of 1939, it was banned by the government as demoralizing. Both the Vichy and the German Occupation authorities upheld the ban throughout the war. Until 1956, it seemed that only the mutilated version of the film was extant. Then two young French cinema enthusiasts who had acquired the rights to the film found hundreds of boxes of untouched footage in a warehouse. After two years of editing, under Renoir's supervision, they were able to reconstruct his original film. When it was first shown again publicly, I saw someone who had worked on it in 1939 sitting with tears running down his cheeks at the sight of it restored.

The plot is a pattern of three triangles—two of them above-stairs, one below—seen mostly at a château during a big house party for the shooting season. The Marquis de la Chesnaye, played by Dalio, is a dapper man who collects eighteenth-century clockwork toys. He has Jewish blood, as his male servants point out behind the baize door to demonstrate that he can't be relied upon always to know the rules of being an aristocrat. His wife, Christine, played by Nora Gregor, is a high-bred Austrian woman, frightened to find herself fond of an aviator who has just flown solo across the Atlantic and let out an angry declaration of love to her at Le Bourget during the radio interview. This is one of the triangles. The second is made up of the Marquis, his wife, and his mistress, a dark, overanimated society girl whose most sober thought is that she wants to be happy; she says it sadly two or three times during the film, between spasms of social chatter. "How are your factories?" she gabbles brightly, blotting out pain to greet a moneyed woman at the château. The third triangle is formed by Schumacher, the Marquis' gamekeeper; his wife, Lisette, the Marquise's maid, who is based in Paris away from her husband and living a surrogate life because of her loyalty to her mistress; and a poacher who crosses the lines to respectability and becomes a bootboy, because the Marquis has been tepidly attracted by the fact that the man is more efficient than the gamekeeper at trapping the rabbits that lower the tone of the shoot. With Lisette's adored mistress in town so much, Schumacher feels he might as well be a widower. He tries to get the Marquis to pay heed to the problem, in a desolately comic scene on the château doorstep while they move between car and front door, but the Marquis has guests and rococo and rabbits on his mind. This ignored third triangle is to intersect fatally with the others when Schumacher, run amok with loss and jealousy, mistakenly kills the aviator because he thinks it is Lisette rather than the Marquise who is with him. And through it all—through the bright welcomes and the glances and the melancholy accommodations to loveless social rules, through the shooting party and the amateur theatricals and the good-night scenes in long corridors where nobly born men horse around with hunting horns while a lordlier-looking servant walks impassively past them—through the whole intricate gavotte of the film wanders the solicitous figure of Octave, played by Renoir. Octave is the eternal extra man, the buffoon who really has both more sense and more passion than the others of his class, the one who best loves the Marquise and pines to look after her in memory of her father, who taught him music in Austria long ago. He would have liked to be a conductor. The man whom everyone idly holds dear for being the perfect guest suddenly speaks of himself with hatred for living the life of a sponger. How would he eat if it were not for his friends? The thing is to forget it and get drunk. Though then, after feeling better, he feels worse—that's the nasty part. But he will grow accustomed, as necessary. He used to dream of having something to offer. Of having contact with an audience. It would have been overwhelming. . . .

The house party's formal shooting scene has its double later on, in the desperately actual one when Schumacher runs among the guests and tries to kill the poacher. The amateur theatricals that everyone treats so seriously have their mirror image also in this drama, which the house party takes for play. The intrusion of the aviator into an alien society—the romantic hero thrust among skeptics trained in old rules, the pure among the impure—has its counterpart in the poacher, catapulted into a world of snobbery-by-proxy and of a chef's adopted airs about making potato salad with white wine. He accepted the Marquis' offer gratefully, because he had always dreamed of being a servant. Limited hopes, delusory debts. He had always liked the clothes. Julien Carette plays him wonderfully. When he is seen in the servants' hall for the first time, a vagrant corralled within the laws of the housebound, his right arm wheels with embarrassment as he introduces himself. There is a shot of him in front of a palm tree with the Marquis during the evening fête, straightening the master's tie. "Did you ever want to be an Arab?" asks the Marquis. They are both thinking about women. The Marquis, with two on his mind, envies Arabs for not having to throw out one for another. "I hate hurting people," he says, and he means it, in his fashion. "Ah, but a harem takes money," says the poacher. "If I want to have a woman, or to get rid of her, I try to make her laugh. Why don't you try it?" "That takes talent," says the Marquis.

Le Règle du Jeu is delicately good to every character in it, even to the most spoiled or stilted. For people driven to their limits it has the special eye that Renoir always reserves for men nearly beyond what they can manage. There is a wonderful shot of Schumacher, the violent, rigid gamekeeper, now sacked from his job because of the shooting affair, and thus separated completely from the lady's-maid wife he was trying to save for himself. She chose to stay with Madame. He stands with his forehead against a tree, stiffly, finished, like a propped scarecrow. The game has gone wrong. The rules of the game—for him as for the aviator—were so much dead wood, but he was deceived in hoping to hack his way back to life by violent action. For the others the game still holds, although the idea of honor has petered out into the advisability of avoiding open indiscretion, and the idea of happiness into being amused. The *crime passionnel* of the plot, terrible for all three triangles, is given the labeling of his class by the Marquis. It is called "an unfortunate accident." He tells his guests that the gamekeeper, who was actually egged on by the poacher to shoot the aviator because they thought he was poaching Lisette from them both, "fired in the course of duty" on an intruder suspected of the only kind of poaching that gamekeepers are supposed to deal with. Renoir's formal command of his film is beautiful. During the last part of the picture, the camera moves about almost like another guest. It must be some quality of Renoir's that makes his camera lens seem always a witness and never a voyeur. The witness here communicates a powerful mixture of amusement and disquiet. The picture was made in 1939, after all; it is not only a wonderful piece of film-making, not only a great work of humanism and social comedy in a perfect rococo frame, but also an act of historical testimony.

SEPTEMBER 20, 1969

Shakespeare in Italy

In staging *Much Ado about Nothing*, Franco Zeffirelli has had the dazzlingly simple idea of placing it exactly where Shakespeare laid it himself: not in an elocutory limbo, which is where it usually happens, but in Messina. This is bound to raise hackles. Whenever a producer seizes on a specific social context for Shakespearean plays instead of letting it roam vaguely somewhere between Mummerset and a sort of Tudor Harrods, he will always be accused of wrecking the poetry.

There exists now in England a passionate small faction which almost seems to wish that Shakespeare had nothing to do with the theater. Denying that he was an actor, and numb to the plain vulgar theatricality of his genius, the party-members sometimes seem to be striving for the day when productions of his plays could be limited to readings from lecterns in libraries. Any imaginative vision of a text, such as Peter Brook's *Lear*, is dismissed as intrusive. By such dogma, clarifications like Robert Graves's three hundred changes for this *Much Ado*—which struck me as no heresy—come into the category of scribbling on the Koran; this applies especially in the case of anyone refurbishing an obsolete joke. The guard-word of the Shakespeare-to-be-read-as-literature agitators is "gimmick," and the main plank in the platform is a project known as "letting the verse speak for itself," as though the plays were a prison for some literary characteristic that sorely needed liberating from the human beings in whom Shakespeare incarcerated it.

Franco Zeffirelli passionately disagrees. What he responds to in the plays is exactly the opposite. It is their theatricality, their humanity, and their instinctive recourse to the concrete. In this *Much Ado* there are two details that could legitimately be called gimmicky (comic business with animated mermaids in a statue, and a Don John with a tic); but they are the stray drops in a prodigal rain of invention, and prodigality has much more to do with the spirit of Shakespeare than pinching caution.

It has become a truism about *Much Ado* to say that it is made up of three fatally distinct stylistic units: the yokel machinations of Dogberry, the notion of romantic love in the Hero-Claudio plot, and the freebooting antiromanticism of Beatrice and Benedick. When the play is produced as it often is in England, with Dogberry speaking like a yokel actor advertising country eggs on the telly, a repining Hero out of refined drama school, and two classical stars trying to make the small-town banter of Beatrice and Benedick sound like Oscar Wilde, no wonder *Much Ado* is held to be organically a failure. But Zeffirelli has had the blessed simple-mindedness to see the characters not as sources for critics' puzzles, but as the citizens of a single small town; and the moment the play is localized, it meshes as precisely as a watch. Instead of being the proponent of a distant ethic of love that now lies pickled in troubadour poetry, Hero becomes a wretchedly believable girl trapped in perfectly recognizable Sicily where the same ferocious code of chastity endures to this day: cf. Pietro Germi's last film, *Seduced and Abandoned*.

In the same way, Beatrice for once seems credible as her cousin. In Maggie Smith's performance she is not the usual alien sophisticate, free of the rules that bind Hero and unrelatedly caustic, but a product of the same culture who simply happens to have more spirit and a pelting tongue. Placing the play as exactly as this at once makes sense of the Hero-Claudio drama: in logic it is absurd that the accusation against Hero is unanswered (as Lewis Carroll once complained in a letter to Ellen Terry, why didn't anyone use the abundant material for an alibi?), but in Sicily a slur is enough.

Zeffirelli tears into the play as though it were a fiesta. It is rather like the way Beecham belted into the Hallelujah Chorus; the pouncing speed is breathtaking. The play begins and ends with a local brass band, wheeling past an enthralled populace on a stage that is rimmed with fairy lights like a small town welcoming a hero. The Latin sense of self-importance is rife, and so is the endearing Latin unconsciousness that to anyone else this sense may well be conspicuously unfounded. The military characters wear magnificently brave uniforms that have obviously never sniffed battle, and Leonato has a mayoral suit apparently tailored for a duck.

The men are mostly dashing, especially Robert Stephens as Benedick, even if the pomp of their chesty uniforms does tend to run out as they near the ground, the costume designer having done miracles in turning Englishmen into no-leg Latins. The women are unimaginably plain, especially Hero, and Beatrice is blithely blowzy. Dogberry—Frank Finlay—sweetly seems to see himself as Napoleon in a greatcoat. The character's furious tears about his insulted position as a householder are so accurately

Italian that they almost settle the question of whether Shakespeare ever went to Italy.

Not for years has the human substance of Shakespeare been reflected like this in a production. Nearly all the small parts are superlatively played; Tom Kempinski's Borachio, for one. As Zeffirelli hinted before in the difference between his historic *Romeo and Juliet* of 1960 and his *Othello* with Gielgud, he seems to work better with a young permanent company than with imported great actors, for Albert Finney's Don Pedro is oddly external. But even here there is one extraordinary moment, inexplicable except in the unique terms of what can happen in a theater, when the light holds and then slowly fades on the character sitting alone, smoking a cigar, and simply looking after Beatrice and Benedick. The moment swivels the mood of the play, a pause full of death set into a gala ending, and it demonstrates the balance of feeling that is the commanding gift of the production. Half the time the characters' obsession with wooing is made to seem absurd, as it is in the tears of the pear-shaped tenor who turns "Sigh No More" into a richly maudlin piece of boudoir verse; but if romanticism is to be mocked, love is made to seem mortally serious. The "Kill Claudio" scene can never have worked with more bitter energy.

FEBRUARY 21, 1965
LONDON

In Luigi Barzini's book on *The Italians* there is an interesting page about the national use of the words *sistemare* and *sistemazione*. Italians *sistemano* unruly nature, mountain torrents, and spoiled children; mothers want to *sistemare* their daughters with steady husbands. Streetwalkers and high-born mistresses yearn for a *sistemazione* that will allow them to pose as widows and bring up their illegitimate children respectably; industrialists long to *sistemare* competition through cartels. The land of misrule and scrambling improvisation dreams of itself as imposing order and stately master plans. It is genuinely comic, like a man yelling at the top of his voice in praise of restraint.

"*Ti sistemo io*" ("I will curb your rebellious instincts") is a common Italian threat that sums up Petruchio's piece of swagger in *The Taming of the Shrew*. His bullying is funny as soon as the play is firmly planted in Italy, because he is then a hot-air disciplinarian whose ability to curb his shrew occurs in the midst of bouts of yelling and chaos in himself. His attempts at a masterful coolness are more like fatigue and about as impressive as hangovers in the life a drunk.

Franco Zeffirelli's film with the Burtons has the same brilliantly obvious comic source as his stage production of *Much Ado;* he simply takes Shakespeare to have meant precisely Padua when he wrote the word, and he makes the cast behave literally like Italians. They are buffoons dreaming of dignity, careful tacticians with a picture of themselves as heroic risk-takers, romantics believing in their talent for logic and *sistemazione* as devoutly as fat Neapolitans believe that *lasagne verde* is slimming because it is coloured with spinach.

The film is very captivating. The editing of the brawl scenes is a bit like vaudeville. The picture is enticing to look at, with a sunny-natured opening scene in a gauzy drizzle, high shots of rapt onlookers and crankily angled passages, brownish tints through the reds, and Burton in a bucolic make-up that looks like a Venetian portrait when it isn't obscured by his great foot kicking over a goblet on the table. (The photography is by Oswald Morris and Luciana Trasatti; the art directors were Giuseppe Mariani and Elven Webb.)

Michael Hordern as Baptista, father of Elizabeth Taylor's exquisite Shrew and Natasha Pyne's pastoral Bianca, looks sick at the havoc but keeps cheerful. "How speed you to your wooing?" he bawls nonchalantly to Petruchio, who is staggering about on the roof of a house with one foot off balance, vilifying some happy cats and a far from wooed Kate. The bond between the lovers is one of benign disgust. Their discontent has nothing dismal in it, but merely blessed adrenalin for another good day of battles. Every now and again the fury is reined back and there is a pause of docility between them, like the finely felt moment when the Shrew tempers Petruchio's violence and kisses him on the nose. Comparisons with the fights in *Who's Afraid of Virginia Woolf?* are silly and have to do with nothing but the casting. The jibes in Zeffirelli's film leave no wound, because they are about nothing private; they are simply variants on a community convention, devised by two virtuosos of insult flailing about for a way of making the awful admission that living together might work.

It is a feat of this production to make it seem purblind for anyone to grind on with the old saw about *The Shrew* being a male suprematist tract. The play's last part can seem boorish; but Zeffirelli fastidiously twists it around, mostly by Elizabeth Taylor's performance, which quietly sends up Petruchio for putting her through hoops. In the end the triumph is really hers, and it is one of emotional taste, because she chooses to tell the steady truth about love in the banquet scene where everyone else is effect-making. It is a debonair way to end a gentle-spirited film.

Zeffirelli and his writers have cut the Christopher Sly induction and done a lot else to aggravate literary purists; what the film proffers instead is buoyancy, control of mood, Shakespearean performances where the actors unusually seem not to be listening to what they are saying but tumbling out with what they are thinking, and some joyous comic sequences about the Italian character, especially the wedding. The congregation's mood quickly switches from piety to seething boredom, and a priest hoping to *sistemare* the noisy couple loses his nerve in the face of a Petruchio who has dropped off into a sloshed doze on the altar rail.

MARCH 5, 1967

Hamlet the Husband

Chekhov wrote *Ivanov* when he was twenty-seven. He conceived it as a sort of comic Russian *Hamlet*, an account of a man plagued by Hamlet's temperament and unredeemed by Hamlet's circumstances. Ivanov is cripplingly aware that there is nothing to account for his grief: no stolen crown, no treachery within a month, nothing but debts and samovars and a brooding suspicion at thirty-five that his hair is going gray.

His painful modern capacity to see himself as everyone else sees him, and his alertness to the possibility of tragedy being a nuisance, seem to have been things that Chekhov shared. Shockingly soon after he wrote *Ivanov*, Chekhov started to have trouble with his heart: after one attack, at twenty-nine, he said that he "walked quickly across the terrace with one idea in my mind, the idea of how awkward it would be to fall down and die in the presence of strangers."

The character is played presently by John Gielgud in his own adaptation. Like all Russian stage characters, Ivanov knows everyone in the play almost as well as he knows his wife, and lives with a good half of them. (How could Chekhov write now, when people live without aunts or uncles or estate managers and see their friends once a month?) One bawdy relation manages his land. A senile jokester uncle uses his room for schoolboy feasts. His Jewish wife, unaware that she is dying of consumption, clings to the memory of the time when they were happy and tries to forget her parents, who cast her off without a dowry in return for marrying out of her religion. There is a marvelous scene in the first act when an unkind young doctor is attacking her for choosing such a husband; Yvonne Mitchell suddenly smiles in the middle of the lecture because something in it has reminded her of what Ivanov's gaiety used to be like.

He has settled down with his Ophelia now into a nagging, rancorous melancholy. There is something about her Jewish intensity that makes him uncomfortable, and though he loathes himself for wanting to escape her he cannot for the life of him stop himself fleeing every night to the stuffy parties at the Lebedevs', where the gossips of the district play bridge and daydream viciously of an Ivanov who shuts up his alien wife in a cellar and stuffs her with garlic until she reeks. His personality obsesses them. They speak of little else. The Lebedev daughter (Claire Bloom) is inescapably mesmerized by him and proposes love, and at the end of an act his wife disastrously discovers them.

One of the destructive effects of the even intelligence of John Gielgud's performance is that it makes scenes like this seem melodramatic instead of the natural reflection of a character who attracts flamboyant events like a magnet. The style has the same effect on the next act; the shock at the end seems inserted, because the staggeringly constructed series of collisions before it are played too levelly to precipitate it. By this time Ivanov's mood is supposed to be half-mad, caustic, elated, and rotted with contempt for himself, and if the pile-up of scenes were played with less inhibition there would be more than enough violence released to explain his vengeful impulse to tell his wife she is dying. But in this production nothing cannons into anything; everything happens in isolation, surrounded by dead air, which has become the hallowed Anglo-Saxon way of playing Chekhov. There is one inspired actor's moment in the last act when Gielgud suddenly twirls round like a child being spun for blindman's buff; but most of the time it seems an oddly one-note performance, packed with intellectual concentration but always repining. The suicidal insights are harrowingly there, but not Ivanov's sense of being an exceptional man, nor his galvanic energy, nor his self-mocking hypochondria.

Chekhov's charity often seems to blind the foreign actors who most love his toughness. *Ivanov* is a chart of a gentle-seeming world that is really a killer. The old wag in it has moments of the most evil erotic suspicions, the obtusely plain-speaking doctor has the sensibility of a man waving a rope in the house of a man about to be hanged, and the sweet girl vowing love is already crabbed with fear about the course of her life if she stays unmarried. The observation is ferociously sharp, like the eye of some of the short stories.

OCTOBER 3, 1965
LONDON

Czech at Home

Intimate Lighting is a gentle Czech picture by Ivan Passer, the man who was Miloš Forman's assistant director and co-screen writer on *Loves of a Blonde*. The immediate material is the Czechs' passion for music. A musician from Prague is visiting an old music-college friend in the provinces to give a concert. The film has a character that will one day belong as definably to Czech films of the 1960s as certain domestic qualities mark the Dutch school in painting. The editing is plain and serene. The dialogue often seems improvised, and the characters' oddities aren't at all precious. I'm not sure how it happens. The film's absorption has a lot to do with it.

At the opening of the film the members of an amateur orchestra are rehearsing hammer and tongs to get themselves up to scratch for the visiting soloist. In the first passage a wind player commits a harrowing note for the nth time. The conductor, grim with control, says "We'll drown you afterwards." When the soloist arrives he stays with his old friend from the Conservatoire days, whose dulled family life now appalls him. To his eyes it visibly reduces mostly to squabbles about who is to have which joint of the goose, and to tactics about keeping the peace with Grandpa. People's tetchiness becomes genuinely comic in the film because it is made dogged and self-aware. A string quartet fumes with civil war without even stopping playing. "Either we play or we fight," says one of them, carrying on with the score. About music the Czechs like to be serious. The characters are possessed by it, bossing a girl friend on the topic of how to sound a motor-horn more rhythmically, enthralled when drunk by the musicality of a pause between Grandpa's snores, and gently elevated by the gloom of a funeral tune. Under their sealed-off idiosyncrasies they express a feeling of seriousness about life, regret about lost chances, the blight of bodies that time and hard work have spoiled for earlier pleasures. There is one little scene, when a stout grandmother making a bed suddenly tries to demonstrate a ballet position she could once do, that I suppose only a Slav film could achieve with such a true mixture of ridiculousness, grief, and lightness. The characters address themselves to art rather as Chekhov's people address their furniture, hailing it every now and then in a sort of elegiac vocative. "People say you can travel the world with one sad song," says a character in a funeral cortège behind a brass band, suddenly revived by musical melancholy. "If this car ran on tears—my goodness . . . " He falls excitably silent, like a Chekhov character struck by the tragic sense implicit in a family bookcase.

NOVEMBER 27, 1966
APRIL 9, 1967

Czech in America

Two very young girls dressed in the Stars and Stripes are piping away at a talent contest, slightly out of tune. Aged twelve, maybe. "Love, love, love, why don't people believe in it?" Plump faces, pacifying: flower children in the bud. The orange-juice-and-Vietnam generation, the only generation in history to grow up on war protest and vitamin tablets simultaneously. Their eyes slide off-camera helplessly at the forthright end of the song, pining for approval from the audition panel. Then a hard-pressed suburban father (Larry Tyne, played by Buck Henry) is seen in a chair at a hypnotist's, trying to conquer smoking. Everyone has his own Everest. He concentrates on letting his hand float up, soberly. "Are you for living or are you not?" says the hypnotist, an inexpressive, kindly, somewhat bald man with a voice that lies there on the floor like a piece of very dead herring. He has a look that is an unholy mixture of priest and woman traffic warden. One has to respect the body, he says magisterially. "Slowly make a fist, with the hand itself." The characters in this film—*Taking Off*, by the Czech Miloš Forman, working in American for the first time, with a script by himself, John Guare, Jean-Claude Carrière, and John Klein—have been directed so that they speak most painstakingly, at the deliberate pace that is so striking to elliptical Middle Europeans, with its long pauses for thought and its retreadings and its exquisitely careful redundancies. "A fist, *with the hand itself.*" No room for a mistake there. After a bit more of the same, the hypnotist switches on a record of his own speech, methodically using his patient's preoccupation in trance as an opportunity to give a rest to, er, the voice. Like most of the people in Forman's picture—like the tranquil girl who occasionally slips into the picture for a pleasant flash, stark naked and immersed in playing the cello—the hypnotist lives in sweet obliviousness of making an ass of himself. Teaching the patient how to roll his eyeballs upward in coma as the next part of the antismoking session, he explains that the exercise can be done anywhere by closing the eyes first, "so that the roll is private." The patient takes the earnest idiocy with due gratitude; he is a bashful man. A while later, a child of the generation gap—the patient's own daughter, secretly at the audition, about to run away from home but not really so unlike him—stands in front of the mike and can't get out a note. The number she has practiced gags in her throat like a candy swallowed by a small child running. "I'm sorry," she says. "Can I come back?"

Among other things, Forman's recklessly funny anecdote about the apocalyptic nation is about people's shyness, their shaggy-dog purposefulness, and their punishing stamina for more. Forman sees privileged human beings as having an instinct to continue that is fortunate for the life term of the species but ill-conceived for their own comfort, and he makes the observation in a style of charred comedy that is very Slavic. It is fine that he could work abroad with the same convincing and bitter funniness as in the Czechoslovakia where he made *Loves of a Blonde* and *The Firemen's Ball.*

In *Taking Off*, he is much gentler toward his American characters than an American film-maker would be likely to be at the moment. The characters are engaged, to his mind, in idiosyncratic and testing concerns, and we are not reminded a second of any of the other films that have washed over us about the nation's characteristics in crisis. Small endeavors of no necessity, answering the conventions of a society that Forman sees as if it were some instinctively Rabelaisian village gone out of kilter and hedged by tragedy, are embarked upon with solemnity and ardor. There is the obligation upon an American wife to enjoy sex, for instance. Two wives chat about husbands' animal impulses in an appalled *sotto voce*, and then throw themselves into splendidly affectionate and stilted spasms of Dionysian dance in their bedrooms for these animals' sakes. When Larry Tyne gets drunk about the disappearance of his daughter he begins to eat a hard-boiled egg to sop up the booze because there is a matching ritual obligation on American middle-aged fathers to drown sorrow in drink; you see him eying the egg beadily as it rolls off the counter onto the floor, correctly recognizing the impossibility of bending down to get it, salting another one with dignity, and then eating that without getting the shell off, clinging to insane proprieties about spitting it out. A vestigial politeness reigns in impossible, ludicrous and sometimes desperate circumstances. When four parents have been through a racking night of cheer —pot-smoking under tutelage to learn about their mystifying children, and then strip poker—the half-naked Larry, ill at ease about behaving with a kid's sort of abandon, still goes through the form of shaking hands at the door, though reeling and also struggling into a shirt cuff that has the button done up.

In *The Firemen's Ball*, Forman directed a celebrated wan scene of a beauty queens' contest. He has an eye for the damp way people try to sparkle at social functions. The parents in *Taking Off* have been programed all their lives to dress up in black tie and sequins and to look as if they were enjoying themselves when a hundred of them are gathered together. So when the function happens to be a horribly unhappy meeting of parents whose children have run away—the Society for the Parents of Fugitive Children—the grief is hidden and the rules are served. There is a girl hippie at the dinner whom the orotund host in a dinner jacket introduces as if she were something on a television jackpot show. She may have seen *your* lost child. Parting her long weeping-willow branches of hair hanging in front of her eyes, she bends down to look at each in turn of the photographs that are worn like cameos on the parents' spangled breasts. As the man at the microphone says, any one of the people in the queue may be the lucky one. The executive faces and the stiff hairdos affectingly express a generation and a class. The guests are made to seem no more ridiculous than any other prisoners of a period, and they are exonerated from complacency. Forman looks at the two sides of the age war and finds it a poignant conflict, with the parents faintly the more interesting because more formed, and more coerced by ineloquent conventions. The pop songs that the kids sing have a voice. There is one fine song that sets an unpublishable, metrically prim lyric to a madrigal warble, sung by a nice girl who looks as if she were majoring in ceramics; it will be agreeable if the record business has the humor to release it.

And meanwhile the parents in the film, crippled by politesse and fake office bonhomie and high heels, recover whatever rusting scraps of force and grown-up love they can from the wreck of their age group's self-esteem. They have old souls, but their world makes them behave like pre-1939 adolescents, giggling and dressing up and having to grapple with a paralyzing secret diffidence. Lynn Carlin, the runaway's mother, is delicately hipped on modesty in the middle of the strip-poker romp; it is a lovable performance of someone longing for fun and prudish mostly for her husband's sake. The bereft parents have gone blissfully off the rails after a solemn indoctrination into dope at the SPFC meeting, where they have learned how to smoke pot from a bossy and rather mournful expert called in from the ranks of arcane youth. ("A joint has two ends. . . . Put the *closed* end into your *mouth*," says the pedagogue patiently, following it with a little lecture on not hanging on to the joint after a drag without passing it on to a neighbor. "That is very *rude*.") In the end it is the parents who are financially worsted, the parents who turn out to be the underdogs of the capitalist system that they are held to be running.

But they have the last word. The runaway's song-writing boy friend comes to a conciliatory dinner; the oldies do their best to make things work, the father faltering rather when he hears what the boy earns because he gracefully expected him to be on his uppers. "Two hundred and ninety thousand," says the lad. Larry splutters into the wine. (A pause would have been better, maybe.) "Before taxes," says the boy, equally graceful. After dinner the young pro declines to play the piano himself, so Larry and his wife take over and finish with a terrific brave rendering of "Stranger in Paradise."

Perhaps it takes a foreigner to see New Yorkers not as the tense, mercurial, backchatting go-getters that native legend makes them but as Forman's lovingly cemented couples, moving slowly through their city with clogged tongues and admirably little ambition. Forman's film is another view of the land that most of its inhabitant film-makers now mechanically despair of; for instance, there is another new film this week, called *Making It* and indoctrinated in native self-depreciation, which deals in the usual machine-made way with a student and the generation gap and permissiveness. One might as well shut up about the movie, but one has to wonder if the American film industry knows how special it is in its obsession with the journalistically topical. Fiction usually assumes the freedom to move away. Shakespeare left his own time and place in nearly every play; Tolstoi went backwards in *War and Peace;* Truffaut went backwards in *Jules et*

Jim and *L'Enfant Sauvage;* Kurosawa, Wajda, Renoir, Visconti, the same. But apart from *Bonnie and Clyde* and Westerns, the American cinema at the moment is scared enough to keep newsworthiness and film-financing as close together as foreign correspondents clustering in a bar and refusing to leave one another in the middle of an interesting strange country. It has fallen to a Czech visitor to take the curse off films about the generation gap. Forman really likes America. He could probably make us see raw nerve-ends in a drum-majorette rally.

APRIL 3, 1971

8½

It would be a waste of time to wonder how precisely autobiographical Fellini was being when he made *8½*, his famous film about a famous film director. As he said once himself, there is a sense in which he would be autobiographical even if he were telling the life story of a sole.

What is certain is that this film is constructed so as to *seem* autobiographical, no matter what the facts are: it uses a scarcely veiled first-person as a deliberate artistic device. People are forever talking about subjective films, but the surprising thing is that nothing like *8½* has ever been done before in the cinema. The only work I can think of that has the same grim comic capacity for self-exposure in Evelyn Waugh's *The Ordeal of Gilbert Pinfold*.

8½ is a rueful account of a peculiarly contemporary kind of man, imaginative, openly greedy, riddled with the bullet holes of his self-accusations, and almost dying of neurotic sloth. It has been made by a poet whose genius for film-making spills out of his ears, and I hope its courage isn't going to be dismissed because it is flamboyant and comic. Intellectuals here are hard on Fellini, especially since the words *la dolce vita* passed into the gossip-columnists' language. Sometimes they seem to feel his humor is something he should try to get over, something diminishing and vulgar: and my impression is that he would be much more respected if he would stop implying that sex can be cheerful and start concentrating on the misery of it, like Antonioni. (I remember once standing in the snow trying to pass on my enthusiasm for *La Dolce Vita* to an austere acquaintance who happened to be out enjoying the cold: he gave a short, hard bark through his nose and said severely that the film left him uncertain about how Fellini voted, which seemed to him to clinch the whole thing.)

The film director-hero of *8½*, played by Marcello Mastroianni, has hit an immovable creative block. Living in the bedlam of preparing for a big picture, he hasn't an idea in his head. Sets are already being built, rival actresses are acting their heads off to each other in the pretense that they have parts, but no one has seen a page of his script. His imagination keeps submerging into the past, remembering the huge hips of a woman he once saw doing a rhumba when he was a small boy, and the punishment he got afterward from the priests at school.

Coming up gasping from this daydream and shaking the drops off himself, he thinks perhaps he may at last have rescued something off the ocean bed. But when he timidly describes his trophies to a critic-figure who seems to be working on the film, the critic-figure sternly replies that there's no point in thinking of using this kind of childhood memory to say something about the Catholic conscience in Italy because there's nothing for reviewers to get their teeth into. You think again of Gilbert Pinfold, who is made dogged in his illness by awful critical utterances like this and has hallucinations of wet, snarling boobies carving him up on the BBC. The man in *8½* is the real arch nitpicker, the enemy of art whom all artists would like to murder, the one so glutted that he thinks anyone in danger of producing second-rate art should control himself and produce no art at all.

Like all creative people who are stuck, the director in *8½* finds himself feeling too many things at once. He is lonely for his wife, but as soon as she has arrived on the set they start to have bleak quarrels. He has also sent for his mistress, a plump, amiable girl with a mole on her chest that disconcertingly matches a spot on her eye veil, but though he feels tenderly toward her he can't help seeing her as absurd. He hates hurting his wife with his affairs, but he can't truthfully say that it stops him enjoying them: what he dreams of is not of being able to give them up but of seeing his wife and dozens of mistresses sweetly getting on in a harem. This is a very, very funny sequence, and funny because it is aghast: he doesn't approve of himself at all for thinking what paradise it would be if his wife accepted polygamy and his actresses were longing to be whipped.

At one point, in despair, he arrives at the particularly modern notion that perfect happiness would lie in being able to tell the total truth without hurting anyone. But at other times—after he has talked to an aging cardinal in the steam room of a health spa, for instance—his dozing Catholic conscience is booted into life and he believes that happiness shouldn't be a goal anyway. Nor perhaps truth-telling, he begins to think. In the best scene in the film he is watching some screen tests with his wife, whose misery about his lying he has transcribed as justly as he can in a film character who speaks with his wife's words. But when she hears her own lines coming back at her from the screen it doesn't seem to her an offering to the truth; it strikes her as the most terrible of all her husband's betrayals.

Anouk Aimée as the wife, gray-faced and biting her nails, gives a scrupulous performance. So does Mastroianni. Apart from him none of the actors was allowed to see a full script, which sounds like a despotic piece of director's trickery, but I see now why Fellini did it. *8½* is about the way the world looks to a humorous man on the edge of a breakdown, a world full of extravagantly self-absorbed people who seem to him more like gargoyles than human beings. By putting the actors into a vacuum, Fellini has forced them to give performances that are almost uncannily narcissistic, which is the distortion he wanted. The camera work by Gianni di Venanzo is enthralling; so is the editing, and the whole organization of the film.

AUGUST 25, 1963

Lighting Up the East End

For years now people seem to have been saying that they are bored with working-class films and that kitchen-sink drama, whatever that may be, is washed up. But the truth is, of course, that there have been nothing like as many working-class English or American films in the last few years as, say, comedies about car-minded and sexually bashful members of the middle classes.

I think the feeling of exhaustion is partly because there has been such a huge output of mean-spirited housewife-plays on television, and partly because some of the working-class films that we have had seemed bogus. Joan Littlewood's *Sparrows Can't Sing* is the real thing: tough-minded, instinctive, and very reviving. It is also hilariously funny and has some of the bluest jokes since the music halls closed. It would be easy to describe it in a way that made it sound like a hoydenish romp, but I think this would be misleading. Her film of the play she directed is really about a way of living: about gaiety, and staunchness, and sexiness, and being good to people. The Stepney characters in it live as well as they can, unrancorously, with fury and humor and a lot of pleasure. A sailor comes home from the sea to find that his wife has had a baby and left him for another man. To get her back—and whether the baby is his or not seems to him no reason to ruin anyone's life—he does the obvious thing: he buys her a double bed.

Stephen Lewis's play was first produced at Theatre Workshop in 1960. Stepney has changed since then, and so has the story. The hero doesn't recognize the place. When he whips through one house he used to know, on the first floor he finds two Indians politely cooking something on the carpet, farther up a lot of Africans who seem to be living in a private farce, and in another room a woman probation officer talking sternly about "forcing an entrance and being drunk on the premises" who turns out to be speaking to an eight-year-old child.

New flats have gone up and the squealing girls in their tight skirts and high heels now have packets of frozen food in the back of the pram. "There's frozen corn. . . ." Barbara Windsor says blithely through the kitchen door to her lover—beautifully played by George Sewell—who is nursing flu and needing attention. "I think I'll have cheese and pickles," he says. "Oh, don't have anything cold!" she cries lovingly. I can't think of any other actress with the innocence to make frozen corn sound better than cheese and pickles.

The original play had no central plot; it described a series of people who revolved around a grandmother. It says something about the way modern blocks of flats break up the East End family pattern that in the film the grandmother scarcely matters. It also says a lot about Joan Littlewood's talent as a writer that the screenplay she has done with Stephen Lewis has a narrative backbone. The film is just as free as the play, but much stronger; and the acting is quite simply the only *company* acting I have seen so far in an English film. It is done by people who are used to working together; this kind of invention and expressiveness can't be achieved any other way. We have grown too used to being fobbed off with performances that are about a hundredth as good as anything we would respect on stage, given by actors who have had no chance to rehearse properly, no chance to work in sequence, and sometimes no chance even to meet until they find themselves spliced together in celluloid. The acting in films matters. It is one of the most dangerous half-truths in the cinema to say that films are made in the cutting room; you can't cut what was never shot.

Joan Littlewood obviously has a revolutionary instinct for film-making. She knows in her bones, praise be, that ordinary audiences are observant and sharp-eared when they are looking at films. But on the other hand she obviously had no technical mastery at the beginning, and you need a lot of it to beat the mediocrity that is built into the British film industry. On the first picture made by one of the very few dramatic geniuses alive, it seems a crime not to have given her better technical help. The lighting is vile; the interiors look as though they have died slowly in a refrigerator, and some of the dubbing must give her a pain every time she hears it. If we don't make it possible for her to direct another film as she wants, with the unit she needs, we don't deserve her. Perhaps we don't. But after this, surely some producer must be itching.

MARCH 3, 1963

Beatrix Potter

Falstaff and Prince Hal, Papageno and Papagena, Popeye and Olive Oyl, Lear and Fool, Don Quixote and Sancho Panza, Peter Rabbit and Benjamin Bunny. The ringing characters in fiction are often the paired opposites. Beatrix Potter, creator of the last two, has just been celebrated in the Royal Ballet's film *Tales of Beatrix Potter*. The onlie begetter of Peter Rabbit, Mrs. Tiggy-Winkle, Pigling Bland, the tenebrous Mr. Tod, the neurotically housewifely frog called Mr. Jeremy Fisher, whose cautious mackintosh saves him from the guts of a large trout because trouts are displeased with the taste of mackintosh —Miss Potter belongs in the list of great authors of comic fiction. She wrote about animals endowed with distinct purposes and with identities as clear and convivial as the summer light of Cumberland and Westmorland, where her classics are set. We are in the Lake District, but it isn't Wordsworth's. Miss Potter would never care to tell us that a cloud can be lonely. Her characters are placed in predicaments as concrete as the way she writes English, which has the beat of a grandfather clock. Jemima Puddle-Duck is thwarted by a farmer's wife from hatching her own eggs:

> . . . she set off on a fine spring afternoon along the cartroad that leads over the hill.
>
> She was wearing a shawl and a poke bonnet.

In Beatrix Potter's watercolors, which are made to seem an even greater wonder in the film's devoted use of them, we see Jemima excitably in flight and then alighting rather heavily after the exercise to try some nesting on a tree stump amongst the tall foxgloves. A fox, however, is already sitting on the stump. He is an elegantly dressed gentleman, as Jemima sees him, with sandy-colored whiskers, reading a newspaper.

> The gentleman raised his eyes above his newspaper and looked curiously at Jemima—
>
> "Madam, have you lost your way?" said he. He had a long bushy tail which he was sitting upon, as the stump was somewhat damp.

The crisp details, the alliteration, the firmness of the pretty paragraphing are part of Beatrix Potter's genius. Her characters create a world of human beings transposed, busy with private endeavors, terse about the soporific effects on rabbits of eating too much lettuce, devoted to picnics. The social system is a fixed one, and the vernacular is unmuddied. Her washerwoman hedgehog introduces herself:

> "My name is Mrs. Tiggy-Winkle; oh yes if you please'm, I'm an excellent clear-starcher!"

Obsolete skills come up, or long words like "conscientious" and "superfluous," but no five-year-old ever jibs. The rhythm is local, sunlit, aphoristic. This is English as it can best be. No wonder so many phrases have lodged in the back of so many million grown-up heads. "A minnow! A minnow! I have him by the nose." "No teeth. No teeth. No teeth."

Beatrix Potter was born in 1866. She was brought up in some

loneliness in London, reprieved by holidays in the North Country that she came from by heredity and by nature. The books, which began to be published only when she was thirty-five, describe a world that she created with the lucidity of exile. The vision has a peculiar social exactness. Her smiling, foxy villains, like the one who sends Jemima Puddle-Duck in search of sage and onions with the intention of later roasting her with the traditional flavor, foretell genteel English murder suspects like Dr. John Bodkin Adams and Christie of Rillington Place. The friendships in her books are unbreakable, and the tales avoid the fatal, though not the loss of a beloved pair of galoshes; all the same, she records a world of force, classically passionate, where the eyes of a hypocrite occasionally glitter dangerously through the woods. Characters go on vivid quests, to lay forbidden eggs or to steal lettuce or to furnish a nursery mousehole with booty dragged from an unguarded doll's house.

Miss Potter's mind communicates itself as both downright and delicate. She was to remain on her own, after a forbidden engagement that was ended by her fiancé's death, until her late forties. Then she married a Lake District lawyer who handled some sheep-farm property she had bought. It seems they were greatly happy. She is described by people who remember her as shrewd and practical, dressed usually in a tweed skirt fastened at the back with a safety pin. The historic things in her stories are extremely matter-of-fact. The movie shares her likings. She was devoted to the excitement of precise catalogues. She will go through the account of an animal duel as if she were doing an inventory. She is magically accurate—so is the Royal Ballet's picture—about the mayhem created by the Two Bad Mice when they break a load of dolls'-house plates in fury at plaster hams and fishes that only bend the dolls'-house lead knives, and then explode the dolls' bedroom mattress in a storm of feathers, though prudently saving a bolster that may yet go down their mousehole.

The film is a day off, halcyon, prodigious. Sir Frederick Ashton plays Mrs. Tiggy-Winkle, bustling about in an apron with a hand-knitted muffler tucked into the front straps. His hedgehog mask, by Rotislav Doboujinsky—this is the best mask-making outside Russia—looks domestic and piercing. The picture was shot partly in Cumberland, partly in a wonderfully created studio world where scale is everything. The Royal Ballet mice, using their tails as skipping ropes, measure up to a little above the skirting boards of a farm kitchen where an iron frying pan hung beside a range throws a shadow in a huge and golden room. We see Jemima Puddle-Duck and the fox (Ann Howard and Robert Mead), and then the love affair between the slope-shouldered Pigling Bland and his adored Black Berkshire lady pig (Alexander Grant and Brenda Last). The two of them have a pigs' *pas de deux* that is as joyful as any picnic in the world. It ends, as good picnics do, with dark falling, and Pigling Bland leads his love along a Cumberland road in a navy-blue dusk in front of a lit stone farmhouse.

We go to Jeremy Fisher, the dapper-toed, hypochondriac frog who wears pointed galoshes and who braves the rain to fish from a water-lily leaf, equipped with a butterfly sandwich in a brown wicker basket. Jeremy Fisher, danced by Michael Coleman, does the most elating leaps in the picture. He has an elegant brocade waistcoat and Belle Époque thighs; he is a dream of frogness. Then the Two Bad Mice—Wayne Sleep and Lesley Collier—creep into a nursery that has a Victorian rocking horse looming into the right-hand side of the frame, and a replica of Beatrix Potter's famous drawing of a dolls' house in the essential faded pink that she immortalized. The dolls' house is big enough for the mouse dancers to rifle but much smaller than the rocking horse; the burglars look alert and radical.

In the finale, everyone satisfactorily meets. Peter Rabbit runs riot in a field of lettuces before he finds the whole cast having tea; he hides, being of a shy nature. A squirrel pelts the eaters with nuts and then paddles away in a squirrel flotilla across a Cumberland lake. The pigs lean against each other in a pyramid of dozy affection. A dapper town mouse with a rolled umbrella and a pale-blue frock coat does a dazzling solo, kicking the umbrella as if it were the third leg in a tripod. The unmanageable rural mice trample in jam tarts, and Pigling Bland leads his crinolined beloved in an opiate love duet. Pigs' trotters transform perfectly into feet doing point work. John Lanchbery's music is pastoral and rowdy, full of brilliant turns, like a court scene in a nineteenth-century ballet. The design is by Christine Edzard, the direction by Reginald Mills; the choreography is by Sir Frederick Ashton himself, that droll, spirited man now officially called retired, whose work at Covent Garden has so often skimmed into the blue of fun and dressing-up. The last glimpse in the film is a pull-away from a huge Cumberland field with the figure of Sir Frederick's washerwoman hedgehog hurrying rather rheumatically toward a far-off dry-stone wall, bent on some errand of her own as twilight thickens the end of an undimmed summer day.

JUNE 26, 1971

Bergman

Ingmar Bergman's *The Passion of Anna*, which is a masterpiece, is one of the most specifically modern films I have ever seen, yet there is barely a modern object in sight. No traffic, no frozen food, no push-button sophisticated speech. It is the characters' plight that seems so modern. The people in the film live on an island off the Swedish coast. Bergman presents their world as theologically created, but the Theos is mute about what to do next. Blunders have the weight of heresy; idle errors have barbarous consequences.

I am not religious, but I can see how much our atheist epoch may have impoverished Western art by formulating no substitute order of good and evil. The flower children are about the only people poetic enough to have tried. The reign of black comedy, satanic comedy, has diminished literature, on the whole; it is very easy to write about evil, very hard to write about good and evil. The reason why so many rollicking antiwar films are nothing very much—the reason why they offer no convincing account of the diabolical—is that they present war as a given and uncontrollable condition outside any system of cause and effect, and therefore morally as banal as awful weather. They show within that condition no one who makes you suppose that he and his like might have created it. The lack of religion in a nontheistic sense—of a bond between a man and his scruples—has led lately to many rather absurd attempts to manufacture a plastic sort of heresy instead. We have had, for instance, our glum orgies of blue films, which represent a supremely comic effort to blaspheme, considering that the effort is instantly scuttled by its own liberal argument that there is nothing blasphemous about pornography. And in the amoral world of our new, "liberated," but really rather line-toeing wacky comedies that specialize in the far-out, where nothing in the presented world remotely works but where anything goes, one simply misses somewhere to put one's feet; it seems that there is no floor, only falling.

The Passion of Anna is Bergman's second feature film in color. We see Max von Sydow at the start as a withdrawn, droll-looking hermit called Andreas Winkelman, with reddish hair and beard. He is mending a roof. The sunlight comes and goes. He has few friends. There are brief reprieves, but his soul lives mostly in the cold. We hear that he is divorced, "in a way." Much later, when he is living with someone, he has a terrified daydream about an unidentified woman. The image mixes up love-making and hospitals, and he comes out of the daydream to say that he was thinking of cancer. So did he leave his wife when she was deathly ill? Is that a part of his own mortal unease? His ex-wife's pottery barn, where we then see him twirling the potter's wheel and getting as drunk as he can, is "left exactly as it always was," except that he is now boozed out of his mind in it. On sacrilege, he and Bergman's film are experts.

As time goes on, Andreas gets to know two women. One of them is Eva (Bibi Andersson), married to a bilious architect called Elis. She has a brief and pretty melancholy affair with Andreas. The other is Anna (Liv Ullman), lame after a car accident that occurred when she was driving and that killed both her child and her husband, who was also called Andreas. Anna and the visible Andreas start living together, more or less happily. "There was violent dissension," she later says of this period, "but we never infected each other with cruelty or suspicion." She says the same thing of her first marriage, and we believe every word of it for a while. In a technically amazing monologue at a dinner party, she turns her head swiftly to the off-screen Elis, Andreas, and Eva, and the camera, unlooked at, presses in on her, close up, like the stare of conscience, as she talks about her marriage and about "living in the truth." She looks transparently honest but she is really lying in her teeth, for her marriage was a bad one and she half-consciously meant to kill the husband and child whose deaths now genuinely make her suffer so much—just as she means, later on, to try to kill the present Andreas in the same accidental way.

The film has partly to do with the malign hold that the past can have. The people in it wreck the present by too much re-enacting. They can't escape. The past has a grip on their feet like mud in dreams. They can't make a move, and past behavior consumes the possibility of present action, just as the old, unseen Andreas begins so to requisition the present Andreas that there is a moment when von Sydow actually goes out into the garden and shouts his name to himself to call back his swallowed soul. And the two women—Anna, an angel-faced liar who at first seems really anxious for the truth, and Eva, a girl who thinks herself shabby-natured but who talks miserably well of sorts of puniness that are beyond the first one's comprehension—actually fit together like the halves of a walnut. They are described as inseparables, and their personalities flow in and out of each other like the psychic exchangings of the two women in *The Silence* and *Persona*. So do the temperaments of every other pair in the picture, which is sexually geometric. (It even emerges, when the architect is talking to Andreas, that Eva, the architect's wife, also slept with the Andreas whom Anna killed.) There are extraordinary close-up two-shots—again like the ones in *The Silence* and *Persona*—in which two faces will move across each other in talk and sometimes slightly hide each other. (The cameraman, as always, is Sven Nykvist.) The composition is a little like a Picasso Cubist painting, one face often in full front view and one in profile; it is also entirely theatrical—an image of power in flux between one person and another, like the theme of Strindberg's *The Stronger*, in which a silent woman slowly takes over the authority from a prattler.

One of the more trite questions of modern art is whether one can be two different people at the same time. Bergman is more interested in the opposite: can two people melt into one? And, if so, what about the simultaneous deadly combat to remain separated? He has made, again and again, films that are about people's terror of being eaten alive spiritually and about their mesmerized longing to risk it all the same. In the old days, he often went into that notion in stories full of charades, magic shows, apparitions, and the occult. Now he does it simply. Alma, in *Hour of the Wolf*, typically pointed out that old people who have lived together all their lives begin to look like each other. In *Persona*, in the scene when the two women are picking over mushrooms and their sunhats tip across each other, the characters quietly hum tunes pitted against one another in contradiction of the merging image. Bergman makes films that are about girls half formed until they are with other and stronger women, about men's abiding terror that the women loved in their maturity are going to eat them up and return them to the immurement known before birth. In this film, Andreas tells us that he has claustrophobia and that he used to dream of falling down potholes.

Andreas has no perceptible job. Now and again he writes at a desk. The hero of *Hour of the Wolf* was a painter, the hero of *Shame* a musician; like Andreas, both were not working and seemed obscurely stalemated. People sometimes assume that because Bergman so often makes films about artists he is being autobiographical and self-important about creativity, but I think the artists are there because they are the most natural examples of men who work on their own and who can easily hit rock, in a way that moves and interests Bergman about people in general. The universe in his films is god-made, the invention of a being who keeps his own counsel about how to live in it, and the inmates are hard-pressed by that silence. It rings in their ears. There are moments of conviviality that break up the isolation. Friendship. Love (never very erotic, and always tinctured with some dread of departure). Great tenderness (Andreas gently looks after a puppy that some madman loose on the island has horribly strung up by the neck from a tree). But such warmth of the sun is fast gone, and Bergman's people are again left to cope for themselves on a loftily conceived planet where they feel perpetually humiliated. Lately, his heroes have often spoken of that—of a humiliation that he sees as the companion of modern humanity, and hard to bear. Our social system is based on it, he says: the law, the carrying out of sentences, the kind of education we have, the Christian religion. Andreas feels himself stifled and spat upon, but without an alternative. He has a police record, the punishment for minimal crimes of rebellion. "I am a whipped cur," he says quite proudly, rage his only weapon. Does he bite? We'll see. The god whom Bergman's characters now rather prefer not to believe in is implacable and unexplanatory, much like an artist who declines to interpret his work. This creator will not be his own exegete, and there are no footnotes. He remains entirely mute, without the ghost of a smile. Meanwhile, the inhabitants of his order stumble around in it, aware that there are rules, damned for breaking them; and sometimes powerfully longing to be out of the game. Evald in *Wild Strawberries* said, "My need is to be dead. Absolutely, totally dead."

In this supreme new work, Anna is the character who has been closest to death, and who is therefore—as people are—the least enlightening about it to anyone else. She talks of the car crash distantly. She remembers herself walking away, and her child's head in "a funny position." She speaks of thinking, "What a ghastly accident," and of wondering "why someone wasn't coming to help those poor people," including herself. The alienation is complete and rather frightening. And then we see a dream of hers, in black and white, starting off in a boat that is like the boat in *Shame*. She runs up a road, longing greatly for company and knowing somehow that it has gone forever. There is nowhere to go. A woman on the road is hurrying; she might be someone to befriend, but she turns aside and says, "I've changed all the locks." Then Anna sees another woman, sitting dead-silent with a face of stone. Someone says that the woman's son is going to be executed. Anna falls on her knees in front of her and says, out of nowhere, "Forgive me. Forgive me." One remembers then that she was at the wheel of the car that killed her own child, and remembers having been told that this dream troubled her at Easter.

The word "Passion" in Bergman's title is certainly theological as well as vernacular. Bergman has always been one of the most Christian of film-makers, but his old and rather affected apparatus of symbolism has now been replaced by pure human behavior, both more direct and more truly mysterious. He is also pulling further and further away from orthodoxy. There can seldom have been a Christian artist who held out less hope of an afterlife. It is as though he felt that if people can already be so troubled and so barbarous when they are in the temporal world, eternity must be unthinkable. ("For if they do these things in a green tree, what shall be done in the dry?" Saint Luke wrote. Bergman makes one dredge up verses from the Gospels that one didn't know one remembered.) The un-Christian possibility of suicide also comes up, when the four main actors jump out of character and speak directly to the camera about what they think of the people they are playing. Bibi Andersson says that she thinks Eva might try to kill herself. "I hope they'll manage to save her," she says, and adds that she hopes Eva will look at her own old ego with affection. This is one of the warmths in Bergman—his wish for people to extend charity to themselves. He does something amazing at the end of the sequence, just after Bibi Andersson speaks about Eva's possibly someday becoming a teacher and feeling blessed: on the word "blessed" Bergman changes the exposure and floods the screen with light. There are other halcyon seconds in the film that make you catch your breath. In the middle of violence and carnage—sheep killed by the madman, a gentle peasant called Johan committing suicide because he can't bear being accused of the outbreak of animal slaughter on the island—Andreas and Anna suddenly look after a dying bird that threw itself with a thud against their window while they were watching war news on television.

The island is racked with "physical and psychical acts of violence": we keep seeing the words tapped out on a typewriter, part of a letter left by the first Andreas, which reveals a good deal of prescience and also a dangerous degree of truth about the marriage that his widow has coaxed herself into thinking ideal. Bergman now seems free of the dank respect for passivity and the gluttony for suffering that clung to his earlier films. We hear in this film, after a stable has been set on fire, of "a horse that ran around blazing" and "damned well wouldn't die." There is another line, spoken by Andreas, in the same spirit of admiration for mute refusal to give up in extremity: "Has it ever occurred to you that the worse off people are, the less they complain? At last, they are quite silent." Silence. Bergman's obdurate theme for many pictures now.

The Passion of Anna (called *A Passion* in Swedish) is a wonderful piece of work, even better than *The Silence* and *Persona*. Again and again, Bergman effortlessly tops some amazing piece of invention. The material is complex, but everything seems simple and lucid. The human details are often strange but are always convincing, in a slightly shattering way. Andreas, for instance, lets out a terrific wordless roar when he is lying alone on a bed after the insufficient, saddened Eva has left his place to take the ferry. "It's not enough," the roar says. "None of it's enough." Andreas and Anna don't love each other enough; Eva is out of reach.

Eva talks hopelessly about her cynic architect husband, who is building a culture center in Italy. "Building a mausoleum over the meaninglessness of Milan," he has said earlier, at their dinner all together. The scene seems improvised. The actors look a little flushed with wine and with the fire behind them. Bergman is one of the very great directors of acting. When the commentary here suddenly goes into the present tense and talks about Andreas as feeling "a rush of affection for these people," the affection is really there—even for Elis, the alien. Eva's husband is a pagan in Bergman's world of unwilling agnostics, and a further element in the film's scheme of the devouring and the devoured: Eva talks about herself as "nothing but a small part of his sarcasm." (When she is alone with Andreas, playing some rather horrible old dance music, she suddenly says, "What is to become of us?" Of all of them, she seems to mean.) Her husband, more buoyant, cheerfully collects photographs of people in the midst of violent emotion, which is his study. He arranges the pictures neatly in indexed boxes. The subject disagreeably fascinates him. "You can't read people with any certainty. Not even physical pain gives a reaction," he says, showing Andreas a picture of Eva looking beautiful. "She was just starting a migraine," he goes on—this aesthete of pain, one of the jaded, the out-of-heart, dead from the neck up and trying to quicken himself with snapshots of other people's intensity.

The whole movie is pitched very high, and is made by a man technically at the top of his powers. He catches people in fibs that ricochet: in a tiny stinginess about pretending to have asked a telephone operator what a call cost on someone else's phone, in a lie about not having had an affair, in a lie that everything is fine. The method of the film forces the characters into absolute clarity of intention. It is as if they were pressed up against some invisible wall, with the camera unremittingly on their faces. Few films can have had so many close-ups. Instead of flashbacks, people describe things; Bergman is loosening the traditional film links between sound track and image. The moments when the actors slip out of their parts to talk about their characters are not modish, not neo-Godard, but brilliantly necessary. They have much the same effect as the showing of film stock breaking in *Persona*—it is as though the dramatic medium itself had for the moment snapped under stress. Like the work of Renoir, Beckett, Buñuel, and Satyajit Ray, Bergman's new film is religious in the sense that it restores a lost weight to the human act, and an essential existence to its characters that is more significant than their existence in the eyes of the people they are addressing. There is agony in the material, but the attentiveness and the talent of the film-maker are altogether reviving.

JUNE 13, 1970

INDEX